TABITHA

R. Kenward Jones

WATERTOWER HILL PUBLISHING

Also by R. Kenward Jones

The Face in the Grave
Tabitha
Buried at Sea

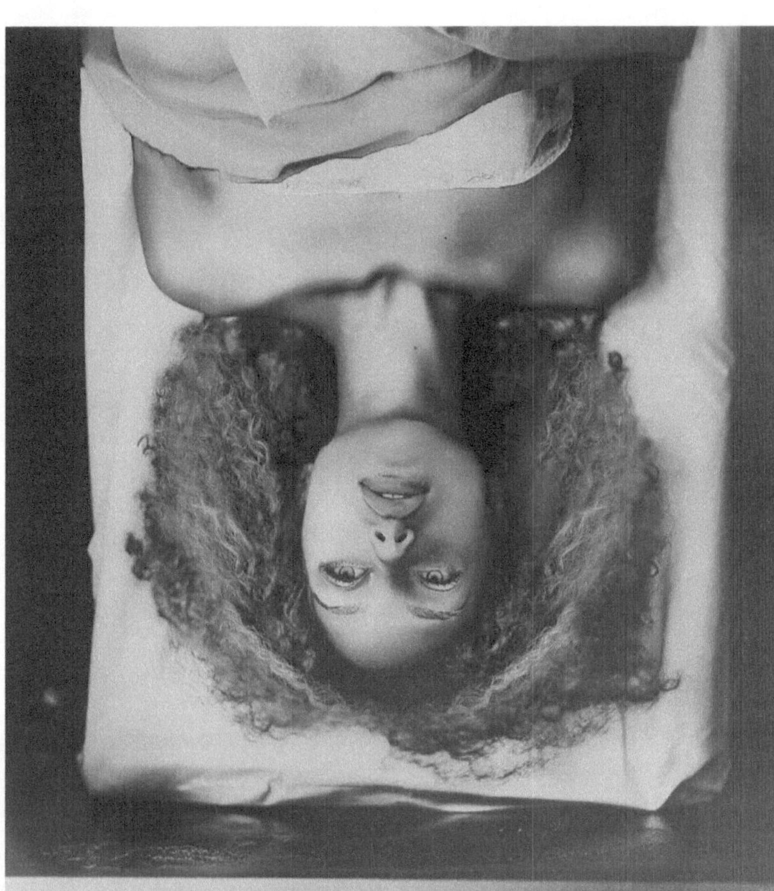

TABITHA

R. KENWARD JONES

Published by Watertower Hill Publishing
Tulsa, OK
Joshua Daughrity - Publisher
www.watertowerhill.com

Cover wrap by Susan Roddey
at The Snark Shop by Pheonix and Fae Creations.
Cover Artwork by Christy Aldridge, Grim Poppy Design.
Cover design and internal format/editing by Joshua Loyd Fox and Heather
Daughrity at Watertower Hill Publishing.

<u>*Author's Note*</u>
*All character and names in this book are fictional and are not designed,
patterned after, nor descriptive of any named person, living or deceased.
Any similarities to people, living or deceased is purely by coincidence.
Author and Publisher are not liable for any likeness described herein.*

Library of Congress Control Number: 2025930684

Hardback ISBN: 978-1-965546-07-9
Paperback ISBN: 978-1-965546-08-6
eBook ASIN: B0DTZNZXQG

Printed in the United States of America
10 9 8 7 6 5 4 3 2 1

This book is dedicated to:

My best friend, who said "I have it" at the lowest point in my life. You did, and you do. Thank God I heard you and thank you for walking me out of the Valley of the Shadow of Death. Life is worth the living just because you live.

Acknowledgements:

There are so many characters that live inside me because so many men and women took the time to write their stories. Starman Jones, Jean Valjean, Scout, and Sydney Carton. Edmund Dantes, Willie Keith, Christine, and Aslan.

How can I ever repay you for giving me such good friends? So much authentic emotion? I humbly acknowledge you and pray I will do for others what you have done for me.

CHAPTER ONE

Doug Windsor was driving home from work, his radio turned down and tuned to his local talk station. The top-of-the-hour newsreader came on. Somebody was dead; the tone said it.

He turned up the volume. He didn't know why; usually he'd do the opposite. Why add worse news to bad? Thinking back a few days later, sitting in a jail cell in Raleigh, North Carolina, he would note that it was the first of many actions to follow that were unlike him.

The dead person was a twelve-year-old girl, the daughter of the charismatic young governor of North Carolina who had wrapped up the Republican nomination for president, and whom many said was a shoo-in to win the national election.

Doug already knew about her. The girl had contracted a freakishly rare case of a brain-eating amoeba after swimming in Smith Mountain Lake in Virginia. The girl's treatment and fight for life was national news. It was impossible to ignore. Images of Tabitha Treeright and her famous father were everywhere on the 24/7 cable news cycle. Media outlets had formed a tent city surrounding Duke University Hospital where she fought for her life.

Governor Treeright's family was a picture of Reconstructed Camelot. Beautiful. New-photograph-frame filler. The first African-

American elected governor in the state, it wasn't hard to see why he was elected and why he was a formidable politician. Pundits gushed that his smile alone was worth electoral votes. And, as the old folks said, he could speechify—a true natural.

Put that smile and those gifts in front of that family, and the left and right wings of the country fluttered; one side in fear and the other in glee.

Daniel Treeright was going to be the president unless something very unexpected happened. It was a Titleist on a golden tee. But now his daughter, his only child, was dead. And Treeright was not there.

The governor, with the nomination locked up, had turned to state business. He went on a junket to Africa, purportedly to promote ties to businesses in Namibia, but also to boost the lightly-traveled candidate's image as an international figure. It would not hurt him with the African-American community to be seen in "the motherland," either, his chief of staff told him.

At the invitation of the Namibian president, he'd gone on a sightseeing trip deep into the bush, out of range of normal communications, and right off the grid. It literally took a runner, a native man on foot from the village nearest the capital, a three-hour hike to find and inform the official party of the sudden illness of Treeright's daughter.

This was only the beginning of woes for the governor. The trip back to civilization was slowed by the onset of an out-of-season monsoon-like rain that flooded roads barely passable under good weather conditions. Treeright, desperate to get home to his sick child, felt as if he was running in waist-deep mud.

Everything conspired to slow his journey home.

The delay receiving word of his daughter's condition, combined with the weather and breakdown of vehicles trying desperately to get back to civilization, could not be overcome. A wealthy donor dispatched his personal 757 to bring Treeright home, but the girl was two days dead before the plane left the runway.

As Windsor listened in his car, Daniel Treeright watched on a grainy television in the VIP lounge of the Windhoek International Airport in the capital city of Namibia. His daughter's medical team held a news conference before an auditorium filled with reporters from every major news outlet. Tabitha Treeright, aged twelve, was dead. Cause of death was a catastrophic brain infection known as primary amebic meningoencephalitis (PAM) caused by the so-called "brain-eating amoeba" *Naegleria fowleri*.

"Miss Treeright died at 1205," a white-coated hospital spokeswoman said. "We believe she was exposed to the amoeba while on vacation with friends last week at Smith Mountain Lake in Virginia. Exposure to *Naegleria fowleri* is extremely rare and the chances of becoming ill from it are minuscule.

"The amoeba enters through the nasal cavity and by the time any symptoms are recognizable, treatment is usually ineffective. The damage Miss Treeright suffered to her brain was irreversible and rapid. We would like to express our deep sorrow and support for Governor Treeright and his family in this difficult time and we ask that you respect the privacy of the family as they mourn their loss."

The spokeswoman left the microphone. A profound silence ensued momentarily, then, as if waking from a collective dream, the assembled reporters roared to life with questions shouted to an empty podium. No one returned to satiate their thirst for answers.

Doug shut off the radio. He was no fan of Treeright. He hated the man's politics and feared seeing him in the White House, but this was not happy news for any man.

He knew in the days to come, perhaps even in a few hours, the sting of the tragedy would dull enough for the wags to begin discussing the political ramifications of Treeright's loss and his absence at the critical moment. They would be unsparing, unblinking.

Nothing was sacred to them and this too would be weaponized by left and right.

The more he considered it the more he leaned toward hours rather than days before it happened. *For God's sake*, he thought, *a child is dead*. A mother and a father are dying inside. Leave them alone! Suddenly he hated it all. Left and right. Positions. Pundits. Campaigns. Our side. Their side.

He hated it and he hated what it did to people, to him, for on the edge of his mind he was aware of his own loathsome, shadowy thoughts. This wounded Treeright. This slowed him down. This would make him vulnerable. It would slow his momentum and might even keep him out of the White House.

The shadow thoughts were undeniably there.

Six time zones away, Daniel Treeright stared at the television unseeing, helpless, choked with despair and anger. His race against his worst fear was lost. He was exhausted.

The phone call he'd managed to get through to his wife was choppy and disconnected after a few painful moments. She sounded resigned, distant, and empty. She cycled through every emotion with him and then she was gone.

Wanda was a strong woman. A beautiful woman. She was also sleeping with his chief of staff; an open secret in his inner circle of friends and advisors.

He didn't grudge her these foibles, and she in her turn kept her eyes turned from his.

They had the picture-perfect family and relationship but it was a snapshot; a made-for-TV family, and it wasn't built for stormy weather.

CHAPTER TWO

Wanda Treeright, a former Miss North Carolina, was headshot glossy perfection. Naturally blonde in the shade women buy from bottles, built for comfort with a lithe beach body, a product of heredity that didn't just endure middle age, but made it look good.

She'd grown up in Manteo, North Carolina like a whale in a koi pond.

She and Daniel met, fell in love, and married at East Carolina University, following her freshman and his junior year. The fact that he was black and she white caused more eyebrows to raise in Greenville than it did in either of the small towns they came from; an oddity that amused but didn't surprise them.

They knew from experience that there was more veiled racism on college campuses than real racism in rural Carolina.

It was a good match. Daniel was going places he couldn't yet see. Wanda saw where he could go long before he did and had the course plotted in her head.

They had one child, Tabitha. She was sharp. She was the kid on the playground who lined up all the others, younger and older alike, and got them to play her game. When people referred to being born with "it," they meant Tabitha Treeright and her kindred.

She was a markedly unattractive infant given the attractiveness of both parents, so much so that even old ladies who lie about how beautiful every baby is were reduced to using adjectives like "character" and "cute" to describe her features.

It was in the eyes, which were a nice almond shape, and a truly other-worldly blue, but too big for her face and too widely spaced; so widely they appeared to slant downward from high cheek bones as if they would fall off her face.

The slant unfortunately drew attention to a huge nose, long and angular, leaving the impression of a lion's muzzle; an impression that wasn't helped as the child's hair grew into an abundant and untameably rich mop of yellow kinky curls.

The overall effect was a baby and little girl who looked for all the world like a caricature artist's sketch. But in the same manner Tabitha's mother aged from beauty to more beauty, Tabitha aged from odd-looking to rare beauty.

Her eyes in particular drew unabashed stares from complete strangers, and the wild yellow hair crowning her milky brown complexion gave her the aura of a rare gemstone.

Coming to the Governor's Mansion at nine years old when her father handily won his first term, she was an instant celebrity, often walking into Treeright's press conferences as if she were a prized advisor, to the delight of everyone in attendance.

Tabitha had the instincts—and ability to use them—of people well beyond her years. She knew when things were untrue or pretentious. The Treerights built a pretty life, and it fooled almost everyone, but not their daughter.

She saw everything and she wasn't afraid to say what she saw. She was unusual in that she didn't identify with one or the other of her parents. She doled out scorn equally, and, Daniel realized, showed a blossoming political skill in using what she knew to get what she wanted.

The trip to Smith Mountain Lake was the latest example of this skill. Knowing her father was going to Africa and that her mother used his absences to spend a lot of quality time with "Uncle Syd"—Sydney DeVito, the chief of staff—Tabitha pushed for the trip.

She knew her mother preferred having her out of the way when Syd was around and she knew her father was too preoccupied with his own trip to put up much of a fight.

Timing her approach perfectly, she waited for the night before her father left and pressed all the right buttons. They weren't taking a vacation this year because of the campaign.

Her friend was moving to a new school and she wouldn't see her. She already had permission from the friend's family.

So Tabitha got her way, Daniel set off for Africa, and "Uncle Syd" brought his overnight bag to the Governor's Mansion.

CHAPTER THREE

Syd DeVito looked at his buzzing cell phone. It was Wanda. He hesitated and then sent the call to voicemail. He had a lot to think about right now and he needed space to do it.

Twenty years' worth of work was resting on a knife edge. It could go either way. He knew the Treerights before they were the made-for-TV family. He knew them now better than anyone in the country.

His affair with Wanda had not been remotely on the table back then, back when they were in college.

Syd was a fast-talking, hard-edged, ambitious kid from Jersey. He grew up street smart and came south to school because it was affordable and because his Uncle Joey, a man of "connections" as the guys in East Orange, New Jersey liked to call them, had ideas about extending those connections to territory in Virginia and the Carolinas.

There were a few small time operations running in Norfolk, Charlotte, and a few more in Raleigh, and he wanted his favorite nephew to put them together in a new and powerful way. It was the family business.

Not exactly old world organized crime, but organized enough to keep the DeVito family living pretty well.

Giving Syd this opportunity was a two-sided affair. The boy was smart, very smart, and Joey foresaw him taking over the local scene if things ran their natural course.

But Joey had sons of his own. They were smart too, but not Syd smart, and, he admitted, not as ruthless. The youngest son of his youngest brother would be trouble for them.

Syd had an edge about him from a young age that belied his altar-boy looks. A priest that had tried some monkey business with the boy when he was only twelve ended up in the hospital with a broken jaw. Joey liked the boy a lot. Sending him away would keep his own boys from an unpleasant intersection with Syd as he came of age, and hooking him up with the minor leagues down south would give him plenty of space to build the family business from a safe distance.

After starting the kid out in Norfolk at Old Dominion University for a couple years he decided East Carolina University was a better fit. ECU wasn't prestigious, but it had the advantage of being in a town where some of the DeVito family minor leaguers lived. Joey had no idea exiling his nephew to ECU and Greenville would connect Syd with the man who would turn national politics on its ear.

Politics and petty crime mixed in the South in different ways than the well-grooved palms and agreements of the Northeast. Syd brought the two together in innovative ways Joey admired.

By the time Syd and Daniel Treeright met and became friends in their junior year at ECU, he was already running the most profitable protection racket in the history of the family and was on a first name basis with sheriffs in seventy-three out of one hundred counties in the state.

The key had been tapping into a basic truth: the sheriffs, while woefully underpaid, loved their hayseed jobs and titles and wanted more than anything else to get reelected every cycle. Syd showed them how, with a little ingenuity and a little shutting of the eyes and bending of the rules, they could have their cakes and eat them too.

He found working with southerners to be a walk in the park compared to the self-important layers of law enforcement and entitled politicians in Jersey. These guys were friendly. They liked people. They also were incredibly trusting.

Syd exploited every advantage he could find, and came to own one after another of them. It helped that he looked older than he was and after some serious work drained all the Jersey out of his accent, an accomplishment of which he was particularly proud.

His interest in Daniel Treeright was purely hormonal at first. The man attracted beautiful women like the swarms of bees on the multitude of cherry blossom trees on the ECU campus. Hanging around Treeright guaranteed any young man a satisfying amount of collateral sex.

Daniel's natural political gifts soon got Syd to thinking of a different kind of power and money than he'd considered possible in the minors. Like all thieves who talk amongst themselves as if their line of work were a natural part of the human condition and nothing to hide, he wanted to live in the light, be legitimized and recognized for his gifts.

He set out to make Daniel the class president as a test of his ability to translate organized crime into organizing a political organization. And they became an unbeatable team. After watching the movie *Carlito's Way* one night, Daniel told Syd he was Carlito; in any situation he was figuring the angles.

"You're my Carlito, Syd." It was a sobriquet that stuck and came up whenever they found themselves searching for a way through the deadliest jungle: politics.

Daniel, for his part, walked amongst the beasts without a scratch. A few strokes of his man's ego was all it took for Syd to set them on the path that had led them all the way to the door of the White House, and Syd's family business was booming.

But now, everything was on the line; a very thin one. Syd had extended himself in ways that required major quid pro quos. Nothing short of the presidency would satisfy the people who had made Treeright's nomination a reality. There were favors on top of favors all across the fruited plains with people his Uncle Joey liked to refer to as "serious," but who Syd thought were more aptly described as dangerous.

His history with the Treerights taught him that Daniel, always smooth on the surface, was an emotional powder keg. Taking Wanda as a lover had been, strangely enough, a way to keep a lit match away from Daniel by giving her a place to find revenge while keeping her "on the reservation."

Politics made strange bedfellows as it always had, but she wasn't complaining and Syd got what he had wanted from the first time he'd laid eyes on the unattainable beauty that fell into his best friend's hands shortly after they met.

The juggling he'd done to keep them together had been a work of art, but it was nothing compared to what he saw coming.

CHAPTER FOUR

Doug woke up in a sweat in his dark bedroom and talked himself down.

I'm not in solitary. I'm not in prison. I'm in my own apartment. I can walk out of here whenever I want to.

But the mental engine whined and whirled too much. His heart took up the spinning cycle and raced along, keeping up with his brain.

He got up, threw on a pair of sweatpants and a dri-fit t-shirt he'd left beside the bed the night before. He padded to the bedroom door and slipped on a worn pair of running shoes. Going to the front door, he stuffed his keys and wallet into his pockets out of habit and descended the stairs.

His car, an old Camry, was sitting in the parking lot. At the angle he saw it, coming from the apartment, it appeared he'd left the map light burning. Mumbling to himself, he went to the car and let himself in.

The switches in the overheads of these cars always stumped him. Which push of the button set the light to go out after the driver departed and closed the door? And how long was it supposed to stay on?

He sat in the driver's seat, closed the door with a satisfying clunk, and felt his heart rate begin to fall. A car was a sort of sanctuary with all the windows up and the doors closed; like the booth they stuck you in for a hearing test. The stillness calmed him.

He fiddled with the switch for the map light, unable to discern the right button or number of pushes to get it to go out. He gave up and started the car. The radio crackled to life, perpetually tuned to his news talk station. The drone of a sleepy-sounding host came on. Tabitha Treeright again. No escaping it even at this ungodly hour.

He checked the time; two a.m. Saturday night. *Sunday morning,* he corrected himself. "Might as well go for a ride," he heard himself mumble, surprised by the sound of his own voice. Yeah. Why not?

He pulled out of the apartment complex in Ocean View—a quaint name for the neighborhood with the highest crime rate in the city—and headed north on Shore Drive with no destination in mind, just driving.

He barely registered that he was getting on Interstate 64. He vaguely thought he might drive the entire outer loop around Suffolk, through the two tunnels and back to Norfolk. The driving was the point, not the route. It was working to bring him down. The rhythm of the road.

He rolled the windows down and turned off the radio. The road sound and his heartbeat merged into one thing.

He felt it and he heard it, then it detached itself from the road and became something else.

A voice?

Keep going.

Keep going? He was at the intersection of 64 and 58.

South.

South? He made the exit, his arms moving without thinking. And he drove on, alone into the night, the voice melding back into the sound of his heart and the road.

Doug was familiar with being alone. He was an ex-con. When it became known to his fellow inmates exactly why he was a guest of the state of Virginia in the Coffeewood penitentiary, he spent a lot of time in isolation. It was a necessary evil that probably saved his life.

He was a child molester—a "cho-mo" to the other cons; that was the official line and the unavoidable moniker that went with his crimes. The truth was he got caught with seven detachable hard drives full of porn; porn which included lots of underage girls.

He didn't know how he got from passively looking at computer screens to connecting online with girls, to the final act of trying to arrange face-to-face meetings. For that matter he didn't know how he ended up spending most of his waking hours watching porn. But he did.

Before a police sting hoovered him up, he spent so much time in a darkened room in front of his computer that he couldn't go out in the daylight without dark shades.

One thing leads to another, the song said. Yes. A little porn. All his friends did it. All of them. They'd all grow out of it right? It was just what boys did. But Doug never stopped. He never could and never did until he got stopped by the Greater Hampton Roads Taskforce To End Child Pornography implemented by the law-and-order governor of the great state of Virginia.

He tried to tell the state-mandated counselor what it felt like; being addicted to porn. One image only made his eyes hungry for a new image. It was like the cursed buccaneers in the first *Pirates of the Caribbean* movie. They could eat and never taste; swallow and never be full.

It was the same with his eyes and porn, he told the moon-faced middle-aged woman assigned to help him. At some point the images eating holes in his eyes made him so hungry he went looking for something to make it stop, something more... substantive, something that would quench him for more than a few seconds.

It was then he started surfing more specific and explicit sites. Why underage girls? Why not? Even in his seventh year of sobriety (including five behind bars), he didn't understand why.

But now he had peace. Mostly. He found his higher power. He walked the twelve steps. He was a friend of Bill W. Yeah. Maybe Bill W. was his only friend. They say addiction stunts your personality. You get stuck at an age and you don't grow.

That was probably true, he thought. *I mean who has time to grow up and become an "adult" when all you do is use and use and use some more?*

It isolated him from everyone and everything. He survived going away and copious amounts of time in solitary, but in truth, he was cut off from any meaningful relationships long before a cell door made it official.

He had no family and no friends. No one knew where he was or asked where he was with the exception of his parole officer. He was in the registry. His walks and drives were always calculated to maintain the legal distance from schools or kids.

The Ocean View apartment was his third since getting out. The first two had been blown down by the huffing and puffing of a couple of friendly neighborhood soccer moms with too much time on their hands and an eye out for any bad actors moving into their little fiefdoms. And who could be a worse actor than Douglas Windsor, convicted felon?

After the second grim-faced landlord came and politely suggested he move on he began to wonder if he was supposed to have a place to live. Maybe he deserved to be kicked out and to stay away from normal people. He didn't know.

His porn-addicted personality was frozen at thirteen or fourteen. It took tremendous effort to think and do what a thirty-year-old should think and do: just to have and keep a job, feed himself and keep a mostly clean appearance.

A thirty-year-old teenager. Weren't moms supposed to kind of take care of someone that age? These soccer moms wanted him gone. They looked at him like a piece of trash the wind blew into their yard.

The third apartment, he changed tactics. He lied about his name on the apartment application. He dropped his last name and used his middle name as his last. He knew this was a parole violation but he didn't care. He had to live. It worked. He doubted the apartment manager ever checked up on him.

He got a job hauling bricks for a mason. It was cliché, but he really had hit the weights hard in prison. He filled out. He was no longer a sun-starved shriveled-up straw of a man. He was a tanned, athletic-looking, almost six-footer.

He kept to himself. He went to his mandated meetings and toed the line. For two years he'd meticulously kept every requirement of his parole. But right now he was leaving his designated parole area without notifying anyone; a clear violation.

He felt pulled down the road south like a barge under tow. All he did was keep his hand on the tiller.

CHAPTER FIVE

Wanda Treeright sat alone in her car in the parking lot of the Governor's Mansion. A light rain fell, distorting her view in the early evening darkness. The car was a haven away from the Governor's Mansion where Tabitha's forever-empty room mocked her.

She felt the weight of her daughter's death and all that began to accumulate behind it like deep waters piling up behind a dam. Funeral? Would there be an autopsy? Should there be? People would want answers. She didn't know how to give them because she had none herself.

Her official self and her private self had so much to do and to process. She wanted comfort. She needed it. Her husband wasn't here. That was normal, but she felt the reality of their fractured relationship more intensely in this darkness, this shadow of death. She needed light. She needed touch. And she knew, more clearly than ever, that these things were not in her lover. She laughed at that even as she cried.

She wondered if any lover she'd ever had was equal to a moment like this. No, she decided, none. It shocked her to think the only honest comfort she had in any relationship had been with her Tabitha; now that was lost to her forever.

"I'm empty," she said, startling herself with the sound of her own voice. She was hoarse with crying. Raw voice. Raw life.

"I'm empty," she repeated, louder. "And I'm alone." Her cell phone buzzed in her purse as if on cue. It was her husband. She punched the button to accept the call.

"Where are you?" she said without waiting for his greeting.

"Just touching down. And you? Bennet said you slipped security again. You know we can't afford any... ahh, embarrassments. Especially right now."

There it was. Contempt and suspicion served up with a touch of sarcasm.

She gave it back to him. "I'm at home. Right here where you haven't been while your daughter was dying." There was a long pause. She thought he had hung up.

"I'm sorry," he said. He was crying. "I'm sorry. I'm sorry." And there was a momentary ceasefire in their open warfare. Hostility and condescension dimmed under the huge shadow of their mutual loss. But the years conspired against the days and the way of peace was obscure while the well-rutted pathway of blame and shame looked inviting. She took it.

"Yeah. Yes. You are sorry," she said. "But the people, they love you don't they?" Now it was the knife fighting she was used to. "I'm sure this will help you in the polls."

Another long pause.

Daniel said, "We need to be seen together." The official husband was back. The mourning father was gone. "I want you to meet me at the hospital, or are you too busy to get off your back and make an appearance?"

Equilibrium. The balance of power in their personal Cold War was restored. She knew how to live in this world. This was comfortable in its sick broken way; this was normal. Without another word, she hung up the phone.

Now that Daniel had accounted for Wanda's whereabouts he was free to go to the Governor's Mansion or the medical center. She was the wildcard in his day-to-day calculations. Although he counted on Syd to keep her in check, their "arrangement" was always a potential hand grenade. When she was off the grid he had to consider the chance she was the target of a journo looking for a story that could blow up his life.

He sat in his limo considering his next move. Tabitha was dead and nothing would change that. He knew it was a cold thought and he shuddered at his icy calculations. Wanda's rebuff had been a defibrillator jolt to his political heart. The tears had been real enough but she had recalibrated him, put him back on his game. It wasn't a time for weakness. She showed him that. Enemies were waiting for weakness and this moment of vulnerability would be theirs if he gave them room.

"Thank you, Wanda," he said to himself.

What was the right move? The right picture to project? He needed to be seen with his mourning wife but he needed to be seen caring for Tabitha too. Going directly to the mansion might appear callous. He didn't want any cameras in his face until he got a grip on both his emotions and his words.

He dialed Syd. Strange to say it, but he trusted the man who slept with his wife more than anyone in his life. Syd answered on the first ring.

"Yeah, Tree."

"I'm in the car leaving the airport now. Thinking through what I need to do first." Daniel paused and Syd did too.

"Jeez, Tree," he said, "you scare me sometimes. You never turn off. Go to the hospital, man. Go see your daughter." DeVito trailed off.

Daniel thought he heard a sob. He tightened his grip on his phone and fought down sobs of his own.

"Syd, we need a plan. It won't help anyone if we fall apart now. This is bigger than us. Isn't that what you've been saying? I need my Carlito."

He paused. There was a world hanging in the silence. He knew Syd adored Tabitha and was hurting. He also knew there was no way forward without DeVito. He needed him and he needed him right now. The man that emerged out of the silence was the one he needed, the wise guy gone political operator. His Carlito.

"The press is camping out around both the mansion and the medical center," Syd said. "With Wanda not willing to play her part it would make better sense to go to the hospital. I think we can explain her absence from the hospital, and it's the place you'll get the least invasive press presence while giving them something to talk about that will make you look good."

He paused and then went on, warming up, looking for the angles. "It's late, anyway. Not much viewership this time of night. We can use the time at the hospital and the rest of the night to let Wanda settle out. By the time we get back to Raleigh and get some sleep, I'll get her onboard with making an appearance with you that'll hit with the next news cycle."

Treeright pushed the intercom for the driver. "Head for Duke," he said, then, "Meet me at the hospital, Syd. I don't want to see her alone."

CHAPTER SIX

There was a sound growing in his chest. It wasn't in his head or his ears. It was in his chest. It thrummed; it synced with his heartbeat. Although he felt it, it was more than that; it was a voice. It had personality. It had resonance and vocabulary. As it grew he realized it was familiar. He knew he had heard it before.

It was drawing him south and west. From the thrumming he heard at first; a name emerged: *Durham.*

Durham?

Durham. He knew it was the place. The goal. The goal of what though? Here he was risking a parole violation and jail time on a vibration in his chest that he thought was a voice. He could picture it now.

Judge: Mr. Windsor, you're here today because you violated the terms of your parole. What do you have to say for yourself?

Doug: Well, Your Honor, I woke up in the middle of the night and went for a drive. Then I had this urge to keep driving and while I was driving something told me to go west and while I was going west a voice said I should go to Durham...

Yeah. That didn't sound like a scenario that would turn out well. A convicted child molester hearing voices telling him to break the law. That sounded like a scenario ending with him back in jail. But it wasn't *voices*. It was *a* voice. A singular voice, familiar and somehow authoritative.

He felt like obeying the voice. It wasn't demanding like the speed limit sign or the terms of his parole, but it was commanding. The thought of turning away didn't occur to him.

He checked himself. Was this sane? Was he going insane? Did he just want to leave town? Was this him speaking or was it a suggestion he got from someone? He put that away. Durham wasn't a garden spot, and although he liked long drives, there were plenty of places to go that wouldn't jeopardize his parole.

He didn't know anyone there. He really didn't know anyone anywhere. He had no money and no place to stay. He wondered how he would pay for gas and food. He kept driving. West and south. Durham. It would be okay. It would be fine.

A misty rain fell. The annoying kind, just enough to obscure the windshield but lacking sufficient moisture to keep the wipers from shuddering across the glass even when they were set to the longest interval.

His headlights splashed Route 58. He was on the section known as Suicide Strip between Suffolk and Emporia.

He still called it by that name although the state of Virginia and local authorities had re-engineered it from its murderous origin as a two lane ribbon of black asphalt where passenger cars jockeying for position on its alternating passing zones had too often met head-on with tin can family sedans to a divided four-lane highway.

At one count over a twenty year span, more than one hundred people had lost their lives in these parts until the residents, wearied of the horrors deposited in their front yards, began posting homemade road signs complete with running statistics under a skull and crossbones warning any who ventured onto the road that it was taking your life into your own hands to drive this way.

The tipping point came in the early eighties when two spinsters from Pennsylvania and a whole family of four from Virginia Beach were splattered by trucks within the same week in the span of a single mile marker.

The slaughter of the family was particularly horrendous with the mother hovering near death, encased in the crumpled remains of their van as paramedics attempted to extract her from the midst of her ruined family.

Her twelve-year-old daughter's body had fused on impact with the rear of her passenger-side seat. It was said that the men responding to the scene took turns between the jaws of life and stints throwing up in the roadside ditch.

The nice four-lane, he realized, was paved with blood and loss, and although he never had a penchant for speed anyway, he kept the car at a pedestrian crawl compared to those rushing past him. Death haunted this road.

Because of his slow pace, he saw the woman and stopped to help. She was on the inside shoulder in a gentle left-rounded curve just outside Franklin. She was barely off the road; her gold Honda Odyssey hobbled with a flat on the rear driver's side. Middle-aged attractive black woman. Obama/Biden sticker visible on the frame of the rear hatch.

He took this in like a Snap Chat and pulled over before it had time to disappear. He walked back to her as two cars sped by, throwing fine mist up from the wet road. Halfway there, he turned back to his car, thinking he better flip on his hazards. The woman cried out. It caught him by surprise.

"Please don't go! Please help me!" She actually started to jog toward him as if to stop him from leaving.

"What? Oh I'm not going anywhere, lady. just turning on my flashers. You should do the same."

"My what?" she said.

"Your flashers. Your emergency lights. Hazard lights?" Her puzzled expression didn't change.

"Wait a sec," he said and flicked on his flashers.

He met her at the rear of his car and her expression changed from puzzled to relief. She began to talk in a stream of words that flowed over Doug like a breached dam. She never mentioned the flashers or the flat tire. She was a download with no cancel button. There wasn't room for *uh-huh* or even grunts.

He felt that nods of the head were drowned in the flood of verbiage. He knew he wasn't socially adept and was unused to talking with people but this person was more defective than he. Something was missing.

An hour later, mowing down miles again in the silence of his own car, it clicked. It wasn't just the amount of words she used or the disconnection from the present situation, it was the utter one-sidedness of the words. She began by saying her name—she was Nancy from Ohio—and seamlessly told him her unabridged life story while he moved mechanically to replace the wounded tire.

She talked as if her life depended on getting this information out. He was a tire-changing 911 operator and Nancy from Ohio acted as if he were sent there to both hear her and to get her back on the road again as surely as if he were her therapist who moonlighted at AAA.

He played the part. There wasn't space to do anything else. He found the semi-worthless donut spare, the cleverly hidden scissor jack, and lug wrench. He got the van off the ground about the time Nancy graduated from high school. The flat removed and examined for the cause of losing its wind came at the birth of her two children and return to school to earn a degree in something business related.

The divorce from husband number one happened when he discovered the donut was completely useless and they needed to take the blown tire into Franklin to search out a service station that still did tire patches.

The drive to town and back was husband two, a move to Utah, and another return to school, this time to become a lawyer.

He paid for the patch out of the last of his money as much out of desperation to get this experience over as exasperation over how to get her to stop talking long enough to ask her to pay up. It was twenty-one dollars and fifty-one cents and he scrapped the last of the change in his Camry's console to come up with it.

He drove seven miles back toward Suffolk to get back on 58 on the right side of the road. By the time he got back to her car he felt as if his ears might actually be bleeding. But if prison had taught him anything, it taught him you can keep your head down and get through almost anything. And so he did.

Nancy's new career as a lawyer was going well by the time he lowered her van onto the repaired tire, restored all the tire changing paraphernalia, and shut the back hatch. He took a moment to look at her to see if she was going to release him from the lasso of words or if he would have to cut himself free with a jaunt to the car and flee the scene.

She stopped. The silence was louder than a passing semi. She had kind eyes and he almost felt sorry for wanting so badly to get away from this human robocall.

Without hesitation or reservation she pulled him to herself in a full embrace. It was so unexpected and so complete that he returned it in kind.

One moment he was a block of sculptors clay; square and hard, untouched and untouchable, and then, then he was rounded and pressed into humanity. Electric coils melted him into the shape of a man. It was the most humanly intimate moment of his adult life. It was sensuously unsenuous.

She released him and he drifted to his car, unaware for the moment that she had not said another word. That all the Nancy words cut off like a spigot with his look in her eyes and her embrace.

As his car door thumped shut and shut out the sound of the rain and the road and the traffic, it closed him into a silent capsule of the afterglow of her embrace. He felt it radiating from him in the darkness.

Nancy's gold van slipped past him back onto the wet ribbon of 58. He sat there unthinking, only feeling for what seemed like a long time. When he turned over the ignition and the blue green digital clock on the dash flickered to life, it surprised him to see barely an hour had passed.

He was accustomed to so little life spread over so much dead time that so much life compressed into so short a time stretched his imagination.

He eased the Camry back onto the road and continued west and south.

CHAPTER SEVEN

The sound; the voice, was still there. Still affirming. *Durham.* As he thumped across the rumble strips on the shoulder, two things happened at once. The low fuel indicator came on and two rectangles of paper fluttered out of the passenger side sun visor, landing in his lap.

Both startled him. The yellow pin prick of light told him he didn't have far to go, voice or no voice. The paper told him differently. It was two one-hundred dollar bills. Crisp the way only new bills are.

He was positive they weren't his and he was also positive the only way they could've gotten there was Nancy, but she must have had street-magician close-up magic skills. There was no time she hadn't been in full view and full voice. Yet here it was. Here they were.

He did a quick calculation and decided he could make it to Emporia before fueling up. It would make a good one-stop shop. There was a restaurant in a truck stop in Emporia he remembered from trips with his family growing up.

Mom and Dad and Dad's kid brother who was so much younger than Dad he was like one of his children. *Family is so slippery*, he thought. It has so many things it's supposed to be and yet it wasn't for him.

His sister, the first born, had a whole different family than Doug. She had the same father and mother and yet she didn't. Dee wasn't a bright star in school or talent or looks but she was the bright star of the family.

As Doug's light dimmed, her light got brighter until the moment the sheriff served the warrant for his arrest. Then his light went out. They couldn't see him anymore. He wasn't just dim, he was done. Or they were done with him. So strange. Families were so strange.

He couldn't tell if he fell into porn like an unsupervised toddler falls into a backyard pool; he only knew that no one noticed and no one came to rescue him. At the last gasp, when all he had left was porn and a basement bedroom, it was the Law and not his family that pulled him out of the pool and only then to punish him, not to save him.

Mom, Dad, and Dee disappeared. The police search of the house in the cul-de-sac, taking out boxes of evidence, broke the ties that bind so completely that Doug did not know where they lived any more. They sold the house and moved to another state. He was a black hole sucking them into his darkness. They couldn't let it happen.

So complete was their disappearing act that he came out of prison with no idea where they were. They weren't to be found on social media either. The only way he came to know their whereabouts was through Uncle Tommy, who was the only member of the family left in the area and the only one who contacted Doug after prison.

He had pondered once about the possibility that embarrassment could kill a person. He didn't know if it could or not but he was sure of this: embarrassment could kill a family. Or at the very least bury an embarrassing person like him alive. He wondered at his detachment from the loss, from the burial. He didn't feel a sense of absence. He didn't feel anything really. He added that to the tally of things addiction had stolen.

He personified addiction. In his mind, addiction was a person who had been a friend, had come into his life and shared a lot of years of pleasure with him. Was pleasure the right word? He thought so. It was pleasurable until it wasn't.

Addiction began causing problems when it—he—got jealous. He didn't want to share Doug with schoolmates or hobbies or even with the sunlight. Then Addiction turned nasty, controlling and demanding. He tied Doug up in a basement in the dimness and stole everything he had. Took his money, his time, his family, and in the end, his freedom. Took his life.

Through all of this, Doug had come to a kind of calmness. His anger, an ever-present companion from earliest memory, burned down to ash in prison. He didn't blame his family for leaving him. He thought he probably deserved to be left, though he couldn't quite reconcile himself to that thought.

There was something he couldn't settle, a little ripple in the surface of the calm he mostly enjoyed, but for now he didn't see a need to stir it. He had enough work to do, forgiving himself. He didn't want to discover he had a whole other group of people to forgive. Forgiveness was hard work.

CHAPTER EIGHT

He snapped back to reality when the yellow low-fuel light began to flash accompanied by a beep. He had hoped to make one stop to fuel the car and his grumbling belly, but it looked like a bad idea. It was still raining.

The thrum of the windshield washers was in sync with the two syllables pronounced by the voice: *thwip-thwap, Dur-ham*. He pulled off at the next exit and rolled to a stop at a gas station that had seen better days.

He sat at the fuel pumps listening to the engine tick as it cooled. He got out of the car and went in to pre-pay for his fuel. A grimy, frayed sign on the register said no bills larger than fifties accepted after dark. He fingered the crisp bills in his pocket.

A mummified-looking Asian woman sat at the counter, perched like a cat on a stool too tall for her.

"I need to fill up my car," he said, "Pump 4."

Not a hint of movement. He thought she might be a stuffed and mounted mummy. The barest flicker in the eyes gave it away that she was alive and awake.

"You pay cash?" she said through lips that barely moved.

"Yes, but I only have a hundred dollar bill," he said, gesturing at the sign and placing one of the two bills on the counter. A hand shot out and snatched the money so quickly it made him think of a lizard picking a fly out of the air. He thought too late it had been a mistake to put half his stash where it could disappear so quickly.

He paused half a beat—a habit he picked up in jail—before responding. The mummy cashier held the hundred very close to her face as if smelling it.

"This a new bill," she said. "Real?"

He nodded. He hadn't the slightest idea if it was real or not. It never occurred to him that it could be a fake. A talkative angel left it in his car, that's all. It couldn't be anything other than the genuine article.

"Can you take it then?" he asked.

"How much gas you need? I only have fifty dollar change in register at night."

Seeing Doug hesitate, she added, "Too many thief. All people pay with card all time. Too dangerous to have cash money after dark."

He did a quick calculation. His car would take about thirty-five dollars to fill. If the mummy emptied her till to make change, he'd lose fifteen bucks. He looked at the weathered face and saw greed written into its lines. He held her gaze. His face was hot, hating the woman, hating the rip-off, finally hating that fifteen dollars could do this to anyone. Something inside him let go.

"How about you just let me fill up and you can keep the change, whatever it is?"

Immediately greed morphed into suspicion.

"Fake! she said. "You give me fake money!"

"No," he said. "It's not. It's real. Look, don't you have one of those markers they use to show money is real?"

The woman's countenance changed again, this time to revelation. She opened a drawer and rummaged through its contents, pulling out the pen Doug mentioned.

"Daughter say this is foolproof but I never use it before. I say I can feel and smell better than pen can show me. Now I see. This seem real…" She trailed off as she rubbed the bill again before her old eyes.

"I already got picture of your license plate on my security camera. If this fake money I gonna call police and give them your number unless you tell me right now it fake." She took the pen and uncapped it. "My daughter say, 'If it turn black give it back.'"

She stared him down, daring him to confess. He considered his situation. He had no fuel to go on or to go back. The debit card in his wallet gave him access to about two dollars and sixty cents until he got paid day after tomorrow and even then wouldn't be good till he deposited the under-the-table cash he was paid. He was well out of his travel-restricted parole area and he was following a voice to a city he knew nothing about for no reason.

"Go for it," he said.

She appeared to savor the moment. She had a sucker in front of her either way. Then she stroked the pen across the bill. A translucent purple band appeared in the pen's wake. Doug realized he had been holding his breath and exhaled.

"You see?" he said.

She hesitated ever so slightly with disappointment, he thought. And said nothing. Then as if talking with the fool she was sure stood in front of her, she gestured to the pumps.

"Go. I turn on pump. I still have you on my camera."

Why this mattered to her he never knew. He went back to the pump and filled it till he ran out of clicks and gas splashed on his shoes. His Nissan's tank was manufacturer rated to hold fifteen gallons.

The pump read 16.3.

"Guess it was closer than I thought," he said to the pump.

CHAPTER NINE

He got in, shut the door, and considered what to do next. He was hungry and couldn't remember when he last ate. He still had twenty miles to make Emporia and he figured another hundred to Durham. He rolled out of the gas station back onto 58 and decided to find a place to eat in Emporia.

He never thought of the lost money or the woman who ripped him off until much later and when he did it was as if it had happened to someone else with someone else's money.

In a way, he told himself, it felt like what should have happened.

The remaining drive to Emporia was uneventful, only the steady reminder of Durham in his ears and a flashing blue light on the other side of the highway warning him to keep it under the limit in the famously over-patrolled environs of the town.

Soon he was at the counter of a twenty-four-hour greasy spoon diner ordering a meal. It was a soup kind of night and he could smell a crock of chicken dumpling simmering nearby. He added a grilled cheese and unsweetened iced tea and propped his elbows on the well-worn counter.

Several TVs faced the room, all tuned to different broadcasts and none with sound. The one closest to him was set to CNN where an obviously animated panel discussion proceeded. A bright red chyron scrolling across the bottom of the screen caught his eye:

Will Governor's Absence Effect Polls?

The scene changed to a reporter under bright lights outside a large brick building. The caption told him he was looking at a live shot at the Duke University Medical Center in Durham, North Carolina.

He felt a surge and heard the ocean in his ears. And he knew this was his destination. From the truck stop on, the thrumming voice calling out *Durham* would be replaced by *Duke*.

He hated Duke as a matter of course. He was an old-line Duke hater. He was a pre-Christian Laettner Duke hater. He was a Duke hater when hating Duke wasn't a thing. The thought of being on campus was like showing Dracula the cross. He was a UVA fan even though he reflected he would not be welcome in that hallowed button-down-khakis-with-no-socks ground.

All of this flashed through his mind while he contemplated the new destination. He thought about the voices he heard in his head. He guessed there were only four possible voices.

He could hear his own self and often did talk to himself alone.

Then there were the voices of others that had an echoey quality about them—in other words they were reflected rather than direct voices. For instance, he often had the reverberations of a slight received from a random person he encountered in public, like a salesperson who was rude to him. He could hear their words and their exact voice sometimes for a whole day.

Sometimes, if he tried, he could recall others voices from many years ago. His mother's voice was a prime candidate for this kind of recall. It came uninvited into many otherwise peaceful moments. He wondered at this. So negative.

But there were also some voices he heard that said good things; positive things. He had a twelve-step sponsor who said many good things and whose voice came to him.

So there were two voices he felt he knew well: his own and the echoes of those he had heard in the past. Then there were the other two. If God was one, the other must be the devil. He couldn't see that there could be one without the other.

He never thought about God or the devil before prison. He met both there in person and discovered he knew them both better than he thought he did. There were people in prison who insisted they heard one or the other speak audibly to them, and some claimed it as a regular occurrence. Doug never heard either God or the devil speaking out loud but he believed both did.

He came to believe the devil spoke to him a lot and suggested a lot of things to him. A visiting minister gave a talk about it. He said something about the sheep of God knowing his voice and following him.

He also said that only two kinds of people speak to sheep, shepherds and butchers, and you had to figure out first if you were a sheep and then who you belonged to. The butcher says harsh things and driving things to move sheep to the slaughterhouse and the shepherd says soothing things and kind things to get the sheep to follow him to pastures.

Doug didn't know why this affected him as it did but he found himself crying and saying a prayer at the end of that minister's talk. He was a sheep. God called and he heard it.

He thought about it later and decided that the reason he knew it was God was because the other voice was so clearly driving him to destruction.

God and the devil. He went back to the twelve-step meetings and told them he found his higher power. Things changed then. Slowly he felt the change. He didn't know how to describe what happened to him. He had a long talk with an inmate who carried a Bible around all the time.

Four voices. Self. Others. The devil. God. He could hear them all. Which one was which was the question. Others seemed easy to know. Their voices went with their faces and moments he knew them. Self and God and the devil all felt intertwined. How to know?

He took his time with the soup and sandwich. The soup smelled much better than it tasted and it tasted impossibly like aluminum kettle. He tried to improve it with saltines and then pieces of shredded grilled cheese but nothing helped. He left it for dead and finished the sandwich.

Now that he had a defined destination, he felt a sense of urgency growing in him although he still didn't know what he was to do when he got there. Along with this he also sensed he was on a mission of some sort. God was talking to him? That sounded weird when he said it in his head.

He paid for his food with the second magic hundred-dollar bill without suspicion and received back eighty-six ordinary dollars and some change. He put a ten dollar tip on the counter near the terrible soup and made his way back to the car.

He typed Duke Medical Center into his phone's map app. It told him he had a two-hour drive. He checked the time. It was just after eleven p.m. He wasn't tired and didn't think he could sleep now any way.

He sat for a moment and thought over what was happening. From a drive home to a drive to nowhere to a drive south and west to a drive to Durham to a drive to Duke. And the last little bit convinced him he was hearing from God. He said it out loud to the rearview mirror.

"I'm on a mission from God." He thought it would sound funny. He thought he would replay a scene from the *Blues Brothers* and laugh at himself and maybe turn around. But it didn't sound funny. It sounded true. It rang with affirmation. He said it again, "I'm on a mission from God," and added, "I'm going to Durham. To Duke."

CHAPTER TEN

Doug turned over the ignition. Nothing but a long, ugly, metallic grind like someone shaking a can half-full of nuts, bolts, and washers. He knew next to nothing about cars but he knew this wasn't good. He tried it again and got the same result.

On the third try he was startled by a knock on the glass half an inch from the back side of his head. He stabbed at the power window button realizing a second late that there was no power. Opening the car door, he stood up into the still-misting night and came face-to-face with the blackest human being he had ever laid eyes on.

"Can't keep on doing that, son. Starter's give up the ghost, sounds like. Won't help to keep grinding it."

Doug looked at the man blankly. He looked back with a question on his face Doug couldn't read.

"My name is Doug Windsor. I'm on my way to Duke Medical Center." He had no idea why he said it or what it had to do with a busted starter or this man.

"My name is Ivory White," the man said. "I drive a truck." He pointed to a rig about a hundred yards across the black top. "I just finished hauling a load to Norfolk and I'm headed home for a few days." Before he finished speaking, Doug knew where he lived and that he was going to offer him a ride.

"Home's Greensboro," Doug said. "Wouldn't mind some company for the last bit of your drive. Been all over the northeast for the past three weeks."

Ivory White didn't look surprised or impressed. His face remained in that barely perceptible hint of a question.

Doug took the change from his meal out of his pocket and offered it to the man. He took it, examined the folded bills and extracted a twenty and handed the remainder back. He gestured toward his truck and said, "Let's be going then."

Doug reached in the still-open car door and started to retrieve his keys, hesitated, and instead got his work ball cap.

""I'm with you. Let's go," he said.

Ivory White turned out to be as laconic as the flat-tire woman was loquacious. After he situated Doug in the truck cab and ascertained his exact destination as the medical center proper, he didn't make another sound for ninety miles. Ivory preferred cool jazz to idle chatter. It suited Doug but also made him sleepy. He dozed while the big rig hummed along and woke with a start when Ivory White's rich baritone voice broke in on him.

"Durham exit," he said. "Ten minutes to the med center."

Doug stirred and checked his watch. He had been out for about an hour but it felt like he was coming up out of a deep well of sleep. He checked himself for drool. Clear. The taste of the meal from the Emporia diner lingered in his mouth. He wished he had a stick of gum. Ivory didn't seem like the gum chewing type but he asked anyway.

"No. No gum. But…" He reached into a compartment in the door and pulled out a bottle of yellowish mouthwash and offered it. Doug took a sizable mouthful of the strong-smelling stuff and swished it around, thinking of a guy he knew on the job site who drank it when he couldn't get booze. *Awful-tasting stuff*, he thought, and realized he was stuck with a mouthful. Ivory took notice.

"Comin' to a stoplight. Roll down your window and spit it out." He did.

"Here's the place," Ivory said a minute later. "Can't pull in there. Not made for rigs. But that's the main entrance right there." He gestured at a well-lit glass-covered causeway resembling an airport drop-off lane. *Duke University Hospital* stood out above one end in two-foot high stainless steel lettering.

"Can't miss it from here," Doug said.

"Guess not," was all Ivory White said back.

Doug shook his hand because this familiarity seemed the right thing to do to end this strange ride on this strange night. He got out and crawled down from the rig. The door hardly clunked shut before the big machine rumbled off, leaving behind the scent of diesel.

CHAPTER ELEVEN

Now what? He had gone to sleep with a destination in mind and nothing else. He walked to the nearest glass door, which opened onto an inevitably bright lobby and the antiseptic smell of hospital. It was too quiet in the way only large spaces made for many people are when they are empty, as if the furniture and walls themselves were lonely.

He sat down on a couch and tried to hear the voice. It was as silent as the lobby. *This can't be the point*, he thought. *I didn't come here to sit on a couch.* He got up and began to walk around the perimeter of the lobby. When he stopped to get a drink from the water fountain, he glanced up and found himself just outside the door of the hospital chapel.

It was closed. He tried it. It wasn't locked. *This was too clichéd*, he thought. *Going into a church to search out the voice of God. Is that what I'm doing? Is this God?* He realized that until this moment he hadn't assigned an identity to the voice. He only knew it wasn't himself and it didn't feel malevolent like the driving voice of addiction or the repeated voices of mean people he often fought to silence. God then? Maybe. So maybe it was right to go in and listen for it or him to speak.

The chapel door swung shut behind him. It was a small room with old-fashioned wooden pews that could probably seat twenty-five on either side of the center aisle. Backlit stained glass panels adorned each wall and there was a table and lectern on a slightly raised dais at the front. The table was ornamented with two imitation brass candle stick holders with tall white unit candles in them. The center of the table held a gold cross with the always puzzling letters IHS on it.

Everything looked like it could move in an instant. He had been in old churches where everything was obviously weighty. They said, *We are immovable and we are here to remind you that God doesn't change*. Here everything gave off the essence of mutability. Like a scene set for a play, all of this could move in an instant. Even the stained glass panels looked as if they could flicker to a new image at the push of a switch.

Doug took this all in and felt disappointed. It didn't feel like a place to hear God. He completed his advance to the table however and was about to turn to go when he saw the lectern held a large, illustrated Bible so big its sides spilled over the wooden edges. He approached it and found it was open to the Gospel of Luke.

On the left-hand leaf, taking up the entire page, was a colored print of Jesus. He was bending over a bed where a girl lay. The girl's eyes captured Doug's attention. The artist had managed to stop time in such a way that you couldn't tell whether she was awake or asleep. Her whole body was positioned in a way suggesting complete repose; no action or hint of movement past, present ,or future. Yet her eyes were open and so full of life that they created movement all their own. And her eyes were fixed on the man bent over her bed.

Jesus appeared to have just spoken. There was tension in his lips but nowhere else. His body language was easy; his hands at his side. His eyes met hers. To Doug it looked like there was a look of jest between them; as if they knew something funny no one else in the picture knew.

Doug was lost in the painting. He let himself go as the picture called him. It was the first time in his life he ever fell into a work of art and it exhilarated him. The fact that it was here on cheap paper without any setting or accoutrement was irrelevant. He drank it in completely.

Finally, as his eyes began to wander about the painting and out to its edges, his reverie was interrupted by a clunky label centered at the bottom of the page. It said "Talitha Koum" in too-fancy script lettering.

"Tah-lith-a Koom," he said out loud to the empty chapel, wondering if he'd pronounced the odd words correctly.

The sound of his own voice startled him for an instant. It fell on muffled walls and sounded dead in the room.

The voice was back and clear.

This is you. This is what you're here to do.

And it all came clear. He saw it as he heard it. He heard it as clearly as he saw the picture.

He gave one more look at the open Bible, sucked in a deep breath, and started back out of the chapel. At the door he noticed a stack of paperback New Testaments. He picked one up and returned to the lectern. Thumbing through the newly acquired book, he came to the matching passage, folded a corner of the page to mark it, and shoved the book into his pocket. It might come in handy to know where this was.

CHAPTER TWELVE

The hospitality desk was manned with a sleepy-looking woman in her sixties with horn rimmed glasses. She wore a salmon-colored vest and, as Doug approached, stirred herself into an attitude of practiced hospitality. *Funny word*, he thought. *Never considered a hospital as a hospitable environment.* He approached the rounded wooden counter considering how to ask for the information he needed. He decided on an indirect tack.

"Hello, ma'am. Do you have a map of the hospital I could use?" He knew it sounded stupid as it came out of his mouth. The woman scrunched her lips to one side in a movement that made her face look like a leather bag with a draw string in it pulling it shut.

"We do," she said, reaching into a drawer and withdrawing a trifold color pamphlet. "But normally we can direct people wherever they need to go." She raised her eyebrows inquiringly.

He met her eyes and felt the question but turned it down. He reached instead for the pamphlet, trying not to look as sheepish as he felt. He felt the insistence of the voice and the outrageousness of what he was about to do couldn't stand up to any scrutiny or he would stall out.

The woman handed the map over and stood up, unfolding it to reveal its contents. She was the type who helped you no matter how much you insisted you didn't need help or how little she knew about what you actually needed.

"Here we are," she said, pinning the map down with a bony finger, "and here are the main elevators. The cafe is here and restrooms are here. If you want to visit a patient you'll have to wait for normal visiting hours to start at nine." She met his eye again with the question and he again avoided it.

"Thank you," he said, taking the map and folding it back together. He turned and walked away before she could continue helping. He had not noticed any security in the lobby but he assumed they were near. He hoped the woman would keep her curiosity to herself.

He knew this was a busy hospital and he couldn't be the only person roaming around in the middle of the night. Still, she had given him a look that made him feel like a suspect and he wanted to get away quickly to his task. He slipped around a corner and entered the restroom she had indicated. He spread out the map on the handy baby changing station next to the paper towels.

He thought he knew the name of the location he was looking for but it wasn't listed where it should have been alphabetically. He switched back to the top of the legend and proceeded to go through it line by line. He found what he was looking for under "D."

Decedent Care. That must be it. *Guess we don't call it the morgue any more. What an odd name. Made it sound like just another department. Another medical department.* But the location said more than the name. Decedent Care was on something called Sublevel Zero. Obviously the basement. Under everything and everyone else.

A quick scan of the map showed that it was also in the back side of the building and a loading dock was just outside the door. *Okay. Now to make my way there.* The voice was pounding now. Louder than ever. What it said was ridiculous but it was at the same time so clear and clearly not something he would ever say to himself he knew it must be God.

He exited the bathroom, leaving the map where it lay. There was nothing else on Sublevel Zero so he had no doubt he would find what he was looking for as soon as he found the way down to it. That turned out to be simple enough. Getting into the main elevator, the panel showed two levels below the lobby, the bottom-most button labeled Sublevel Zero.

He punched it and the doors closed him in with his thoughts. The sense of being a trespasser grew moment by moment although he had done nothing any other person in the hospital might not do. But he was getting ready to do something no one in any hospital would ever do and that awareness made him feel like it was written on his forehead and beeping like a truck backing up as he descended to the bottom floor.

When the doors opened he was so lost in his own thoughts that he stepped out of the elevator car without looking and ran straight into three men coming the opposite direction.

The frontmost man in the group came face to face with Doug and they were both momentarily knocked off balance. Each instinctively reached out to steady the other and keep them from falling. The result was two men in an awkward embrace half in and half out of the elevator. Their faces were inches apart.

Under other circumstances it would have been comical and possibly would have elicited laughter from the right kind of people. In this moment Doug wanted to disappear and the man in his grip looked like he couldn't get away from this place fast enough.

The man, a nice-looking black man in a suit sans neck tie, had been crying, his chocolate brown eyes swollen and bloodshot. One of the men behind him was a doctor in green scrubs with a white lab coat, the other was dressed almost exactly like the one in Doug's grasp except his tie was still around his neck although loosened.

The front man found his voice first. His face went from surprised to angered to full control so quickly and expertly Doug doubted he would have seen it had he not been mere inches away.

"Whoa, there," he said in a distinctly paced voice. He squeezed Doug's arms a little tighter from the accidental grip and went to a purposeful hold. He set Doug back on his balance as he deftly set himself aright.

"We've got to be more careful or we'll end up in the papers."

Doug had no idea what this meant until he stepped fully back and got the measure of the man. Recognition dawned on him. He was face to face with the governor or North Carolina and likely-presidential-candidate Daniel Treeright. Doug recognized him at the same instant the trailing man pushed forward and broke their mutual grasp with a not-too-gentle shove to Doug's chest. The medical man looked on at the scene, frozen in place.

"Whoa, Syd," Treeright said. "No need for that. This young man and I are just going different directions in the same space. No harm intended, I'm sure." His voice and his demeanor were now full politician. In control and assessing the advantages and disadvantages of the moment while wearing an implacable though weary and wary smile.

Doug felt as if he were watching all of this from outside his own body, observing it rather than participating in it. It fascinated him to see this man, who had just a moment ago stepped out of a room where his daughter lay dead and cold, snap from grief and distraction into focused politician. It was frightening as much as it was amazing.

Doug was yanked back into the here and now with the bump from the governor's sidekick—a man he also recognized from Treeright's television appearances—and the next words from the governor.

"Where you headed in such a hurry?"

Doug was stymied. He couldn't say he was headed to see the dead girl himself and he couldn't think of anything plausible to say otherwise.

He stammered "Ahhh, I'm ahhh…"

And here the doctor chimed in unhelpfully, "I think you must be lost." He looked Doug up and down, scanning for some identification and deciding he must be a misplaced visitor.

"Nothing down here except the morgue."

The man glanced regretfully toward Treeright at the mention of that place. "Unless you're here to…." He trailed off, leaving the obvious reason unstated.

Doug, still reeling, took an extra beat to catch on to the end of that line. Oh. Unless he was here to identify someone in the morgue. Or to see someone there.

"Ah, yeah. My, ah, sister is here." He grasped the line and tried to pull himself from this situation. "I just got here from out of town."

The tone around him changed immediately. Shared grief replaced manly posturing. Each man's face reflected it back to him.

Treeright morphed again and this time it felt to Doug that he became his true self for an instant. A human among humans. He didn't have time to consider how odd it was that death should produce this kind of authenticity. The doctor was talking again and inquiring.

"I'm sorry. What is your sister's name?"

Doug spit out the first thing that came to his mind, hoping it sounded convincing.

"Sara Anderson"

The doctor nodded and gestured. "Down the hall to the right. There's a place to sign in. The attendant on duty will help you to find your sister."

Doug made himself smile and nod while his mind began to spin. He had not thought through any of this. Once he heard the last word from the voice he had assumed he would walk into the morgue and do this ridiculous thing alone.

Why would there be anyone tending to dead people? Why set a watch over a person who was never again going to be able to get up and walk away or guard a person who could never be hurt again? Doug had pictured a dark room with rows of tables and sheets covering inert bodies. The only difficulties he anticipated were locating the morgue, and once in there, pulling up sheets one by one, searching until he found her. Now he realized it wasn't so simple.

He managed to mumble his thanks and began to slip past the group of men. Treeright gripped his arm again and purposefully met his eyes. The human being was still present and Doug saw the grieving father looking at him through those eyes. All pretense was gone, all barriers down.

He looked back, barely able to meet that gaze. He wondered what his eyes said. He wondered if the deceit showed. But then he thought of his task and the voice and the command and he wanted to say, "Don't worry. It's going to be alright." He tried to put this thought into his return look. But he realized it was in vain. Did he believe that himself?

Syd DeVito broke the moment by throwing his arm against the elevator door as it tried to close for the third time.

"Let's go, Dan."

CHAPTER THIRTEEN

In an instant Doug was alone in a long, empty hallway. He hesitated and then began to walk in the direction the doctor had indicated. The voice was clear about what to do but now that he was here he needed to know how to do it. He said this out loud, raising his hands over his head in exasperation.

"What am I supposed to do? Walk in there and tell them I'm here to see Tabitha Treeright? This is crazy! This is nuts. I can't do this."

Silence. He felt the silence as clearly as he'd felt the voice. There was nothing more to say. He was here and the way was set. Go or don't go. No more direction.

He came to the entrance to the morgue. A large white sign with stark black lettering stuck out over the double wide doorway: Decedent Care. The two swinging doors were paneled with stainless steel kick plates. The shiny metal was marred with scratches from gurneys carrying decedents to their last stop on the hospital hospitality train.

The scarred doors held his eyes for a second. Saddened, he thought to the people coming through these doors; the last mark they'd leave on the world was a scratch on a cold piece of metal. Looking through the window in the door he saw a glass-fronted booth like a movie theater ticket booth. He couldn't see anyone behind the glass but he assumed the attendant would be there.

He wavered. Yes or no? Go on or quit? Was this real or was he a fool? Why was he standing in the morgue of Duke Medical Center trying to see the body of a dead girl he didn't know? He had no earthly reason for being here, and should anyone question him, he could give no account for being here and for being out of bounds from the limits of his parole.

His feet were cement. Go on? He had no car. No easy way of retreat. No money to get back home. No place to regroup and form a new plan. He laughed in spite of himself. There was no plan; had not been a plan. He wasn't here because of a plan, he was here because of a voice.

God's voice? He went from sure to unsure like the flickering of a battery gauge. Still, as he stood there, he found he had no real choice. No way back and only this insane task before him. He reached out and pushed the door open and advanced into the morgue, suddenly resolved to keep going until he was physically restrained or had completed the task.

As he approached the ticket booth, a middle-aged Hispanic man appeared, framed by harsh fluorescent light. He wore a white lab coat over green scrubs and had a tired expression. His ID badge was visible through the wire hatching crisscrossing the glass. It said Romeo Carnell.

"Cool name," Doug said, nodding toward the man's chest.

The man looked down at his name badge and back up, nodding. "Glad you think so," he said. "Caused me enough grief when I was a kid. I guess we can't account for what our mothers and fathers are thinking when they name us. How can I help you?"

Doug decided to drop any pretense and embrace the moment. If he was crazy he needed someone to stop his craziness and if he was really hearing God a way would open up for him to keep going, right?

"I need to see Tabitha," he said. And added "Tabitha Treeright."

Romeo's eyes narrowed and hardened. He looked Doug up and down.

"And who are you?"

Doug saw his reflection in the glass, and for the first time since he rolled out of bed and into his car some five or so hours ago, saw what Romeo and everyone else he'd run into had seen: a disheveled mop of brown hair stuffed up under a dirty green Jay's Masonry Inc ball cap, an unchecked growth of scraggly beard flowing from his face down his neck and disappearing into the frayed collar of a wrinkled t-shirt, black sweatpants sporting stains from various snacks eaten over the course of too many nights in front of the television, and worn out New Balance running shoes with no socks.

Looking into his own large brown eyes, nervous and wide, the only thing convincing him he wasn't seeing a homeless man who wandered in off the street was the still lingering smell of his Old Spice body wash in his nostrils.

"I'm nobody. I mean I'm not anyone to her or... I just need to see her." He faded off into a silence that quickly grew pregnant as Romeo continued to look him over. The morgue attendant's face grew weary and he seemed to reach a decision. Doug thought the door was going to open. Then Romeo spoke.

"Look, man," he said. "I don't want to have to hassle with you or get the security guys up at"—he glanced at his watch—"two in the morning. Why don't you get lost?" He looked at Doug not unkindly but with resolution.

"I know what I look like and I know this is strange but I need to see her. It's not for anything bad." He couldn't bring himself to say out loud to another person what he was here to do.

Romeo sighed and reached for the phone on the counter before him. He mumbled to himself as he did, "They told me sickos from the press might try to get in here. Didn't think there'd be sickos right off the street."

He glanced up and to the side looking for a phone number posted there. Not finding it, he turned away and rifled through some papers on the desk behind him.

Doug decided not to wait for whatever was coming next. He looked to the left of the booth and saw what he presumed was the door to the morgue itself.

When Carnell found the number and looked up again, Doug was gone from view. He decided to forego the call to security, assuming he had discouraged the unwanted intruder.

Doug entered the morgue fully expecting to meet resistance; a locked door, or another attendant or Carnell, but the door swung inward easily under his hand, and he found himself alone in a room so brilliantly lit he momentarily shielded his eyes as if emerging out of doors into full summer sunlight .

The space was longer than it was wide with two rows of stainless steel doors on either side; one row at knee level and the second at chest level. The room smelled like hospital with a hint of Pine-Sol and something that reminded him of his high school biology class.

The floor was pure white tile and spotless. His shoes squeaked as he approached the set of doors to his left. There was an index card-sized frame set in the center of each door. Glancing around the room, he saw that half the doors had white cards filling these frames. He was relieved. Maybe it would be easier to find her than he thought. These must identify whoever was behind each door.

He puzzled over the lack of a handle, then running his hands along the edges of the steel square at his knees, he discovered insets on either side where he could grip the door. He pulled back and the whole door came riding back smoothly toward him. It was the front of a drawer like a large filing cabinet except this drawer was a flat slab of silver metal. As it slid out, a light flickered on, illuminating the slab and confirming its emptiness.

He pushed it back in and moved to the nearest drawer that had a white label posted on it. *Doe, John*, it said, with an eight-digit number under the name. He quickly worked out that the number equated to a date with the month, day, and year running together. An electric current began surging through his body as he felt the awareness of trespassing. Involuntarily he glanced over his shoulder to see if he was still alone. He spotted a video camera mounted over the door through which he had entered.

Quickly he began searching labels. The girl had to be here. Treeright's presence made that a certainty. Where was she? Just then the lights in the room seemed to dim and his heart went from racing with fear about trespassing to pounding with anticipation. The far side of the room felt like it went down a tunnel. His vision went with it. He focused in on the last drawer on the top and he knew it would be her.

He went to it and read the label. *Treeright, Tabitha*. Here she was. Now could he follow through and do this? His reason screamed at him to run out the back and find a way home but he saw his own hands, as if they belonged to someone else, grip the sides of the drawer and pull it out to its full length.

A black rubber bag lay there, stitched closed by a wide silver zipper. He could see the outline of its contents. A body. The oversized tab of the zipper stuck out at the top of the bag where a small mound suggested the girl's head must be.

Again, hands that felt detached from his body reached out and grasped the zipper tab. The zipper came back easily with a muffled *click click click*. He noticed the cold now for the first time. The room was chilly but the inside of this drawer was as cold as opening a door into winter.

He shivered involuntarily, not knowing if it was a reaction to the cold or to the corpse, realizing at this moment that he had never before seen a dead body. He reached up with both hands and separated the edges of the black rubber. The silver zipper grinned against the black like awful metallic teeth forced open to reveal what death had swallowed.

He hesitated with the thought that the girl would be naked under this bag. He did not want to see that. The demons of his past screamed at him full throated, but he quickly shook them off. The incongruency of this place and time thrown at his mind as something sexual had the opposite effect. It drew him into the utter reality of the sorrow before him. The loss. The offense of death itself.

He gently opened the bag to reveal the girl.

A white sheet was pulled up to her shoulders, leaving the barest part of her thin neck showing. He was struck by her peaceful expression. Painless. Calm. No worry on her face. No fear. Her olive skin was tinged blue around the edges of her mouth and nostrils. The stillness of the body unsettled him. He was unprepared to see a dead body for the first time; confronted with its complete immobility.

He discovered that he'd been holding his breath and let out a long exhale. Reaching out a tingling hand, he touched the girl's face. It was reflexive; checking to see if she was real, if all this was real.

The unnatural cold skin caused him to quickly withdraw the hand as if it had been the exact opposite temperature. Glancing over his shoulder to see if he was still alone, he shook his head, clearing the sense of being in a dream. This was all real enough, and he forced himself to lean in close to the dead girl. The height of the drawer forced him to bend slightly to bring his face close to hers. She smelled faintly of some medicine-y antiseptic. He sucked in a big shaky gulp of air and whispered out her name.

"Tabitha."

Again. "Tabitha?"

Chill air poured from the black opening at the girl's feet. The whir of the ventilation was the only sound. Doug looked intensely at the girl. Her eyelids, her mouth, her nose. Nothing.

"Tabitha. I came here for you," he said.

The words felt stilted, as if his mouth were full of marbles. It all felt ridiculous. He felt exposed. Embarrassed. Stupid. The girl was so obviously dead. So utterly dead. So immovably dead. And he tried to muster the slightest feeling of belief that he could do anything about that fact. He found none. Stupid, stupid, stupid. Crazy.

He moved to push the drawer shut, ready to run from this place, to retreat far away and hide. Suddenly the picture from the Bible in the hospital chapel flashed through his mind in unworldly vividness. Each detail sprung to life as if it were in three dimensions and he could see it moving. The script title under the picture became like a flashing neon sign.

Talitha koum.

He paused. He had no idea what the words meant. He dimly thought of the Harry Potter books he'd read. Maybe these were magic words? He pulled the paperback New Testament from his pocket, opened it to his folded book mark, and found the words. *Talitha koum.*

Without further thought, he reached under the sheet covering the girl and found her cold hand, rigid by her side. He had to lean over further to get his arm down the side of the bag as he tried to keep the sheet from coming off of her and exposing her nakedness. In this position his face came down to a hair's breadth from hers. He started to cry. All of this odd night pressed into his heart with a surge of sadness and frustration and something else.

Hopelessness.

He realized he had come to this moment with an insane hope. It wasn't just a response to hearing the voice. He had come here for his own redemption. He had come hoping he could be part of a story that would change the course of his own story. That his life would have meaning and his past would shrink away under the weight of a miracle.

A full sob caught in his throat and he tried to suppress it. Nothing could stop the flood of emotion, though, and his cries echoed out into the room of the dead. Involuntarily, he put words to the cries as if they were an ancient dirge. He squeezed the girl's dead hand and put his head on her chest.

"Tabitha! *Talitha koum! Talitha koum! Koum koum koum*!! *Tali...*"

His cry was cut off as he was struck on the back of his head. He crumpled to the ground like a felled tree. His grasp of the girl's hand was tight and his arm was entangled in the sheet. As he fell, the girl's arm was pulled out of the body bag and up over her head in half of a grotesque touchdown gesture. The sheet came out of the bag and draped over the shelf like a white tongue hanging from a snake's mouth.

Doug was dazed. He was on his hands and knees. He couldn't see and his head felt as if it would explode with the radiating pain. He threw up the remnants of the Emporia dinner in a slimy mess.

Someone was standing over him screaming at him but it came through muffled, like a broken speaker in a fast food drive through. Even so, the intensity of the voice told him another blow was likely coming, and he grasped the back of his head with both hands and tried to make himself small.

There was wetness on his hair and he dully guessed it was blood. Then a booted foot crashed into his exposed side with enough force that he felt ribs break. All his breath escaped. He rolled over, gasping in his own vomit, still attempting to shield his head and face from further blows.

Romeo stood over Doug, wielding the industrial-strength three-hole punch he had just used on his head. It was the nearest thing he found when he noticed an intruder in the morgue and guessed it was the homeless guy he thought he had run off by threatening to call security. How had he gotten back here so fast and what was he doing to the governor's daughter?

The man had been draped over the dead girl in an embrace with one hand down inside the body bag, kissing her and calling out her name and saying… What it sounded like he didn't want to think of. Was this man trying to have sex with a dead twelve-year-old??!! *God, the world was getting too sick to live in.* Well he had put an end to that. He screamed at the prone man.

"Stay down! Don't move!"

Romeo raised his improvised metal club to emphasize what would happen if the man didn't comply. There was a phone mounted on the wall at the far end of the room. Romeo walked backward to it so he could keep his eyes on the intruder. He felt adrenalin racing through his body as an invitation to beat this creep to a bloody pulp if he gave him any reason at all, but it seemed the man had passed out. He made no move.

Romeo picked up the phone and punched in the number for security he had looked up only moments ago. A gruff, sleepy voice answered.

"I need help in the morgue," Romeo said. "I've got an intruder here."

The voice didn't respond with a sense of urgency but incredulously repeated the location.

"Yes, the morgue. It's someone messing with the governor's daughter."

Mentioning the governor's daughter seemed to get the energy level amped up on the other end of the line.

"Right. Decedent Care. Sublevel Zero. I've got him."

Romeo hung up the phone, started to turn away but thought better of it. He punched in a nine to get an outside line. Then he called 9-1-1 and asked for local police to respond. He was again met with skepticism claiming a break in at a morgue as if he were pranking the cops, but again, the mention of Governor Treeright got the attention he wanted. He was sure by the time he turned back to the pervert laying in his own puke, he had back up coming from near and far.

He approached the inert form cautiously. The man was beginning to stir. A low moan escaped his mouth. He rolled from his side onto his back and stared up with blinking, dumbfounded eyes. Romeo stood with his feet on either side of his head and looked at him upside down. The man was trying to talk.

"You don't…" he gasped, and winced in pain. *That kick must have cracked a rib or two,* Romeo thought. *Good.*

"You don't understand," he gasped.

"No, and I don't want to, you sick bastard," Romeo said. "Keep your mouth shut. Cops are on their way."

The man's eyes widened at that and he tried to get up. Romeo moved to one side and kicked his elbow out from under him, sending him flat on his back again.

"Not goin' anywhere," he said.

"I'm… not… a pervert. I'm here to help. I'm… here to help… her." Doug said.

Romeo saw to his surprise that tears were flooding into the man's upturned eye sockets and spilling over his cheeks. For an instant Romeo flashed back to the girl's father's face. It was the same grief reflected here in the pervert's face. He shook that thought off with a shudder of revulsion. Couldn't be the same.

"Help her?! Help her? She's dead, man! There's no helping her!"

He leaned down to look more closely into Doug's eyes, wondering now if he was seeing madness instead of evil. He didn't know if one was worse than the other if it drove a man to do what this one was setting out to do.

But the face he saw before him upon this closer examination triggered a completely different response. The face looking back at him had no guile, no cunning, no insanity. The face didn't even contain a hint of malice for the injuries the man had sustained at Romeo's hands and feet. The eyes were tear-filled but unpleading. Grief stricken but calm.

Romeo felt something like pity start up in his chest. He tried to suppress it, but unreasonably, it grew. Seemingly against his will he dropped to a knee next to Doug. He yanked the sheet still dangling from the body bag all the way out and used a corner to wipe blood and vomit from his face. He took out his pocketknife and made a cut so he could rip it. He bunched half of it up, making it into a makeshift pillow for the man's bleeding head.

What am I doing? he thought. *This is nuts. This guy is a creep, a sicko. But he's not.* Somehow Romeo knew it. Something in the man's eyes said it wasn't so and Romeo believed what he saw in those eyes more than what he had seen with his own eyes. It was a look that Romeo would remember the rest of his life.

There was blood spreading out like a red halo on the white sheet behind Doug's head. Romeo gently lifted his head and turned it to one side to examine the place where he had clubbed him. There was a jagged two-inch gash in the scalp he could see through blood-soaked hair. It looked nasty and was bleeding profusely. Romeo cut another strip off the sheet, folded it over several thicknesses and pressed it to the wound. Doug winced at the pressure.

"Here," Romeo said, taking one of Doug's hands and placing it over the improvised bandage.

"Keep pressure on it while I go and get the first aid kit. You're bleeding a lot."

Doug complied. He said, "Thank you, Romeo."

Romeo was mildly jolted to hear his name come from the bleeding stranger and it must have shown on his face. Doug directed a glance to the name tag he was wearing.

"Not a name that's easy to forget," he said, smiling weakly in spite of the fog in his broken head.

CHAPTER FOURTEEN

Doug's pain had eased from swelling thunder claps to sharp throbbing and his eyesight was clearing of the red edges that accompanied the initial blow to his head. He rested his head on top of his hand and the bandage, using its weight to add pressure and stop the flow of blood.

Romeo got up and jogged back out the door to search for the first aid kit. A sense of urgency grasped Doug and he struggled to get to his feet. He followed Romeo's retreat with his eyes and then took in the scene in the room. Tabitha still lay with her right arm posed over her head where Doug had pulled it out as he fell.

She was naked now, the sheet having been ripped away in the tumult, and she lay exposed to her belly; her lower half covered by the half-unzipped body bag. Doug retrieved the balled up remnant of the sheet which was stained red with his blood and tried to cover her.

He scanned the girl's face for signs of life. The job was not complete if she was still dead, right? He was sure he was here to help her. To raise her. The name. The picture in the lectern Bible. The urgency to come to this place. Maybe he didn't get something right. Tabitha lay still. No breath. No life. No fluttering eyelids.

Doug took her outstretched arm and laid it atop the bloody sheet he had spread over her nakedness, grasped her hand again, and said, "Tabitha, please wake up. Please wake up. I think I was sent here to wake you up."

Nothing. He knew he must be out of time. Security or police or both would be flooding in here any second. He looked to the back end of the room and saw a door marked with a sign: *Exit to loading bay - never leave this door open.*

He could run for it now and make an escape. It was possible. This was obviously a failure. At best it was God playing a sick joke on him. At worst... he didn't want to consider the worst but he did anyway—at worst he really was losing his mind.

He took all this in in an instant and for the second time tonight decided there was no retreat for him. This was an all-or-nothing moment. A moment he could and would live with no matter what came next. He threw himself on Tabitha's dead body, embracing her. His head was on her chest and he was draped over her when he shouted, his voice cracking with intensity:

"Tabitha!!!! *KOUM*!!!!"

Two things happened at once. For the second time in five minutes, Doug was clubbed in the head; this time a punch to his right ear which ruptured his eardrum and would leave him deaf on that side for the rest of his life.

And, in the barest sliver of a second before he crumpled to the floor, he thought he heard, in his left ear pressed to the girl's chest, a faint thump. It disappeared from his hearing and his thoughts as he again fell to the cold white tile floor.

Chaos ensued in the morgue. Two patrol cars had been lingering near the hospital in the wake of the media circus that had attended Tabitha's struggle and eventual death. Both were stocked with two Durham police officers.

They had responded to the 9-1-1 immediately, and because the hospital security office was located on the opposite end of the large complex of buildings from the morgue, the police officers and security force converged on Sublevel Zero at the same moment.

While Romeo was vainly trying to locate the office first aid kit, four Durham cops and three hospital security guards crashed through the same door Doug had used to get into the morgue. They saw a bloody man embracing a dead girl screaming gibberish—or something much worse.

The nearest cop had tried to taser the man but the youngest security guard crossed his line of fire, ran up to the man, and without stopping crashed a fist into his ear. As the man fell prostrate, Romeo ran into the room yelling for them to stop but it was a melee.

Shouting to each other, guards to guards, cops to cops, and cops to guards, it was a testosterone-infused cacophony.

One cop cursing above the chaos fell on the prone figure and started landing punches on his upturned defenseless face. It looked like the end of an MMA fight when one of the combatants had succumbed but there was no referee to call the match.

A beefy security guard landed a kick to Doug's side that landed with such force it flipped his unconscious body onto its side.

Romeo screamed, "Nooooooo!!!!" and launched himself into the middle of the scrum, trying to use his own body to shield Doug from more blows.

He got a partial punch to the small of his back for his trouble from a cop or guard in mid-swing when he jumped into the fray.

The closest cop grabbed him and tried to drag him off Doug but he held on, still yelling at them to stop. He had broken the momentum of the men's anger like a breakwater in a storm surge. The lead cop took charge, moving in quickly to bring order.

"Cuff him," he said to a young cop who had been on the verge of landing some punches of his own. When he hesitated, the leader shouted, "Do it! Now!"

Unbelievably, Doug stirred and opened his eyes. He was staring at black boots inches from his face. His head was beyond hurting now. It felt as if it must either cease to ache or cease to be attached to his body.

He heard a ringing in the ear that the guard had punched but the voices around him were muffled and distant. He tried to move his hands to get them under him and push up to his knees but he discovered both arms were trussed behind his back and his wrists were pinched together.

As he discovered this, he was lifted roughly to his feet by hands gripping him under either arm. He was set on his feet but his legs didn't want to cooperate and his knees buckled.

He also discovered that he had urinated on himself involuntarily at the last kick to his side, the warm wet legs of his sweatpants informing him of the fact.

He looked for all the world as if he had lived on the street for months when in reality he had walked into the hospital less than thirty minutes ago clean, well fed, and more in control of his life than he had been for most of his thirty-three years.

His eyes were swelling shut from the rain of punches to his face. The man who had clubbed him on the head and then strangely comforted him was standing in front of him and trying to get his attention.

Romeo, he thought. *Right. Head hurts like hell but the brain is still working. That's a good thing right?* Doug tried to understand what Romeo was saying and turned his head so the still functioning ear was facing him.

"Tell them what you told me," Romeo said.

Doug was puzzled. "Wha…?" he mumbled through swollen, broken, bleeding lips. He hadn't told Romeo anything. He was blank. All that came to mind was the last thing that came out of his mouth before the beat down began. So he said it. *"Talitha koum…? Tabitha. Koum!"*

This was not what Romeo had in mind. He wanted Doug to tell them he had come to help the girl and then he wanted Doug to tell them... what? Something he said with his eyes. Something untranslatable and transcendent. Something that had flipped a switch in Romeo that would never get unflipped. But it wasn't in words and it wasn't in this battered face now. It was gone.

The reaction to Doug's words had the opposite effect to the one Romeo hoped for; it reignited the smoldering fire of indignation in the guards and the cops.

"The perv is still talking about getting off on this dead girl!" the beefy guard who had lifted Doug off the ground with his kick shouted. The two cops who had pulled him off the floor and held him upright by either arm simultaneously squeezed down hard.

It felt to Doug that his biceps would pop like balloons if they kept it up. He cried out in pain but it was cut short when the lead cop pushed past Romeo and punched him in his unprotected stomach. Doug buckled with the blow, all the air escaping his lungs, the room, the universe. He lurched forward but the men jerked him back upright. He thought he would die then.

Romeo thought the men would swarm Doug again and this time wouldn't stop until they had killed him. In desperation he pointed to the security cameras mounted in the four corners of the room.

"Look! Look! Video! All this is on tape, man! You guys are gonna catch hell for this if you don't stop now! You're beating an unarmed man who didn't threaten you at all!! You'll get sued. You'll get canned!"

Romeo 's words lowered the temperature in the room instantly, his appeal to their self-interests hitting the mark. The lead cop was the first to back off and he called the others down with both hands raised, palms out in a gesture like he was in the middle of an intersection.

All stop all directions.

He looked into the nearest camera, knowing Romeo was right. This wasn't going to look good for any of them. He spotted the same sign for the back exit Doug had earlier.

"Harris, Jordan," he barked. "Take this son of a bitch out back."

Romeo thought for a moment the cop was giving them permission to continue the beat down out of view of the cameras, maybe even finish Doug off. He started to protest but the cop cut him off with a finger in his face.

"Rogers, go up and get my cruiser from in front of the hospital and bring it around to the loading dock back here. Hurry up."

The storm was past.

CHAPTER FIFTEEN

Doug was treated at the jail by an unconcerned-looking medic who accompanied him and one of the arresting officers around booking. He was given a tan jumpsuit and an inflexible pair of shower shoes in exchange for his soiled clothes.

The process and the holding cell they deposited him in were all familiar and carried both a sense of nightmarish unreality and the soothing comfort of routine. He had spent almost a third of his life incarcerated, after all. *Shawshank Redemption* scenes where Brooks and Red got out of prison and struggled to adapt to the outside were close things for Doug. He knew the feeling.

All jails must have a sameness to them, he thought. And all the pap about being innocent until proven guilty showed up for the farce it was as soon as you stepped out of your shoes and into those shower shoes. You might not be a dead man walking Death Row but you were a criminal walking a yellow line to wherever they said to walk, and step out of line and you'd find out what guilt felt like. Innocent or no. Inside, you were guilty.

Doug also knew about the cardinal rule of prison life for anyone who carried a whiff of child abuse on them: beat their ass first, second, and third, and don't ask questions later. He was sure, now that he had time to reflect on the scene in the morgue and the beat down he had received that it was this rule the cops and guards applied upon finding him bent over the half-naked dead girl.

Talitha koum, he had said. He had screamed it the second time.

It clicked. They thought he was getting his rocks off on her. *Koum*. Cum. He got it. Oh he got it.

The shaved patch on the back of his head where the medic super-glued closed Romeo's gash told the start of that story, and the swollen face and dull ringing in his punched-out ear told the rest.

Touching the shaved spot, he thought through the odd bit that didn't fit the rest of the story. He remembered Romeo. What happened to that dude? *First he first knocks me down and kicks me and then wants to comfort me and patch me up.*

Doug didn't think he had done or said anything that would have changed the man's mind about him in the flash of an eye. He was too stunned and trying to keep his head from exploding to say much. What had he said? Just that he didn't understand.

Well there was an understatement. Who would understand? Doug didn't. So why would anyone else? He said what else? He said he was there to help Tabitha. But that didn't turn out to be true, did it? Help a dead girl.

Doug felt a strain on his heart rising up as it had lingering over the girl. She looked asleep. She was pretty. Young. He reflected that none of this aroused him. He double checked himself for the demon. No. This was something different. It was an attraction to her tragedy. It was the orbit of loss, of grief. It had pulled him in then and it was here again.

Tabitha. He loved her. He loved her? How could that be true? He didn't know her at all, never met her, never came close to meeting her until he stood over her dead body. And who was there to love when there was no one there but you and a corpse? Where could the love be?

The catch in his chest rose into sobs as it had before, overwhelming him. He got to his knees and rested his head on the cot chained to the wall. The grief more than the lack of rest or the blows to the head made him retreat into a troubled sleep.

CHAPTER SIXTEEN

As quickly as the melee came to the morgue, it was gone. Silence reigned more loudly in the wake of the disturbance. The mid shift in the morgue could be busy but it was never loud. The hospital morgue was never loud on any shift. Even when relatives visited a dead loved one, their grieving was muted. Romeo guessed this might be because it was rare for a person to end up in his morgue without some warning.

The hospital morgue wasn't like the city morgue where accident victims regularly arrived before anyone knew they were there. He had a friend who worked the city morgue. He told Romeo of pulling still ringing cell phones out of the pockets of dead people. The ringing would stop and then start again; a connection that would never be made again.

But here the bodies arrived from failed treatments to sustain life, and most of the time the significant others were keenly aware of the impending loss. He liked to say that people didn't end up in his morgue by accident—a little play on words he thought was clever.

But his morgue looked like the scene of an accident now.

The cops had tracked blood out the back door and the guards had done the same out the front. Tabitha Treeright's dead body lay on the stainless steel drawer, splayed half in and half out of the body bag.

The torn sheet he'd used to staunch the flow of blood from the intruder's head was puddled under the drawer where the girl lay, soaked in his vomit and blood. The sick sweet smell of the vomit lingered in the air along with the locker room odor of the sweaty cops. The place was a disorderly mess.

Romeo liked his morgue to stay in order. He wondered at the fact that two times tonight something had been out of place when he needed it; first the yellow sticky note containing important numbers—always on the wall next to the desk—had gone missing, causing him to turn his back on the man who slipped into his morgue, and second, the first aid kit wasn't where it was supposed to be, making him go looking for it at the moment the cops and guards crashed the place.

He would put things right now. He was sure there were going to be lots of questions to answer and he realized he was in hot water. He should probably get ahead of it and call his supervisor. He hesitated, then decided the dead girl had to be taken care of before he did anything else.

He went to a supply room and retrieved a fresh sheet. He went to the drawer holding Tabitha Treeright's body, unzipped the black rubber bag all the way to her feet, and examined the body for any obvious damage. He was used to looking at dead people of all ages, races, and genders, and it didn't disconcert him.

The girl's body was unchanged as far as he could see. He remembered what he had initially thought the intruder was doing to the girl, and what the cops and guards were sure he had been doing. He examined her groin carefully without touching her. There were no marks on her that indicated she had been violated sexually. He hadn't expected to see any.

He wondered vaguely what it would look like to order a rape kit for a dead girl. This led him to think of the events of the past quarter hour—he double checked the wall clock, incredulous to the scant passage of time—in a new light.

The cops had left the scene so quickly it didn't occur to Romeo they might have muffed their job. He had been relieved to get them under control and out the door without killing the intruder. He didn't think of this as a crime scene.

Though he was sure by some means beyond his ability to explain that the man had not been attempting to sexually violate the body, he had sudden doubts about disturbing the room. Was he destroying evidence by cleaning up and putting the girl back where she belonged? He contemplated this but went on replacing the sheet.

Starting at the girl's feet, he gently wrapped her in it, stuffing the edges tightly under her on each side. She wasn't going to be autopsied; her father had said it on his viewing only minutes before the melee broke out.

Romeo had a slap-your-forehead moment. This wasn't just any dead girl! He realized with a growing sense of dread that this would be a news story and it wouldn't take long. He resolved to get his boss up immediately. He might have to fight off real members of the press before his shift ended. All it would take would be one of the guards talking or some hack monitoring police dispatch and tracking to the same hospital that had just been front and center of a national press gaggle for the past week.

He hustled to finish with the corpse, the urgency of the phone call he needed to make growing by the second. He repositioned her arms at her sides and tucked the sheet tightly around her back. The top of the sheet came to her neck just under her chin. He zipped the body bag to her face and paused.

Some subtlety caught his attention. Something here was different somehow but it was ethereal, like trying to find the differences in those picture games. He was puzzling over it when the phone in his office started ringing. Reflexively, he slid the drawer into its recess and closed the door. He caught the phone on the third ring.

"What the hell's going on?! I've got the Oh-Oh up my ass about somebody invading the morgue?" Romeo heard his boss's voice, sleepy and irritated.

"Oh-Oh" was hospital slang for the Director's office in general but sometimes referred to the Director herself. Romeo feared it was the latter in this case and he was right.

"Called me herself. Two-thirty in the morning, Rom…"

His boss paused. Romeo had never known the guy to raise his voice. It was like the morgue protocol was his permanent volume control, but now it sounded like he was really forcing himself to keep it there.

"Would've been good to have a heads up."

Romeo had no answer ready and he was disappointed in himself for letting his leadership down. He really liked his boss and he chafed at letting him down even if it wasn't, strictly speaking, his fault.

"Frank, I was getting ready to call you but the place is a mess and we had a body out of storage and I couldn't leave it all the way it was. I'm sorry. I should've called you first thing. I don't even know how the Director got the word."

Frank broke in. "Security has a protocol that she's to be called any time law enforcement responds to a call initiated by us." He sounded exasperated but calming a bit. "I take it that the 9-1-1 went out from you?

"Yes, sir, it did."

"And you're all right? No weapons involved? Nobody on our team is hurt?"

Good guy, Romeo thought. *Always had his priorities set on his people.*

"No sir. I'm not sure what version of the story you got, so I can fill you in."

"Please," said Frank.

Romeo began at the governor's visit and told him all that had transpired.

CHAPTER SEVENTEEN

Daniel Treeright and his chief of staff were almost to the Governor's Mansion when Syd got a call.

Daniel was numb, a state unfamiliar to his active mind and body. He felt like he had no life energy left in the tank. No plotting. No strategizing. No spinning. Seeing Tabitha had been like nothing he had ever experienced. He thought he could handle it like a leader handles any crisis—with a reserve of energy and detachment even if it was slight. But it had pulled the plug on his reserves and forced its way into his mind and heart so completely that he had no room for detachment. It went all the way in like the coldest winter chill and left him drained and disoriented.

He found himself momentarily when he collided with the stranger at the elevator, some deep-seated automated political muscle memory kicked in like getting hit in the knee at the doctor's office. But that was it. He barely made it to the car and slumped against the back seat window in a semi-fetal position.

If he could get home and get the door closed behind him, he thought he would not go further than the foyer before giving in and lying face down on the carpeted floor until the sun burned out. No more and nothing. *I am nothing and I can do nothing.*

Syd was getting animated, he could tell, but that wasn't unusual and what could it matter anyway? Nothing. The one-sided conversation he was hearing but not hearing ended. Syd looked at him with an expression he couldn't read and didn't want to try. His chief of staff hesitated, then spoke.

"There's been an incident at the hospital. That was their head of PR." Syd scanned his boss's face for signs of comprehension and decided to plow on.

"Someone broke into the morgue. Must've been right after we left." This got Daniel to at least raise his head and look at Syd.

"The intruder... the guy…" He either could not bring himself to say it or did not know how to say it. Syd was not normally reticent about anything.

Daniel was roused enough to see his friend needed permission to go on. When he met his gaze fully he was surprised to see tears in Syd's eyes.

"What? What happened?"

"They say a man broke in... he was touching Tabitha... her, ah. He was… touching her and argh…." Syd trailed off in a garbled moan of sorrow laced with seething anger.

Daniel was fully engaged now. "What?! He did what?!"

"He was putting his fingers in her and shouting at her to have an orgasm." Syd slumped against his own side of the car.

Daniel was reeling; his life already felt like it must be at the lowest point it could possibly go, and now the bottom had dropped out of even that unthinkably low place. Could this go lower? Could he go lower? A white hot fist gripped his heart and lungs. He could barely breathe. In choked off words he said. "Where? Where?!"

Syd knew instantly what he was asking and regained enough composure to head him off.

"There's nothing you can do about this right now. Nothing good would come of seeing the guy.

"Damn right," Daniel said. "Nothing good will come of it. I don't intend there to be any good. Where is he? County? Where, Syd? I'll get to him with or without you."

Syd considered this and knew it was true. No one was going to keep the perp's location from the governor. He had ten numbers in his cell he could call and get the information right now. He decided it was best for him to stay with his boss and walk through this rather than get tossed from the car and hear about what Treeright did on the news later. If he was there at least he could mitigate it somewhat.

"County," he said. "They took him to County."

Treeright tapped on the glass divider to the driver. It slid back immediately.

"Take us to the Durham County Jail."

"From the sounds of it, they beat the guy pretty badly. Messed him up." Syd said.

Treeright said nothing. His eyes were black coals, dangerously hot and focused. Syd was worried about what the man would do once they got to the jail, but for right now he thought this might be better than the husk of a man who was slumped next to him only moments ago. At least Daniel still had something left in him, some fuel still left to burn even if it was burning with hatred.

"Does Wanda know?" Daniel said.

"I don't think so," Syd said. "Pretty sure this hasn't gotten out to anyone. He paused, then added, "Yet. I told their head of PR to hold it as long as they could but it won't last much past sunrise. Too many story hungry reporters still in town. To many noses in the wind. One of 'em will catch the scent."

Treeright considered this. "Better let her know." Syd looked confused as to who was to accomplish this.

Daniel said, "I'll do it." He took out his phone and called his wife.

Wanda Treeright was lying on the floor in her dead daughter's bedroom, where she had collapsed. She had come to the mansion, ordered that every television be shut off, and made it to their family quarters before wandering back here, drawn as if by a magnet.

Could there be an existence where this mental anguish, this relentless weight crushed you but left you alive? She thought it would subside but she didn't know how. There was nothing to hope for in this circumstance. No redemption. No changing it. The facts were like the ocean coming to the shore of her thoughts over and over. The tide was coming in and it might go out again but it would never stop. They were relentless and merciless.

When her cell buzzed it took her several moments to reconnect to the here and now. Stretching to reach it, she tilted it up to see who it was. Her husband. She considered punching decline but decided to take the call. They were going to talk one way or another in the midst of this shipwreck. Might as well accept it. Daniel wasted no time when he got her on the line.

"Wanda, there's been an incident at the hospital. The details are sketchy but I wanted to give you a heads up. It will probably leak soon."

What could he possibly say next that would matter? she thought. She kept silent. She was familiar with this Daniel. This was the executive. This was the partner in the business of politics. Her husband had long ago disappeared into this man and she had no time for him tonight. She might have no time for him ever again in any context, business or otherwise. She waited.

He ran through the details in a monotone. She listened as if hearing someone tell her a nightmare. Hot tears filled her eyes as Daniel finished. The silence grew. He waited. She waited. Then he broke the connection.

She got up and found her keys. It seemed ludicrous to run to the aid of a dead child, but life was ludicrous, or worse than that, life was meaningless; either way she was on the edge of a knife that was slowly cutting her apart. Movement seemed superior to stillness in this state. She stumbled to her car and started out for the hospital.

CHAPTER EIGHTEEN

It was cold. She was cold. This was the first thing she thought. Cold and dark. This was a big contrast to the last things she remembered.

She had been consumed with heat that wouldn't let up, heat that came from inside her body, not from the sun or a campfire, but from some unseen furnace inside her. Her brain was burning inside her skull with an intensity that she couldn't endure. Her eyes melted. Her ears blew out. Her mouth turned to dust. There was no amount of water in the world to extinguish the fire.

And then there was light brighter than the sun. It was a light that she didn't need her melted eyes to see. It was a thing of awful beauty and intensity. It was inevitable. It was inescapable. It was consuming her. The light and the fire merged into one thing and then became the only thing. There was no more here or her. There was only the Light.

Tabitha? Who was that? What was that? Light, pulsing like a beating heart was all. Then there was sound like the rushing waters of ten thousand waterfalls and it spoke her name but not her name. A name she knew was hers but also knew she had never heard before.

She was again.

She emerged from the Light into the light of the Light. She came out of the shadowland into the land where no shadows could exist. She saw herself emerging as if she had walked through the rushing waters and realized it had been light, cascading light. Liquid light flowing from immense heights and down to forever. And she had passed through it.

How? She didn't know and never knew. She was sure it wasn't on her own feet. She had not walked. She had simply moved without any sense of motion, carried to a place she could never go on her own. More of herself came to her like pieces to a multidimensional puzzle; a puzzle with an image she had never seen and never imagined its completion.

Pieces of a self infinitely more than the girl…? Tabitha?

Yes, that was the name she was called before in the shadowland. It was not the name she heard from the lightfall. Tabitha. Nothing wrong with her old name. It was just too small for her. It couldn't hold her meaning. It couldn't express her full self. It was a cup and she was an ocean. Tabitha. It echoed into the light and bounced off it falling to bits of sound like a dropped glass. *Talitha koum*. What? *Talitha koum*! *Tabitha*!!!!

Darkness. Darkness made more dark by the Light. Darkness more worn than seen or felt. She was a shadow in shadow. She was waking from reality into dream. She wanted to go back, to fall awake, but couldn't will herself to it. It wouldn't come. The cold persisted. She shivered against it and tried to hug herself for warmth. Her arms were pinned to her side. She felt the flesh of her hands touching her legs and realized she was naked.

It all came to her then. She was dead. She died? She was alive. She lived? She was Tabitha the sick girl. The very sick girl in the hospital. So many people coming and going, faces over her face. Her mother. *Mom*! And then the burning heat and the journey to Light and back.

Did she die? Was that what it was? It wasn't like anything she expected it to be. Then again was this living? This cold dark place where there was no light? Life and death were not what she thought they were if all of this was true—all of this what?

Time seemed to be something other, something unreal. She could not grasp it. She had no sense for how long she had been in Light and out of shadow. The sense of urgency hadn't existed there but it crept into her here in the dark, and it grew uncomfortably. She felt it and fought it but it was as real in this land as breathing.

Breathing. She was breathing. That was strange. Breathing again with no sense she had been holding her breath. She thought that phrase was upside down. It was really more true to say that breath held you. Inescapable. But only for shadowland. No breathing in Light land.

She sucked in a huge breath and filled her lungs. The compression on her chest restricted her. She was wrapped in something. The need to be mobile and free took her. She began to roll slightly side to side and felt the grip of whatever held her lessen. Her hands started to come away from her sides and as they did she realized she was wrapped in cloth.

She grasped handfuls of the cloth and pulled. She felt no panic and felt the absence of the panic as a thing. Shouldn't she be afraid? It was as if she had been inoculated by Light. She had experienced peace of a quality that made her at least temporarily immune to fear. She continued to breathe and to roll and to pull and little by little she freed herself.

What next? She was still cold. Still in utter darkness. And still encased in something close and dark and smelling of rubber. —She felt it all around her now that the wrap—a sheet? Yes. Now that the sheet was loose she felt the next layer. It was unpleasant and clammy.

She realized her head wasn't completely enclosed. Her breath was going somewhere. Somewhere out. There was an outside. For a moment she had begun to think she had fallen out of the Light and into the opposite. It made sense. If Light was more real than she ever imagined, wouldn't Dark be the same? But her breath escaped into somewhere out, so out was a possibility. How did this work?

She found she had room to maneuver inside this casement and reached both hands to her mouth. She pushed them forward and outward like a swimmer making the shortest possible breaststroke. Her fingers encountered an opening that was cold and jagged. She parted it and heard a noise that startled her because it was so near and so familiar. A zipper unzipping.

She was in a sleeping bag? What other bag would have a zipper in it? But this was the most uncomfortable sleeping bag. No fluff. No padding. No soft material. Stinky, thin, flat rubber. She found the zipper tab and pulled it down as far as she could reach. She tried to sit up and hit her head on something a foot above her. It clanged with a dull, gong-like sound and she saw stars. It hurt and reflexively she said, "Owwww!"

The sound of her own voice threw her off balance. It was her voice but it felt like it was coming from inside a trash can. It echoed too close and died out too fast. She reached up to feel what she had hit and felt smooth metal in every direction.

Was she in a metal box? In a sheet in a bag in a box... this was very strange. Well, if there was an outside of the sheet and an outside of the bag there must be an outside for this metal box too.

She decided at first to try going toward the far end of the box at her feet to see if it led somewhere. Alternating between pushing up on her elbows and heels, she managed to go only inches before her feet encountered a solid metal wall. The end of the box. She pushed herself back to her starting point and reached behind her head to see if she could feel the other end of the box and there it was, only half a foot from the top of her head.

On impulse she pushed against it. Light flooded into her metallic cave. After so much time in utter darkness it should have hurt her eyes. She should have flinched back from it and covered her face. She knew this and her body tensed for the reality of the light but it died out like a stillborn sneeze.

No. This light was pretend light. Her eyes had seen the real thing and this was make believe. It didn't really illuminate anything.

Reaching a hand on either side of the square opening at her head, she pulled herself out. To her surprise, she discovered she was on some kind of rolling bed that slid easily out of the box. It rolled to a stop. She swung her legs around, dangling them over the side of the bed, and sat up. She stretched her arms and neck. She took in the unfamiliar room with its rows of square metal doors like the one she just opened.

Her surroundings and her identity echoed in and out like a coin slowly rolling to a stop; one moment she felt part of this world and remembered being here, the next she felt so alien it was as if she should don a space suit.

Her belly rumbled. That was familiar enough. She didn't know where she was but she hoped there was food.

CHAPTER NINETEEN

Doug woke still on his knees, slumped over his prison cell cot. Both legs were deeply asleep and refused to even consider getting up when he tried to rise. He elbowed his way onto the cot and sat there, trying to rub life into his legs and sleep out of his eyes.

How long had he been out? He didn't know. His watch and the rest of his meager possessions were in a Durham County Jail processing envelope down the hall. That was something. How did that work? Listen to God (?) Go and do what God (?) says to do. Wake up in jail with your face beat to a pulp and your Casio in a manila envelope.

He touched his face gingerly. It wasn't the first beating he'd taken. Prison was a fairly steady diet of physical abuse in one form or another. A basement-bound porn addict who had not participated in any voluntary form of physical activity after rec league basketball in seventh grade, he had been utterly unprepared and defenseless in the face of the focused violence that rained down on the "cho-mo."

It had occurred to him, watching the perverse elation on the faces of the inmates who violated him, that by finding a victim who garnered no sympathy they were free to express their perversions and pass them off as punishments for a "real" pervert. Being a convicted child abuser gave him no protection and his tormentors no fear. The result was Doug becoming very fit in a short period of time as a simple matter of self-preservation.

It took the better part of his first eighteen months inside, but he had a large frame and surprised himself with the discovery of some hibernating athletic ability that awoke in the weight room. He found that it was the one place he was allowed to be a normal inmate. The cons there were serious about what they were doing. It was a sanctuary, and like other places of worship it had a set of rules automatically accepted by anyone who entered.

Doug exchanged focus on porn for focus on weights. The repetition of movements he copied from other worshippers made sense to him and he spent every possible moment he could there. The result at first was a string of injuries that slowed his progress, but he caught on to the rhythm of work and rest; leg days and arm days and chest and back days.

He grew stronger faster than he realized. It showed up one day when he completely demolished a man's nose who tried to back him into a dark corner for some fun. It wasn't the first time he ever threw a punch. He fought back every time. But this time it felt different.

This time, when his first blow glanced off his attacker's shoulder as it went wild and right of the mark, he felt something different and saw it in the man's expression. That swing missed the mark but it hurt the guy. Doug felt something shift in his brain. He threw the next punch believing.

It was well aimed and thrown with a year and a half of emotional release behind it. The attacker's nose exploded like a villain's in an old Batman comic. He went down like he had been shot. Doug walked out of the dark corner with blood smeared on his right hand and splattering his chambray shirt.

After that, the abuse had slowed to a trickle and then stopped. Strength wasn't attractive to the second tier perverts and they moved on to other, easier targets.

Doug got up and shuffled to the lidless metal toilet. He relieved himself, surprised not to see blood. There was activity outside his cell and he heard the electrically-controlled lock release. Two sheriff's deputies stepped into the cell simultaneously.

Doug tensed for a confrontation but none came. The deputies split and stood on either side of the open door, waiting. Doug saw the reason for their waiting. Three men hovered just before the door, speaking in low tones. The middle of the three was a head taller than the other two and seemed to be listening more than talking. Doug recognized him as he broke away from the other two men and stepped into his cell. It was the Governor of North Carolina.

Daniel Treeright came to the jail without a plan. He was running on no sleep for enough days that he had lost count. Adrenaline kept him upright and going forward. He wanted to see the man who violated his dead daughter, that's all. He wanted to look in his eyes and... and... what?

He thought there would be something there that would tell him what to do next. Lunacy? Insanity? If he found that in those eyes the fire might go out. The deadly rage in his heart might hit that like a lightning strike hitting a grounding rod. But if he looked into those eyes and saw something else—intentional evil? intelligent malice?— or if he saw unrepentant joy... the lightning strike might find another more violent place to discharge.

He used all his considerable political skills to convince the shift commander to let him see the prisoner. That and a little bribery implying the shift super was obviously suited to a more important role in law enforcement, perhaps with the governor's personal security detail? Syd tried to get in the way and demanded the shift get permission from the sheriff, but Daniel won out and they were escorted to the cell where Syd insisted on bringing along two deputies to keep things from getting out of control.

Daniel stepped into the dimly lit cell. Doug turned to meet him. The face the governor saw was swollen and bruised. The lips, broken in several places, were grotesquely fat. He strained to see the man's eyes through slits.

Then he knew him. His politician's eye for cataloguing faces registered this one and dialed it in to the latest viewing. The elevator outside the morgue. The near collision. This was that man.

Daniel had a momentary flash to the scene from *Spider-Man* where Peter Parker lets the criminal get away—the one who shoots and kills Uncle Ben. He shook it off and took a step toward this criminal. This animal.

The white heat built in his face and his hands followed. He was not a violent man. Had never raised his hands to strike another person. Never understood the things that drove the people who did. In an instant he shed any inhibition he ever felt toward violence or the violent. He was going to cool the fire in his hands by bathing them in this man's blood.

There was the sound of rushing wind in his ears as if the storm in his emotions had created its own tornado weather system around him. The man stood fast against his advancing form, moving neither to nor from the storm. He was not passive. His posture was not defenseless, it was what? It was sure. The man stood there without any shred of doubt.

Syd shouted above the tornado winds of Daniel's rage and the deputies shrugged off their static poses. Doug watched with detachment. He was as surprised as anyone else in the cell at his lack of reaction to the governor. He felt the utter calm of a person who might have been sitting on a beach watching waves come ashore.

In the same instant the storm rose in Daniel and he came on, Doug knew this wave couldn't wet him. He didn't know why and couldn't have explained it but he knew. His heart rate dropped. He waited and watched.

The expression on the governor's face became Doug's focal point. The layers he had observed outside the elevator appeared to work in reverse. It was as though Doug possessed an emotional X-ray vision allowing him to peel away the face coming at him. He saw that the raging mask overlay a pain unlike any Doug had ever seen on any person's face.

It was so terrible that Doug felt his own heart seize as if it would refuse to go on beating. The pain went to his own bruised and battered eyes as if he were a mirror. The governor's hands were at his throat, poised to take hold, to rip, to shred, to destroy, when their eyes met.

Daniel's hands slid past Doug's neck and he fell against him for the second time this night. Hot tears streaked both men's faces. Doug wrapped his arms around Daniel's prone, barely upright body and held him.

Then they were buried under the barrage of men screaming and trying to separate them. Doug held on to the governor even as the deputies and shift commander knocked them to the ground. He got the worst of the fall, landing on his back on the smooth hard cement floor of the cell without being able to brace himself.

Eager hands pried his hands away from the governor's back, finally separating the two men. They threw Daniel back and he landed on his hands and knees in the center of the cell. He was crying and laughing at the same time. Syd had never seen a nervous breakdown but he guessed this is what it looked like.

The guards were subduing the inmate although he wasn't resisting and was trying to obey their conflicting commands to stay down and back away and get on the cot. One of the two guards kicked the inmate with an audible thump. This snapped Daniel out of his crazed stupor. He got to one knee and ordered the guards to stop.

"Get away from him!" he said. "Get away from him now!"

The guards seemed as confused by Daniel's commands as the inmate was by theirs. They looked to the shift commander who was half a second from delivering his own kick to Doug's side. He shouted at them, "Do it!"

Doug staggered to his feet and slumped on the cot. The calm of the moment before the storm was still there. He breathed in and out easily. He had no anger or sense of offense at being beaten again for the third time tonight.

The calm was so real and complete that he didn't notice the absence of "normal" emotions and reactions until much later. When he did, he thought his ideas of normal were forever changed in the few seconds that passed in that jail cell encounter with the Governor of North Carolina.

CHAPTER TWENTY

Tabitha sat on the edge of the metal drawer for what seemed like a long time. She had lost or misplaced her sense of time in the land of Light. She felt no urgency but she did feel hungry.

She had never been in a morgue. She had no idea where she was or how she got there. The room was strange enough to go along with the strangeness of waking up in the cold and the dark and semi-imprisonment, so that she thought she might be dreaming.

Even though the cold and the dark and the escape from the stinky rubber sleeping bag felt like she was awake, the white room with its many doors seemed to her to be a gateway to anywhere. Maybe this was part of heaven. Maybe she had to find her way out of this like she found her way out of the metal box.

She dropped to the floor, a full two feet from her dangling legs, and the thwack of her bare feet slapping the white tiles made her reassess the situation. It stung her feet the way jumping off the cliffs at Smith Mountain Lake did when she hit the water flat footed.

I'm not asleep, she thought. Her belly growled in agreement at the same time she became aware of her nakedness. She took the sheet, still bunched up where she'd shed it in the black body bag, folded it neatly in half, and wrapped it around herself, tucking it in on itself like a bath towel. She glanced at the weird drawer she had emerged from once more now that she was sure she was awake. It still puzzled her. Where was everybody?

She walked to the front of the room and found a door leading out. She opened it and felt a rush of warm air. It was delicious. Going through it, she viewed another door she guessed was the exit and she went through it too.

She found herself in a dim hallway and saw that there was an elevator and not much else. There didn't seem to be anything on this floor except the empty place she just left. She hesitated at the head of the hallway and slapped her own side through the sheet to reassure herself one last time that she was awake. The dull thump got her going again.

She got on the elevator and went to the floor marked "Main," where she got off. As soon as she got out of the elevator her nose took over all guidance.

The scent of frying bacon wafted through the air and led her to the hospital café like a cartoon character floating on the air toward the delicious smell.

There were no other people in the cafe. A steam table with the morning breakfast bar was newly filled with bacon, scrambled eggs, country fries, muffins, and French toast. Tabitha picked a piece of bacon out of the heaping pile in the nearest pan and ate it without a thought. She ate three more pieces in this manner before she slowed down enough to get a plate and scoop a mountain of scrambled eggs onto it and wolfed it down as well.

It was as if her stomach took on a life of its own and took charge. The more she ate the more she wanted more to eat. She didn't know she could be this hungry. She hadn't bothered to sit down during this feeding frenzy, and remained standing at the breakfast bar not much different than a barnyard animal at a trough.

When the morning line cook came out of the kitchen moments later to discover the dent Tabitha had made in the morning offerings, she didn't have a clue where it had all gone. She thought some men from the night shift must have devoured it and would come by later to settle up.

Tabitha walked out of the cafe just ahead of the line cook's discovery. She took a chocolate milk and two small apples.

The spinning coin of identity rolled around again to the here and now. She was Tabitha Treeright. This was the hospital. Knowing where she was and that none of her family was with her kickstarted her nascent sense of timelessness. Now she wanted to see someone she knew and she wanted to be somewhere other than this place. The fact that she had been awake for—how long?—and not seen another soul restarted another lost feeling: loneliness.

The volunteer at the information desk greeted Tabitha with a glance up and down. Her naturally curly hair usually had a life of its own that was hard to tame. Being stuffed in a bag for who-knew-how-long had not helped it calm down. It was a mass of auburn with light streaks of summer-bleached highlights that surrounded her head like a wild bush. Her young face was recovering its color as she warmed up, but the weeks' worth of illness had left her cheeks sunken in and aged her well beyond her twelve years.

The sheet she had made into a makeshift dress was clean enough but her bare arms both bore the traces of needle marks from IVs. Her feet were dirty from walking around the hospital with no shoes or socks.

The woman had spent many nights behind this desk and she knew what she was looking at. The only question was how the girl was coming from the direction of the hospital's interior instead of from the front door. It was always sad when street people came here looking for help. And this one was so young. Pitiful.

She said, "Honey, you can't be in here, you know. I'm sorry but you have to leave."

Tabitha was surprised at this greeting. She was about to ask the woman to call for her mother. She was used to alternately using or hiding her identity as the daughter of the state's chief executive as it suited her purposes. It could lock her out of some places but it could also open doors to others. In this moment she wasn't ready for calculations and evaluations. She just wanted to be a girl in her mom or dad's arms, a feeling that had become more rare in the past year or so. The feeling fell back into her heart like a stone and she began to cry.

"I just want my mom and dad," she said. "I want them to come and get me out of here."

The tears of the girl pierced the woman's motherhood like a dart in a bullseye.

"Oh!" she said. "Oh, it's okay. It's okay. I'll help you. Where are your mother and father? How long have you been away? Do they know where you are?"

Tabitha accepted the woman's embrace and felt the warmth of it filling her up in a way she didn't know she had been empty. She sniffled and caught her breath and said into her shoulder, "I'm Tabitha Treeright. You know my father, I'm sure. Can you please call him or my mother? I know the number if you can let me use the phone."

Tabitha did not notice how the embrace went cold and rigid halfway into her explanation. The woman's embrace changed into a clinch as she backed out and held Tabitha at arm's length. All the motherhood drained from her eyes. There was a severity to her look that Tabitha didn't understand.

"That's not funny," the woman said. "You sick fiends think you can say anything and do anything in this day and age. Not to me. Not here you can't. You either get out of here now or I'll call security. I'll call security," she repeated and seemed to make up her mind with each punctuated step toward the phone. "I'll have you off the streets anyway. I won't have you upsetting those nice people, the Treerights."

Tabitha watched the woman dial the phone with detachment. She couldn't comprehend the yo-yo of emotions this woman was going through. What had she said wrong? Why the anger? The police??

"I just need to use the phone. I can give you my mother's direct number... or my father's."

"You just stay right there where you are and keep quiet. This is not the time for jokes. You think it's okay to pretend to be the governor's dead daughter?! I tell you what. I tell you I will make sure you don't upset anyone else with your stories."

"But I'm not…"

"Stop it right now! You're either a very sick person or just evil."

This was more than enough for Tabitha. She turned her back on the hysterical woman and walked out the front doors that swooshed out of her way and closed behind her. She could hear the woman yelling at her to stop. It was still misting and the ground was wet but she didn't slow down or look back. Someone would help her. She didn't need this crazy woman.

For the first time since coming to herself in the dark she felt the absence of her phone. Where had it gone? And her clothes? She started to wish this was a dream and she could wake up but the misty rain seeping into her mop of hair and dripping down into her eyes insisted it was real.

Durham was not normally a happening town but this night it was even more asleep than usual. It was as if it had wrung itself out. All the focus and the lights and the breathless members of the media breaking the slightest bit of news minute by minute had exhausted the town.

It was exhaling after one long and intense breath. It was sighing and asking itself if it really wanted all this attention and couldn't things just go back to normal?

Their girl was dead.

The doctors had been forced to give graphic descriptions of her demise under the relentless probing questions of desensitized reporters who cared nothing for the humans in the story and next to nothing for the humans hearing the story.

It didn't phase them to insist on having the lead physician explain how the brain eating amoeba in Tabitha's skull had feasted on her neurons, literally turning her frontal lobe to jelly. And at the very end they did what this breed always did best; they pivoted to what if's and blame.

Who was to blame for the girl's death? Did she receive the proper procedures? A girl in Alabama had received a radical new treatment for this condition and she had survived. Why hadn't this medical team tried it? Did global warming play a role in the number of cases of this brain-eating amoeba we are seeing? Did the absence of the girl's father have any impact on medical decisions that were made?

It was endless and relentless and ridiculous. It had worn the hospital staff and the city to a frazzle. But now most of the press gaggle was headed back to their more natural environs; New York, Washington, and Los Angeles. Little ol' Durham could settle back down to the pace of a southern college town and Duke Hospital could go back to being the best hospital in the region.

But tonight everyone was tired and sad. Tabitha was not a patient they couldn't help. She grew up in the Governor's Mansion and she had the gift—that thing entertainers and politicians try to install post production but only comes with the original equipment. She had the seed of a Lady Diana smile in a child's face and it was plain to see it would come into full bloom.

But it didn't. It hadn't. It was cut off like a half-budded rose. The loss of one so full of life was felt as an offense against ongoing life. The info desk woman was the city itself, pushed too far. Enough was enough.

Tabitha stood outside the main doors and looked out on the town. It was not home although she had been here many times. If she had been in Raleigh there would have been half a dozen places she would think of going to get help. Here she had none.

As she stood there, she felt as if this place in its shadowy reality was draining away her name. She was losing definition again. It was like she had fallen out of this world into light and somehow lost all darkness.

The Light had been so powerfully cleansing it had scrubbed away the old Tabitha and left the new… what was that name she heard there? The name she knew had always been her real name but never heard it before she went to the land of Light?

She felt the darkness of this place holding her feet to the ground. From somewhere behind her, close yet far away, she heard a woman shouting.

"There she is!"

CHAPTER TWENTY-ONE

Wanda drove to Durham in silence. Like her husband's journey to the jail, she had no plan. She had no idea what she would find there or what she would do. She was glad for the drive because it was something to do and she needed something to do.

It took her just under an hour to get there and she drove up to the drop off area right in front of the main entrance to the hospital.

Her phone buzzed as she parked. It was a number she didn't recognize. She rejected the call and dropped her phone in the car's cup holder. No more interruptions. She left her phone and her car, not caring if either were there when she got back.

As she walked in, she realized she didn't know where she was going. She had not accompanied Tabitha's body to the morgue. Was that bad? Was that the last guilt trip of all the mother guilt trips she put herself on? She walked to the information desk and questioned a disheveled-looking volunteer. Must have been a long night. Well, so what? Wanda was having the longest night of her life; a night with no hope for dawn to come.

"Where is the morgue?" she asked.

The woman looked up, immediately recognizing Wanda. Her face contorted into a pain-filled expression. She started to speak. Wanda wasn't in the mood for sympathy from strangers. She cut off the volunteer's response with an outstretched hand.

"The morgue, please?"

The woman looked pained but said, "Sublevel Zero. Take the C Bank elevators around the corner and to your right and hit the button for Sublevel Zero. Decedent Care is out the elevator and to the left."

It took Wanda a second to register that Decedent Care was the morgue.

"Thank you. Got it," she said and headed for the elevators, without giving the volunteer room to say another word. She found them and punched the button and was deposited in the same corridor her husband and Doug had collided in a few hours ago, though she didn't know any of Daniel's movements on this awful night.

She reflected again on how alone she was as she approached the door marked Decedent Care. She pushed it open and came to the glassed-in information desk. There was no one in it and she could not see a way to summon the attendant. She knocked on the glass with a clunking tin can sound.

"Hello? Anyone there?"

A man stood up from under the desk. They startled each other as they came face to face on either side of the glass.

"Oh!" Wanda said.

"Sorry, I… ah… was looking for something," the man said. Recognition dawned on his face. "Mrs. Treeright!" he stammered. "Ah, what…? Can I help you?"

She was still not in the mood to deal with the public or anything like it.

"Where's my daughter?" she said.

"She's here. She's…" He was about to say, "She's all right," but checked himself. There was nothing all right about a twelve-year-old girl lying in one of the slots in the room behind him.

"She is back here." He gestured to the room.

"I'll see her," Wanda said without leaving room for discussion.

Romeo didn't hesitate. He was shaken from all that had transpired this evening, the conversation with his boss not the least thing to shake him. He had strongly implied that Romeo was going to have to give a thorough account for his actions and it was likely to lead to some disciplinary action.

The fact that the door from the holding area out front, where this woman now stood, into the back where the bodies were stored had been left open was high on the list of questions to be answered.

No matter that it had been SOP since he had arrived to leave the door unlocked on the night shift when only hospital cleaning crews were coming and going.

He wanted nothing to do with getting on the wrong side of the governor's wife. He guessed he was already there but no use in getting himself further in the doghouse.

He said, "If you go around to your left I will buzz you in."

Wanda did and as soon as Romeo spotted her in front of the door on his security monitor he hit the button. He felt the electric lock vibrating through the wall and walked out of the rear door to meet her.

Wanda walked into the brightly lit room as Romeo approached. She took it all in at a glance. She had never been in a morgue before but she quickly understood what she was looking at. And something was wrong, she knew. Her gaze locked on it as Romeo began to address her.

"What's that?" she said, pointing over his shoulder.

Romeo turned to see what Wanda was looking at. It was one of the unit drawers pulled out to its full length. It was empty except for a black rubber body bag.

A blood-spattered paperback New Testament was all it contained.

CHAPTER TWENTY-TWO

The security force, like the rest of the hospital staff, was stretched thin by the demands of the week-long national media circus they'd just endured. All of them pulled extra shifts and all of them were chased down by reporters determined to get access to places they were not allowed to go.

Perhaps the worst part of it was kissing the asses of the media rats they found scurrying around out of bounds. *Don't make a story* was the Chief's warning. Don't give them any room to say they were manhandled or treated roughly.

It tested them and contributed to the violent beat down of the pervert discovered in the morgue. It was a week's worth of being polite to assholes and stuffing it every time they had been called names and accused of interfering with the press. It broke out in the morgue and they broke the pervert's head.

It also contributed to Jackie Smith, the midnight shift lead - a straight-laced by-the-book security officer if there ever was one - deciding to zip into the morgue's office and pull the security camera storage drive.

It would be missed, obviously, but it would be better to answer questions about a missing drive than an out-of-control beat down. He didn't feel good about the beat down, but he'd be damned after all his guys had been through this week if he would let them go down over a sick pervert.

He'd keep it to himself and if there was heat over it, he'd take it.

As Jackie and his crew completed their turnover and got ready to go home, the day shift supervisor was trying to get some answers out of a used up looking street girl who had been caught wandering around the hospital.

"So what's your name? Tell me your name and I will get you home. Promise," he said.

Whether it was the shock of being taken into custody or her addled brain flickering back to life as she spent more time in this shadow world, Tabitha Treeright emerged again. She caught a little of her old flame, a little of the power of that name.

"I told you who I am. I'm not going to keep repeating myself. If you know what's good for you you'll get me a phone and let me make a call," she said.

"Okay. Okay. Don't lose it," he said, using that tone designed to make anything the other person says sound insane or aggressive or both.

He put a phone in front of her on the desk and said, "Hit nine to get out."

The girl held the phone away from her head in one hand and the other hand hovered over the dial. She appeared to be trying to recall a number. The guard grunted. Smart phones were making people stupid, he thought; hard to remember numbers they only punched in once and never have to again. He could remember his own home phone number from when he was a kid. He dialed it thousands of times. This girl never would know a number that way. But as he watched, something clicked for her and she punched in a number.

"Hit that button to the side right there so we can all hear if you don't mind," he said.

She did. The phone was ringing. A woman answered.

"Hello…"

The girl jumped. "Mom!" she said.

"I'm away from my phone right now. Leave me a message and I'll get back to you as soon as I can."

Huge tears welled up in the girl's eyes. A sob caught in her throat. She struggled to regain composure to say something as the beep prompted her.

"Maaa!" It came out sounding like a cat's cry. "Maaom… I'm here, Mom. It's Tabitha. These people don't know who I am. I need you to come tell them—to come get me."

Another sob caught in her throat and she dropped the phone. She seemed to shrink in front of the guard's eyes, all her bluster and confidence draining away like a punctured tire. She put her head down on the desk next to the dropped handset and spoke in a muffled whisper.

He leaned down closer to make out what the girl was saying. She was repeating lowly and slowly: *I am Tabitha. I am Tabitha. I am Tabitha.* He took the phone, broke the connection, and dialed the hospital information line. They connected him directly to the number he asked for. The woman who answered was too chipper for his tired ears.

"Hellooo, Psychiatric Ward! This is Marge, how may I help you?!"

"Yeah, ah, Marge, this is Benson in security," he said and started to explain his situation.

"Good morning!" she interrupted before he could continue.

He looked at his watch and saw that it was just after six. "Ah, yeah. Morning," he said and went on without leaving space for any more niceties. "We've got a young lady down here, ah from her looks I'd say she was twelve or thirteen years old, who needs some help I think."

He glanced down at the still muttering girl. "Could you send someone to check her out or should we bring her up to you?"

Marge was undeterred by his brusqueness.

"Of course we'd love to help her if we can, Mr. Benson! What seems to be the matter? Who is she? Where did she come from?"

"That's the problem, lady. We don't know where she came from. She just showed up at the front desk."

Marge interrupted him again. "Sounds like a case for CPS. Why is she wandering around in the middle of the night alone? Where are the girl's parents?"

"Yeah, Marge. That's kind of the thing. The girl says her parents are, ahhh…" He hesitated to say it in front of the girl and went down to a whisper. "She says her dad is the governor... she says that she is Tabitha Treeright."

"Whaaa?!!" Marge blasted into his ear. "She doesn't!"

"Yeah. Yeah. She does. She says she lives in the Governor's Mansion and she goes to school in Raleigh and she just went to Smith Mountain Lake. All of it. The whole story. She's repeating everything we all heard the past week on the TV."

Marge lost a bit of her chipper. In fact she sounded a little angry when she spoke again.

"That's awful. That's terrible. I know kids these days will do anything for attention but this is the worst. The absolute worst."

"I don't know, Marge. This don't look like an act to me. Y'all are the experts though. I think someone oughta check her out. I think she's, ahhh, broken."

There was a pause and then Marge said, "We'll send someone down to get her."

Fifteen minutes later an orderly collected Tabitha in a wheelchair and rolled her to the psych ward.

CHAPTER TWENTY-THREE

Wanda was screaming at Romeo. He had no answers, no explanation for the empty drawer where Tabitha Treeright had been. It was impossibly barren.

He peered vainly, stupidly, into the square mouth of the compartment as if the body could be misplaced like an extra sock hiding in a drawer. He opened the two empty compartments on either side of the compartment labeled with her name. He went to the back door and checked it. Locked. Secure.

There were four other corpses in the morgue. He went to each one and identified them. Everyone was where they were supposed to be. In desperation he opened every compartment in the morgue one by one. Wanda followed in his wake each step crying and screaming obscenities at him, barely restraining herself from striking him.

No body. No Tabitha.

"Where is she! What did you do with her?!"

Romeo was struck dumb. His frenetic searching wound down and he came to a stand, still as a statue in the center of the morgue. Wanda was in his face but he couldn't hear her. He stared into nowhere.

She collapsed at his feet in a heap sobbing incoherently. Romeo bent to her and found that he was crying too. The weight of all this night's events sat down on him and he had nothing left to hold it up or keep it back.

Wanda got up off the floor and pushed Romeo away. He was useless, she decided. It was his fault her daughter was molested. It was his fault her daughter was now missing.

She didn't want him touching her. His tears were meaningless. She needed someone who could do something. Get things done. Make things work. Find her daughter. Fix this.

She needed Daniel. She needed him. She felt the strangeness of needing her husband who she had no use for. But she knew he would fix this. She reached for her purse, dropped at the door when she had seen the empty slab where her daughter was supposed to be, and searched it for her phone before remembering she'd left it in the car.

"Idiot!" she screamed at the morgue attendant, before running out of the morgue and back to her car.

When she got there she pulled out her phone and ignored the notification that she had a missed call and had a new voicemail. She would deal with that later. She told the phone to call Daniel. It made the connection. Daniel answered before she heard it ring.

"Yes?" he said

"I'm at the hospital."

"What?"

"I had to see for myself. I had to see she was all right."

"Wanda…"

"Daniel, she's gone! She's not here!"

Daniel was disoriented. He was still sorting through the encounter with the man in the jail who they said molested his dead daughter. He was going to kill him. He went there to kill him unless he found a reason not to. But he had seen something in the man's eyes that stopped him. It put out Daniel's rage like a snuffed candle.

He couldn't understand it but those eyes, that look said something to Daniel's heart that he couldn't translate. Whatever it was, whatever it said, it had put his heart at rest in a way that he never felt before. His daughter was dead but it was okay. Somehow it was okay. He was okay.

It made no sense whatsoever but every time his mind tried to lock onto the hopelessness of "the facts," he couldn't keep a grip on them. Had he slipped a gear? Peace was the last thing he should feel right now. Now another fact was pushing its way into his thinking.

"Gone?" he said.

Syd was next to him and his eyebrows shot up in a question. Daniel put Wanda on speaker.

"I went to the hospital to see her after you called. I'm here now. I went to the morgue. And she's not here, Daniel. She's not here." Wanda sounded exhausted and on the verge of hysteria.

"Wanda, I put you on speaker. Syd is here with me. We're headed back to Raleigh. We went to the jail to see the man who…" He trailed off, not knowing what to say. The sad absurdity of the moment struck them all silent. The married couple that had no relationship. The lovers who had no future. The friends who had no trust. The grieving ones who had no body to mourn over.

Syd spoke. "Wanda, stay right there. We will be there as quickly as possible. Don't do anything without us." He looked at his boss who nodded agreement.

Wanda was silent.

Syd said "Wanda?"

"Okay," she said, barely audible.

Daniel said, "It's going to be okay." And somehow, he believed it.

CHAPTER TWENTY-FOUR

Doug was lying in his cell on his cot. He guessed it must be getting light out by now although he still had no way to tell time.

His visit with the governor had been short but intense. He felt drained in a way he had never felt before as if all his life energy had leaked out of his body in that one look they shared. His head felt like a bowling ball, heavy and fat and swollen.

He tried to recall the events of the evening. To get some perspective on where he was and where he might be going from here. No one had asked him if he wanted to make a phone call. That wasn't right. But he had long ago released his sense of justice being fair or orderly.

Sifting through the last part of the wild night and the arrest he also remembered that he had not been read his rights. That would be enough to get him set free in the world of television cop shows.

He knew better than to believe it was going to get him anywhere here. Three cops would all agree that the fourth Mirandized the suspect. Cover for each other. That was the way of things.

He had an itchy thought. That's what he called those things that floated around the edge of his mind just out of reach, teasing his brain. Playing hide and seek but not coming out when he cried uncle. Something was there. He should give the old brain a break, he thought. It had taken a few nasty thumps tonight.

He couldn't help the replay that ran through his battered head. The morgue attendant Romeo drawing first blood with the ancient three hole punch that looked as if it had been made to inflict punishment on flesh and blood more than reams of paper. Then it was the cop who clubbed him clean on his upturned ear. The blow that was still ringing in that same ear right now.

It rang along in sync with his heartbeat like a bee buzzing him. *Beat ring beat ring beat ring.*

Beat.

He sat up.

Her heart beat. He heard it. He knew it.

Tabitha was alive.

A torrent of nausea rushed over him from sitting up too fast. His head swam. His logic revolted. He had an argument with himself.

You got hit on the head one too many times. You can't even hear right out of your good ear. You've been hearing things for the past twelve hours. God talking to you. Come on. You're a fool or worse you've lost it.

He held his head with both hands as the blood circulated to his addled brain and the wave of sickness passed. No. He heard it. He heard her heart start beating. He knew it as surely as the throbbing in his head. It was real.

And she was in that awful place in a bag. Did they know she was alive? Would she get up on her own? Did she need help? He didn't know any of the answers to these questions. With an effort he got up and went to the cell door. He was inviting another beating he knew, but this was too important. He beat on the door.

"Hey! Hey! I need someone. I've got to talk to someone!"

The inmates around him shouted back at him. Some mocked him and others told him to shut up. He was surprised when a guard responded. The slot in his cell door opened and he saw the framed face of one of the two deputies who had been in his cell with the governor.

"What's all this noise?" he said.

Doug said, "I've got to speak to the governor. I've got information about his daughter he needs to know right away." Even as he said it, Doug thought it was the most ridiculous thing an inmate in this jail had probably ever said. He braced for a verbal or perhaps physical attack. Instead the guard slid the speaking slot closed and opened the full door.

"Do I need to cuff you? Or are you gonna behave yourself?"

Doug stared at him dumbly. This was not the response he expected.

"Well?" the deputy repeated.

"Where are we going?" Doug asked.

The deputy met his eye and sighed an exasperated sigh. "Don't you know that just this minute, when you started beatin' on the door and hollerin' for help, the governor was on the phone with the boss?" He said it in the form of a question no one would ask or believe the answer if they did.

Doug lifted his eyebrows at this.

"Yeah. He did. Said to the boss that if you had anything to say about his daughter we were to get you on the phone with him. Boss was just tellin' us this when you interrupted. Told me to come get you."

Doug considered this and put his hands out to the deputy. "Cuff me if you need to but I'm not going to make trouble. I just need to talk to the governor."

The man indicated he should come out and walked behind him up the row of cells, depositing him in an interrogation room just off the main space near booking. The shift commander came in shortly and unceremoniously handed him a cell phone. He had the look of a man who had given up trying to make sense out of his circumstances and was going to just go for the ride wherever it led.

"Reception isn't great in here, but it's passable. The governor said to use this number." He reached over Doug's shoulder, scrolled through recent calls, and touched the last number.

The phone started to ring. Daniel Treeright answered.

Doug hesitated. He didn't know how to address this man. Didn't know what, if any, relation they had to each other. This was compounded by the magnitude of what he was about to tell the man.

"Governor?" he stammered.

"Yes." The terse response trying to place the caller from an unknown number.

"Governor, this is Doug Windsor. The man from the jail."

"Windsor!" Daniel said.

The doubt and peace inside the governor were at war. This Windsor had to have something to do with Tabitha's disappearance but he also was the only place Daniel had found any relief in this crazy night. He was a convicted child molester—he had discovered this at the jail as they ran a background on the man—who touched his dead daughter.

Now his dead daughter was missing. This couldn't be a coincidence. He had something to do with it. And the demons insisted whatever it was must be wicked. He must have a partner. There must have been an accomplice.

But the peace was there too and it had another story. It was a complete blank. No answers, no scenarios, no possibilities. Just peace. The choice was hard. But he just told his wife it was going to be okay. Did he believe it himself?

Doug said, "Governor, I know what I'm going to say is not believable... I... I can't tell you why to believe me but I can only tell you what I know. You need to get back to the morgue as quickly as possible. Tabitha is alive." He waited, then added, "I heard her heart beating."

Saying this out loud to another human being was clarifying and terrifying. Saying it aloud to the father of a dead girl upped the ante to all in. He really did believe what he was saying. If he was wrong there would be nowhere to hide from himself or anyone else. He would have to embrace his own insanity.

Treeright was silent long enough to make Doug think he had hung up the phone. He started to hand the device to the shift sup who had overheard what he just said.

Treeright said in a measured voice, "My wife called me from the morgue fifteen minutes ago. That's why I called and left word for you. She's at the morgue and Tabitha is missing. I'm headed there now."

His tone was steady and slow.

"Windsor… Windsor, if this is some kind of a set up… if this is a sick scam to get something out of me, out of us, or to make a political point or… or anything else but…" He struggled to find the right words. "If this isn't true, I will personally kill you and anyone else involved. That's a promise from a father and not a politician." He hung up.

Doug handed the phone back to its owner and followed his escort back to his cell. He thought of Treeright's last words. If this was all a lie, Doug hoped the man would keep his promise.

CHAPTER TWENTY-FIVE

The sunrise was muted by low clouds that morning. The persistent mist, almost-but-not-quite-rain made for a wet commute— the kind that's not wet enough for the lowest setting on the interval wipers to sweep away with squealing.

Dr. Fred Robinson wanted to get in early to the psych ward. He had several case notes to catch up, although catching up was always relative in this miserable job. He was perpetually behind with paperwork and hated the feeling of swimming against it like a rip tide.

The ward was usually quiet in the hour before and after dawn and he liked to be alone with his misery. Today the night charge nurse met him at the side entrance he frequented in order to avoid charge nurses.

"Good morning, Doc!" Marge said, giving him a start with her ambush. "Sorry! Didn't mean to scare you!"

"Hey M-Marge," he said, trying and failing to keep the irritation out of his voice. So much for catching up on paperwork.

"Doc, I'm glad you're first in today. I think you'll be interested in a girl that came to us just now."

When he looked doubtful she went on anyway. "She insists that she is Tabitha Treeright." Now she had his attention. This was more interesting than paperwork.

"Where is she? You didn't put her on the ward did you? Anyone else see her? Medicate her?"

"No. Doc Hampton had to run out a few hours early and left me with his number if an emergency came up. But it was quiet all night and the girl wasn't a problem so I decided to wait it out till one of the docs made it in. Girl is in the intake room, sitting quietly.

"Funny thing is she has no ID. No nothing. The only thing she had in her possession was a sheet wrapped around her. Nothing else. Not a thing. I put her into some of our clothes."

Fred nodded at all this and Marge added, "Yeah, pretty strange."

A charge nurse on a psych ward saw more than their fair share of "strange," so he asked, "What in particular is strange? Her claim to be a dead person?"

"No," Marge said. "It's strange that she must have come from off the streets. It's been drizzling like this for a week and she was dry as a Baptist birthday party. Hair. Sheet. Feet. Dry. Don't know how that could've happened."

Fred considered that for a moment. He could think of several explanations for the girl turning up dry but he didn't feel like bantering this around with Marge.

He said, "Let me throw my stuff in my office and I'll come and meet her."

Fifteen minutes later, Fred sat in an intake room with the girl who claimed she was Tabitha Treeright. She was calm and met his gaze easily with no hint of anxiety. She was absent of any ticks or twitches and when she spoke it was with a surprisingly unselfconscious tone for a tweenish girl.

"What's your name?" he asked.

"I'm Tabitha Treeright," she said.

"How long have you been here, Tabitha?"

"I'm not sure. What day is it? I know I came to the hospital on a Sunday but I felt so sick and they put me in a room with no windows… I don't know how long, I guess."

The lack of detail didn't appear to bother the girl. She didn't strain to fill in the gaps or add details to embellish her story.

"How long have you been Tabitha Treeright?"

This confused her as Fred intended it to do, hoping for her to break character.

"All my life," she laughed. And it was an honest, girlish laugh. Robinson immediately found himself liking her. She gave no indication of pretense or affectation.

"Tell me about your life," he said.

And she did. She told him about her mother and father and how it was hard sometimes to be the child of a black father and white mother. She said she liked to swim and play soccer but didn't like either of them enough to spend the time to get really good at them. Her favorite thing was music. Everything music.

When she hit this theme her whole body shifted. Concerts where there were many or few people or anything in between made her feel alive. Seeing concerts with friends was the best. She listened to everything. She said she couldn't find any kind of music she didn't enjoy. It was as if music itself captured her imagination and wouldn't let go.

It was sad, she said, that she had no musical ability of her own—that she was a spectator. She lamented the fact that she couldn't dance at all.

He let her ramble, fascinated at her seemingly sane and innocent enthusiasm. Their discussion finally ran aground when he asked her about her favorite song of all. She sat back from him and appeared to be upset by the question, almost offended by it. Her face contorted with deep thought verging on pain.

"What is it?" he said.

When she spoke again, her eyes were so wide they felt like they could swallow him whole and the expression on her face was otherworldly. It forced its way into his consciousness gently and insistently in and through the face of the girl. Heaven was in her face revealed undeniably and he had no reason or resistance to her or to it. Her sweet alto voice held absolute sway and confidence without insistence. She was an Oracle.

"I heard a song I can't remember. It is the best of all songs. The words would make you cry a cry that would take away any reason to be sad forever. It was so loud the ground shook with it and so low I had to strain to hear it. I could sing it too... even though I'd never heard it before. I could sing and not miss a word or a note. I could sing this song even though I can't sing."

She shrugged a girlish shrug and closed her eyes as if trying to find what to say next. "It was like the song sang me and I went along with it. I know that must sound strange, but it just did. Instruments I never thought of made sounds I never thought of before, sounds that made me want to find that instrument and spend all of my life learning how to play it. It was a song but I think… I think it was real. I think it was the only real music I've ever heard. Everything else is a shadow—everything else is a copy. It's the only original music I've ever heard."

She fell silent and shrank in her chair. Robinson felt as if he'd been flying in a plane that had landed without warning. He thumped down into the moment. He looked the girl over closely. She was sitting back in the chair in psych ward-blue pajamas, hugging her legs to herself. She had declined the white socks Marge had given her and her bare feet were on the seat.

The feet. The toes. He scanned her hands. A sick feeling came over his stomach and rose to a sweat.

He said, "Where did you hear this song?"

The girl stirred but appeared not to hear the question. Her eyes were now as vacant as they had been animated mere moments ago.

Robinson said, "Tabitha? She stirred at the mention of the name, but her eyes remained unfocused on anything in this world.

"Where did you hear this song?"

She smiled, a whole-face smile that radiated warmth and peace, and laughed an easy laugh. When she spoke, it felt to Robinson as if her voice came from someplace other than the girl. It was as if she were a ventriloquist throwing her voice into the ceiling of the room. It was such an odd effect that he caught himself looking up.

"When I was in the Light. When I went to the place that is Light."

The psychologist had difficulty pulling himself back into the room, back to reality. Or what he'd always thought of as reality. The encounter with this girl was fraying his ideas. He shook himself back into his clinical self, his scientific demeanor.

"I've never heard of that place. How did you get there? Where is it? Can you show me?"

"I don't really know how I got there. I was really sick for a while and I came here and I fell asleep and woke up in the place of Light. That's the only way to describe it. I don't remember how I got there and I really don't know how I got back. But I went there and I think someone called me and brought me back here. I woke up in the dark here in a strange place that was cold."

She paused and looked like she was trying to remember something. Robinson leaned in toward the girl.

"There was something that interrupted the song. It made the music skip a beat. I can remember it now. It was the name."

"Name?"

"The Name."

She looked at Robinson. He tensed. The sick feeling grew to a crescendo. This girl before him wasn't off the streets. Her hands and feet—fingernails and toenails alone—testified to it. The puncture marks in her arms were not the scattered scars of an addict, but precise, as if made by a medical professional. Her eyes were unclouded.

He got up suddenly, a chill running through his body. He virtually ran from the room and called for Marge. He stood leaning shakily against the door. The nurse came to him and he asked her to bring the only possession the girl brought to the ward: the sheet. She delivered it in short order, not without giving him a questioning glance.

He knew the psych ward sheets all carried a stencil showing they belonged on the ward. He had asked about it one time and was told it was something the Infectious Disease people demanded as a way to track down potential sources of diseases in the case of an outbreak.

It seemed far-fetched to him, but he needed to see the sheet to make the chill in his heart go away. He nervously examined this sheet, wondering what he would do if he found…

Property of DUMC
Dec. Care Dept

Blue-black stencil. Fresh. Maybe even new or never washed. He held it taut between his hands, stretching the fabric without knowing he was doing it. He looked at it as a man might look at a moon rock. It was here and it was real but…

"Marge!"

She answered down the hallway. "Yes, Doc?"

"Are you sure this is the sheet she was, ah, wearing when she came in?"

The nurse returned up the hallway and looked at the white cloth in his hands. She furrowed her brow.

"Yes. I'm sure. I never got around to throwing it in with the soiled laundry. I was just about to do it when you asked for it. Anything wrong? You don't look well, Doc."

Robinson made an effort and pulled himself together. He smiled an uneasy smile the nurse did not see.

"No. Just wanted to be sure she got it back. It is the only thing she owns."

Marge looked like she had been caught red-handed stealing Momma's cookies.

"Oh, Doc, you're right! I didn't give a thought to it being hers. Looks so much like one of ours that I was gonna throw it right in with the rest of it."

Robinson smiled again, then came to a decision. "It does look a lot like a hospital sheet," he said. "But it's not one of ours. " Technically a true statement. "I will take care of it."

He nodded toward the girl sitting passively in the chair and lowered his voice confidentially to Marge. "It might be useful—a comfort item for her."

Marge nodded herself, glad to be included in this bit of insider information with one of the doctors.

"Let's get a bed ready for her, and a sedative. I think she's had a lot of excitement lately. I'm going to call over to Central Regional and get her moved there. We can't keep her here. That'll be the right place for her."

Marge left to get things set up as Robinson asked. He folded the sheet neatly, covering over the stencil and hiding it deep in the folds. Stepping back into the room, he found the girl sitting exactly as he'd left her, but she was looking at him intently.

Her expression was neither warm nor cold, simply observant and intelligent. He felt uncomfortable under that gaze. He felt undressed as if his thoughts were out in the open and she were browsing through them.

"You don't know the Name," she said. "You've never heard the music or seen the Light."

It was a melancholy statement. It was spoken as something unchallenged and unchallengeable. Nor was it harsh or pleading.

The weight of the words fell on him out of the ceiling like a double portion of gravity. "And you're afraid of it. Of Him. Of what you don't know. You're full of fear."

Marge came into the room with two paper cups. One contained a powder-blue capsule and the other water. She handed both to the girl and said, "Here you go, sweetheart. Take this and I'll get you to a bed where you can rest."

CHAPTER TWENTY-SIX

Dr. Fred Robinson retreated to his office and called the desk at the Central Regional Psychiatric Hospital in Raleigh. He arranged to have "Jane Doe" transferred as soon as they could send transportation. It would be several hours before anyone picked her up.

He buzzed Marge to tell her he would be back in a few minutes and slipped out the side door. He stuffed the folded sheet under his arm like a morning newspaper and made his way to the main lobby. The night volunteer who was the first to meet his Jane Doe had already been replaced by a woman who could have been her twin.

He got the new lady to give him the phone number for the off-going—and reminded himself never to let anyone who worked here get anywhere near his own personal information.

He next made his way to the security office but found the door closed and locked; evidently everyone was out. His last stop was Sublevel Zero. He got on the elevator mumbling to himself.

As he made these stops, his reason began to return and he felt more in charge of his faculties.

Should've gone here first, he thought. *Why all this running around? The girl's managed to get in your head. You just weren't on your game. Just walked in the door. That stupid Marge didn't give you time to get your game face on and your mind set for the nuts in the nut house.*

The elevator doors opened on Sublevel Zero. It was an ant hill of activity. Cops in suits—who couldn't tell one of those?—hospital chieftains, uniforms, everyone talking or moving without going anywhere, some on phones, others writing on note pads. Clumps of two or three huddled together with grim expressions, whispering to one another inaudibly.

No one looked in his direction as he exited the elevator. He decided to apply the "look like you belong here" strategy and approached the door marked Decedent Care.

He felt the sheet under his arm growing conspicuous, like a zit on a teenagers nose. He approached the door and was met by a uniformed policeman who gave him the once over, lingering over the embroidered name on his white lab coat.

"What's your business in the morgue, Doctor Robinson? It's a crime scene. Can't let anyone in unless it's part of the investigation or if you have a, ah, patient to deliver..." The cop paused and gave him a look that suggested he couldn't be delivering what he called a "patient," so what did he have to do with the investigation?

Robinson was unprepared for any of this, having come down here to simply get a quick answer to a question he knew the answer to. This wasn't on his menu.

"Crime? What kind of crime happens in a morgue?" he asked.

The cop leaned in and gave a conspiratorial grin. In a low voice he said, "Fuckin' grave robbery! Well—I guess it's not technically grave robbery until a body is in a grave."

Robinson felt the sick feeling rising again in his belly and the sweat machine came with it. The cop interpreted his change in demeanor as an invitation to go on with his tale. Robinson did not think he was ready for the rest of the story.

He was right.

"Yeah, there was a break in last night—and they stole the governor's daughter. Took her right out of cold storage."

Robinson felt the ground move beneath him and the overhead lights swirled like they were mounted to toy tops. The sheet tucked under his arm became strangely heavy; so heavy he thought he might drop it and run away. The cop was looking at him with concern when his eyes and body got back in sync.

"Are you all right?"

"Yes. Just got a little queasy there for a minute. Never take your vitamins on an empty stomach." He managed a weak smile. "Any idea why someone would pull something like this?" he said, more to make room for his exit than to get the opinion of some halfcocked beat cop with nothing past a high school degree.

Instead of catching the hint the man leaned in and launched into his analysis.

High politics were a no-holds-barred endeavor, he said, raising his eyebrows after each sentence for emphasis or affirmation or both. Governor Treeright was engaged in the highest politics in America and that meant the highest politics in the world. No dirty trick was too dirty. In these kind of politics there was no such thing as dirty at all; there was only effective or ineffective; winning or losing.

While the cop droned on, warming to his theory of what had really happened in the morgue and to Tabitha Treeright's body, Robinson gathered himself and his thoughts.

He pushed away the sickness and the fear. He waited for the man to pause and then said, "Interesting," which was his standard way of addressing people and things that were decidedly uninteresting to him.

He turned on his heel and started to walk away, oblivious to the fact that the cop had asked his opinion. His eye caught sight of something along the ceiling and turned back to the cop. "What about video? Isn't there video of the morgue?"

The cop looked at him with disgust. "I just told you the hard drive for the cameras was taken and hospital security says it's only a local feed stored here. Security office says they have no way of knowing what went on in there unless that drive shows up. It looks like a sophisticated deal."

Robinson grunted and turned to go. He didn't hear the cop mutter, "Pretentious asshole," under his breath.

He hurried back to his office, his mind buzzing with impossibilities and the possibilities that arose out of them. He shoved the sheet from Decedent Care into a half-empty drawer in his desk and then thought better of it.

He got out his briefcase and emptied the file folders out of it to make room, then packed the sheet away. He checked his watch and guessed it would be an hour till the van from Regional showed up to pick up the Jane Doe. He slipped out of his office without Marge seeing him.

The walk to his car gave him time to sift through his cascading and colliding thoughts.

The governor's daughter was three days dead. Everyone knew she was dead. It was a very public tragedy and it played out in the best medical facility in the region. The governor was absent for the tragedy—also a well-known fact.

The girl's body stayed in the medical center morgue instead of being moved to a funeral home because no one would act without his approval and he either couldn't or wouldn't release her body until he got back to the States. There was no autopsy for the same reason.

Governor Treeright had frozen the normal processes in place and no one wanted to tangle with a grieving father who was likely to be the next President of the United States. Tabitha Treeright had literally gone into cold storage pending her father's return. And now she was missing.

She, he thought, was not the right way to think of it. She was gone. Dead. People die and that's it. Her body was missing. He had a girl in his ward claiming to be Tabitha Treeright, conveniently outfitted in only a sheet from the morgue. And no one knew about it but him.

This was explosive. No one outside the hospital knew the body was missing yet. He was sure all the buzz down in Sublevel Zero was a head shed meeting to sort out how to keep a lid on this and what to do when it inevitably blew. He wondered if the girl was in on this or if she was a plant taken off the streets and cleaned up for the job.

She could be an actress, but his Jane Doe was definitely young. It would take real skill to pull this off. Real skill. Or real crazy. One way or the other, the girl had given him a stir. She had him thinking crazy thoughts himself.

There it was. The thought he suppressed. The one that made him sweat and made his stomach sick. *What if it is real? What if she is Tabitha Treeright back from the dead?*

He was in the parking garage almost to his car. He laughed out loud and the sound bounced off the concrete in a hollow echo. He was sure of one thing; near-death experiences were exactly that: near death, not death.

Suggesting that someone who was dead for three days somehow got up and walked out of the morgue on her own, that was not a road he was ever going down. He would never live it down among his peers if he was taken in by a hoax like that—no matter how elaborate it was.

And if a genuinely crazy girl fooled him it would be even worse. No. This was a no-win situation. The only thing to do in a no-win situation was to find a door marked "Exit" as fast as he could.

If someone wanted to embarrass the governor or the hospital or both they could do it without Fred Robinson. If someone had a master plan to take down a presidential contender, they were serious people. Not the kind of people he wanted to know anything about.

The missing drive. He never thought about the morgue as a place where the hospital would put security cameras. But the missing drive. That was the whole thing, wasn't it? That took it to a new level. Made it a sure thing that there must be "serious" people involved.

Who would do that? Who would even know how to do it or that it was the only place the video would be stored? No jack-leg crook would think to do something like that, right? And for that matter, what kind of crook would steal a dead body in the first place? No body and no video meant this was a political operation.

Fred was proud of himself for sorting through the facts and coming to the right conclusion, the perfectly sane and scientific conclusion, before he made a fool of himself.

He used the remote to unlock the trunk of his car. Giving a quick look around to see if anyone was watching, he unsnapped his briefcase and took out the folded sheet.

Rummaging around, he lifted the cover off the spare tire well and dropped the sheet in it. He dropped the lid and spread the detritus of his trunk back over it.

Satisfied, he closed the trunk and walked back to his office. Jane Doe was asleep in her room on the ward.

Much later he would realize the hospital had security cameras in many places he had never considered before.

CHAPTER TWENTY-SEVEN

The meeting with the head of security did not go well. The fact that everyone in the department was worn out from working overtime and chasing down strays all over campus for a week was not interesting to him at all.

He wanted to know how his men let someone steal a dead body from their morgue. He wanted to know exactly what went down with the intruder in the night watch and he wanted to know how the cops had arrived in his hospital without him getting a call.

The chief was a kettle-faced rounded-out man of around fifty who gave the impression that his head might actually pop with red pressure when he was angry. Right now the kettle was on full boil.

Every time it appeared as if he were ready for a response to his profanity-laden questions, he spouted more.

The night watch, having been called back to the hospital from their anticipated sleep, was reduced to numb silence and stood tiredly, looking at their shoes.

Finally he stopped and said, "And the security camera… the drive just goes missing." He let this statement sit in the room like poison gas, seeing who might choke on it. Nobody moved a muscle.

"If that drive turns up in one of you guys' possession, it's gonna be bad. Real bad. But it could get worse. Wouldn't surprise me if we end up with the Feds poking around in this. They'll turn this place inside out. So…" He glared at them, "Better to come clean now than later."

Again he waited and again no one flinched.

"Let's be clear then. If that drive shows up and if it is in any way attached to any of you, I will crucify you. All of you."

The three night guards left the meeting together and walked silently to their cars. They were wrapped in individual cones of silence and self-preservation. Jackie Smith had a particularly grim expression on his face. The other two knew enough to get in their cars and drive away without even looking at each other.

Jackie's phone rang. It was his wife.

"Jackie, where are you? Why aren't you home yet?" He could hear his two toddlers bouncing off the walls while she tried to have a normal grown-up conversation.

"I'm just leaving the hospital, baby. Be home in a few minutes. Just had some things to clear up before we could get out of there this morning." He hoped he sounded steady. His wife had always been a Nervous Nellie and he was careful to keep anxious things an arm's length away from her.

"Okay, honey. Just wondered where you were. Could you stop and pick up a few things for me at the farmers market on your way home?"

"Sure. Text me a list?"

"Yep. See ya in a minute. Love you."

"Love you too."

He started to put the phone down and back out of his parking spot. It was already buzzing. *Wow*, he thought, *Maria must have had that list on the top of her head.*

But it wasn't his wife. It was Todd and then it was Steve; his two guards. They were blowing up his phone. Scared. Panicking. Breaking.

He tried to ignore the onslaught of texts and get out of the parking garage. He hated group texts for this very reason. It was like getting a restaurant placeholder that you couldn't give back to the hostess. Finally he pulled over and texted them both.

Shut it down. I will call you both after I get home. He patted his breast pocket unconsciously, feeling the video drive from the morgue outlined there. He knew it was the most sought-after object in this county right now, and here it was, warm in his pocket. He also wondered what was on it.

The spontaneous beat down his men gave to the intruder in the morgue led to a spur-of-the-moment decision to pull the drive, and he had snuck back down to the morgue just before the shift ended to snatch it.

It turned out to be a simple task. The attendant was occupied with someone in the morgue. He heard them talking as he slipped in and out. The move was instinctive. He was protecting not only his own guys but the cops who jumped in on the beating.

How was he supposed to know a dead body would go missing the same night? And the very same body they were there to protect from the pervert? It was just too bizarre.

He didn't believe in coincidence. Law enforcement had made him into an utter skeptic when it came to that. Where there was smoke there was always fire, and there was usually an arsonist around. Spontaneous combustion wasn't an option.

These two unrelated incidents were not. The break in by the pervert and the disappearance of the governor's daughter were linked even if he didn't see how. Yet. The best piece of evidence was in his possession and that both scared him to death and thrilled him.

The chief was right. The Feds would get involved. And the state police and every other investigative agency that could find an angle and a reason to horn in on the case. It was a juicy case. It had "promotion" written all over it for the person lucky enough to break it.

Jackie Smith, like many other guys in the security guard business, resented being called a rent-a-cop but knew it was an accurate descriptor. All the people he'd met in the five years in his job at the hospital were either rejects from state or local law enforcement agencies or retired cops who couldn't stand being at home.

He was no exception. Everyone had their story about why they couldn't cut it with the big boys; injuries, budget cuts, black-balled by an ornery sheriff who didn't like their face. The stories were both pathetic and endless.

Jackie's own story was simple; a wild and lawless childhood within foster care led to a wilder and more lawless adolescence. He had spent as much time in juvenile as he had in any of the several "homes" the great state of North Carolina sent him to.

He was well known to judges and cops alike in Raleigh-Durham; one of the too-numerous-to-count sad-sack stories of the broken system failing a broken kid from a broken (in his case, non-existent) family.

By the time his peers graduated high school and submitted their transcripts to colleges, Jackie had a rap sheet longer than their list of courses completed. All the offenses were minor—there was the one robbery when a clerk in a Wawa got smart with one of his boys and got smacked around a little—but no one got "stiff" or even permanently broken in any of Jackie's turns.

In a life-is-stranger-than-fiction turn of events, he met his wife through robbing her father. They disagreed on the precise details for several years.

Jackie insisted he found Popa Rodriguez's wallet on the sidewalk in front of the Raleigh municipal building and Paul (Popa or Poppie to friends and family) said he knew he had been pickpocketed and returned to the scene of the crime just in time to catch the crook with the wallet in hand.

Poppie tended to get the benefit of the doubt in this exchange of stories. He was an experienced beat cop of twenty years and knew the ropes. Jackie, in the end, admitted he was the one crook stupid enough to try stealing from a cop on his way into court for a day of testimony.

He got as far as flipping the wallet open to where the folding money should have been and found instead a stack of worn photographs showing the Rodriguez family through the years. It caught him by surprise. In a flash he saw himself standing there on a street corner, cars buzzing past on a day like any day, stealing a man's most prized possession. He choked on it.

Thumbing through the photos, he saw a life he never knew. If he had been with his crew instead of doing a little solo petty thieving, he would have pushed the feelings down and laughed off the idiot who didn't have enough money for parking in his wallet.

Being alone, the feeling had space to grow, and before he knew it the sense of loss, of lack, of missing something vital, grabbed him by the heart and shook him. The last picture in the stack showed the cop's family—two boys and two girls—in front of a Christmas tree. The oldest was a girl. Right then he knew he wanted her and everything she had.

That was the moment he met Poppie Rodriguez.

If it had been any other day with any other cop, things would have gone very differently for Jackie. But he met one of the real good guys, the actual good guys, the ones who come to the force to protect and defend and not to pursue and to punish.

Poppie knew exactly what and who he was looking at when he looked at Jackie, but when he caught the kid staring at his pictures, the kid's face was like an empty well or dry ground begging to be watered. The street and all its hardness fell out of his eyes and for a moment left an orphan standing there alone. Poppie absorbed the awkwardness of the moment and flipped it on its head.

He was a big man with a big voice.

"You like *mi familia*?" he said. "I do too! That's my money! Everyone has these phones with all their pictures. I like my pictures where I can feel them."

He took the wallet from Jackie and picked out one of the more worn photos. "Besides, when I took most of these pictures there were no phones for taking pictures. If you can believe it, there were cameras for making pictures and phones for making calls!"

Jackie took this all in while considering whether or not to run away. There was no doubt in his mind he could easily leave this man behind. But he discovered he didn't want to run away. The weight of desire for what this man had was heavier than the desire to run away again. He'd had a life of running away from nowhere to nowhere.

There on the sidewalk of the municipal building with a stolen wallet in his hand he decided he would stop and find a way to have a picture like this of his own. He started the only way he knew how, by lying.

"I just found this wallet and I was trying to find out who it belonged to. You have a great-looking family."

He was a good-looking kid, and he used his practiced and polite street hustle charm routine. It felt like gravel in his mouth. At least for right now and right here, the hustle was gone.

Poppie, who had shifted unconsciously into perp interrogation posture, felt and saw Jackie start up with the hustle and crumple back to the orphan. He relaxed, and for reasons he could never explain to anyone, including himself, he said, "You look like you're hungry. I'm going in here for a couple of hours but if you meet me at noon on the front steps, I'll buy you lunch."

He was only half surprised when the kid actually showed. The unlikely lunch led to an unlikely friendship that led to the most unlikely thing of all—Jackie meeting Poppie's daughter, falling in love, and starting to create their own version of the picture in Poppie's wallet.

Knowing a lot about the criminal justice system from the inside perspective, combined with a sense of awe and gratitude for what his father-in-law did for him, made Jackie interested in being a cop himself. Years of run-ins with too many of the pursue-and-punish crowd left him little in the way of options for getting hired directly into the force. Even Poppie's string-pulling and cashing in favors couldn't get him a break, but with the help of Poppie and others, he set out to find another way in.

He was used to being an outsider looking for ways to get in; sometimes it took time and creativity to get access. He passed the high school equivalency exam and enrolled in courses for an associate's degree in criminal justice at the community college, and he set out to erase his old record one day at a time.

When the security officer job at the hospital came open, Jackie didn't see it as second best or a boobie prize, he saw it as the next rung on the ladder he was building. He worked hard and he learned the ropes and he treated the job like it was real law enforcement.

This made him both popular and unpopular around the medical center. The medical staff often felt like he was too much like a cop for their taste and complained about him. The administrative staff, including his chain of command, came to depend on him to get the hard jobs done that no one else would touch.

After only a year on the job, they promoted him to the mid watch shift supervisor. He was sure he was on his way up and out, but he discovered the hazard of being too good at his job. It was hard staffing the mid shift and Jackie did such a good job that no one was interested in helping him move up or out.

He finished his associate's degree with no fanfare, promotion, or even a raise. When he asked for a letter of recommendation from the security chief that he could use as an intro to the local PD, he got an empty promise. It had been two years now since he took over the mid watch and he was no closer to a position in real law enforcement.

Reflecting on all this as he drove to the farmers market and tried to keep his guys in check, he considered what to do about the hard drive.

Snatching it from the morgue office was a reflexive move, a street move. He saw how this would go down for him and his crew and for the local cops involved in the beating. It wouldn't go well. So he took care of it.

He didn't like it when his street instincts took over—he fought it like Jekyll fought Hyde. Most of the time he kept it at bay. He especially fought to keep it from his wife. He wanted to be—had to be—better for her, more for her.

She deserved it.

Poppie had given him the best gift and he would not be unworthy of it. Maria was his girl and he was her knight. It was corny but it was true, at least as far as she knew, and that was how he would make it stay.

Bagging up the fresh tomatoes and the ears of corn she wanted, lost in thought, he almost walked out without paying. When he reached for his breast pocket where he kept his folding money as a hedge against pickpockets like his old incarnation, he felt the drive there next to the cash and he made a connection.

Whatever was on this drive was really like money in his pocket. It would increase in value as soon as the right people knew of its existence. Yeah, that was one way to play this.

He didn't like the street reflex that got him into this situation but he was in it now and now he had to decide if the way out would be street or straight or maybe a little of both.

He paid the tab and drove home mulling this over.

CHAPTER TWENTY-EIGHT

Daniel and Wanda Treeright sat together in Daniel's office. Syd DeVito stood. The presence of the three in anything other than an official setting was unusual.

They had learned to dance their dysfunctional private-public tango like all dancers, one step at a time.

As Daniel and Wanda fell out of step and out of love, there had been a time without masks when both shared the confidence of Syd as their friend since college and before their wild ride into politics.

But when Wanda and Syd fell into each other's beds, the masks came on and the movements became complex. The friendships they shared eroded and fused in different places so that they found each other necessary in doing life together—going where they all thought they wanted to go.

They rarely stopped to consider the dehumanizing effect of counting the ends as more important than the means and reducing relationships to useful tools rather than the substance of true life.

Tabitha's death was too real for the dance, too authentic for the masks, and the events of the past evening pressed them together into one room and one dark cloud of emotion they could neither avoid nor embrace but only hope to cling to one another and survive.

Syd, ever the strategist, was grasping for a plan, his way of breathing in the oppressive air of this present darkness. "The press is going to know about this soon. It's amazing it's still quiet." He looked at Daniel for a reaction. There was none. "We can't do nothing. It's not an option."

He took in a deep breath, held it, and slowly released it. He couldn't find a handle on this. It was like sticking his hand in a pile of the homemade goo kids loved. He could touch it and feel it but not take hold of it.

It wasn't just on him. It was on all of them. He had never gotten over the feel of this office, the smell of leather and books, the dark wood of the majestic governor's desk, the huge area carpet with the seal of the state of North Carolina. It was the place the three of them had envisioned as their destiny.

It never got old for Syd, never lost its sense of wonder. A place that felt like he was adventuring and not working, like exploring a dark cave. This morning it was like a cold light found had its way into his cave, ruining all the mystery, exposing everything for mere stones and empty space. No magic here. Just a cave full of lost people and the sound of his own voice echoing off the walls.

Daniel stirred.

"Where would she go?" he said to no one.

"What?" Syd said.

Daniel didn't appear to hear him or see him. He was in a trancelike state, staring into nowhere.

"Where would she go?" Daniel repeated. "Wouldn't she try to find us? Go home?"

Wanda and Syd stared at Daniel and then each other. He had cracked. They were drowning in sorrow, going down for the third time, possibly never to rise again, but Daniel was lost. His mind was broken.

"He said she was alive. He told me. He knew it. He knew it."

Daniel had told them about the phone call from the inmate at Windsor. First he told Syd as they drove to the morgue and then he repeated it to Wanda. The repetition took some of the edge off for Daniel. Saying something so incredible out loud made it seem so childish, so naive. Foolish.

Daniel Treeright was not foolish and he wasn't a child even when he was a child. He had never been able to tolerate it when adults implied he was not up to their level intellectually. It was the possibility of being considered foolish that drove him through school all the way to his LL.D and on to the governorship.

Standing there in the morgue with the empty place where he had seen Tabitha's dead cold body only hours before and watching the police begin to gather evidence had shaken the silliness out of him. This was too real for fantasies. Could the girl be alive?

For Syd, the missing video drive was too real to ignore. Someone committed a crime and was covering it up. Syd and Wanda had eyed Daniel warily when he recounted the inmate's phone call, obviously not taken in by it like he was. Their eyes said, "Shut up," and he had.

That was then, in the face of the bright lights of the morgue and logic. Here in the dark office with no other ideas or hints to go on, it was slipping. Logic was giving way to something else. Peace? Hope?

His heart skipped a beat and his breath caught in his throat. What if? What if? Could there be a way he never considered before? The peace was quietly insistent. It was like the backbeat of a song that got lost in the noise of the club but when it came back you knew it never left—it was always there. Missing video drive—missing daughter.

Missing. He started to pick up the phone on his desk and Syd pounced, forcing his hand back down.

"Who're you calling?" he said.

"State Police. I'm gonna get someone looking for her."

"Looking for her? What the hell do you think every law enforcement agency—local, state, and federal are doing right now? They're all looking for her!"

"They're not gonna be looking in the right places. They're looking for a lost body. We need them looking for a lost girl."

Wanda gasped.

Syd tightened his grip on Daniel's hand and the phone together. "No. No," he said. "I'm not going to let you turn this into a circus. It's not good for you, the state... the campaign. It's not good for Tabitha!"

Daniel didn't resist the pressure Syd exerted on his hand. He didn't raise his voice. He said, "Syd, I know you want what's best for Tabitha. She always loved you. She always loved you... she loves you. We've got to quit speaking about her in the past tense. She isn't in the past tense. She is alive and she walked out of that morgue and we have to find her. She must be in trouble or we would have heard from her by now."

He gathered himself, considered something, and continued. "I'm not losing it. I'm not. I believe what I'm saying sounds crazy. Maybe it's because of our culture. If we were in Africa, maybe we would at least see the possibility. Here we have no room for it. I'm looking at the facts and I believe Tabitha being alive is a reasonable way to account for the facts."

He waited.

Wanda and Syd sat; eyes down, unresponsive.

"Okay," he said. "Give me your story. Give me your way to account for the facts. I'm not losing it. I can listen to other possibilities. Give me some."

Wanda spoke up. "The missing hard drive, Daniel. It's a fact that's hard to get around. What happened to it? Did our dead daughter get up off that slab and steal the only evidence so we wouldn't be able to track her down? Why would that be missing if she was alive? Wouldn't anyone who saw that happen want to show it to everyone? That's it, Daniel. The missing drive is everything here. It says there's a cover up of something and no one would cover up a dead person coming back to life."

Wanda set her jaw and looked at her husband cooly, ready for a fight, expecting the flash in his eyes and knowing their only form of communication for several years had only been a fight.

Instead she got a look of understanding. His eyes had no fight in them; no flash, no anger at being challenged.

"I agree with you," he said. "The missing video is hard to get around. I don't have an answer for it yet." He sighed. "But consider what you're saying if you believe someone took her body and stole the drive to cover it up. What's the motive behind it? Who has something to gain from it and who has something to lose?"

Syd and Wanda recognized the man addressing them now. It was the man they knew, not a lunatic or a father driven to an act of desperation. It was the shrewd politician, the governor, working out a problem and taking people along with him while he did it. Pitching the solution and looking for buy-in from colleagues and constituents. But it was more than that man. He was more than in control. He was above this problem in a way they didn't understand. And this made them curious and attentive.

"Think about the operation this would involve. Think of the logistics of it, the planning. No one knew Tabitha was going to die. They could guess it was coming but no one knew how long the disease would take to kill her. And no one could know I wouldn't make it back in time to be with her. Did we give any hint that she would stay in the hospital morgue until I got back instead of going to a funeral home?"

Syd shook his head.

"Right. So we have to have someone who came up with a plan on the spur of the moment and carried it out to perfection. If it's a political opponent there's almost infinite downside. Get caught at stealing a dead girl's body and everything is over for you, forever. That's high stakes. And what's the upside? What does anyone hope to get out of it? How does it hurt us?" He paused and searched their faces.

"Doesn't it generate sympathy for us? Doesn't it make us look like victims? And it's a good time to be a victim. Isn't it? So it isn't reasonable to think a political opponent did this. Losing Tabitha twice doesn't make us look bad. I thought it might be a way to make me look incompetent—not here when my daughter needed me..." He glanced up at Wanda and corrected himself. "When my family needed me."

He got up and paced, rising more and more to the moment.

"No. I think it would be more reasonable to think this wasn't a professional job at all. It could have been a fanatic who just hates us and wants to hurt us. That might be possible. It makes more sense than giving it to an opponent trying to knock us down. But there are big problems with that too. The biggest is the one you pointed out. Would a fanatic be able to get in and out of the morgue with the body and think to steal the video? Picture the kind of person crazy enough to want to steal a girl's body. Can you conjure up the image of someone stable and slick? I can't. There is one possibility that makes sense."

He mulled it over a second before launching his last pieces of argument.

"Yes. It could have been. If the morgue attendant was the fanatic or if he worked with some nut job, it could make sense. He would know how to get the body out of the morgue and how to get the hard drive from the security camera.

"He would have to work with someone else because he had to be there when it was all over. He could have done it. But he's the guy who cracked the skull of the only other person we know was in the morgue last night. He clocked him because he was disturbing Tabitha's body.

"The cops at the scene all agreed that Windsor was bleeding from a head wound when they got there. Not to mention he was the one who made the 911 call."

He reflected on this. "Doesn't sound like a guy who has something to hide or who wants to hurt us."

Daniel stopped pacing and lowered himself into a chair. They were all silent.

"You see? It's not reasonable to go with those theories. Or… maybe it's better to say we have only unreasonable options to go with."

Syd stirred. He had warmed to the challenge his boss laid down. He wasn't a hack. He considered himself Daniel's equal in every area save for face-to-face political charm and charisma. He prided himself on seeing the angles to exploit that others couldn't or wouldn't see for themselves.

"I think there's another possibility you're not considering," he said. "You're right about the downside of a stunt like this. It's huge. It's beyond huge. Botching it or getting caught is a bottomless pit. But I disagree that it doesn't have an upside—or a potential upside.

"Let's face it. Let's look at the reality of our position. You are untouchable. You are going to cruise to the nomination and it looks like you'll do the same in the general."

Wanda and Daniel eyed Syd. He was breaking a cardinal rule— his own cardinal rule—never under any circumstances let yourself believe you've won an election until every vote is counted. Never say to yourself or anyone else you are the winner until you are the winner.

But here he was putting them in the White House before the campaign got started. This was an anomaly. He met their eyes without blinking.

"Those are the facts. It's ours to lose. The stars are aligned. And there are people who want what we have. It's the greatest prize on earth. Think about it. Really think about it. You have to think about it like that or you'll be vulnerable. We have the toy all the other kids want.

"Better yet—we have the only bone in the pound. The other dogs are not going to let us just have it. It's not in their nature. They don't think it belongs to us. They don't think at all. They smell what they want and they go after it. It's instinct. It's nature. They will take the bone by brute force if they're big enough and believe they can do it without getting killed.

"You're the biggest dog they've ever seen, so that kind of attack is out. But they aren't giving up. They can't. It isn't in them. The bone drives them crazy. It's all they think about. All they live for. They sleep with it in their dreams.

"So they'll wait and watch for any opportunity to get it. Any opening when the big dog isn't holding onto the bone tightly. Or gets distracted.

"They don't have to plan a great deal. They don't need to prepare. See what I'm saying? They are prepared. They aren't doing anything but thinking about how to get that bone. And when they see it, they act without remorse and without hesitation."

Syd stopped to make sure he had their full attention. He did.

"Without remorse. Without hesitation. These dogs live for the bone that we have. There is no such thing as a dirty trick. There's only winning and losing. No rules. Here's what I think you're missing.

"The dogs saw us falter with Tabitha. Saw us weakened and unsure of ourselves. You didn't make it back. We didn't handle the press; they handled us. We hesitated to move Tabitha to a funeral home."

He held his hands up in front of him to show he knew the counter arguments to his case.

"Dogs. Remember it's dogs we're dealing with. It's reflex. Snatch it."

He made a face like a snarl and clenched one hand, mimicking a dog's snout.

"And you forget that you aren't just any candidate for president, Daniel. You are a black man running for the Republican party. A conservative. If you run and get elected, it changes the electorate forever. You are a generational shift. You are a tsunami that will disempower the left in ways they can't allow."

He let this sink in and continued.

"They want to exploit your weakness for Tabitha. I think the explanation is what I just saw in this room. I saw an intelligent man— a reasonable man—turned into a gullible man. A man who would fall for a con.

"I don't think they're trying to embarrass you over not getting here or being out of touch when a moment of crisis arose. I think they're trying to get you to look like a fool. I think they want to make you believe Tabitha is alive so they can prove how stupid you are.

"And when they do, they will expose it all as a hoax and bury you with it."

Syd paused and looked to Wanda for support. She kept her head down.

He went on.

"Daniel, Tabitha is dead. She had the best medical team on the east coast give her every possible chance to survive. They certified her death and if you had been here she would have already been in the ground. It's true. She's gone. Someone has her body but she's not there. She's gone.

"Throwing away your life's work isn't going to bring her back. It's only going to give the bone to some dog—a dog who would go to this length to get it. Think about that. You want that kind of dog sitting in the highest office in the world?"

Daniel found that he had been sitting forward and gripping the arms of his chair as Syd spilled out his thoughts. He relaxed his grip and settled back into the chair. He said nothing.

As the silence grew, Wanda realized Daniel and Syd were both looking at her, waiting.

It was a tie. Syd had not moved Daniel. Daniel had not moved Syd. She was repulsed by the thought of breaking this tie although she had been in this position many times before.

It was natural enough. A force to be reckoned with in her own right, she was the equal of both the men intellectually and possibly superior to Syd as a strategist. Both men knew her to be more ruthless in political fights.

But she also had a subtle charisma, an introverted charm she reserved for her private life and rarely showed to those who didn't know her personally. She had the respect of these two powerful men even as she lost the affection of the one and took it from the other.

Wanda did not want to break this tie. Her mind hurt. Her emotions pounded away at the edge of endurance. She didn't know she could be this tired and not collapse.

Life tired; empty of any life energy yet still living.

She said the only thing she had left.

"Dead or alive, I need her back. Dead or alive, you two are going to find her and bring her back."

CHAPTER TWENTY-NINE

Tabitha Treeright arrived at the Regional Mental Hospital in Raleigh. It was less than a fifteen minute drive from the Governor's Mansion where Syd and Daniel and Wanda were meeting.

She was sedated but awake enough to know she was in a new place. Looking at her wrist, she saw a hospital bracelet. It said, "Doe, Jane," with a date and identification number.

Hadn't she told them who she was? She tried to tell a white-clad orderly who retrieved her from the ambulance and put her in a wheelchair that the bracelet was wrong. She was Tabitha.

She tried again with the nurse in admitting. Why wouldn't anyone believe she was who she said she was? Everyone smiled and nodded and went on with the process of admitting her. They told her to rest and she told them that she'd never been so rested in her life. She told them she felt more alive than ever.

The new room was a shared space with three other beds, two of which were occupied by girls who appeared to be more or less her age. One of the girls was awake and the other snored loudly like a man. Tabitha felt a new dose of sedative start to take hold and fought to keep her eyes open. It went dark.

She awoke disoriented. The room was dimly lit. Waking up in a strange place for the second day in a row was not helpful and it took her several long minutes to put it together.

The edge of the foggy sedation lifted enough to let her feel present in her own present. She sat up and surveyed the room. Snoring girl was gone, leaving a pleasant hole in the background noise. The fans in the far-away ceiling whirred. Shielded light strips above each bed washed fluorescent swaths down the white walls.

Her eyes adjusted to the light and her mind cleared. She saw the girl in the next bed was also awake and sitting up, looking back at her in the gloom. She was expressionless, her moon face and dark eyes vacant. Tabitha wondered if she too was sedated. But she spoke clearly and loudly, blowing a hole in the peaceful atmosphere.

"I'm Janine! Ha! I'm Ja-ja Janine! Aha!" The girl twitched her chin down to the left each time she punctuated her words with a burst of laughter. Comprehension of something flickered through her eyes and she held a finger up to her lips.

"Too loud!" she whispered, too loudly. "Too loud. Ha! White Shoes comes if we're too loud. Ha! They'll makes us eat candy that mmmmakes us sleep! Ha!"

She craned her neck toward the door silhouetted in a white square across the room and rolled over, sniggling to herself. "Yep! Ha! Come and give us the sleeping candy! Aha! Ha ha ha ha!"

Tabitha heard a disturbance outside the door and threw herself down on the bed just as it swung open. It was too late for Janine though. The night nurse scolded her for being too noisy and did make her take some of the "sleeping candy," while Tabitha did her best to be still enough to appear to be asleep.

She was coming fully back into her faculties and she didn't want any more of the candy for herself.

The nurse lingered over her only for a moment and seemed satisfied. She left Tabitha lying next to the slow-breathing Janine, her laughter fading out with progressive breaths as she passed into another drug-induced slumber.

I wonder how much of the time she is drugged, Tabitha thought with a shudder. *And I wonder if that's what they'll do to me. I wonder why she's here and why they put me in a room with her.*

The revelation that someone thought she was as crazy as the girl next to her came clear. It felt like a heavy weight sat down on her chest and pressed her into the mattress of the hospital bed.

She tried to piece together the events of the past day. Day? Was it only a day? She had no idea how long she'd been sedated. Waking up in the Duke hospital and her interaction with the people there had a dream-like quality to it—like she was not really there somehow.

Some part of her was there, it was true, but more of her had been somewhere else. She shook her head at these thoughts as if trying to reset an Etch A Sketch.

She had a flashback to the trip to Smith Mountain Lake with her best friend Hannah. The trip was fun. Hannah's family was more like a real family than her own. She felt easy with them. Hannah's mom and dad liked each other and Hannah liked them.

It was all so normal and they treated her like she belonged with them, not like a guest. They were some of the only people in her life who were not interested in pumping Tabitha for information about her famous parents.

It was all just… easy.

Their regular trip to the lake was the same week every year in the same rented house. They had all the right toys; jet skis that Hannah and Tabitha were just getting to drive for themselves and a boat for hauling water skiers and wake boarders; Hannah's brothers and sisters.

The most fun time was riding the huge four-person float pulled behind the boat, hauling various combinations of the kids. Hannah's mom and dad took turns driving, swinging them back and forth across the water valley created in the boat's wake, bouncing them over the edges of the white water cliffs and sending them flying in a tumult of roller coaster laughter.

Knowing there were no seat belts and no speed limits only enhanced the white-knuckle fun. They screamed for more speed and more air time. Hannah's dad was the more restrained driver but her mom… her mom let it, and them, fly.

Tabitha remembered it now. The last time tubing. It was just her and Hannah with her mom flinging them around in wild arcs, each more thrillingly violent than the last.

Each time they impossibly held on to the float as they crashed down on one pass and waited for the tow line to go taut and snatch them, sending them skittering across the wake again. "More more more!" they screamed.

And they got their wish.

It had happened hundreds of times in their years of lake daredevilry. The float went completely airborne like a child's kite finally springing into the wind. For an exquisite moment, they achieved Wright brothers ecstasy, getting what they wanted and wondering how they'd come down.

Gravity and tension on the tow rope answered that question an instant later, flipping the float on its side while they adopted an each-girl-for-herself scramble to find a handhold and keep from losing their grip.

Hannah found a way. Tabitha didn't. She flailed on the float-turned-kite as it crashed down and came back under power. The inflatable seat back caught her perfectly in the back and flung her out along the arc it had been traveling.

She skipped three times like a smooth stone until her face went straight into the wake from another passing boat.

The force of the impact drove lake water up her nose and half-open mouth as if she had been hit by a stream from a fire hose. It wasn't the first time she had experienced a "skimmer"—their name for it—in fact, it happened once or twice a season to one or the other of the kids, but this time it was different.

It was never comfortable getting a head full of lake water and it often took a day of blowing your nose and clearing your ears to feel normal again and not hear an echo in your head.

This time Tabitha felt like she had been punched in the face. From the moment she sputtered to the surface and waved to the boat to let them know she was okay, she knew she wasn't.

Thinking back on it, she touched her forehead, feeling the phantom of the pain that had started there and expanded. It began as a pinprick of heat in the dull throbbing of pressure in her sinuses.

The fire spread quickly to her eyes and ears. The night of the skimming she lay on the couch watching everyone else play a board game. By bedtime she was unable to stand or to talk.

Hannah's parents had wrapped her head in towels full of ice and her dad had laid her in the back seat of their van and driven her an hour over the circuitous fifteen miles out of the lakefront to a first aid facility in Moneta.

She could remember these things in a relatively straight line; after she got to Moneta pieces of the story went missing. It was like sunshine and shadow chasing each other as you drive past them in the car.

Flashes of light where she could see and hear and remember.

The Food Lion parking lot converted to a helipad. The red-and-white helo setting down in a whirl of wind and noise. Faces over her face. Shadow. Clump-clumping down a hallway on a bed on wheels. More faces, different faces, over her face. Shadow.

Cold compression on her arms and legs, odd-looking and sounding boxes like being in a Legoland of plastic machines. Heat. Her mom's face over her face.

She concentrated on this moment, trying to relive it, to see it, and hear it, and understand. Mom's face. Mom talking to another face. A doctor? She is telling Mom something. It is so hard to hear.

The fire inside is burning like standing too close to a fire pit, and the fire has a sound. It has a sound as a jet flying too close overhead. It drowns out all else.

But she does hear snatches of voices breaking through. She can hear the doctor saying the words: *Tabitha is dying. Nothing more to do. Only a matter of time.*

She felt as well as heard this in her memory. It was like being thumped hard on the chest. Her heart began to race and to hurt. Sweat poured off her face in the chilly darkness of the psych ward. Dead? She died? But she hadn't died. She had lived.

Could this explain why everyone was treating her like she was crazy?

She sat up straight and swung her legs over the edge of the bed. She couldn't remember dying but what did that mean? Who in the world ever said something like that? No one.

No one ever said, *Oh yeah that was the day I died*! Either she didn't die and they thought she did or she did die and… and what?

The Light land was real. She knew in a flash that here was the disconnect; here was the source of her confusion since waking up in the hospital. She had no doubt the Light was real and she had been there, not mystically or magically or spiritually or any of the ways she'd heard people talk about heaven or the spirit world.

She had walked and felt her feet. She had seen with her eyes and heard the music with her ears. All real. How she got there and how she got back were a mystery but the facts were not disputable to her.

And the problem was that this place, this reality was real too, only… it was less real. It was like walking in shadow.

Her hours—days?—back in this shadowy world were more blurry than the time she spent in the Light. There was another problem. Hours in shadow versus how long in Light? She tried to think of the moment she got to Light land and how long she had been there. It didn't fit.

She could not think of Light land and time at once. The two things felt like trying to hold the South pole of two magnets together. They repelled each other right out of her mind. She realized that there were no days or nights in Light land and that she had not slept while she was there.

Whatever sense of time she had existed here in the shadows.

Now that she was in time again she had slowly gained a sense of urgency to go along with being in time. Now there were things to do that couldn't be done if time ran out. She let this settle on her. She didn't like the feeling of being in time compared to the timelessness of Light land.

She thought that this was like coming home from the best vacation ever; one so good that you even forgot you had to go back to school ever again or stop doing anything but having fun.

This was a drag. Going back to "life" when you were really living. It took time to get back in the groove, to begin to feel normal in your own normal ways. Yeah. That's what this was like. Only she had not woken up in her own bed after this vacation, she had woken up in… a morgue!

It snapped into place suddenly and harshly like a slamming iron door. The trip back from Light land happened in no time—it literally couldn't have used up any time there—and going from full and real Light into shadow had done a number on her.

It was as if she had been in the high clear desert consumed by light and been plunged into polar night. Only this had affected her whole person, not just her eyes. It had taken how long for her to dilate enough to see again—who she was, where she had been, where she was now?

Her emotions caught up to her then and she cried. Deep gulping sobs. She cried for her mother's pain at losing her. She cried for the fear of death in this shadowy place. She cried for the loss of the Light.

She lay down exhausted and let the tears wet her pillow. The nurse came in at hearing her cry, and with nursely coos and there-theres, gave her a shot of tranquilizer.

CHAPTER THIRTY

Doug was arraigned on charges of abusing a corpse, sexual abuse of a minor, breaking and entering, and assaulting a police officer. He was assigned a public defender who spent thirty seconds looking at his file and another thirty asking him for his particulars—name, social, address, and phone—before they appeared before a bored-looking judge.

His loud and clear "Not guilty to all charges" startled the attorney into wakefulness. The judge took no notice of his woeful lack of representation. He was busy with his head down scowling at papers on his bench. He looked down at Doug and said, "You're a parole breaker too, Mr. Windsor."

Doug decided to let the implications of the word "too" pass.

"Sir, it is true that I am outside of my assigned parole area by a few miles, but—"

The judge cut him off. "A few miles? Sir, you are two hundred miles away from the court that has jurisdiction over your parole. You are across state lines. My people inquired after you to see if by chance you'd filed for an exemption to travel with your parole officer and the answer was 'no.'"

The judge knit his scraggly white eyebrows together. "You think we don't have enough sex perverts in our state to keep us busy?

Need some more perversion here? No, we don't. I know what we do have here in my courtroom. We have no tolerance for perverts who hurt children. No, sir. None. So I'm gonna keep you locked up till I can get you locked back away somewhere in this state or the next."

In no time Doug was remanded to the custody of the sheriff's deputies, who escorted him back to the same cell he came from. His sleepy public defender mumbled something about getting his case to someone else in the office and his day in court was done.

The only thing they had him on was breaking parole. No way around that. But the other charges? He hadn't broken into the morgue; he'd walked in. Sexually abusing a minor? He didn't want to use a technicality but could a corpse be a minor? He wondered what constituted abuse of a corpse and decided they could construe that any way they wanted.

But that last charge... assaulting a police officer? They must have been afraid of what would happen when he showed up in court looking like Rocky Balboa. They were covering for each other. He remembered that cops were almost all wearing body cameras these days but the ones in the morgue weren't. There were cameras in the morgue though, he was sure of it. There would be proof of what really happened in there. He was the one assaulted by any measure.

Doug didn't know it as his cell door clanked shut, but the beating in the morgue, and everything else that had happened—all the evidence needed to prove not only his innocence but his sanity, was recorded, but it was also in a hard drive that was missing.

CHAPTER THIRTY-ONE

Syd DeVito sat in his office in a black mood. He did not like being out of control. His speech to Daniel had been desperation. Out of control. He saw twenty years of work teetering on the edge. He had violated a primary rule of life in Syd world—never count on anything, and especially never say anything, unless you could prove with the facts—when he told Daniel the presidency was his to lose.

He worked hard to keep Treeright razor sharp. He *made* Daniel Treeright. Created him out of raw materials that were high quality, no doubt, but in Syd's hands the right cuts were made at the right time to turn the man into a diamond.

It had taken all his skill and a good amount of lying to get the Treerights to stand down and let him work this problem. They were resting in the family quarters now, but he knew he had a limited amount of time to make something happen.

In some ways Syd's affair with Wanda was another cut, albeit a cruel one. It was a way to maintain control of the person who could do the most damage to Daniel were she to go off the reservation.

It was Syd who saw the frayed edges of their relationship long before Daniel. He saw the neglect in her eyes. He had warned his friend; had built dates for them into his man's schedule. He had even arranged for the Treerights to participate in a marriage enhancement weekend. None of it penetrated Daniel's perpetual focus on advancing his career. Treeright thought the date nights made for good photo ops and the weekend retreat was a chance to mingle with a few other power couples who attended.

Syd had created a monster with a single eye and that eye never rested upon his increasingly frustrated and lonely wife. Wanda was beautiful in the rare way of women who wake up looking Vogue and never give more attention to a mirror than the time it takes to brush their teeth and hair. She had a body that still looked like it did when she was barely out of her teens. Men noticed her and with that sense certain of them have, they began to catch the scent of an unloved woman.

He did not set out to be her lover, only to be her confidant and protector, but it wasn't long before he knew she was reaching exit velocity from her marriage. The one way to keep his man from destroying his life's work turned out to be having an affair with his wife.

It was not an entirely selfless act nor was it unpleasant. He had to admit to himself that he had wanted Wanda, had thought about her in his bed. The reality of having her was not disappointing. She was a hungry lover and appreciated his every attention.

The affair did keep a lid on the internal unhappiness of the made for television all American couple, but Daniel didn't see things as coldly as his chief strategist and best friend. He was not grateful. It took all of Syd's relational capital and strategic skill to hold their political family together and settle into their uneasy working truce.

Now, after all they had been through, they were on the cusp of the great prize. It had been costly. Having an affair with his best friend's wife was not the worst thing Syd had done to get them here. There was a long list of double dealing, backstabbing, and throat slitting on his ledger; some of it in a literal sense.

He was a student of power, and from early in life had neither illusions nor qualms about the means necessary to obtain it. He also developed a knack for identifying men and women who would apply those means if the price was right and the way to plausible deniability paved for them. As the stakes got higher, he learned to feel less and hide more emotion, like a poker player training himself to keep his pulse steady and keep his carotid covered when he couldn't.

The stakes had never been higher than right now. He had sent Daniel off to Africa in a preemptory strike at political enemies who were angling to target Treeright as an Oreo. Black man married to white girl. Not down for the struggle. Not black enough.

The trip was inspired by Tabitha, who had insisted on getting one of those heritage DNA tests done for both her and Daniel. She had discovered, incredibly white as she was, that she had a strong trace of Namibian blood in her ancestry, and Daniel did too.

The trip was an easy sell to Daniel. The Namibians had been more than happy to accommodate the rising star from America.

It turned out they had been too accommodating. After doing some research of their own, they discovered the exact tribal village of his ancestors and arranged to take him there as a surprise. With Syd running the show stateside and the press hawking his every move, Treeright had been hustled off into the nether regions of the backcountry bush, incommunicado and days away from civilization when tragedy struck.

Yes, Syd thought, this moment was here because he had not been there when it counted. Now the whole process was on the edge of a knife. He needed to take that knife and use it.

The place to start cutting was the man sitting in the Durham city jail. Syd picked up the phone and dialed a man of means.

CHAPTER THIRTY-TWO

The local press had not been treated with much respect during the national media feeding frenzy surrounding Tabitha Treeright's sickness and death. There was too much blood in the water; too many bigger sharks snapping up any little news morsel to leave much for the beat reporters slugging away in the minor market of Raleigh-Durham. It was especially hard on local print journos who were regularly trumped anyway by the local TV journos looking for air time.

Rich Macher was a rare bird in the news business. He was a fifty-something, old-school, street-tromping news man, and he looked the part. His dress was disheveled bachelor and consistent: khaki "no wrinkle" pants (the reason he never ironed them), a t-shirt in summer and a sweatshirt in winter, which rotated between the logos of various professional ball teams and eighties bands.

He was an emotional guy with a kind face that remained less wrinkled with age than his clothes. He had bright, inquisitive eyes that made you feel you would like the man before he ever spoke a word. His beaky nose matched with a nervous twitch that flicked his head to one side and his 6'2" height gave him the appearance of an overgrown bird. He was proud of the fact that he was still hovering around his painfully thin high school weight of one-fifty, a fact that he attributed to his active life haunting Raleigh and hunting up stories.

Macher was a fixture in the local press, having started out delivering papers for the News and Observer and landing a job writing interest stories for them out of college. He never left. He did it because he loved it and he did it because he loved his little city, even with all its warts.

He had a nose for the kind of inside-the-loop stories that others couldn't stomach or didn't care about. It was the kind of work that got you nowhere in the news game but made you beloved by the gritty, down-home kinds of folks who are the only true locals occupying any smallish college town like Raleigh.

It was his devotion to the things others didn't want to see in his city that landed him in the middle of the hottest story in the country.

Ten years ago, when a particular gang of very young and outrageously brazen thieves had terrorized Raleigh, Macher had gone looking for the story under the story. From the way the crimes went down, he figured the gang members were local kids, not imported. They weren't particularly violent and hit places away from the touristy and college dweller parts of the city, sticking instead to convenience stores near older neighborhoods.

True big-city gang activity had not infiltrated Raleigh yet, and Macher was curious if this group of young bandits was the vanguard of something new. It was while he was searching out this gang that he met and became friends with a teenaged hard ass who didn't know he wasn't hard enough to stay on the track he was riding for long.

No, Jackie Smith wasn't a hard ass; but he didn't know it. Macher, who had seen his share of bad men in his years on the beat, did know it. He didn't exactly set out to save Jackie—kids like him were more like feral cats than stray dogs—but he did set out to get close enough to gain his trust.

He accomplished that by listening to the kid over meals in fast food joints. He bought Jackie's confidence for the price of a few value meals and an open ear. Jackie paid him back with the real story of how the system failed a lot of kids like him, and how they survived on their own.

Macher had published a series of articles about Jackie. They were well written but were barely noticed. Rich was proud of the articles for the same reason he was proud of anything he considered good; it was true and it had a heart.

When his phone rang Macher, picked up immediately.

"Rich?"

"Jackie! How you doin', young man? It's good to hear your voice. How's Maria? How's work? How's life?"

Jackie was used to Macher's machine-gun questioning and scooped all the answers into one response.

"All's well, Mach-man. I've got something I need to run by you. Pretty urgent. Could you meet me at Quillens over here by my place?"

"The place that smells like heartburn?" Macher checked his wristwatch. It was too early for the lunch crowd at Quillens.

"Sure, Jackie. I can head out now but I doubt they're open."

"They're not. I know the owner and he'll let us sit while they set up for opening. I was hoping we could be there alone."

"Ohhh," Macher jibed him and said with mock seriousness, "Secret meetings with high level sources."

Jackie let the joke fall flat.

"How soon can you get there?"

Quillens sat back from the street in a part of town that was a collision of industrial park, storefront churches, and single-family homes from the fifties. It was named after the owner of one of those homes who had started out grilling hot dogs in the front yard to feed lunch to the hard hats from a ball bearing factory across the street. Pretty soon the lunch crowd spilled from the yard into the house and then the house stopped being a house and became a true greasy spoon dive.

The factory died but Quillens lived on, a rare case of culinary evolution adapting to the new clientele and times.

Jackie and Macher sat in the greasy dimness on wooden chairs stained with sweat and food cooked before Jackie was born. They could have been father and son in age and in looks.

Jackie picked a spot well away from the entrance in spite of the fact the joint was closed. He sat with his back to the wall and scanned the room furtively.

"Okay, Jackie. What's the deal? Seriously, you're acting like we're in a *Mission Impossible* movie or somethin."

Once again, his friend let the chance to let the air out of the moment go by. Instead Jackie popped up to his feet and hustled over to a waitress who was heading their way with an armload of salt and pepper shakers to set out before open. He relieved her of them and sent her on her way. Sitting down again, he cleared the room visually one more time before locking eyes with Macher.

"I've got something that could be very valuable to the right people," he said.

Macher saw the gravity of whatever Jackie was involved with pulling down the edges of his face. He was worried—no, he was scared—but it was tinged with excitement.

"What is it, kid? What's so heavy? You'd think by looking at you you've gotten on the wrong side of the mob."

Jackie let out a long exhale and looked at the aged green Formica table top. "It's bigger than that, I think. It's at least as dangerous, maybe more. Did you know the governor's daughter is missing?"

Macher looked confused. "What?! But she's dead!"

"Keep it down, Mach-man!" Jackie hissed. "Tabitha Treeright's body is missing. Someone stole it from the morgue last night." He looked to see if Macher was tracking. He was.

"They're trying to keep a lid on this. You can see why. I haven't seen or heard anything about it on the news. Obviously you haven't either."

Macher nodded assent.

"There's more to it. Last night we responded to a disturbance in the morgue and found this guy messing around with the girl's body."

A look of horrified rage crossed Macher's face.

"Yeah. I know. The boys felt the same way. They started to beat the hell out of the guy. Durham's finest got there same time we did. It came close to being two dead bodies instead of just one."

"How…" Macher started to ask. Jackie cut him off.

"The guy on duty in the morgue wasn't paying close enough attention. Left the door unlocked and the pervert just walked right in. Started putting his hands on the dead girl. Jeesh. I saw it with my own eyes. This guy with his hands inside a rubber body bag. The girl's lips…" He pursed his own lips tightly as he saw again what he wanted to forget and couldn't.

"Her lips were blue. The guy was face to face with her, almost like he was gonna kiss those dead blue lips."

He looked at Macher and they shared a wide-eyed look of incredulity. Macher started to clear his throat to speak. Jackie stopped him again.

"It's not the worst. The guy is on top of her... saying... repeating over and over her, the word 'cum.' He was saying her name and telling her that word. I swear to you if I hadn't seen and heard it for myself I would never believe it."

Macher gained some of his journalistic curiosity back from the outrage flooding his mind.

"What happened then? Who else saw this and heard it? Who made the call to get the cops there?" He was reaching into a pocket to get out his notebook. Jackie's expression hardened along with his tone.

"Macher, this is off the record man. Has to be. Let me finish and you'll know why. At least I hope you will. Cause I need you to understand. This is my moment. Could be. Needs to be. If it ain't that tide thing you told me about I don't know what is."

Macher scrunched up his face, trying to connect with this. "Ah, you mean the Shakespeare quote. 'There is a tide in the affairs of men…'"

"Yeah. That's it. There's a tide." Jackie reached into his shirt pocket and took out a black plastic box slightly larger than an old cassette tape and set it on the table between them. "And this is gonna bring a flood."

"What is it?"

"After the perv got knocked around, I knew it wouldn't go down well for the good guys. You know I know how to work that angle. Police brutality. The good guys are bad." He gave a half smirk, remembering his days on the streets. "I knew the place was wired with cameras, and before I left the hospital, after my shift, I snuck back down there and snatched the hard drive out of the security system." He nodded toward the cassette box.

Macher gazed at it, not yet connecting the dots. Jackie did it for him.

"The girl's body disappeared after we left the morgue and before I snatched this." Jackie indicated the black box. "It makes it look like whoever took the body took the drive to cover it up." He let that sink in. "But it was me covering for my guys."

Macher's head twitched in his bird-like manner. He nervously clicked the pen he'd taken out a moment before. He spoke deliberately. "Jackie, you've got to give up that drive. You're right; it is dangerous. It's radioactive." He mmm'd to himself. "That's exactly the right analogy. It's going to hurt more the longer you hold onto it and there are people who know how to find things like this. Serious people. Things like this give off their own signal. It won't stay hidden for long."

He looked up at his young friend and was horrified to see that he didn't look scared any more. He looked excited.

"Right. People will want this and they will come looking for it." Jackie's eyes were weirdly bright, looking off into some brilliantly lit future Macher couldn't see. "I imagine more than one group of people. And some of those people might be interested…" He hesitated before making eye contact with the reporter and finishing the thought with a street wise grin, "…in buying it."

"Jackie, this isn't why you asked to meet me, is it? You've got the wrong guy if it is. I thought you left this kind of hustling behind." Macher looked disappointed. He was disappointed. Jackie was not just a story to him, Jackie was evidence that the right man could make a difference if he tried. Jackie was his investment in human nature come to maturity.

Jackie smiled his winning smile edged with sheepishness. "Mach-man, I'm not gonna say I haven't thought about it. The way up the ladder isn't going fast and the money isn't great. But I'm happy with my life. Money isn't the thing I want. I just want a chance. I want to prove I belong in real police work. That's what I want.

"You know where I've been. You know who I've been. It's a fence too high to get over without some help. It's not right the way a few people keep my past in front of my face—in front of everyone on the force. Hell, I even thought about using what's on that drive to persuade some of them to let up on me. Just seems like I'd always have that hanging over me. Blackmailing someone to get on the police force? Yeah. That's not for me either."

He smiled and added, "You taught me better. You and Poppie showed me the way."

Rich tried to keep the relief and pleasure out of his face but failed when his eyes leaked involuntarily.

"Okay. You've got my attention," he said. "I'm dying to hear what you've got in mind."

CHAPTER THIRTY-THREE

Syd's man answered on the first ring. He knew a call from the governor's chief of staff meant he was needed to clean up a mess or to make a mess. It all depended upon the circumstances. In this case it was a little of both.

He was just one of the many men whom Syd DeVito had groomed over the years as he carefully built the North Carolina branch of the family business. Syd found it the easiest thing in the world to convert those men into the political machinery needed to get Treeright to the Governor's Mansion. They made a lot of money along the way and Syd saw early in the game that money and power were simply two sides of the same coin, and that controlling a man's supply of either was the sure way to control the man.

Right now he needed to tie up a loose end and this man would do it, no questions asked.

There was an inmate in Durham County jail who needed attention.

How much attention?

He needed to be quiet for a long time. But before he went quiet he needed to answer some questions.

The man listened as DeVito laid out the nature of the problem and the proposed solution. It was all very business-like and civilized. He liked doing business with DeVito. He paid good money that came with no trace or taint of corruption on it. No one suspected that a leading business owner in the city was a crime boss.

In a three-minute conversation, Doug Windsor's fate was determined as easily as finalizing the price of a used car.

CHAPTER THIRTY-FOUR

Jackie's plan was outrageous and Rich Macher knew it. He also knew he wasn't talking his young friend out of trying it. He was going to use the security camera hard drive as bait and himself as the hook. Macher hoped he wouldn't disappear down the gullet of a giant fish who wouldn't care about having Jackie slowly digesting in its belly.

The trick was to get the cut outs right. Actually the trick was to make someone believe there were cut outs when it was only Jackie and Macher playing for the home team in this all-or-nothing game.

Rich managed the first part of the scheme by getting in touch with a national contact he knew from out of state. It was a bureau chief for CBN in Washington and he trusted her to feed his story back into the local market. He also counted on the off-the-beaten trail Christian Broadcasting Network throwing a few lazy reporters off for a while. There was a generally smug attitude in the press about CBN and perhaps the story would seep in rather than come as a flood.

That was a miscalculation. The Treeright story was like a red hot coal at the bottom of an ash heap, still too fresh. All it needed was a little fuel and the flame was ready to light off again.

The CBN contact had called into the Raleigh affiliate of ABC and their reporter had called Macher before he made it home from his meeting with Jackie. He had expected to get a call, it was essential to their plan, but he thought it would take a few skips across the water before it got to him. Instead, ABC sent a reporter out to Duke and another to the jail.

Jackie was trying to expose a buyer for his hard drive so he could solve a high profile crime. He wanted his shot at real law enforcement and figured the powers that be couldn't deny him with a big win like this under his belt. He was the only one besides Macher and his men who knew where the hard drive was. It was key to him that the contents never get out because it would reveal a beating that would garner pity even for a perverted pedophile, and perhaps get the man out of being charged.

It was a thin line Jackie was walking and he had convinced Macher to stand on it with him. There wasn't much room for error.

The first thing they had to do was endure the onslaught of media interest needed to get the existence of the drive out there in front of the nose of their rat. They had to do this without either of them appearing to know anything about it.

Jackie was worried about his guys leaking so he had hurried off to brief them up and get them in line as soon as he had left his meeting with Macher.

Macher knew his status as a member of the press would help shield him, but he was under no illusions. In cases like this, the normal rules would only apply for a limited time, and if they were dealing with really bad actors, well, the rules never even began to apply.

By noon, teasers of a new angle on the Treeright tragedy were showing up on local TV, and it turned out there was more to the story than either of them knew. There was a bit about the governor confronting the pervert Doug Windsor at the jail, and there was a rumor that the two had talked on the phone after the confrontation. It was shocking and confusing.

To Jackie and Macher, the story had two distinct parts: there was the pervert in the morgue and there was the theft of a dead body. While these two things happened in close proximity to each other on the clock, neither of them were connected. It was a coincidence, albeit a strange one, that could not be easily put together.

Windsor was obviously crazy or perverted or both, and couldn't be part of a plot to steal the body of Tabitha Treeright. And he was locked up tight by the time the body went missing. It was also unlikely that whoever planned to steal the body would have wanted the distraction of the brouhaha in the morgue drawing attention to the scene of their crime.

Or did they? What if Windsor was in on this?

Macher mulled it over again. Would a man willingly expose himself to the kind of condemnation and punishment Windsor was in for? He couldn't hope to avoid jail time and relentless hatred from the public. What could motivate a person to do that?

Macher thought the right amount of money could do it. Guaranteed money in offshore accounts that would be there ten or fifteen years in the future. That could do it. If the guy had no other prospects, going to jail would be like working a job with a big payday at the end. Walk out of prison with a new suit and Shawshank himself to the Mexican Riviera.

Yes. That could be possible. He kicked himself for ignoring the oldest code in a journalist's book: there are no coincidences. Jackie needed to learn that one too, because it was also the first rule of police work. It looked like they both fell down this time. He hoped it didn't cost them but he had a bad feeling about it.

CHAPTER THIRTY-FIVE

Doug Windsor spent the morning resting. His injuries were stiffening as they always did but he didn't feel too bad considering all he'd been through. The place he'd been kicked in the side gave him the most pain, but he thought it probably wasn't a cracked rib but only a deep bruise.

The deputies took him to medical again after the phone call to the governor where they'd redressed his head wound and given him some Extra Strength Tylenol. All in all he felt surprisingly good.

He stopped short when he realized it. *Why should I feel good*? he thought. *I'm in jail. I'm probably going back to prison. My life is in pieces. What's going to happen next?*

He discovered that he had no real idea how this was all going to play out but at the same time he had a lightness about him he had not felt in a long time. It made no sense. He was sure of what he was sure of. He was sure that Tabitha Treeright was alive and that he had had something to do with it.

A miracle. A real miracle. Who didn't want to see something like that? Everyone talked about them. Everyone asked for them. Here he was in the middle of a miracle. Him. Doug Windsor.

What other people did he know who were part of miracles?

It seemed to him that the people asking for miracles always had a way to explain them away when they happened. There was the boy who drowned and was in a coma when Doug was in elementary school. All the teachers said he was not going to live; it would be a miracle if he survived.

They'd even been asked to pray for him—for a miracle.

But when the boy came out of the coma the next week, all Doug ever heard about was how the doctors and nurses at CHKD had worked so hard to save him. It didn't feel like a miracle.

But then again, what did a miracle feel like? How were you supposed to react to a miracle? What did it mean? Miracles were messy things without well-defined borders.

Doug didn't think he knew enough about miracles to tell anyone else how they worked or why they existed, but here he was, neck deep in the biggest miracle he'd ever heard of. Suddenly he wanted a copy of a Bible so he could look at a record of miracles and see what happened. He wanted to compare notes.

Mostly he wanted to read again the passage about the little girl and the *talitha koum* he found in the Duke chapel right when he needed it.

He wanted to know what happened after the miracle. Maybe that would give a hint at what was going to happen to him.

CHAPTER THIRTY-SIX

Syd DeVito had called in his man. He would not get a return call unless something went wrong. He expected the next thing he would hear about the strange man in the Durham County lockup would be in a news report; hopefully nothing more than a footnote to the evening news.

When a call came in from his staff man who monitored the media for him, it was not unexpected. The story of the missing girl would get out and he was prepared to spin it any way necessary to keep the flow away from Daniel.

Both he and Wanda were too fragile to handle any media right now. He felt like he was keeping watch on too many pots that might simultaneously boil over if he wasn't vigilant.

He picked up the phone and called the one person in the local media he trusted to tip him off to local matters.

"Syd?" she said.

""Hi, Sylvia. Whatcha got for me?" He tried to sound nonplussed... *no story here,* he tried to convey.

"I think you know, Syd. I'm hearing a big story is brewing about the governor's daughter and the Duke morgue and a missing body."

She waited to see if DeVito wanted to play. He waited her out.

"Okay. Not gonna share? There's more. A lot more. There's a man in city lockup who got caught molesting her dead body and caught a beating for it."

She waited again and again DeVito waited her out.

"You know, Syd, this is a two-way street. I'm not feeding this to you for your edification and not my own."

DeVito cleared his throat. "Keep going, Sylvia. So far I'm very interested."

This was Syd's code for "your information is right, but don't quote me." It was their delicate dance. He was waiting to hear just how far this would go and how much the governor was involved.

"The story is strange enough to be the lead on every outlet. Don't believe for a second this is staying with me. As soon as this call ends we're going wall to wall with it. The juicy bits are even better."

So far she was not giving Syd more to worry about than he already knew.

"Two more things before I go, Syd. One is that we had a talk with some friends at the jail and they tell us not only did Treeright visit the man they have locked up for molesting his daughter's dead body, but that the man called the governor after that meeting."

Sylvia had his full attention now and she knew it.

"But the juiciest of all is something no one knows about at all... yet. And you're gonna have to give me a good reason to sit on it. I'm sure you know about the missing security camera drive. Right? Of course you do."

This time she didn't wait for DeVito. She plowed on. "The word I'm getting is that someone is shopping it around. Feeling out what the market might be for it."

Syd knew this might come up—would come up—but he was still unprepared for it.

The video couldn't hurt them for the same reasons he had spelled out to Daniel and Wanda. It was sure to garner sympathy for them and outrage toward anyone who had anything to do with Tabitha's disappearance.

The strange thing was that it should surface at all. It made no sense. The people who stole the body must be the ones with the video and what could they gain by shopping it around? It would surely incriminate them. This was a puzzle.

The much more troubling piece was the knowledge that Daniel's contact with the inmate had leaked. That was going to complicate things. He realized he had been silent while Sylivia had stopped talking.

"Sylvia, all of this is very interesting. The governor is aware of everything you've told me except the surfacing of the video. Of course we are hoping to find the governor's daughter and we condemn this sick act of stealing her dead body..."

Sylvia cut him off with the upper cut she had waited to throw.

"Is she dead? Our same source says that phone call from the inmate to the governor was about his daughter being alive. That the governor believes she is alive. You want to respond to that?"

Syd sputtered. "You can't run with that! That's below the gutter, Slyvia. That's *National Enquirer* UFO shit, not news; not reporting."

"Syd, we've got the man who is most likely the next President of the United States taking phone calls from an inmate who's a convicted child molester. We've got a missing body of a child and we've got missing security camera footage.

"Top it off with a claim that a girl three days dead is alive and walking around... If this isn't the definition of *National Enquirer* shit, I don't know what is.

"The question is, what does your boss believe?"

CHAPTER THIRTY-SEVEN

Tabitha snapped awake. The nurse who doped her up would have been amazed to see it. She had given the girl a dose of tranquilizer that should have lasted a minimum of twelve hours; enough for the nurse to finish binge watching the latest season of her favorite show on Netflix on her phone.

She was well into episode three, season two, when Tabitha slipped out of her bed and out of the ward.

She quickly scouted the hallway and nurse's station and crawled past on her hands and knees. Time was ticking and she was living in it again. The female locker room was empty of people but full of bits and pieces of clothing laying on top of lockers and a communal coat rack.

She cobbled together an outfit she was sure would make her look like a cross between an off-duty nurse and a homeless woman. A worn-out pair of dingy orange Crocs three sizes too large for her were the prize of her locker room raid. She had a long walk in front of her and had hoped for some tennis shoes but was glad for any form of footwear.

She slipped them on and started back toward the door when she was startled by the sight of someone coming at her. Her heart raced and she stifled a cry before she realized the person tracked with her movements.

She was looking in a full length mirror mounted on the door. The sight of herself in the thrown-together outfit was, as she expected, much like a street person, but the girl looking back at her was changed in appearance in a manner far beyond mere clothes.

Her hair, once lionish gold and painfully kinky, a full towering mane, her crown, was now utterly straight and flat against her head. It gave the impression that Tabitha herself had shrunk.

And the color... the color was as if the golden lion had been washed and washed again until there was only a trace of it left in her hair, which had changed to a color not quite little-old-lady white, but barely yellow, like corn silk. She slowly walked up to the reflected image, reaching out a hand as if she could wipe away the changes.

She looked into her own eyes and saw the most shocking change had occurred there. The deep-electric-blue eyes that would make people stop and stare were no longer looking back at her.

Instead she saw dark brown rims circling pools of glowing amber. It was as if the rich yellow of her hair had cooked down and drained into her irises, pooling there.

She looked so... old. It wasn't written in wrinkles, her face was as smooth as it have ever been, it was in those pools that seemed to look back at her from some place so ancient it made time irrelevant.

She felt a panic rising in her chest. Looking at herself in the mirror made her dizzy, as if she were standing on the edge of a high tower with nothing to hold. She felt a vertigo of identity.

Was she still Tabitha Treeright? Had she emerged from the Light back into the world of shadow as some shadowy thing herself? What if she just let go and fell off this tower, would she go back to the place of Light?

As she swayed on her feet and her heart rate increased, she heard someone laughing; the charge nurse still caught up in her Netflix binge. Tabitha snapped out of her spin and looked herself up and down in the mirror.

Her eyes lit upon the filthy orange Crocs. Then she realized in her scavenging she'd donned the only outwear she could find, a yellow rain slicker.

The slicker, combined with the ridiculously large orange monstrosities on her feet made her flash instantly to Sesame Street. She looked like Big Bird. She laughed out loud in spite of herself. The sound filled the locker room.

And it was her laugh. It felt more real than the floor under those silly Crocs. The vertigo fled.

Hair or no hair, eyes or no eyes, that was Tabitha's laugh. It was enough for now. She pushed through the locker room door and peered cautiously into the hallway.

Getting out of the hospital turned out to be easier than she expected. The nurse must have been the front line and only line of defense at this hour. Once past her, Tabitha made her way down a set of stairs and let herself out a door marked Staff Only directly onto the street behind the hospital.

Having no money and no phone, she decided to walk to the Governor's Mansion. She just needed to find herself and get going in the right direction.

In the meantime, she wanted to get some distance between herself and the hospital. She couldn't believe how easy it was to get away and was afraid that any minute someone would come after her.

It felt good to walk in the night air. It felt good to be upright after a day lying in bed in a stupor. The drugs had been like a weight vest on a runner.

Now that she was fully awake and alert, she made fast progress. The mansion was dead center of the city, and once she found the first cross street, she quickly oriented herself and set out at a steady pace.

CHAPTER THIRTY-EIGHT

Daniel Treeright felt as if his insides were turning out. His stomach churned and his mind reeled. He knew the thought that Tabitha was alive was insane but he couldn't put it away. He couldn't rest or stop his mind from wheeling back around to it again. He'd spent the day pacing his study.

Syd made a good case. Although it would be the most incredibly cruel and unusual tactic ever used in politics, Daniel had gotten used to the idea that there was no bottom to the lengths people would go to get the prize—the "bone" Syd talked about.

He had to look no further than his own crazy state of affairs; living the lie of a marriage and family life for the public so that he wouldn't lose his chance at the presidency.

Yes, he thought, *anything was possible*. But that brought him back face to face with the conundrum of Tabitha's fate. If anything was possible then she could be alive, right? Anything.

Suddenly, he was overwhelmed with a need to speak with Wanda. There was little left between them, but they were the parents of the dead missing girl. He wanted to talk with her and share this moment with her somehow. Was there a way back to her too? *Anything is possible.*

He wanted to go back to a place where Tabitha had been their secret delight. When Wanda was pregnant and no one knew it but them. Before they were the picture everyone wanted them to be. Before they let themselves be Photoshopped and Instagrammed into the images that people craved.

Was there a way back to that place? It made no sense to think about this now; in the midst of this hurricane of emotions and failures and loss. But he wanted her now. He wanted it to be possible. And anything was possible.

He slipped out of his office and went up to the family quarters. He found Wanda lying fully clothed on her bed, her arms tucked under her in a pitifully childlike pose. He roused her gently with a touch and for an instant as her eyes opened it was as if the chasm of mistrust and war between them evaporated. Those were the eyes he had come to look for; to see if they were there still.

The instant passed as quickly as it came, draining out of her eyes like the flash of a camera. *But there was a residue of it there*, he thought. *Maybe. Anything is possible.*

"Wanda?"

"What is it?" she said.

"Wanda, I want to ask you if you believe…" He struggled to say what he came here to say. He choked back tears. Wanda looked at him not unkindly but keeping her own emotions in check. This was something she'd not seen in many years; her husband in any way vulnerable.

"I can't stop thinking about the man at the jail. I know it isn't believable but I still can't shake it. Syd made his case, I know. But what do you think? Is it more unbelievable that someone would steal the body of a dead child to hurt us or for Tabitha to somehow be alive?"

"Daniel. You weren't here." There was a hint of accusation in the words, but not her usual vitriol. "You didn't have to see what I saw…" It was Wanda's turn to crack. "It was so horrible watching her suffer. To see her slipping over the edge of this life. To burn up alive in front of my eyes."

She covered her face with both hands. "I didn't ever say this or want to admit it to anyone, but when she, when she finally died, it was almost, no, it was, a relief." She said the last phrase in a barely-audibly whisper choked by a sob.

Great streaks of silent hot tears ran down her cheeks. Daniel reached out to wipe them away, fully expecting her to draw back, but she didn't move away. He stroked her face as he wiped her cheeks dry, feeling a genuine warmth and compassion for her he hadn't known for years.

"I can't let myself go back there," she said. "If I have to see that again I will go over the edge. You see what I mean? Letting myself even think about her being alive is just too, it's too… risky."

Daniel looked deep into her pained eyes. He did understand. He had not seen his daughter die but viewing her body in the morgue had been horrible enough.

To run halfway around the world racing to get to her side and have the path end in that sterile white room with his little girl cold and stiff and horribly blue around her forever-shut eyes and still mouth.

He understood. It was risky. To believe she could be alive and then to find her again as he'd seen her in that place would probably be the end of him. It would take his heart away.

"Wanda, I'm going to go back to the jail and talk with that man again. I want you to come with me. Please. I don't care anymore about what things look like. I just want to see if I'm completely lost. If I'm completely out of my mind. And I realized last night that there isn't anyone I trust to tell me what's true more than you. Will you go with me? Will you take a chance with me?"

Wanda looked up at Daniel, searching for something. She seemed to find it. "You know that Syd is right about this, don't you?" she said.

Daniel felt his heart drop away at the mention of the name. Then he saw a slight grin at the edge of her eyes.

"He is right. This is what they're waiting for you to do if this is a set up. They're waiting for you to show up and tie you with the story that a child molester convinced you our daughter is alive."

Daniel nodded slowly. "I don't care," he said. "I don't care what anyone thinks now. I only care about Tabitha. I only care about you; about us."

She reached out her arms for him to help her get up. On her feet, she stood directly in front of him. Her eyes were weary but her grip was firm. She turned her face up to him. He was always amazed at how he towered over her physically; in his mind's eye she was always taller.

He looked down and saw his wife again, his girl, and he heard the words again; *anything is possible.*

"Let's go," she said. "If we go over the cliff, let's do it together."

CHAPTER THIRTY-NINE

Tabitha made her way steadily toward home. It wasn't exactly cold, but it wasn't warm either, and she found that the walking wearied her a surprising amount.

Maybe the different parts of her body were having to regenerate at a different pace. Her mind had snapped back clearly enough, but her muscles might take longer.

She approached the gatehouse at the Governor's Mansion unsure of herself. Coming and going past the guards here had always happened with her in the back seat of one or other of the official cars her parents rode in. The security officer was not someone she recognized, it was dark, and she had no identification.

She was dressed in what amounted to a street lady's attire. The man scowled at her as she walked up to his post.

"Hello," she said.

"How can I help you?" the guard responded, barely looking up from the YouTube video he was watching on his phone. It was a replay of Jimmy V's NC State Wolfpack winning the NCAA, and it was just getting to the good part.

"Could I get you to call the house and have my mother come out and get me?" she said, going for broke.

The man hit pause on his video and gave her an appraising glance up and down. He said, "Get out of here girl. Your mother doesn't live here. You need to get off the pipe."

Tabitha's temper flared. "Pipe?! I'm not on the pipe, you idiot. I'm Tabitha Treeright and my mother and father live here."

The guard rose from his stool and approached her, holding her in an angry gaze. "Girl, you might not be on the pipe but you're no doubt on something. Tabitha Treeright died three days ago."

Tabitha felt this like a punch in the guts even though she'd already concluded this herself. Her anger flickered out. She was unprepared to hear it said so bluntly, so factually.

It set her mind back and wearied it like her legs, as if she'd been working it too hard too fast. Was she really alive or just a ghost? How could people see her and talk to her if she was a ghost? How could she wear clothes and feel the world around her? And how could she be so hungry again?

"But I am Tabitha Treeright," was all she could say.

The guard put his hands on his hips.

"There's no way I'm calling anyone but the cops for you, girl," he said coldly. "Now either get out of here or wait for a squad car. It's up to you."

"I don't have anywhere to go," she said in a shrinking voice.

"Suit yourself," he said and retreated into his guard shack.

Tabitha looked longingly at the front door of the mansion just out of reach, and it sparked the last of her energy. She bolted for it as the guard looked down to pick up his phone. She was past him and running as fast as she could, the awkward crocs flip flapping on her feet.

She made it three quarters of the way there before the guard tackled her from behind and brought her down hard.

She cut her lip and scraped a sheet of skin off her right knee as they came down in a heap. The guard was cursing. He produced a yellow zip tie from his pocket and snapped Tabitha's wrists together behind her back.

He stood her up and half dragged, half shoved her back to the front gate.

"Crazy girl," he said. "Now you're going for a ride."

Half an hour later, bloodied and looking a lot worse for the wear, Tabitha Treeright was in booking at the same jail as the man who had called her back from the dead.

Syd DeVito was also on his way to the jail.

The phone call from the local snitch left him scrambling to call off the plan to shut up Douglas Windsor. There was no way to keep that from getting too loud and too hot if it was known that the governor had already been seen with him.

His calls to his muscle man had gone unanswered and Syd was not willing to leave it to chance that the plans would be called off in time.

He was going to make sure nothing happened to Windsor by getting there first.

CHAPTER FORTY

The door to Doug's cell opened. A deputy he had not seen before stepped inside. "Got some company for you, ChoMo," he said, stepping aside to allow a towering inmate to enter. "Freddie here is a real nice fella."

The look and tone of the deputy told Doug all he needed to know about why he had a new cell mate and what he could expect from the experience.

ChoMo. He hadn't heard that in a long time. He stood up and the new occupant of the cell advanced as the deputy disappeared. The door clanged shut.

Freddie smiled a gap-toothed grin, and stifled a grotesquely wet cough, wiping it away with a huge paw.

He was a massive man with a watermelon head sprouting a grizzled beard on one end and greasy gray-blond streaks of shoulder-length hair at the other. His sleeveless t-shirt strained against a massive belly. Tattoos crawled up both arms from fingertip to neck. The skin peering out from under the tattoos and on his face was tinged with yellow.

In the dimness of the cell light, he looked like a ghoul. His bulk alone would give Doug all he could handle.

Doug's instincts for prison fighting were good but rusty. He knew the first rule: in a confrontation in a confined space, the first blow was decisive. He went from resting to fully alert in an instant; every sense heightened and razor sharp.

Freddie's eyes swept over him, assessing his prey, confident, cold. They were two dogs in a ring, both knowing a fight was before them; reason and understanding were outside and foreign.

Doug rose to it, determined to strike first. In the split second it took him to get off the cot and move toward Freddie, he heard a voice in his ears, his head, his whole being. It was the same voice that brought him to Durham.

This time it wasn't low, resonating, and gradual; it was loud piercing and insistent, like a radio flipped on, speakers maxxed. It blasted him as if he'd already been struck. He dropped his guard and shook his head. Freddie hesitated half a beat, surprised, then smiled wickedly and advanced on him.

Doug held one hand out, palm first, like a traffic cop stopping the flow of cars. He felt as if all the energy in the room, no, all the energy in all the powerful people colliding around him, shrank to nothing, that with a flip of his outstretched hand he could overturn all of it, all of them, like discarded paper cups tumbling along the highway, tossed here and there by the wake of passing cars.

He heard himself say the words that had blasted into his head, calmly, matter-of-factly.

"You have pancreatic cancer. You found out a week ago. You're dying."

Freddie stopped his advance as if Doug had landed the blow he had intended to throw. A puzzled look came over his face; it passed like a Florida rain shower, replaced by rage that darkened his eyes and spread purple to his cheeks.

He started to say something to Doug as he continued toward him, but Doug spoke again. Again his words were low and calm, unhurried.

"You didn't know the pain in your back was cancer. You ignored it. Now it's going to go away."

Doug's words came. Simple. Calm. Freddie advanced. He reached for Doug's neck. He was going to choke these words out of the *ChoMo*. Make them stop. Take out all his fear and anger at the truth, the diagnosis.

He ran into Doug's outstretched hand. It was like running into a white hot slab of metal. It seared his chest, radiating inward and down. His eyes went wild with shock and pain. He staggered. His hands fell from Doug's neck, limp.

The heat took the form of a ball ricocheting inside his body like he was a pinball machine, bouncing off his organs, finally dropping in an explosion of warmth in his lower back.

A sigh escaped his mouth, low and calm, a locomotive coming to a stop, resting on the tracks. The look on his face went from surprised fear to joyful astonishment.

He shifted from one foot to the other, testing his weight. The yellow in his face and arms drained away.

The huge man went down to his knees on the hard cold cement floor like a tree. Tears welled up and burst out of his eyes, dripping onto the tile floor.

Doug knelt next to him, unsure of what to do next. The man was undone, sobbing with both hands to his giant face, taking great gulps of air between racking sobs. Doug had never seen anything like it in jail or anywhere else.

He put a hand on Freddie's shoulder gingerly, feeling the convulsions as well as hearing them.

He heard the voice again: *Tell him I love him.*

Doug balked. This was too much. How was he supposed to say that? It didn't sound true. He didn't know if he believed it himself. The voice inside insisted. The pressure in his heart and mind increased.

Say it. Tell him.

He decided to split the difference.

"Man, you might not believe this, but I think I may hear things from God sometimes."

The response from Freddie was instant. He looked up at Doug, tears still streaming from his eyes and said, "You think?!" He laughed. "You think!!"

Doug still hesitated. The words caught in his throat. They felt jagged and misplaced.

Say it! Tell him!

"God says he loves you. He wants you to know. He loves you."

In response to this, Freddie fell out fully prostrate on the cell floor and began to wail. It echoed off the walls in the confined space like a banshee in a box.

Doug felt like he had set off a car alarm and didn't know how to make it stop. He tried patting Freddie on the shoulder, but this produced more intense sounds; unbelievable noises that rose and fell and finally began to take on shape.

"Gaaaaaaaawwwd. Ohhhhhhhh Gaaaaaaaawwwd. Ah ah ah gaaaaaaawwwd. Pleassssse."

Doug couldn't tell if Freddie was hearing God for himself or responding to what he had said. Was he glad of this message from God, or despondent?

The cell door opened and slammed against the wall as two deputies responded to what sounded to them like the beginnings of a riot. They both held tasers.

"Get away from him!" one of them shouted at Doug, and without waiting to see if he would or not, tased him in the back.

He went down hard, splitting his head on the concrete floor.

215

CHAPTER FORTY-ONE

Jackie Smith had spent the day at home pretending to sleep. Finally unable to stand more inactivity, he told Maria a story about needing to relieve his day shift counterpart early and drove to the hospital.

It was easy to convince the man to take off for the day and to arrange for the other three guards to leave him alone in the security office. He briefed up his guys and made sure they were not going to panic and let on that they knew he had the security camera hard drive.

He had a few hours before they would report for duty and there was something he wanted to do before things got heated up and he set the bait out in front of the people responsible for stealing Tabitha Treeright's body.

He had to know for himself what was on the drive. It was possible it could end up getting out in the open and he wanted to see it for himself. He needed access to the playback system in the security office and he needed privacy.

The hospital skimped in many areas regarding security, not the least of which was the paltry amount of money they paid the guards, but they had not gone cheap on the video system. It was as if they were more interested in having a record of what happened on tape delay than stopping something from happening with live officers.

The system was state-of-the-art and recorded in ultra-high definition and in full color. It also gave an operator the capability to zoom in on areas of a room that might be many yards from the actual camera.

This feature was there for the main lobby and other large spaces where a camera had to cover wide angles from high perches. The effect was impressive and could clearly capture the image of a person's face at the information desk from a camera along the ceiling twenty yards away.

The effect when the camera was mounted only a few feet across a brightly-lit room like the morgue was even more impressive. This drive covered the cameras on Sublevel Zero at the hallway outside the morgue from where the elevator ran to the front door, the loading dock where the bodies were picked up by funeral homes, and two cameras mounted in the morgue itself.

The feed ran on a forty-eight-hour cycle and recorded over itself unless someone switched out a drive to prevent it. Jackie could look at all four feeds at once or break them out individually. He decided to let all four feeds run at once to see if anything caught his attention.

He input the time he was looking for, subtracted an hour, and queued up the footage. He set the speed to run at two times actual and let it run. There was the governor and someone else; two other men hovering over the open drawer with the girl on it. Then they all left the room. The drawer was pushed back in.

The governor in the hallway waiting for the elevator and then almost bowling over a man getting off the elevator. In double time it was almost comical. Jackie paused the tape and rewound it.

Slowing it down and zooming in, he could see it was Douglas Windsor the governor met as he was leaving the morgue. That was interesting. They could not have mistaken each other if they met again. They had been face to face then.

His cell phone buzzed in his pocket, startling him. It was Macher.

He hesitated to take the call, checking his watch. He didn't have much time alone with the drive and he wanted to get this done.

The phone was insistent. He took the call.

"Jackie?"

"Yeah, Macher, go. I'm in the middle of something."

"You need to hear this. The governor met with the man you guys took down in the morgue last night."

Jackie was confused. "How did you know that? I just saw it for myself."

Now Macher was confused. "What are you talking about?"

"I'm running the tape so I can see what's on it. And I just found a spot in the feed from that night where the governor meets Windsor. He's leaving the morgue when Windsor is getting there. They practically ran each other over."

Macher took this in. "Jackie, that's not what I'm talking about but it's pretty weird. Coincidences again."

"What?"

"You and me are gonna have a long talk about coincidence once we get through this. Forget it for now. I got word that when they first brought Windsor to the jail, the governor went there and met him. Not only that but he took a phone call from Windsor a few hours later."

"What's it mean?" Jackie asked.

"I'm not sure but I'm gonna head over there and see what's going on. It seems like everything in this story is headed back to the man in the cell. He knows something that puts it all together."

"What about our plan? Do you think the word is out there about this tape? Will we get the right people interested?"

"Jackie, I think we are going to have a bad time keeping people from finding out who has the tape. This is going way faster than I expected. I've just heard that since noon, a gaggle of media types have been hanging around the jail.

"I'm headed there now myself. You need to find a place to keep that thing that's out of reach and completely disconnected from you. I'd be real surprised if you aren't in their sights by the end of the day."

Jackie paused and said, "Okay, Macher. I can find a spot for it. Maybe I should just destroy it. It isn't the tape anyone wants any way. Nothing here that's gonna show who stole the body and only footage that's gonna make the cops and my boys look pretty bad."

Macher contemplated the idea. "You know what's best, Jackie. Only thing about that is you get to make that choice once and then you can't take it back. Make real sure there's nothing on it that can help us solve this. The governor running into Windsor may be just one little acorn in this nest."

He hung up and Jackie went back to work on the tape, searching for what he could find.

CHAPTER FORTY-TWO

Tabitha had never seen the inside of a jail before. She was too young for the place and should have been sent to juvenile hall but the lack of identification and the place where she was arrested insured her a ride to the big people jail while the authorities sorted out who she was and what to do with her.

The cut on her lip was deep enough to require a sloppy stitch from the nurse practitioner on duty in medical who barely looked at her or talked to her while he worked.

The scrapes on both knees hurt worse and got little attention beyond a cursory cleaning with hydrogen peroxide. They replaced her stolen, ill-fitting clothes with an ill-fitting orange jumpsuit and deposited her in a holding cell alone.

She felt like she was on a treadmill. She had moved a lot in the past twenty-four hours but she hadn't gotten anywhere. She knew who she was but no one else knew. This was a strange feeling. She thought it over and over.

If I'm the only person in the world who knows who I am—if no one else agrees with me—am I still me? Am I who I say I am even if no one else says it?

She thought about all her friends and her family. Surely someone would know she was Tabitha; someone would believe the unbelievable. But what if they didn't? She felt fear rising. She didn't know if she could live like that; without a name, without anyone believing her. She might not be able to hold on against all the other opinions.

Maybe they were right and she was wrong. Maybe she was crazy and belonged in Regional. Maybe she would lose herself in the flood of all the other opinions. She was breathing rapidly, on the edge of panic. She looked up, taking in a great gulp of air, ready to explode in anguish.

The cell had simple fluorescent lights recessed in the ceiling. The lenses were yellowish with the nicotine of thousands of cigarettes from the days gone by when smoking and jail were synonymous and smoking areas were decades in the future. The effect was a sickly light diffused down to an even more sickly light.

It was all so puny, Tabitha thought. This light was not light at all. Pitiful. It was light only in name. It was an imitation. She knew what light was that was so real you could touch it and taste it. Yes! Light.

There was light that was real and then there was something here that imitated it. There was also a Tabitha who was there. Maybe that was the same for her. Maybe she was like the light. A real Tabitha and a less real Tabitha. Didn't she feel like she was more alive there? When she was dead??

This made no sense. Words felt like they didn't fit into this reality. Then there was the name. She heard the name there. A new name. It was like she had heard another name for herself that was more real than her name here.

Like it didn't feel right to call light in that place "light;" it felt empty. There was another name for light. There was another, more full name for her.

As she sat there alone in the holding cell, she felt the weight of her real self filling her.

A moment before she had felt like a leaf in a rising wind, on the verge of taking flight. Now she was a tree, rooted in a ground no one could see but her. She didn't need them to anchor her anymore.

If no one ever knew her again it wouldn't matter, because she knew herself and knew herself to be more than this time, this place, and this name.

CHAPTER FORTY-THREE

Syd DeVito continued calling while he drove. No luck. He worried he might be too late to stop the wheels he had set in motion from grinding down Doug Windsor, not because he had any compassion on him, but because of the mess it would create.

He had hoped for a nice, quiet intervention that would've put a cap on this loose end, but the breaking news story complicated everything.

He thought of ways to spin the governor's meeting with Windsor. He could explain the initial meeting as a passionate father responding to abuse of his deceased daughter. That would probably garner sympathy if not approval.

The phone call was not going to be so easy. He kicked himself for not taking control of the situation more firmly and keeping his man away from the jail and Windsor. The job always required him to walk a fine line between handler and advisor.

Daniel was not like many politicians. He actually had a core and he was actually a leader. Trying to lead a leader without them knowing it was near impossible. Stopping a leader from pursuing a goal they thought was right and urgent was worse than impossible. It required early intervention.

It meant getting to the ignition point before they did and putting out the fire or snuffing the spark altogether. Vigilance. It meant seeing things no one else looked for and thinking of possibilities no one dreamed of.

He had failed miserably on this one.

He hoped he could find a way to put this genie back in the bottle. Driving up to the rear of the jail, he gave second thought to stopping the plan. Maybe it was best to let Windsor go away.

A quick slice of the knife and it was over.

He slumped at the wheel. This was not like him. *Indecision is a decision.*

He had said it too many times to too many other people. Here he was hanging on the precipice of his highest achievement and he couldn't make a decision.

Drive away and let Windsor die or walk in and take his chances navigating the beehive of stirred-up policemen and reporters in order to get to the right person to keep the man safe.

He turned the car off, got out and walked into the jail.

CHAPTER FORTY-FOUR

Daniel and Wanda parked two blocks away from the jail in an alley. They had slipped their personal security at the mansion and were on their own. They wanted to stay inconspicuous and walked down back streets to get to the jail's rear entrance that Syd had also used only a few moments before.

They were dressed in workout clothes. Both showed the wear and tear of the past several days in their weary expressions and bloodshot eyes, but there was purpose in their steps. They expected to find something here, in this strange man and this unfriendly place.

They gained the back door and found they needed to be buzzed in from inside; a detail that Syd would have taken care of for them. Daniel hit the voicebox speaker button.

"Yeah?" a disembodied man's voice crackled.

Daniel stood back to make sure he was within view of the camera and drew down the hood of his sweats.

"Hey, yes, it's Governor Treeright and my wife. Can someone come and escort us in? I want to see a prisoner."

There was a brief skeptical pause.

"Right. We can have a whole family reunion here. Get lost, you freakin' nutcase, before I send someone out to give you a knot on your head and a kick in your ass."

Daniel's temperature rose instantly but Wanda put a hand on his arm and stepped into view of the camera herself.

"Carl? Carl Reener?" she said. "I know that's you. I'd recognize that voice anywhere. It's me. It's Wanda."

There was silence from the box. The back door buzzed open and an extremely red-faced deputy stepped forward, holding it for them.

"I'm so sorry, Governor and… ah… ah… Wanda…"

Daniel looked at his wife and then the deputy questioningly.

Wanda said, "Daniel, meet Carl Reener, or Carl the Snarl. Jackson High School three years behind me. Still like peeking into women's showers, Snarl? I wonder if they know they've got a sex perv working for them."

Carl the Snarl turned crimson from his neck to his ears. He didn't want to relive high school any more than the next guy. He just wanted this nightmare of a moment to pass.

"Wanda, ah, Missus Governor, I'm sorry for what I just said. And that was a long time ago—boyish hormones. Please. What can I do for you? Who do you want to see? Come this way."

He ushered them inside and shut the door behind them.

Daniel cleared his throat and said, "Can you get us into a room with the prisoner named Windsor without anyone else knowing? Is there press hanging around in the lobby?"

Carl shrugged and looked perplexed.

"Jeez. What's with this guy? Mr. DeVito just came in and asked the same thing. Trouble is Windsor's in the infirmary. Had a bad fall when he got tased. Cracked his head on the cell floor when he went down. Gonna need a couple of stitches to button him up. And press?!

"They've been showing up since noon. Sheriff had to open up the old wing of the jail just to have a place to put them all."

"Tased? Why'd he get tased in a jail cell?" Daniel asked.

"Got into a fight with an inmate. Big dude. Windsor knocked him down and was about to kill'm when the deputies got there and shut'm down."

"Is there a way to get us to the infirmary quietly without a lot of people seeing us?" Wanda asked.

Carl was all too ready to get these two off his hands and out of his hair.

"Sure thing, follow me."

"Where's Syd... ah, Mr. DeVito now?" Daniel didn't know why his chief of staff would be here looking for Windsor but his instincts told him to steer clear of the man.

"He's in one of the interrogation rooms. He didn't want to go to the infirmary. Said he'd wait and we should bring the prisoner to him as soon as he's stitched up. Which we better hurry if we're gonna catch them there. Doc don't waste much time sewin' on inmates. Says they ain't pretty enough to worry over."

Carl led the way to the infirmary with Daniel and Wanda in tow. Something Carl said at the entrance to the jail jogged Wanda's memory.

"Carl, what did you mean by we could have a family reunion here? Were you talking about us and Syd DeVito?"

"Huh? Naw. It's nothin. Shouldn't of said it. Crazy."

"What's crazy, Carl? We've been through a lot in the past couple of days. All of it crazy."

Carl stopped and turned to them. He looked pained.

"This job really shows you stuff about people you don't want to know. Can't really forget when you get off work either. People are sick. People do really sick shit, ah sorry, stuff." He glanced at Wanda.

"Spill it, Carl." she said.

He hesitated once more but the look in Wanda's eyes made him think better of it and he plunged in.

"There's a street woman or girl or whatever—a street person in lock up. Came in just a few hours ago. She says she's your daughter."

Carl winced as he spoke, as if he expected a physical blow in return for his words. Instead he was surprised by their quick response.

"Where is she?" they said in unison.

CHAPTER FORTY-FIVE

Macher could have used the back entrance to the jail that both DeVito and the Treerights had used. Over years of beat reporting he had built enough connections to know every deputy except perhaps the ones hired within the past week, and those quickly learned who he was and knew he was one of the good guys.

He went in the front because it suited him to be seen as part of the press gaggle and in no way associated with the genesis of the story everyone was slathering over.

Based on a talk with some of his contacts in the press, he expected to find a large gathering of print and broadcast media members jostling for position. The jail was old and lacked most modern amenities, including any semblance of a briefing room for events attracting more than the odd reporter or two.

The sheriff tried to use the lobby to contain the trickle of media that started around noon, but as the tide of reporters rolled in, he'd been forced to improvise in order to get them out of the way so the jail could conduct its normal business.

An old section of the jail, put out of service for renovation, was hastily cleared of surplus office equipment and pressed into service. It had a common area with stainless steel tables and benches bolted in place. The walls were wet with seepage through cracks in aged cinderblock, and peeling paint hung in long strips that looked as if a giant set of fingernails had raked across them.

It smelled somewhere between a locker room and a urinal.

Ricky Rome was a wily old school sheriff who knew how to walk the interesting line between enforcer of laws and obtainer of votes. He was not shy of the press until or unless there was a chance for the stench of failure or blame to attach itself to his person, and he had a wickedly well-developed sense of smell. He owed much to this instinct, winning five straight elections.

He owed more to Syd DeVito, who had recruited him out of the rank and file of Raleigh deputies and made sure he always had enough cash to quell any challengers.

He had been deflecting questions and promising to speak with the press while dealing with the disturbance in Windsor's cell and the arrival of the girl claiming she was Tabitha Treeright.

His instincts told him there was a lot of downside and limited upside to talking to the press right now; nevertheless, he'd waffled all afternoon over doing it. He was attracted to publicity like a moth to a flame, and it nagged him to miss a chance like this.

He finally settled on making a non-statement at the same instant he'd gotten word that DeVito was in the building.

Macher was identified by the watch commander as he entered the front door and directed to the makeshift press room where the clucking brood of journalists were milling about, growing restless as Rome grew late for the promised statement.

At a glance, he saw the national big leaguers had not caught wind of the new twist to the story they'd fed on and abandoned like a picked-over carcass on the Serengeti. It didn't surprise Macher.

Most of them were lazy parasites anyway; waiting for people like Macher and the others in this room to turn over the rocks and pound the bushes until a real story popped out; then swooping in to take it like a vulture stealing a dead rabbit from a raven, not out of cunning or skill but merely out of bulk.

Immediately he realized the wisdom of coming in person. With his reputation, it would have been fatal to be a no-show when a local story like this one was breaking. It would have looked very suspicious.

He exchanged nods and pleasantries with several acquaintances before settling down at a table opposite the entrance to the makeshift briefing room. He was careful to keep a healthy distance from the woman who had tipped him off earlier in the day.

His phone rang. It was Jackie. He sent it to voicemail and slipped the phone into his pocket. The last thing he could afford in this room full of piranha would be any possible connection to Jackie.

The phone vibrated again immediately and he sent it to voicemail again. Whatever it was Jackie thought was so urgent would have to wait.

CHAPTER FORTY-SIX

Syd DeVito had developed an instinct over the years for knowing the right place to be and the right time to be there. He grew uneasy sitting in the interrogation room. He was missing the action somehow.

He got up and wandered into the interior of the jail, searching for the infirmary. The fact that Windsor had disabled Syd's man was unnerving. How much did Windsor know? Did he guess the man was an assassin or just another child perv hater? And what happened before Windsor was tased?

Syd had given specific instructions to question Windsor before he was permanently silenced and to use whatever means necessary to get him to tell what he knew about the disappearance of Tabitha's body.

If what the deputies told him was true, he could expect to find both Windsor and the assassin in the infirmary. They said Windsor had beaten the man into the ground. Maybe Syd would be able to find both there and gather the information he needed.

He wandered down a few hallways, trying to look like he belonged. His nose tipped him off that he was near the place when he caught a whiff of rubbing alcohol and bleach. The door was cracked slightly and he peered in, attempting to catch a glimpse of Windsor before he entered.

"Can I help you?" came a voice behind him. Syd gave a start and jerked around to see a gnarly-faced man who looked as if he'd been cut out of a knotted old oak tree.

Syd recovered quickly and shifted into his official business voice and tone.

"Yes. Doctor? Are you the prison sawbones?" He threw in a probing smile here, fishing to see what he was up against.

"Yep. I am," the knotty face said unsmilingly. "Who're you and what're you doin' back here?"

"Syd DeVito. Governor Treeright's chief of staff. I'm looking to speak with the inmate Windsor. Is he in there?" Syd gestured over his shoulder.

"He is. Popular fella. Seems like half the jail wants to see 'em. Tell you what I told everyone that's come lookin for 'em; he's fine. And he ain't goin' anywhere soon so you'll get your chance to see 'em soon enough if you'll let me do my job and stay away." He said this last emphatically and obviously not for the first time.

"I'm sorry, Doctor. I'm not sure we're talking about the same person. Windsor? Who is trying to see him? Reporters?"

The Doctor raised one eyebrow. "Reporters? Hell no, man! We aren't in the habit of letting reporters walk around in our jail! We aren't in the habit of letting politicians do it either." He swept Syd up and down with a disapproving glance. "No. Not reporters. Deputies and trustees. They all want to see him after what he did to Freddie Sage."

And without another word, the doctor pushed past Syd and closed the infirmary door behind him.

What had he done? Syd wondered as he retraced his steps to the front of the jail. A deputy almost ran him over. Syd recognized the man as one of the two who'd accompanied the governor to Windsor's cell.

"Whoa, Jones!" Syd said, dodging out of his way.

"Mr. DeVito! Y'all are both here again?!"

"Both? Who? Is the governor here?"

"Yep. He got here just a while ago. Him and his wife. They're goin' ta see the crazy girl; one that claims she's their kid."

Syd's blood ran cold.

"What girl? Where?"

CHAPTER FORTY-SEVEN

Jackie pored over the security footage. He rewound and zoomed in and rewound it again and again.

Before he was done, he retrieved all the footage from the night of the incident and the following twelve hours. He called a friend in the hospital IT department and asked for help converting the video into a format he could download and use on any computer.

They walked through the process together over the phone and by the time his security guard coworkers finished up their rounds, he was finishing up with a video compiled from several different feeds in the hospital on the night of the girl's disappearance.

His fingers trembled as he uploaded the file to his personal storage in the cloud. He watched the blue progress bar until it said one hundred percent, logged off the machine he'd been using, and pocketed the hard drive.

Macher was still not answering his phone. He was on his way to the jail the last time they spoke.

Jackie decided it would be as good a place as any to show him what he'd found.

CHAPTER FOURTY-EIGHT

Daniel and Wanda entered the interrogation room together. The girl sat with her back to them on a bolted-down stool at a bolted-down stainless steel table.

The room was lit in the same icy fluorescent glare as the Duke Hospital morgue. Same stainless steel. Same white tile. They glanced at each other, immediately sensing this room was as empty of hope as the morgue.

This person couldn't be their daughter; their Tabby.

One look, even from the rear, told them that truth. The hair. It was all wrong. No one had ever tamed that golden mop; there was no taming it.

If the girl sitting before them had been bald they'd have held out more hope that it was their daughter. They shuffled forward into the room out of inertia more than any hope.

The girl did not stir. Her hands rested on the table before her as if she were praying. Wanda and Daniel had the sensation of walking into a nightmare as they crossed the room and stopped in front of the girl. Her eyes were open but focused somewhere beyond them; beyond the room itself. She looked serene.

Daniel studied her face carefully. The girl's eyes were like molten gold brown; the color of his lost daughter's hair. Wanda starred into the far-away eyes, set in a face that made her think of ancient sunsets in spite of its youth.

The girl shuddered involuntarily, breaking her reverie. Her eyes focused on Daniel, then Wanda.

Daniel's heart hammered in his throat. His vision narrowed. Wanda sucked in an enormous gasp and tears cascaded down her cheeks. All doubts exploded. The eyes were the wrong color. The hair was wrong. The face aged and altered in some real-life photoshop trick.

But neither doubted this was their daughter, impossibly present; alive. They were fixed in place in a bubble of impossibility; neither wanted to say or do anything for fear it would burst and they would find it was nothing more than a waking dream.

Then several things happened at once.

Tabitha stood up and held her arms out to her parents, who cried out her name and moved to embrace her. The door behind them crashed open. Syd DeVito exploded into the room with two deputies. He screamed at them to stay away from the girl and thrust himself between them.

"It's a fraud! She's a fraud!" Syd shouted. Turning to Tabitha he shoved her and said, "Don't touch them!"

The girl missed the chair she'd been sitting in and fell sprawling to the floor. She began to cry. Daniel and Wanda recovered from the shock of DeVito' entrance into their dream. They started toward Tabitha. DeVito blocked their way.

"It's a fraud, Daniel! Wanda!" He looked to his lover for support and got an acid stare.

"She's part of a set up to ruin us. She's not your daughter. Think about it. Think! You saw for yourself. I saw. We saw her. She's gone. Dead!"

His tone was pleading and desperate.

"Look at her! Just look! That's NOT Tabitha! I know you want her back. I want her back. But it's not possible. She's gone. This…"—he poked an accusing finger in Tabitha's direction—"is a cruel joke. I know it is. I've got firsthand information about this plot. I can prove it."

Daniel and Wanda halted in their tracks. Getting the response he needed from this lie, Syd pushed on.

"The press is already here in force. This is all part of the plan. Put her here. Get you to fall for her story. Shove you in front of the cameras with this... this sorry excuse of a doppelganger."

He sneered at the girl crying on the floor.

"Before you even get out of the building, their plan is to expose the truth. That she's an actress or a deranged look-alike, it doesn't matter which—they'll be able to say you are gullible and foolish. That you'll believe anything. That you don't even know your own daughter well enough to keep from being duped."

He paused to catch his breath.

Behind him, the girl slowly got to her feet and stood unsteadily.

She said softly but resolutely, "Uncle Syd."

He wheeled on her, ready to rain down epithets, but they caught in his throat as their eyes locked. For an instant his confidence wavered. He slipped on the edge of belief. His heart pounded.

The voice and the inflection and the eyes conspired to pull him over the edge.

At this moment, all of who he was slid toward a new definition; a completely new possibility and a new world requiring a completely new Syd DeVito.

Icy terror clawed at him in competition with the familiar warmth of those eyes.

It took all his self-control and discipline to push down the impossible and lay hold of reason again. He came to himself like a rock climber who has just teetered on the edge of plunging into an abyss; adrenalin poured through his veins. He set his jaw.

He was determined to keep anyone else from falling, especially Treeright and Wanda.

If he was the only one still holding to the rope of reality, that was fine. He'd hold them all up. Someone had to save them from ruining their lives and it would be him; the only one who kept hold of reality while everyone was ready to slip off into fantasy.

No. No one was going to make a fool of Syd DeVito.

"Don't you call me that, you filthy lying pig," he said. "You're no one and nothing to me. What are they paying you to sell your soul? Or do you get off on this? Want to be famous? Want to be the one who takes down a president? You're disgusting."

His eyes were wild. He was on the edge, barely realizing he was installing his man as president before a vote was cast. His soul was bared.

He was the dog with the bone and no one would take it from him.

The girl recoiled at Syd's rebuke. A look of horror spread across her face but she remained silent. Tears welled up in her eyes and spilled down her cheeks. Daniel and Wanda remained caught in the in-between, shocked into immobility.

Syd sensed he had blunted the worst of this attack and took charge. He looked to the deputies.

"You two take this girl and put her in a cell away from anyone else. Keep her isolated. I don't want her spreading her lies anywhere else."

The deputies obeyed. He turned to the Treerights.

"You need to come with me and get out of here before anyone else sees you. We are already on thin ice as it is. This will get out no matter what we do. What we need to avoid is any video or photos of you here."

Tabitha reached out to her parents as the deputies took her by either arm and began walking her out. She called out, "Mom, Dad, it's me! I promise it's me!"

DeVito shouted her down. "Shut up! Get her out of here!"

"Please! I'm Tabitha! It's me!"

Daniel Treeright came unfrozen. He too felt like he was teetering on the edge of reason and sanity.

The accumulated fatigue and emotional turmoil of the past week felt as if he were in a dive suit passing crush depth. He struggled to find something to grasp that would support him now on the brink.

From nowhere he heard the words of Doug Windsor. *She's alive.*

He tried to push it away but it was there and insistent. He threw up his hands.

"Stop!" he said in a voice that commanded obedience. Everyone in the room froze.

"Sit her down here. Go and get me Doug Windsor. I want him in here. We're going to put all the pieces together right now."

The deputies let go of Tabitha. They didn't look at DeVito. They knew the bark of a bigger dog when they heard it and hurried to obey it.

DeVito started to object. Treeright silenced him with a wave of his arm.

"Sit down, Syd. Wanda, could you see if you can find some Kleenex for the young lady?"

Wanda wanted to fall upon this girl and embrace her with everything she had, but Syd was, until an hour ago, the person she trusted most in the world and he was leaving no room for doubt.

This was not Tabitha.

How could she, the girl's mother, not see her own daughter? Shouldn't she be the final authority on who was or who was not her daughter? Yet she couldn't commit. She couldn't believe her own eyes and ears.

She left the room and slipped into the office across the hall looking for tissues, feeling like she was having a heart attack. Caught on a barbed wire fence fixed between belief and unbelief.

CHAPTER FORTY-NINE

Jackie Smith greeted a deputy he knew by name as he entered the jail. He asked if Rich Macher was there and was told he was with all the gathered reporters in the old, abandoned wing of the jail.

He found his friend sitting at the rear of the gaggle of reporters. Jackie was surprised to see so many gathered here so quickly. This was not the plan he and Macher had laid out, but then again the video he had uploaded to his Dropbox account was going to make any of that plan disappear like a butterfly in a hurricane.

He trusted Macher and wanted him to see it first as one final check on his discovery; one more set of eyes to confirm the impossible.

"Hey, Macher-man," Jackie said and nodded for him to move away to a spot further from the pack of sweaty men and women waiting for a morsel of information on the new story.

Macher raised his eyebrows in a surreptitious gesture which said, 'Why the hell are you here and have you lost your mind?'

Jackie ignored this and pointed for Macher to join him. They huddled up in the open mouth of the nearest abandoned cell with Macher trying to look nonchalant and Jackie not caring.

"You shouldn't be here," Macher said in the lowest tone he could muster without whispering.

"Doesn't matter," Jackie said.

"What doesn't matter? Your job? Your life? This has gone way over our heads. Look around! We can't be seen together…"

"Doesn't matter. None of it. Things are way different than we thought. I got something you need to see." Jackie pulled out his phone. "It's gonna be a little hard to see it on this but you'll see enough."

Macher scanned the room behind them to see if anyone had caught a whiff of anything. No one was stirring yet.

"Jackie…"

"Just watch."

Jackie clicked on the link to the video he had compiled in the hospital watch commander's office. It consisted of several different views of the morgue and the hospital lobby. It was edited to show only the moments of activity on the night Tabitha Treeright's body disappeared.

Macher watched as the morgue attendant escorted the governor and his chief of staff to the side of the dead girl's drawer and pulled it out, unzipping the black rubber body bag and revealing her corpse.

The video was high quality enough to show the colors in the room and specifically the bluish color of the girl in the bag. It was a gruesome sight.

The governor wavered as he stood over her and the man with him steadied him, propping him up in an embrace. The men left the morgue hurriedly then and the video switched to the hallway outside the morgue entrance where they waited to board the elevator.

The near collision between the governor and a man rushing out of the elevator caught Macher by surprise and he asked Jackie to pause it.

"Who is that? And where is Treeright's security? How is he alone?"

"Dunno about security. Look at the guy's face. You don't know who that is? That's right! I forgot you've never seen him yet."

"Seen who?"

"The man everyone is here to see. That's Douglas Windsor."

"What?"

"Yeah. Pretty weird coincidence, isn't it? Trust me, that's nothing. Keep watching."

Macher was fully engrossed now, forgetting everyone around them.

Jackie hit play and the video showed Windsor approaching the morgue entrance and then slipping in while the attendant was preoccupied. The video showed him searching the morgue and finding Tabitha.

Macher found this part of the tape very disturbing and wanted to look away, but his journalistic curiosity kept him watching.

"The guy is obviously a sick bastard," he said aloud to himself as much as to Jackie. It felt like he had to say it or it would eat him inside.

"Maybe not," Jackie said mysteriously. "Keep watching."

Windsor was crouched over the girl when the morgue attendant flew into the room, almost a blur.

The blow to the back of Windsor's head with the massive metal three-hole punch made Macher wince, although he wanted it to happen as if he were watching a movie and the villain was getting his comeuppance.

"It's about to get very interesting," Jackie said. "Watch closely."

Amazingly Windsor got back to his feet and went back to abusing the dead girl even more. He groped inside the bag grotesquely and appeared to kiss her or get so close to it that he might as well be kissing her.

Macher for all his years on the streets and everything he'd seen was getting queasy.

When Windsor was clubbed away from the girl a second time and fell to the ground, Macher was ready for it to end. He could see the girl's body naked to the waist, her right arm wrenched out of the body bag over her head like a macabre Barbie doll.

There was blood on the floor, starkly red against the white tile, dripping from Windsor's head wounds.

"I don't think you're gonna have a problem with any police brutality claims when people see this," Macher said.

"When people see what you're about to see there won't be any discussion about brutality or abuse at all," Jackie said.

The video continued to roll. There was a great deal of confusion and movement that was hard to follow as Windsor was arrested and removed from the morgue.

Macher was breathing heavily, gulping down air, the whole scene too bizarre and brutal; sick and sickening. "I've seen enough, Jackie."

"You haven't seen anything, Macher," Jackie said.

As the scene settled down, the morgue attendant scurried in and out of the frame, cleaning up the floor, repositioning the girl's body, sliding the stainless steel drawer back into its place in the wall.

When the drawer moved seemingly on its own and the girl sat up on the metal slab, Macher gasped.

Macher hissed out loud in spite of himself, "Holy shit! Holy shit! It's her!"

The room full of reporters started to stir. Jackie saw several heads turn in their direction.

He said, "What do we do, Macher? What do we do now?"

CHAPTER FIFTY

Doug Windsor shuffled down the hall with a guard on either arm. They handled him differently than he'd ever been handled in custody. It was a mixture of gentleness and fear; two things anyone in a corrections uniform would drive out of their behavior within a week of breaking in—or they'd have it driven out for them.

He was both an oddity and a celebrity in the jail.

Word had spread quickly about what he'd done to Freddie, an inmate who'd left a trail of carnage in his wake during half a dozen stints in the city lock up, but the word was confusing.

The two deputies who'd tased Windsor claimed he'd beaten the ogre senseless in less than three minutes. They'd found Doug on top of Freddie, pounding him relentlessly as the huge man cried for mercy. They had to taze him to get him to stop.

For his part, Freddie told anyone who'd listen that the strange inmate who got visits from the state's top executive could talk to God and heal cancer with a touch.

The cross-pollination of stories between inmates and guards made for a curiosity to see Doug, but to keep him at arm's length. He might be a wizard who had power to heal you or crush you.

Nevertheless, a dozen or more people had braved getting close enough to him to touch him, first as his head got stitched up in the infirmary and then as he'd been escorted to a new cell.

These deputies seemed nervous. It amused him. He couldn't remember a time when anyone gave him a second glance or cared about what he had to say.

For the most part, Doug felt invisible, a spare tire only useful when people needed him and then put back away back out of sight. He was unsure of how to handle his new found necessity.

"Know where we're taking you?" one of the guards asked in an odd tone that made Doug eye him..

"No," he said. "Why would I?"

The man appeared disappointed. Doug puzzled over it a second and then a light bulb went on. *Wizard.*

"You think I know things before they happen? Like I'm psychic or something?" He laughed. It made his head hurt.

The second guard chimed in, "Freddie said you saw things no one could see. He said God talks to you. That's the hardest man that's ever been in this jail. He's been in and out of here a dozen times since I've been workin' here. No one comes out of a cell with him in one piece."

The deputy lowered his voice to a conspiratorial whisper.

"But he's connected. Nothing sticks to him. It's like he comes here to rough people up and he walks out a week or a month later with no charges."

Doug considered this. Why would someone want to harm him? He was still puzzling over it when the trio arrived at the door to Interrogation Room Three.

The door opened and Doug saw the governor and the man who had been with him at the morgue and the jail. There was also a woman who, although obviously tired and a bit disheveled, was very attractive.

He entered the room before he realized there was another person, a young girl sitting with her back to him.

"Come in, Mr. Windsor," the governor said. "Please leave us alone," he said to the deputies, who looked at each other hesitatingly.

One of them volunteered, "Should we handcuff him to the table, sir?"

Treeright looked carefully at Doug. Their eyes met.

"No, that's not necessary. I take responsibility for him and for our safety. If you like you can station yourselves right outside the door."

This placated the deputies and they stepped out, closing the door behind them. Syd DeVito stepped between Daniel and Douglas and said, "One more time, Daniel. I'm telling you this is a bad idea.

"This pervert is not going to help us and now you've gotten even more people involved who will go and tell the press you're meeting him. Let's cut our losses and get out of here."

"Shut up and sit down, Syd," Treeright said.

Daniel watched as the chief of staff moved to sit opposite the girl. The girl! His heart jumped into his throat. It was The Girl.

He rubbed his eyes. Here she was. He knew she was alive but he didn't know she was alive until this moment. The reality flooded his mind, overwhelming all he'd been through.

"Tabitha!" he cried. "I knew it! I knew it. You're alive! God told me. He told me."

Wanda and Daniel watched in amazement as Tabitha stood and reached out to embrace the man. Syd let out a strangled scream and tried to block them.

"It's an act! It's a hoax!"

Daniel grasped him by the shoulder and forced him to sit. Tabitha and Doug hugged each other tightly. She was sobbing and laughing at the same time, all muffled as she buried her face in his chest.

Doug felt a warmth flow through him; something he had never felt before, or something from so long ago it was forgotten, he couldn't say which.

This girl was really here, really in his arms, really breathing. Alive. No one could doubt him now. He wasn't crazy.

And even if they didn't believe, he knew. But it wasn't the vindication that warmed him, it was love for the girl, joy for the parents looking on at the lost daughter recovered, and a sense of belonging that was difficult to understand, but real enough. Tears streamed down his face.

Daniel recovered himself enough to say, "How could you know each other? You never met!"

Looking over Doug's shoulder, Tabitha said, "I know his voice. He called me when I was in the Light. He said the name and told me to come back. He said I should wake up. I didn't know I was asleep. But I guess I was."

"What name?" Wanda asked. "He said the 'name'?"

"Mom," Tabitha said. "Do you know me now? Dad?" She faced them.

They fell on their knees at her feet as Doug moved aside. Their upturned faces reflected a kaleidoscope of emotion; wonder, fear, joy, and regret.

Tabitha put a hand on each of their faces and wiped away tears.

"The name is Jesus. I heard this man calling me and saying, 'Wake up,' but I couldn't. Then he said I should wake up because Jesus wanted me to wake up. And then I did wake up."

She said this simply, matter-of-factly, as if anyone should understand it. It was so innocently childlike that when Syd spoke it was like a slap to all of their faces.

He stood and stuck out an accusing finger at Doug.

"This is the worst scam ever. Can't you see it? They'll make us look like religious freaks! Crackpots! *Jesus*." He spit the name out contemptuously.

"This is the whole plot! Where is the body, you son of a bitch! Look at her! Anyone can see she's not Tabitha! Where did you put Tabitha's body? Who are you working for? Who is paying you? I swear I'll find out and it won't matter if you've ruined us or not, I'll make you suffer. Both of you."

Doug stared at DeVito dumbly. Another God word came to him. He was gaining confidence in what he heard now. He pointed back at him.

"You ordered a hit on me in this jail. You called for a man to come and kill me. And that's not the only time you've ordered a hit. I see you've done this many times before. I hear names… Rogers. Ben Rogers. And… and… and Mike Donnelly and…"

Syd's expression turned deadly.

He had not gotten himself to the height of political influence without being able to think on his feet and, most of all, to spin.

"You see, Daniel? You see? This man is part of a political operation. How else would he know those names? And to accuse us of setting up hits? He's part of this con job."

Treeright didn't acknowledge Syd. He was embracing Tabitha, who had stooped to her mother and father at her knees.

Syd felt the situation slipping through his fingers, out of control. It would be a complete disaster. He could see it. Why couldn't anyone else? The press would eat them alive.

But... but the press might be his solution.

He abruptly turned and left the room, telling the deputies to stay out and keep everyone out of the interrogation room until he came back.

In the hallway going toward the lobby of the jail, he met Ricky Rome.

"Where are you keeping the press people?" he said.
"Got them all in the old wing," the sheriff replied.
"Show me," DeVito demanded.

CHAPTER FIFTY-ONE

The sheriff led DeVito through a corridor to the old wing of the jail. They entered to chaos. Reporters shouted at each other and pressed around a small knot of people in the back of the room near an empty cell.

A swell of people all tried to get into the tiny space at once. It felt as if they'd walked in on a prison riot. Syd asked, "What's happening?"

Rome said, "Don't know. I left here a minute ago and it was quiet."

They waded through the tangle of journalists and got shoved and elbowed until two reporters recognized Syd and turned their attention to him. Half the crowd continued to press into the cell and the other half surrounded him and the sheriff. It took several minutes for Syd to begin discerning the questions they screamed over each other.

"We have a man here—back there"—they indicated the direction of the cell in the rear—"who says there's a video of the morgue on the night Tabitha Treeright disappeared! Do you know about the existence of the video??!!"

DeVito took this in without giving away anything in his expression. He hissed in Rome's ear, "Get some men and find out who they're talking about—it's got to be whoever is in that cell. Arrest them. "

Rome dutifully slipped away, Syd raised both arms over his head and motioned for quiet. Microphones and cameras sprouted in front of him like mushrooms on a damp lawn. He decided to stall for time in order for the sheriff to get his men.

"Okay, okay. Please. I know you all have been waiting for some word from us about the occurrence in the morgue," he intoned, shifting smoothly into his practiced official voice.

"I'm sure you want to respect the privacy of the Treerights in this traumatic and tragic time. The loss of a child is obviously the worst thing any parent can imagine."

He scanned the crowd gravely. The knot of people in the cell at the rear thinned noticeably as more of the crowd realized who was speaking.

"We ask that you continue to give privacy to the family as they mourn and make necessary arrangements…"

A man in the crowd interrupted. He was a local television station favorite known for his flamethrower style of "gotcha" journalism.

"Arrangements for what? We hear the girl's body is missing! What's the word on that? Can't have a funeral without a body, Syd."

The blunt force of the statement on the crowd was interesting to see. Most of the group were veterans, but they all felt a sense of unease with this story. Syd sensed their discomfort and immediately and deftly turned it back on the flamethrower. He retrieved a handkerchief from his coat pocket and held it to his eyes for an exaggerated moment. When he looked out from behind it he could sense the anger in the crowd toward his questioner. He managed to put a tear in his voice.

"Ed, I, uh, we understand how much, ah, interest there is in this story." He paused to wipe his eyes again and was proud to think he still had the ability to squeeze out a real tear or two when he needed it. "We want to be as responsive as possible while remaining sensitive to the needs of the governor."

Out of the corner of his eye, he saw the sheriff skirting the edge of the room with a cadre of tough-looking deputies. It was time to get all the focus in the room off whoever was in that cell and onto him. He raised his voice to project throughout the space.

"Even though there are still many questions about the morgue and what transpired there, I am prepared to give you a statement." This had his desired effect and almost the whole room shifted to face him.

"There was in fact an incident in the Duke University hospital morgue involving a known sexual predator, Douglas Windsor, who was on parole in a neighboring state and traveled here in violation of that parole. This man was apprehended in the morgue by our own local police after he was discovered trespassing in the morgue and was confronted by hospital security forces.

"The suspect, Douglas Windsor—again, who is a convicted child molester and sexual predator—was engaged in conducting sexual acts upon the body of Tabitha Treeright…"

There was an audible groan in the crowd of reporters. His words had the exact effect he hoped. He wanted to poison anything and everything associated with Douglas Windsor so that he would be swimming against an ocean of ill will when and if he was presented to the press.

He let the statement settle on them fully before beginning again. The sheriff entered the cell. Syd needed all eyes firmly on him.

"As to the existence of a video of the events in the morgue, it is something we were aware of from the evening of the assault on Tabitha's body." He had them now. He could see it in their eyes. Hungry worthless skags. Dogs he fed scraps; only useful when he set them on the scent of something he needed chewed up or chased down.

"Yes, we knew of the video…" he continued.

"Did you know the video is out? It's here. People in this room have seen it!" It was the same reporter. A space opened around him in the crowd as if the man was radioactive.

"I've seen it. Have you seen it? Do you know what's on it? Does the governor know?"

This was unexpected. DeVito struggled to keep his press face. As he did, Rome and his men tried to escort two men from the cell and retrace their steps along the edge of the crowd. He recognized one of them as Rich Macher. He didn't know the other younger man.

Many things happened at once.

Macher began to shout.

"They're trying to arrest us for showing a video of the governor's daughter!"

The local flamethrower continued haranguing DeVito, shouting himself. "The video shows that Tabitha Treeright is alive! They put her in the morgue and she wasn't dead!"

The crowd responded to both of these exclamations at once. The sheriff's men tried to drag Macher and Jackie out of the room. Half the group of reporters surged toward their colleague and the other half toward DeVito. It was pandemonium.

Both DeVito and the sheriff gave up the fight and fled the room, elbowing and shoving their way out. Soon Macher and Jackie were standing in front of cameras and mics with a crowd of journos screaming questions and restraining the remaining two deputies who struggled to get free of the tangle of people.

Macher had gambled on his fellow journalists coming to his aid when they were confronted with being arrested, but he had no plan for what to do next. The whole plan had gone sideways from the moment Jackie arrived.

He did not want to be drawn out on what he had seen. He had too many questions. There was no doubt the video Jackie had obtained showed something strange but Macher reminded himself to keep his reporter's skepticism intact. If something appeared to be impossible it probably was.

And there were no coincidences.

He had to admit that in this case it was hard to reconcile those two principles. He wanted to get away from the jail and assess the possibilities. It was obvious to him that the governor's chief of staff was responsible for ordering their arrest. He knew DeVito was a formidable political force and he played rough but he didn't know why he would try to stifle information about Tabitha before he knew what it was.

He guessed it must be simple. Control. DeVito wanted to control any and every narrative that had to do with Daniel Treeright.

Macher assessed the situation and decided to cut and run. Grabbing Jackie by the arm, he pulled him through the crowd and shoved his way to the exit.

CHAPTER FIFTY-TWO

Doug felt awkward watching the reunion of Tabitha and her family. Although he did not know any of them, he felt a strange intimacy while at the same time seeing himself as an intruder in this incredible moment.

Tabitha broke away from her parents and embraced him again, completely self-forgetful, completely child-like. As the girl hugged him, the tension of the past several days drained away like dirty bath water.

He felt clean, accepted and acceptable in her grasp. He had no words and sensed no need for them. This was communication enough.

Wanda broke the silence.

"I guess I'm the only one here who hasn't met you yet," she said. "I'm Tabitha's mother, Wanda."

She moved toward him and joined her daughter's embrace.

"I'm Doug," he sputtered. "I guess I wouldn't say me and Tabitha met…" He looked to her for confirmation but she returned the look quizzically.

"Of course we met. Just not the way people here understand it," she said.

"I guess I'm confused then," Doug said. "When I, uh, left the morgue, I never saw you wake up or anything."

Tabitha said, "I don't understand it either but when you walked in here and spoke it was like"—she searched for the words—"it was like your voice hit a note in my heart. You know how when you're at a concert and they play so loud that the ground shakes? And you feel it in your feet and your chest? That's it! Except it isn't loud it's just... real. Your voice is so real to me that it makes my heart move."

Doug, Wanda, and Daniel considered this and fell silent. There was something so profoundly simple in Tabitha's explanation that each of them understood it and accepted it without needing more.

Wanda said to Doug and Tabitha, "How did this happen? I saw you—I saw her die, didn't I? There were doctors and nurses and machines… and you were in that place, in the morgue, for three days. How?"

Tabitha said, "That's the whole problem. I don't think I died. At least not what I thought was dying. And I don't know what happened to time. Time didn't happen while I was there."

Daniel spoke up, "Maybe we should work backward from where we are right now? There are so many questions. I'd like to know about the three days you were, ah, away, but I'd like to know how you got here and what happened after you woke up in the morgue. And," he said, looking to Doug, "We need to know how to explain his part in this so we can get him out of here."

Tabitha told the story of waking up in the dark and cold of the morgue and her stops along the way. She described how she came to herself more and more until she remembered who she was. The stop in the psychiatric ward at the hospital and the Regional mental hospital, her escape from there and attempt to get into the Governor's Mansion.

"It was not what you think. When I try to tell you, I'm not getting it right. I'm sorry. It's so hard to explain. I say I 'woke up' in the dark in the morgue but it actually feels more like I was awake in the other place; the Light place and the no time place. I was awake there and then I kind of came back to this place. This place feels like a dream to me now—at least it did when I first came back. It felt just like I was in a dream.

"You know how strange dreams are but how parts of them feel real and normal but parts are crazy? That's how it was at first. But then time started to get real again. I felt it start up again. That was the first thing I noticed. Time. Then the rest of this place stopped being so fuzzy. I was telling people who I was but it was hard to tell them because I didn't believe it myself—or I guess I didn't think it was as real as the person I was in the Light. There I was someone else but also me.

"I don't know. It's almost like there I was grown up but not the way people grow up here. I was grown up into what all of us are supposed to be; not older or taller but fuller." She sighed and looked exasperated. "It's so hard to tell. But the longer I'm back here the more time is taking hold of me. I can feel it. And I can feel my old me getting clearer."

Doug said, "I think you're doing a good job explaining something nobody else knows how to explain. But there are going to be a lot of people wanting to hear this. I think you should be careful... you could get flooded with questions before you're ready to talk. I mean people are gonna want to get a piece of you..."

He looked to Daniel. "You understand this, sir. You know what celebrity does. She isn't ready for the level of attention she'll get if she just walks out of here into the public."

Treeright had a new respect for this strange man who came from nowhere to bring his daughter back to him.

"You're right. But we can't keep this secret, either. There's already two dozen or more reporters here waiting on this story to fill in. They know something happened at the morgue and they know I visited you. They are not going to go away. They'll do the same thing to you, Windsor. They'll hound you. You might be better off here than on the street." He paused and thought. "But you haven't told us your part of the story yet. How did you get here and what did you do in the morgue?"

Doug touched the bandage on his stitched-up nose and considered the question. How *had* he ended up here?

"I just went for a drive and I kept going," he said. "I never set out to be here. I just heard a voice… I heard God."

He looked up to see their expressions. No one blinked or scoffed.

"I'm not a very religious man, but I'm a Christian. I became a Christian when I was in prison. But I never really prayed much or even knew how to pray or hear God. And since I've been out of prison it's been hard. People don't want to be around a sex offender. Don't want me near their children. Even though I never, I *never*, I didn't have anything to do with touching a child. It was underage porn I got caught with and it wasn't little kids…"

He had a miserable look on his face. He knew where all these conversations went. He knew the looks on people's faces; when they started to back up from him even if their bodies never moved an inch. Why was he telling them this? He just had to. It was part of the story. It was part of his story and he needed to tell it. These people had to know who he was.

At that moment, Wanda did something Doug would never forget for the rest of his life. She came to him and took both his hands in hers and stood straight in front of him. She waited for him to look up and make eye contact.

"Doug. Whatever you did in the past is past and you've paid the price for it. Don't be afraid. We won't leave you alone. I promise." She said this with such a fierce tenderness that Doug felt his heart melt and his walls come down. He felt safe among the strangers who knew his secrets. It was a first.

"I believe you. I don't want you to be surprised at what they will say about me. I want you to know the truth. I'm not a good person. I'm nobody. I am not special. I want you to know that too. Because of what happened in the morgue. People might say other things about me... they might try to make me out to be someone I'm not in another way; say I'm special or something. Okay? I'm just trying to be me. I'm trying to know who I am. And I guess you should also know"—he smiled sheepishly at Daniel—"I'm not a fan of your politics at all."

For some reason they all laughed at this.

Doug went on, "It's all just weird, how all this happened. I heard the story on the radio about Tabitha and how you couldn't make it back in time. Later, I woke up in the night and couldn't sleep. I went for a drive. Then I heard something tell me to go to Durham. It's funny telling it now because now it seems so clear what was happening but then I couldn't say why I was doing it. Why I was driving to Durham.

"I don't think I knew it was God until I got to the chapel at the hospital. It was when I read the Bible in the chapel. I knew it was God then. Do you know where the Bible in the chapel was opened to?! It was opened right to the story about Tabitha. It was Tabitha. By the time I got there I was hearing God but I didn't know it was God.

"Have you ever heard God? I think it's like this. I think God sounds so normal that we don't know it's Him. I think He talks to us so much that it's almost like the backbeat in a song. It's like the bass line. If you don't stop and pay attention you might not even notice it.

But once in a while there's a bass solo and it's all you hear. It's so extraordinarily ordinary. It's not what you expect.

"Now I'm thinking He says a lot more things to us than we know. More things than we are even willing to listen to or believe. And I think the stuff He says isn't all that important maybe. Just everyday stuff. Yeah. Now that I know it, now that I'm listening for it, for Him, I can hear Him saying lots of things."

He looked up at their faces again, searching for signs of scorn or unbelief, but he saw interest and kindness. He went on.

"The Bible told the story of Jesus going to a little girl named Tabitha and telling her to arise. But she wasn't asleep, she was dead. Her father came to get Jesus and brought him home because she was dying. And Jesus went there and they laughed at him!

"I've thought about that in the past few days. I went to our Tabitha and they didn't laugh at me; they beat me up! But even Jesus got laughed at! Can you blame them? I don't blame the people who beat me up. Who would believe a dead girl was asleep if they really knew she was dead? No one. I wouldn't. The only way I believe it now is that I'm looking at her!"

He pointed at Tabitha. "I don't have any great religious belief. I don't know how she's alive. All I know is that God told me to come here and when I got here He showed me the Tabitha story and I acted it out. That's all."

"You left out what you said," Tabitha interrupted. "You left out the Name. His name. I heard you talking to me. I heard you calling me but I wasn't going to come back."

She looked to her parents and saw their expressions. "Don't be sad. It isn't that I didn't want to be with you. It's so hard to explain. In that place it doesn't make sense to leave. No one would ever leave if they didn't have to and I don't think many ever have left it. I don't think anyone can unless He opens the door.

"And when he"—she indicated Doug—"called out to me and said Jesus wanted me to come back, it was as if I couldn't say 'no.' I felt like it was right. It was good even though I didn't want to leave there."

Her parents looked at her, dumbfounded. They were not a religious family in any sense of the word. Not that they were hostile to religion; politically speaking they had learned to give lip service to it in order to get and hold power in a state that was part of the ever-loosening but not-quite-disappearing Bible Belt.

They infrequently attended a nice safe Lutheran church where they could make an appearance on occasions. Tabitha had no religious training and no exposure to the church other than those few times. Where had all this come from?

"You saw Him?" Doug asked.

Tabitha screwed up her face into a half grin, half puzzle. "It's not that I saw him so much as I knew him. It's like being in a room where you know everything that's there and you can walk through it in the dark and not see where you're going but know where you are and what's there beside you each step. It's like that except it's in the Light.

"There's so much light there that it fills up every space so fully there's no room for dark; there's not room for a shadow. Jesus is there but there is everywhere and I just knew it. I knew it was Him. It was like I always knew Jesus and he always knew me. That's strange, but it's how it felt."

Daniel said, "Why did you use the name of Jesus, Doug?"

Doug said, "When I tried to wake her up in the morgue, nothing was happening. I was saying the words in the story, '*Talitha koum,*' but she didn't come back. I said it a few times and then I realized the big difference between the Bible story and what I was doing. It was Jesus calling. I thought it must be the difference. So I just called it out.

"I called out in Jesus's name that she would rise. Then they hit me and knocked me down. But just before they did, I heard her heartbeat. Now that I think about it, there's no way in that moment I could've heard it. There was shouting and people running and coming at me. But I'm sure I did hear it. I knew she was alive right then."

"And then they beat you up and threw you in here," Wanda said.

"Yeah. I thought about that since I got here. I think maybe it's good for me to be here for now. What would happen to me if people believed I could raise the dead? If people believed I could raise the dead…"

Daniel considered this. "There's no way around it, though. That's what people will believe. And it's true, isn't it? You did raise the dead. Tabitha's here and there's no denying the part you played in it."

"I didn't do it. I don't know how to do it. I don't want any credit for it. I just want to be myself. There are places in the Bible where Jesus heals people and he tells them to go away and not let anybody know he did it. That's what I want. I don't want anybody to know I had anything to do with this. I'll never be able to go out in public again. I'll never be able to be a normal person again."

"Think about what you're saying, Doug," Treeright said.

"If you don't have something to do with Tabitha coming back to life, where does that leave you? You're a convicted child molester abusing the dead body of a child. A child that was famous before this happened. When people see her now she's going to be even more famous. This will be a worldwide story. And you'll be the creep who tried to abuse her dead body. It will be the opposite of wanting to see you do miracles. People will hate you. I don't see how you get a normal life that way either."

They all fell silent again. The magnitude of this event settled on them, each in their own unique way. All their identities boiled on the stove of this miracle; father, mother, daughter, governor, wife, husband, convict, candidate, citizen.

It seemed nothing would be the same again. Everything was redefined in an instant.

"Anything is possible," Daniel said to himself, to his family, to Doug Windsor, to the world.

CHAPTER FIFTY-THREE

Syd DeVito seethed as he drove himself to the Governor's Mansion in retreat. His first instinct in a crisis was to gather allies and assess enemies. He worked under the assumption of ongoing political warfare.

This had been his modus operandi from the time he had taken on the task of getting Daniel Treeright elected as their college class president.

The players on that chess board were cardboard lions easily beaten into submission before the idiots knew they'd been in his crosshairs. But the principles were always the same.

Control the narrative before there was a narrative. Identify the enemy early and their weaknesses earlier. Compartmentalize trust; allies were only allies for this battle and never entrusted with the whole plan of war.

It had served him well. He had developed a political omniscience that friends and foes alike admired, hated, and feared. Now he needed all his skill to rescue the battle and probably the war.

He considered his options, and drawing on his favorite leadership motto, decided upon an audacious move. He picked up the phone and told his secretary to find a number for him. Ten minutes later he was talking with Rich Macher. They agreed to a meeting in a very public spot, a coffee shop across the street from Macher's office at the paper.

The two men sat across from one another, eyeing each other. Neither had taken pains to mask their identity. They expected it wouldn't take long before one or more members of the jilted pack of press people caught their scent. Macher counted on it to keep him safe and to keep this meeting short.

"You tried to have me arrested," Macher opened.

"For your protection. I thought that room might get out of control. All I wanted to do was get you to a safe place. From the looks of it I'd say I was making a good call," Syd said. "Where's your young friend? What's his name?"

"I decided to get him to a safe place myself. And I think I'll keep his name out of this for now."

"His name is Jackie Smith. He's a former street rat who's now a rent-a-cop at the Duke University hospital. He wants to be a real officer of the law when he grows up." DeVito paused for effect and went on.

"He lives in a nice little rented house in a decent neighborhood on the east side with a cute but nervous wife and a couple of kids. And, uh, he's your little social project. Rich. You know this is too big for him. It'll swallow him and his family without chewing.

Rich Macher fought to keep his face impassive. His guts churned. DeVito went on.

"How long do you think it'll take for someone else to connect the dots? His life is over. The only way he has a video from inside the morgue is that he took it. And if he took it, whatever is on it must be bad news for him. I have a good idea what it is. Probably a CYA for the guys that cracked Windsor's skull. Yeah, that's it.

"Well that's gonna be a problem for him and his dreams. And when the boys and girls from the jail—your friends in the press—get hold of him, they're gonna turn him inside out. They'll probably find things out about Jackie Smith he doesn't even know about his own self. No doubt things the wife doesn't know. It's too bad."

He waited. Each man contemplated the other. Both knew the course of this conversation could affect the fate of the world, but they thought this based upon completely different premises. DeVito had the next leader of the free world on his mind. Macher had the greatest miracle imaginable on his.

Macher decided he had the trump hand and could afford to wait out whatever DeVito threw at him. He remained silent.

"Of course we could help each other out. What the governor wants is not unreasonable. He wants to find out who's responsible for his daughter's disappearance. I'm sure you don't want to be a party to body snatching for political gain. What's in it for you? You want a story. You want to make it to the big leagues yourself. You and Jackie. Same thing.

"And you want a payout. You guys had a chance to make a lot of money off this if you played it right. Sell the tape. Got to be worth six figures or more to the right organization. Look Macher... Rich, we've got a good idea who did this and why. You and Jackie come along with us and the sky's the limit for the both of you. You want to work in the White House and be part of our media team? Or you want to stay on that side of the fence and be a reporter with direct access to POTUS? Jackie? Forget local yokel law enforcement. He can be Secret Service. It looks like an easy choice. We can work together and things go great for you two..."

"Or what?" Macher finished for him.

"Or we can go about this in a messier way. A way that hurts people. You really want to be on the side of the body snatchers?" DeVito said. He still didn't know if the pair were in on the scam or were just trying to turn lemons into lemonade. Macher wasn't giving anything away in his face or posture, even after the veiled threat.

Macher puzzled over all DeVito had said. His brain was in overdrive, sorting through the bits and pieces of information he had just received and fitting them with what he knew.

"Body snatchers? You think someone stole the girl's body. If you think that you must believe this is a political plot…" He trailed off.

"What else would it be? It's a Hail Mary. It's a wild punch in the dark. My man is unbeatable and this is a weakness to exploit. It's the only chance they have to knock him down. The only question I have right now is how you're connected to it."

"You've got the wrong idea. So wrong. Tabitha is alive." Rich said this with a straight face, but in his reporter's soul, it was anything but straight.

Syd let this fall flat between them. Now he knew Macher and Smith were in on the conspiracy to make the governor out to be a fool. It was his turn to play poker though, so he kept silent and let Macher continue.

"You're right about the tape and you're right about Jackie. He did take it to cover for his guys and the cops that responded to the morgue that night. It was a stupid move but from a good heart. He wasn't trying to cover up a major crime.

"And who could blame him for protecting the good guys from a perp like Windsor? So he went in and snatched the drive out of the morgue office. Who knew it would turn out like it did? Did you know that the morgue is the only place in the hospital that has its own separate system? What are the chances?

"It was just a perfect set of circumstances. We have the evidence."

"Listen Macher. I get it now. I see how this is gonna go down. You're working for them. Which one of them is it? Madison? Or Gulkey? Either one would try this. They've got nothing to lose. And then there's Kramer. Or maybe it's all of them. Do you even know who's using you?"

It was not lost on Macher that DeVito had gone from confidently asserting he knew who was behind the "body snatching" political stunt to fishing with the names of the governor's chief rivals.

"You've got it wrong, DeVito. This is no set up. This is real. I saw it myself. Jackie has the tape to prove it. Not just in the morgue. There is more. Tabitha's alive and I've seen it. It's a miracle."

"Would you listen to yourself, Macher? You're not gonna sit here and keep up this charade, are you? Are you that stupid? The girl's dead. Dead. Three days dead. The girl they've hired to be part of this game doesn't even look like Tabitha Treeright. It isn't like the girl's an unknown quantity! She's a fixture. No one's going to go for this."

"Wait. What? You've seen her? You've seen the governor's daughter?"

"I've seen the girl... woman... that they're trying to pass off as Tabitha Treeright."

"Where? When?"

"You're not listening, Macher. Or you're a great actor. Maybe I underestimated them. I guess it would make sense to keep as many people guessing as possible."

"Who are you talking about? I'm telling you this is a miracle and I've got proof! I'm not part of a conspiracy and neither is the governor! We're part of seeing something no one has ever seen. Can't you see it?!"

"What I see is a sucker being used to tear down a good man who is going to be the next President of the United States. A sucker. Who are you anyway? I thought you were a real reporter. A guy who gave up the big time and stayed local because you wanted to be a genuine reporter, not a show clown like those national ass hats. A purist. A truth seeker. And here you are, falling for the biggest lie that's ever been perpetrated on the public in the history of our country.

"I'm surprised. I'm shocked. There are plenty of them out there I could see who'd easily go along with this, but you? You're the last one I'd believe would allow themselves to be used like this. Maybe that's why they picked you."

Macher steamed at these accusations. "The story is a lot bigger than your politics or your candidate... or our country for that matter. This is a miracle."

"Listen to yourself. Listen. Miracles! Since when do you believe in miracles? Since when do you believe in coincidences? Isn't that rule number one in your business and mine? There are no coincidences. Tabitha Treeright died. Two doctors, not just one, independently verified her death and signed the death certificate. And not just any old hack MDs. Both are nationally recognized experts.

"She wasn't just brain dead. She didn't get unplugged, either. She suffered a catastrophic brain failure that led to a total collapse of her vital organs. The description they gave me—because I was there, I had to see this happen up close and personal—is that the amoeba and the infection *ate* her brain. Turned it to jelly like the yellow scum in a can of Beanie Weenies.

"And you know what else, Macher? The infection and inflammation in the brain is so intense it literally squeezes the brain like a python. It crushes it down like a trash compactor until the brain is stuffed down into the brainstem at the base of the skull. The neck. You can't turn your head because it's where your brains are.

"I watched it. I watched her lose her mind and hallucinate and thrash. They tied her down and pumped her full of morphine. It didn't do anything. Her body couldn't process it through the compacted jellied brain. So she thrashed and cried and we couldn't talk to her and tell her we were there because it took away her hearing too.

"Yeah. And then the end, the end... what happens in the end is the pressure in the cranium gets so high that it cuts the brain off from the spinal cord and you lose the ability to breathe. After everything else, all the hell of having your brain lit on fire with no extinguisher and then crushed relentlessly, and the loss of hearing and speech, after all that you choke to death slowly.

"That's what happened to Tabitha Treeright, Macher. That's the body they wheeled down to the Duke morgue and put on a slab. A broken rag doll of a thing. A ruined thing. An irreparable thing. I don't care what you think you saw on a video. I know what I saw in person. Nothing could change that. Nothing did change that. Get a grip. You're part of a hoax whether you know it or not. Whether you're in on it or not. You've got a choice and a chance to help me stop this."

Macher was sobered by Phillip's description of Tabitha's demise. He considered how he would feel if he was witness to the same things the man had seen and then presented with Jackie's tape.

"Tell me what you think the truth is," Macher said.

"The truth? Someone is trying to derail the governor's candidacy. They're out to make him look like a gullible fool. They want him to come out and identify this girl as his dead daughter, make him believe she's alive, make him look wild-eyed crazy. Once he does they'll produce the dead body or offer irrefutable proof that she's not Tabitha.

"Either way, they score. Not to mention what it will do to him emotionally if he's shown that she is really dead. It's an evil idea. It's near impossible to believe anyone would attempt it. But it's true. I don't believe in coincidence. Windsor isn't here by coincidence. The girl. The body disappearing. The emergence of the tape. I do my own arithmetic. I make my own calculations and it adds up this way: there's a conspiracy to take down the governor. As hard as that is to believe, it's more reasonable than believing a dead girl—the girl I just described to you—got up and walked out of a morgue."

"I admit both things are hard to believe," Macher said. "But won't you at least look at the video?"

DeVito said. "Yes. I'll look at it, Macher. But you see the issue yourself, don't you? Your boy had the drive to himself for days. All of a sudden he comes up with these images. Who's to say what he did with it? Who edited it? How can we be sure it's original? These things have a way of catching everyone's attention for a hot minute and then we find out it was all a fake. In my experience, 'unexplained' videos always turn out to be doctored videos one way or another. It's more likely you've got the latest version of the Bigfoot video on your hands than anything else."

Macher wasn't ready to give up on Jackie so fast. "I don't think Jackie has the skill to do what you're suggesting," he said. "And what's his motive? He's not a political operative. I can tell you that."

"Can you? How about this: he's applied for the state police and the local police half a dozen times each and been turned down cold. His record as a minor has followed him. He's caused so much trouble for so many people for so long that they've black balled him even with all of his reforms and connection with his father-in-law.

"He makes squat at his job—really doesn't make a living wage even though he's a shift boss. He has two kids and a wife who stays at home with them. He's stuck. He doesn't have a way up or out. No, Jackie might not be a political operative, but I can see how he'd be a good target for people who wanted to use him.

"Money motivates. Lots of money can buy a lot of motivation. As to fixing the video himself, well, these days software can do incredible things. Doesn't take any skill at all. Ever heard of deep fake videos?"

When Macher hesitated, DeVito went on to explain.

CHAPTER FIFTY-FOUR

"We've already fought off several of these things. Deep fakes. It started as most new technology starts; with sex. A guy on Reddit took an idea from artificial intelligence researchers and used it to make porn videos with faces of celebrities. He posted them online and they were so real, no one could tell the difference. The guy did it using an open source program from Google called TensorFlow.

"Before they could shut him down, he developed an app that could do what he did and he put it on the web. It's called FakeApp. Anyone with access to the web and some pictures can use it. We've gotten our fair share of them thrown at us. You can imagine what kinds of things can be done with this technology. It's deadly serious stuff. It takes the possibility of blackmail to a whole new level."

DeVito saw the impact of his words on Macher.

"Maybe your friend isn't the one manipulating the video. He doesn't have to be. It's possible someone got to him and altered it themselves. All he has to do is get it into the right channels."

Macher felt a gnawing at his gut. He knew Jackie. He knew what he had been and what he was now. The street savvy gang banger was capable of much worse than manipulating the press. That guy, the one Rich met all those years ago, was capable of anything.

He didn't want to think that guy was still around. He wanted to believe Jackie was the feel-good story he'd seen unfold in the last ten years.

But doubt began in the corner of his heart even as he tried to suppress it. It came on like a black snake slithering out of a hole. It chilled him. He didn't want it to be true and that was the problem.

His instincts fought down the desire. He had trained himself never to let his desire for a story to be true to lead him to acceptance. It was his enemy. Doubt was his friend. Jackie was no different than other men. Change was possible but if it was possible to change in one direction it was always possible to change back.

Once he let the whole story lay open in his mind he felt silly for believing Tabitha Treeright was alive. This had all the earmarks of a high tech hoax. Was he falling into the trap? He grasped at the one thread that appeared to offer a different path.

"What about the girl? It seems she could be exposed easily with some direct questioning. There must be things only the real Tabitha could know that a phony couldn't. And where could they find someone able to pull it off? We're talking about an incredible coincidence, not to mention an actor who could do it and would do something so horrible."

DeVito grimaced. "Yes. All true. But listen, Macher, you're getting some real inside stuff here, see? I'm showing you my cards; our cards. Some of the deep fake videos we've dealt with involved Tabitha. We thought there might be a body double or even a girl who resembled her so much it would fool the public. It was really sick stuff. Really sick. Showed her going into an abortion clinic and had her saying she was there to abort her father's—Treerights—child."

DeVito screwed up his face in disgust at this last statement. Macher mirrored the expression.

"Yeah. It's total warfare. No rules. No boundaries. Nothing off limits. You can see why I'm not falling for anything anymore. I figure this must be the girl from their deep fake videos and she must be more than just a body double. She must be a real doppelgänger. How good does she have to be? People see what they want to see. The governor and his wife want to believe and they'll see Tabitha. Others will want them to accept her too. Ever see the movie *Changeling*?"

Macher shook his head no.

"Based on a true story out in California in the 1920ss. Same type of thing. Kid goes missing and another kid shows up taking his place. His mom isn't sure it's her son and points out the discrepancies in their looks and physique, then everyone piles on her. Says she doesn't know her own child. Police tell her he's hers and doctors even give reasons why he's changed appearance.

"The press got involved too; published articles about her being an unfit mother. Woman ended up in an insane ward because she wouldn't accept the kid as her son!"

"Okay," Macher said. "What can we do to get to the bottom of this? If it's a deep fake, how do we know? There must be a way. What did you do with the videos of Tabitha from before?"

DeVito didn't betray anything in his expression. He knew how to manipulate these people. He congratulated himself. He still had it. Could still spin it.

For the first time in days he felt himself regaining control of the narrative. All it took was a little creativity and thinking on his feet. He thought the story of a deep fake video of Tabitha was a nice touch. Amazing how those things came to him in the spur of the moment. Now he was going to take that spur and plant it in this sucker's mind. He needed that story running in every media outlet available within the next hour.

He said, "I need you to let all your colleagues know what's going on. Tell them about the deep fakes and tell them you've got information about a conspiracy to ruin Governor Treeright's credibility."

Macher raised his eyebrows.

DeVito set the hook.

"Use me as a source. Quote me. I'll back you up." He added, "And keep your phone close. Before the day is out, I'll give you the name of the people behind this sham. You can break the story."

CHAPTER FIFTY-FIVE

Daniel drove Wanda and Tabitha back to the Governor's Mansion in silence. Tabitha was exhausted and found it hard to keep her eyes open. She leaned against Wanda in the back seat.

As he drove, Daniel reflected how good—how normal—it felt to simply drive his family somewhere. It made him melancholy, remembering the early days of their marriage and life together.

Wanda kept an arm around her daughter. She watched the girl's chest move up and down, and also remembered. She thought of trips to the side of her baby daughter's crib in the night, checking to see if she was breathing, staring in wonder at the person who had come from her own body.

She didn't know what might come next for herself or for Tabitha or Daniel but she determined in that moment never to lose the wonder of it all again. Never to let it slip into the category of assumption.

All of it was a miracle. All of it had been miraculous; every moment of it; every second. Life itself and life together; one great miracle. She caught her breath and let out a long ,contented sigh. In this bubble of time she let the world go by and just lived.

Their return to the mansion did not go unnoticed. The zoo from the last days of Tabitha's hospital stay was sprouting again on the perimeter of the grounds of the house. Cameras were everywhere. Daniel bypassed the front entrance and phoned security to let them enter via the service alley.

Rousing Tabitha, they threw a windbreaker over her head, ran into the house and up to their private quarters. Tabitha lay down on her bed and was out in seconds. Daniel and Wanda sat down in Wanda's office near the master bedroom.

"Do we have a Bible somewhere?" he asked.

"Wait a minute," Wanda said, disappearing down the hall. She came back holding a paperback New Testament bearing some nasty looking black spatters. To his questioning look she said, "I forgot about this. This was laying in the empty body bag at the morgue. I picked it up. I don't know why. It was sitting there where our daughter was supposed to be."

Daniel stared at the book like it was a moon rock, then took it from his wife and examined it.

"Is this… this looks like blood." he said.

Wanda shrugged. "Doug Windsor's, I'd guess."

"Do you know anything about the story Windsor told us about? The one he found in the chapel Bible?"

"No. I haven't read the Bible much."

"I got a good dose of it in Sunday School growing up... not much since. I did read it through for a class on religion I took in college, but that was more like flipping pages so I could say I'd done it. I guess we can google it and see what comes up."

He took his phone and typed in 'girl comes back to life in Bible' and scanned the results. The first two pages were filled with links to stories about near-death experiences, a scattering of links referring to Bible passages about Jesus raising people from the dead, and one to a movie called *Elvis and Annabel* about a girl who comes back to life when a mortician kisses her.

"It looks like there are a couple of places it could be in the Bible," he said.

"What about calling the minister at the Lutheran church?" Wanda asked. "We need a Bible expert, right? Let's get one."

Daniel thought about it. "Ministers are the same as lawyers when it comes to confidences. We need to be careful what we say right now and who we talk to. Windsor is right about Tabitha. You see how exhausted she is. When this breaks, it'll be next to impossible to keep her from a flood of people wanting to see her. We need to take this slowly and carefully for her sake. I know Syd has been culling through religious leaders trying to find us one who would be the right fit."

Wanda shot him a suspicious glance. She was used to her husband calculating with an eye to the political, not the relational bottom line. What she saw in his face turned away her doubts. He was thinking of their daughter.

"We don't even know that minister," he said. "Do we know anyone who is in a church? Anyone we trust that has a minister they'd suggest?"

Wanda said, "Alicia goes to a church in the city. She mentions the services sometimes. Actually, she's invited me and Tabby to come, but you know what complications that causes."

"What does she say about the minister?" Daniel asked.

"Loves him. Thinks he's funny, smart, and spiritual. Tell the truth, it's a little creepy the way she talks about him. Makes me feel like it's a cult kind of thing; like he's on a pedestal pretty high up. But that's just me taking what she's said and running with it. Probably not fair."

"What about Tabitha's friend's family? They go to church, don't they? Aren't they Catholic? We could get their priest to come talk with us."

He paused, the wheels turning in his head. "What if we got all three to come? It helps me make decisions when I have lots of input." He looked at his wife. "What do you think?

Without thinking about it, they had slipped into their previous life; the way they loved one another before the love of politics surpassed it, the way they collaborated over parenting, the work, the home.

Wanda felt the bitter wall of their long winter melting and also felt its loss as a great relief and its long presence as an offense in itself.

She said, "I think we need help. We don't just need political advice. We need someone to tell us about miracles. It isn't something I've ever thought about before. I know I've said out loud that something was a miracle but I don't know that I ever believed it. I think I've always tucked away the idea somewhere in my mind that there was an explanation for everything that happens. This? There's no explaining it."

"Right. And that's the problem isn't it? We are in the business of explanation and spin. Not only what happened but what it means, and hopefully it means something good for us. I don't know how to explain what happened with Tabitha and I don't know what it means. It is good, though. It's good."

Daniel sat down next to Wanda and slipped his arm around her. He squeezed and she responded by putting her head on his shoulder.

"Yes. It is good," she said.

CHAPTER FIFTY-SIX

Father Mullenix, a thin grey man who blended into his priest's suit as if he were a black-and-white photo, was the first of the governor's religious confab to arrive.

Wanda and Daniel had decided to hold their meeting with the three men in the family quarters of the mansion. The Reverend Jarry Daly of the Lutheran Church they infrequently attended, and Martin Hammond, the megachurch pastor who shunned religious titles and preferred being called Marty, arrived simultaneously, each dressed casually in jeans and polo.

Daly was a middle-aged man with a round middle and a round reddish face topped by sparse blond hair. His blue eyes were so recessed they brought to mind an eerie sense that their owner might be blind.

Hammond was thirty-something. He had intense brown-black eyes set in a bearded face that looked like a field gone to seed.

The Treerights settled their guests into a semicircle of chairs scrounged from other rooms in the private quarters. Each eyed the others with marked curiosity; none knew why they had been summoned to this meeting, hustled surreptitiously into the Governor's Mansion.

Hammond lounged in his chair, legs thrust forward carelessly. Mullenix sat stiffly upright, gray hands spread on his black suit pant legs before him. Daly, although he had no real relationship with the state's first couple, assumed the lead role out of a highly developed sense of self-importance as much as by dint of being able to say they "attended" his church.

"Governor. Mrs. Treeright," Daly said in a crackling, adolescent tone mismatched to his size and age, "let me say I am so sorry for your loss. There's no pain like the pain of losing a child. We at Saint Mark's and the entire diocese will provide any support you need during this terribly sad time. We have already been in discussions with your chief of staff about protocol and how to handle the anticipated interest from the press. I'm sure you know the church has a long history of serving the needs of our community's public servants."

Daniel couldn't tell if it was the man's voice or manner or both that affected him, but he got the impression Daly wasn't as worried about Tabitha's death as he was about selling them on using St Mark's for a very public and important funeral.

Wanda started to interrupt—to spell out the true nature of this meeting—but Daniel gently reached out and touched her arm, halting her. The truth could wait. They might be able to discern a lot about these religious leaders if they let them talk a bit.

Daly continued his sales pitch, oblivious.

"Of course we offer in-house grief counseling individually and in support groups." He paused and sucked in a breath.

Mullenix took the opportunity to speak. He had not missed the subtle interaction between husband and wife. His voice had a young man's vigor and timbre that communicated both authority and peace.

"I'm also very saddened by the passing of your daughter, Mr. and Mrs. Treeright. All children are God's gift to all of us. I'm sorry to say I never met her. The Taylors loved her. They spoke highly of her. I've met with them this week to speak with their daughter, Tabitha's friend, Hannah. She's not doing well, I'm afraid, as you can imagine. Very sad. Very sad."

He looked sideways at the other two ministers and said, slightly embarrassed, "We too are available to help any way we can, but I didn't know you had any affiliation with the church?" The last came out as a question more than a statement.

Wanda glanced at Daniel, understanding what he wanted to say, and more importantly for now, not say.

"Thank you, Father Mullenix. We hope Hannah is getting the care she needs right now. The Taylors are so special to Tabitha. No, we aren't Catholic. We appreciate you coming here today. It's very kind of you to offer to help even if we aren't part of the church."

Marty Hammond carefully examined his shoes while the other two men spoke. He raised his eyebrows in the silence following Wanda's statement. He was used to high-energy environments with a couple thousand people hanging on his every word.

As a rule, he avoided awkward meetings with small groups and preferred to set the agenda when he was in one. He especially disliked sad or despondent people and farmed out counseling to underlings under the guise of being efficient. He had no idea how he ended up here as he only knew of the family through what he heard and read in the media. He was unaware that the first family was served by one of his congregants.

"I'm also sorry, folks. Didn't know your girl. Sad case. Rare. Makes you wonder what God's doing, doesn't it?" His voice was a surprisingly rich baritone that filled up the room with its resonance like the smell of moist pipe tobacco.

Daniel answered, "Yes. It does. We are definitely wondering what God is doing."

He let this sentence fall in between the religious men like a basketball on a playground. Who would pick it up first? Who would try to do something with it?

Wanda shifted in her seat, not completely comfortable with the game Daniel was playing.

Hammond felt a sense of obligation to answer since he was the one who brought God into it.

"I get it. I've been there. Me and the man upstairs have had it out a few times when I didn't know why things were going sideways. Me and my lady lost a child ourselves."

Wanda said, "Oh? You did? I'm so sorry. That's horrible."

"Yeah. Bad times. Miscarriage. Had to fight to stay hopeful. Had so many people depending on us to stay strong. My lady though, she was a champion. Got right up in front of the church and told the people how God was making all things new and God would get us through this too.

"Quite a time. Quite a time. Church just grew a ton when that happened. You see, God took the darkness and brought light. So many people heard the message and wanted to know about how we were so together in the midst of a trial. Mmmm. Yeah…" He trailed off and looked intently at both Daniel and Wanda as if he'd answered all their questions.

Wanda considered whether or not miscarriages were comparable to losing a grown child and decided not to linger over this right now. She wasn't liking this one very much.

Daly was incensed to have the younger and obviously unqualified megachurch pastor taking the lead with *his* people. He was also a closet atheist who didn't want this discussion to run down a rabbit hole of worthless discussions about God. He cleared his throat to speak, but before he could, the priest said, "God is inscrutable but He isn't merciless. The one thing we can't say if we are Christians is that God doesn't care."

He paused and held the Treerights in the gaze of his pale blue eyes, intense against the black suit and gray face.

"As Christians we can see that God so loved us that He got involved personally in our fallen world. He got involved in our sadness. I've thought of this often in times of grief and loss when I miss the hand of God. In Jesus Christ I've discovered that the Holy God of heaven who never needed to experience loss or sorrow or any bad thing became like us.

"I know that I don't know why this terrible thing happened and I am tempted to turn away from God in anger or despair, but two things I see: turning away from God doesn't take away the sorrow or the questions about why bad things happen, it only leaves me with no hope for any explanation in the end—no redemption story. And in Christ at least I have evidence that God cares and so I can trust His heart when I don't see His hand."

The weight of the priest's words settled on the room like the heavy air before a great storm. No one moved for a long minute. Wanda never heard anyone explain Jesus like this before. She wanted to hear more. She felt her mind thawing in a place it was long ago frozen. Daniel and the priest were locked eye to eye, not in Daniel's natural assessing stare, but in appreciative wonder.

Hammond broke the silence. "Deep, man. Good stuff."

Daly didn't like the direction this was taking. He said, "Jesus was a good man who showed us the way to live; the way of love. I believe people are good and we have the power to lift ourselves out of the ooze of the past and overcome superstitions that hold us down. It's what he showed us. God is love."

The old priest maintained eye contact with Daniel, his eyes clear and piercing. Daniel felt peace in those eyes. The priest's words sliced open the veil between this world and another and he knew it. He felt no need to pull open the flaps on either side of his statement but his demeanor suggested they walk through this gap together.

Daniel involuntarily reached out for Wanda's hand and she reciprocated. They both gave a little start as there was a knock at the door and then smiled sheepishly at each other. The door opened and an attendant wheeled in a cart with the makings for tea and coffee with Danishes.

"Excuse me, ma'am, sir. Alicia said I should bring you some refreshments."

"Thank you, Sarah," Daniel said. "That's great. Exactly what I need; a good cup of coffee." He gestured to the cart. "Gentlemen, please help yourselves. The pastries are deadly though. Costs me an extra thirty minutes a week on the Stairmaster to pay them off."

The rich smell of coffee wafted into the room with the cart and the men stood up. The governor led the way, pouring a cup for his wife and for each of the ministers in turn.

All refused the pastries except for Wanda, who said, "Don't be shy, guys. These are the best you'll have in a month of Sundays, I promise. And I'm starving." She swallowed a raspberry danish with a voraciousness that surprised Daly and Hammond, both of whom had wives who ate barely enough to keep a bird alive. They weren't used to seeing a woman eat anything more than a morsel of salad.

It occurred to the Lutheran minister that most people he dealt with in this situation had no appetite at all. Wanda's example nudged all three of the ministers to follow her lead. The food and drink moved the group conversation into the mundane; weather - Father Mullenix, local sports - Hammond, and traffic problems - Daly.

Wanda watched her husband watching these men, reading him as he read them and guessing what he was thinking.

They had called this confab to help them get a grip on the miracle lying asleep in the bedroom down the hall. She thought that so far the jury was out on which, if any, of these men could help them navigate this new reality.

What should they do next? She was unsure and being unsure was not familiar territory for either herself or Daniel. What was he thinking? What was the next move?

Daniel, sipping his steaming coffee, gave her a sidewise glance then said, "I... we are interested in what you can tell us about miracles. Are they possible? Have any of you ever seen one? Something absolutely inexplicable?"

None of the ministers saw this coming. Daniel saw it in their expressions and it was exactly what he intended to do with his question. If they were going to get advice from these men, he needed to know their starting point. No sense in showing his hand before they saw a miracle; then it would be too late.

Hammond the megachurch pastor jumped in.

"Sure, I believe in miracles. God is a God of miracles. He does them all the time. Life is a miracle. The sun coming up is a miracle. Have I seen a miracle? Yes! Last year we needed five hundred thousand dollars to get our new worship center built—half a million bones! I told everyone it would take a miracle to get that money. We had bupkis for collateral for a loan and something like 75-K in the bank.

"So we prayed and asked God for the money and told everyone to pray and ask God what they should do about it—I mean what they should give. So about six months went by and we had this big meeting planned when the owners of the property were gonna ask us to either put up or shut up. We had a special service and asked everyone to bring their offerings. We named it the Chest of Joash service after the story in the Bible about Israel trying to get money to build the temple."

He looked at the Lutheran and the Catholic ministers to see if they knew the story. Daly had busied himself with a second danish the minute Daniel raised the question and didn't look up. Mullenix smiled noncommittally although he was familiar with the story.

"Anyway, we had special music by this really good singer and got a guest speaker that everyone was hot to hear—both of those cost us almost all we had in the bank, but hey, you've got to break eggs to make an omelet right? We even built this mockup of a big wooden chest for people to come up and drop in their money. Well, it was amazing what happened. We got almost all the money we needed to get into our new place. It was a miracle. A real miracle. We never had an offering like that one before.

"When I told the church about it they flipped out! We all agreed God is with us and has great things in mind for us." Hammond paused and looked at each of them in turn, a broad grin on his face.

Daniel said, "Mmm."

Wanda said, "You must have been very excited."

Daly continued munching on his danish.

Hammond looked deflated at the reception to his story and slumped back into his chair.

Mullenix started to speak but Daly suddenly found his voice, cutting the priest off.

"I'm not sure I'd call that a miracle," he said in a scholarly tone. "It sounds like you worked pretty hard to produce that outcome!" He glanced at Daniel with a sly look. "The difficulty with miracles, Governor, is that by their nature they're outside of natural cause and effect and so they're outside of scientific inquiry—outside of what we'd call 'proof.'

"Lots of people call an event a 'miracle' but what that usually means is they lack the means to prove why a particular thing happened. In my experience, the lack of proof is usually a result of people not having all the facts, or overlooking a key fact. I understand why people want to see a miracle. Who wouldn't? But that's the problem, isn't it? Don't we all see what we want to see? No offense, Pastor Hammond," he added condescendingly.

Daniel interjected, "You're saying there are no such things as miracles then? Aren't you a Christian minister? Isn't the church built on miracles? Red Sea parting? Virgins giving birth? Jesus rising from the dead?"

His last example caught in his throat like he had dry swallowed an aspirin. His mind whirled around the implications of his daughter's resurrection. To this point he had only considered her return to him and the joy of having her back. Suddenly he saw he must reconsider Christ and Christianity.

The Lutheran minister sat back as he heaved in a huge gulp of air. Exhaling and maintaining his annoying, condescending school master tone he said, "Well the church was steeped in much mysticism and the belief in miracles was part of that. But we've evolved. I'd say we've become more authentic in our beliefs. After all, it isn't the miraculous things that are the most important part of our faith."

He arched his eyebrows and continued, "The core of Christian belief is the moral teaching of the Bible, you see? Not the miraculous but the moral. The Ten Commandments in the Old Testament. The golden rule of Jesus in the New. These are the pillars of the church. These are what we teach people and how we encourage them to make the world a better place. And, if I might, I'd say that whenever a person loves his neighbor as himself, it's a little miracle. Kindness and love are miraculous."

It was Daly's turn to strike a pose and wait for the acknowledgement of the room. It was also his turn to see his words fall flat like a Christmas inflatable decoration with the plug pulled. He slumped back into his seat, sipping his tepid coffee.

Daniel barely heard Daly's soliloquy, lost in his contemplation of resurrection. He did not notice the pregnant silence growing in the room. It began to rain hard outside and the room grew darker as the wind whipped huge raindrops against the floor-to-ceiling windows. It thrummed with an uneven rhythm that kept the company momentarily speechless. The clink of someone's cup and saucer chimed like a bell breaking the spell.

Wanda noted the Catholic priest's posture. He was neither sitting forward nor completely reclined. She was used to seeing men eager for her husband's attention, leaning into every opportunity to be close or closer to the great man.

She sensed this in Daly's body language and speech. She also sensed Hammond's slack posture was a poorly-concealed attempt to appear nonchalant when he actually craved more of Daniel's attention. The grey priest in the black suit waited without stirring, his kind eyes blinking the only indication he was not sleeping sitting up.

She asked him, "Reverend Mullenix, aren't you going to tell us what you think about miracles?"

Stirring himself, the priest said, "I'm just sitting here wondering what use you have for miracles."

"Use?" Wanda said with surprise. "I don't understand. I think the question is about whether any of you believe in miracles; what they are—how they happen…"

The old priest smiled. "Pardon me if I'm speaking out of turn, Mrs. Treeright." He paused as if deciding to take a plunge into uncertain territory and she could see him measuring his next words carefully.

"But if I understand what I read in the news, I'm sitting in a room with the next President of the United States." He tilted his head toward Daniel. "Nothing to sneeze at. When it comes to power, there isn't anything to compare to politics. Power and politics. I love science fiction. The first book I ever read my mom got for me. It was *Tunnel in the Sky* by Robert Heinlein. After that, I read everything he wrote I could get my hands on.

"I know," he said a little sheepishly, "not standard fare for the clergy. A little racy and fanciful for some in my order, but I always thought I could find God in the story even if Heinlein didn't put Him there.

"Well, Heinlein actually had a lot to say about religion and politics. He wrote something that stuck with me. This isn't exact, but close. He said any religion would legislate its creed into law if it acquired enough political power to do it, and after they did it they would persecute anyone who didn't hold their particular beliefs— they would outlaw the 'heretics.'

"You see, he had a healthy distrust of religion and political power and I think he was right. Christianity as a religion is good. Christianity as a political system has been pretty abusive. And one of the ways Christianity morphed into a political power was through manipulating miracles."

He peered sharply at Treeright. "I'm not skeptical about miracles at all, Governor. I fully embrace them. Seas parting. Virgin birth. Resurrection from the dead. All of it. But I'm highly skeptical of politicians who are interested in miracles. I'd like to know what use they'd like to make out of them. I guess you could say because I have such a high view of miracles and the miraculous that I'm protective of them. They are potent. They are full of power to move the masses."

He paused again and pursed his lips as if what he was about to say pained him. "And if I could be blunt sir, I'm skeptical of your politics," he said. "Well, that's not the exact truth. Actually, I'm skeptical of you. I'm not sure what kind of leader you really are. What would you do with all that power? What would that power do to you?" He looked uncomfortable having to say these words.

Daly, embarrassed by the old priest's impudence, tried to cut him off. "Show some respect…"

Mullenix never missed a beat or raised his voice. He continued addressing Treeright.

"Please don't take it personally. I would say this to anyone seeking this kind of political power. It's not a Republican or a Democrat thing with me. From where I sit, there's little difference in the parties. What I see is a group of people who've already accumulated enough political power to persecute anyone who doesn't hold their beliefs; a group of people who already legislate their creed into law and are beginning to outlaw anyone who disagrees with them.

"I see our political class at the head of their own religion, a secular religion that isn't friendly to any other religion, and who are downright hostile to one religion in particular; Christianity. Christians are at the top of their list of heretics. And here you are asking about miracles? I think my question about the usefulness of miracles is perfectly reasonable."

Treeright bristled. He started to respond to the impertinent little man. Wanda subtly touched his hand.

"I see," said Wanda gently. "You make some good points. This whole meeting must be disorienting to all of you. I don't blame you for being suspicious of politicians. My favorite Heinlein quote is, 'Love your country but never trust its government.' She paused to relish the priest's surprise.

"I'm a fan of the Dean, myself, Reverend Mullenix. *Starship Troopers* and *Farnham's Freehold* for me."

The three pastors and her husband all had bemused expressions on their faces. Mullenix grinned widely and visibly relaxed. Wanda quickly reflected on how much of "boots on the ground" politics was really as simple as a shared love of a thing totally unrelated to the issue at hand. She continued.

"It makes sense the miraculous could be abused. Politicians are storytellers and connecting to a powerful story is a sure way to motivate followers. But we aren't looking to use a miracle for anything."

Another awkward silence descended on the group; each of them pondering where this meeting was headed.

The religious leaders, thinking they had been summoned to speak into a moment of grief, were disoriented by the left turn into a discussion about miracles.

The Treerights, who were trying to find help from the religious leaders for navigating the miraculous return of their daughter, were unsure these experts added anything helpful to their situation.

The clink of cups on saucers magnified the growing silence. Daniel started to get up to signal an end to the meeting when the door swung slowly open and Tabitha stepped into the room, yawning.

CHAPTER FIFTY-SEVEN

Jackie Smith was shaking. The adrenalin rush over what he'd discovered on the security video had died down on the drive from the hospital to the jail. It had been pumped back up by the scrum of reporters and the attempted arrest. His legs felt like jelly.

Rich Macher sat with him at his kitchen table, stirring honey into a cup of tea, sloshing some of it onto the blue-and-white checkered tablecloth.

"It won't take them long to track us down," Macher was saying, his brow creased with worry. The day's events had steamrolled his plans to manage the release of information about the disappearance of Tabitha Treeright's body and the missing security camera hard drive Jackie had stolen. He stirred the tea nervously and wished for the hundredth time that day that he hadn't quit smoking.

"Guess I should've stayed away from the jail," Jackie said. "I got so excited over what I found I had to show you." He looked at Macher expecting a rebuke.

"Spilled milk. I don't blame you," Macher said. "Our whole plan was blown up before it started any way. The governor and the chief of staff both at the jail… I didn't see that coming. No one could've. This is the strangest story I've ever been part of. I don't know what to think.

"Syd DeVito wants a lid on it. Why? Is it a fraud? Who's the guy they've got locked up? Where'd he come from? Seems we've got to do some work on him—what's his name? Douglas Windsor? I'll call in some favors with some friends in Norfolk. I know that's where he's from."

He didn't see the distressed look on Jackie's face.

"Fraud?! Rich, you've seen the video! How can you say this is a fraud? Are you saying I'd lie about something like this?!" His voice and temperature were rising. His wife pushed the kitchen door open slightly and shushed him. *Kids asleep. Keep it down*, she said, as all mothers know how to do without words.

Macher met his friend's fiery eyes and saw the young street tough he'd first met years ago. No, Jackie wasn't a liar or a fraud even in those days. He had somehow, in spite of having no family and no good examples, developed a high sense of honor and loyalty. It was one of the reasons Rich was drawn to him.

"I'm sorry, Jackie," he said in a fatherly tone. "I don't question your integrity. At least that's not what I'm trying to do. I'm sorry if it sounded that way."

He watched as the fire lowered in Jackie's expression. "It's just so incredible. So… yeah. I've used that word many times in my life but never felt like it does coming out of my mouth now. Incredible, Jackie. It's like as soon as I quit looking at the video my mind immediately starts to tell me it can't be real."

Jackie softened his tone. "I know, Macher. I know. But it is real. That girl is alive. She walked out of that morgue!"

"Right. So where did she go? Where is she now? How could she just disappear? There were people who saw her. Why didn't they say anything? Do anything? Help her? Why didn't that woman at the info desk tell someone? You can see them talking. She must have known something odd was happening! The girl was only wearing a sheet, for God's sake! Wouldn't that tell you she needed help?"

The mention of the info desk woman triggered a response from both men. They looked at each other and said, "We've got to talk to that woman," as they stood up.

"I'll drive," Macher said.

Macher used the time in the car to connect with his contact in Norfolk, a retired reporter for the local rag, the Ledger Star. Macher put him on speaker phone while driving.

The man was grateful for something to do and punctuated his sentences with colorful obscenities, causing both Macher and Jackie to laugh out loud. He was sure he could get the dope on Windsor. He knew all the right people to track down a perv like him. He would call back as soon as he got the goods. The conversation ended as they drove into the hospital parking garage.

They were disappointed to find the information desk manned by a woman who was singularly uninformed about her fellow volunteers and who refused to let them see the schedule book or the phone list which would have given them access to the person they were seeking.

After a fruitless conversation with a human version of a business phone menu looping back to nowhere, Jackie pulled Rich away and said, "I can find out who she is with the records in the security shack. She has to get an ID badge through us so there will be a record there. We'll just have to sort through the files and see if we can match a picture to the woman on the video."

Walking to the security shack, something occurred to Macher.

"Jackie, does the security system cover just the big common areas in the hospital?" Answering himself he said, "That can't be true. There are cameras in the morgue and the hallway outside of it too. But they can't be in areas where there are patients. That has to be a violation of privacy, right?" No one was ever sure about the presence of cameras anymore and the legality of where they could and couldn't be.

Jackie said, "The morgue is a special case. The system down there was installed after the main system in the rest of the hospital. That's why there is a local control panel and a separate hard drive. The cameras only cover common areas on the main floor—no cameras in any area where patients might be. Privacy," he affirmed. "We do have cameras on the exterior of the complex. Parking lots. Parking garage. Loading ramps."

Jackie had a thought. "I got so wrapped up in seeing the girl alive and walking around I didn't think about anything else. If she left the building…" He gave Rich a big-eyed look. "Macher! What if she never left the hospital! What if she's still here?!"

Macher felt his heartrate bump up. They'd been going on the assumption Tabitha Treeright had exited the building after her encounter with the woman at the information desk. In his excitement at what he'd seen, Jackie had stopped looking when he'd seen the girl walk out the front doors.

What if she didn't leave?

"Where would she have gone? We have to go on the assumption the woman working the desk didn't know who she was… How does that make sense? Everyone knows the story. You'd have to live under a rock to not know. Especially someone working in this hospital after the media zoo all week."

"I've been thinking about that, too. You can see they are face to face on the video. As close as you and me right now. How could she miss it? I don't know but maybe it's like you said. Your mind can't see what it can't believe."

They arrived at the door to the security shack with these thoughts hanging in the air.

Jackie said, "This is gonna be weird, me coming in during my off-duty time. And these guys are sharp. I can't fool them with some bullshit story. I don't want to. I think it's too big to keep to ourselves."

Macher met his gaze. "So what do you want to do?"

"I'm gonna own it. Stealing the hard drive. What went down in the morgue. And then I'm gonna show them the video and ask them to help us find Tabitha Treeright."

"What if they can't believe what they see either?"

"I can live with it. I believe it. I believe the girl is alive and since she hasn't shown up anywhere else, she could be in trouble. And I couldn't live with something happening to her after all she's already been through."

Rich looked admiringly at his young friend and put an arm around his shoulders. One had no father and the other had no son but they had found their own way to this father-son relationship, forged in the streets, each adopting the other, each at ease with the thought that what the world denied them naturally they'd found somehow, maybe even supernaturally.

"Let's go. I'm with you," he said.

CHAPTER FIFTY-EIGHT

Syd DeVito sat in his car in the parking lot of the Governor's Mansion. His head hurt badly and he dry swallowed two extra strength aspirin. Not a good idea. The oversized tablets settled securely in his throat and repeated gulps did not move them in the slightest. He cursed out loud.

Great metaphor for this debacle; a bone stuck in his throat he couldn't touch. Couldn't move it. Every attempt to take hold of the narrative had only jammed the bone further into his gullet.

He reached in the glove box and pulled out a flask. He took a pull from it and let the whiskey set in his mouth to build up a mouthful of liquor and saliva before giving another hard swallow. The liquid burned his throat and had no effect on the tablets.

Yeah. Perfect metaphor.

From where he sat, he could see the lights to the private residence burning. He noted three unknown cars parked near the rear entrance. Daniel must be meeting with someone and Wanda must be with him.

Funny how quickly he'd gone from insider to outsider. Any crisis in this house or with these people for the last twenty years they'd faced together, even the crisis of a failed marriage. He had thought himself indifferent to the emotional aspect of his affair with his friend's wife. It was a political expediency; keep her on the reservation.

But in the face of seeing Wanda and Daniel reunited, even if only temporarily, he felt the stirrings of jealousy. Maybe it wasn't all politics and sex and convenience.

No time for those thoughts. Their plans were hanging by a thread and emotions were not going to help. It was emotion that was jeopardizing their plans.

Syd reflected on that. Daniel Treeright was the most rational man he knew. Perhaps the smartest. A true anomaly of human nature. Unquestionably the most charismatic person on the scene, he was also a gifted thinker. Able to kiss babies and debate intricate policy seamlessly. And on top of it all a physically attractive man without the vanity of attractive men.

When they had started down this road together, Syd had thought he would find a hole in Daniel's armor, a place where he needed a guardian. But Daniel didn't have a weakness unless it was the weakness of a strong magnet to collect every bit of magnetic material around it.

He did sleep with a lot of women but he didn't flaunt it. And what was wrong with that? Powerful men were always surrounded by women. The wife of a powerful man had to get used to sharing him in many ways. Sex was just sex after all, and marriage was marriage. Syd's Catholic school education taught him at least that much.

Even the great kings in the Bible had lots of wives and concubines. This was the primary argument he had made to Wanda when she first threatened to blow up the Treerights' marriage very publicly. It had taken lots of persuasion and in the end allowing her to transfer her emotional needs on to him to keep her settled.

Syd wondered if it was Wanda's emotions that were derailing Daniel at this critical moment. Had she infected him with the unbearable sorrow of seeing their daughter die? Had that burden so crushed them both as to cause them to see ghosts? Maybe. Anything to get out from under that weight.

He was certain that someone had calculated the effect and rolled the dice. A shrewd enemy and ruthless. Dead people stay dead and that's that. Seeing the faux Tabitha at the jail had at first shocked him until he reminded himself of the facts.

This was not what some called a near-death experience. It wasn't a matter of life support being removed and a patient holding on, or of someone's heart stopping for a few hours or a boy drowning in a cold pond suddenly reviving.

This was a girl dying a gruesome death in the best hospital in the region from an irreversible infection that destroyed her brain. A girl declared dead by not less than three expert physicians. Dead. Brain dead. Body dead. Heart stopped. Cranium full of gelatinized white matter. Not even a question of donating organs because they were also damaged beyond usefulness to anyone else. And that body had sat in a morgue for three full days waiting for Daniel to return from Africa.

He took another slug of whiskey, remembering the trip to the morgue and the viewing of the body. No. That body did not get up and walk out of there. No.

As crazy as it sounded and as unlikely as it might be that a political enemy could steal the body and send an impersonator to fool the Treerights, it was more believable than that.

He had to expose whoever it was before they flipped the switch and exposed Daniel Treeright as an irrational idiot who couldn't recognize his own daughter.

Syd knew how to play this game. He knew how to play rough and he knew that sometimes you made a dirty play knowing ahead of time you'd get penalized. Oh, well. Take out their knees and get a "roughing the passer call." But make sure the quarterback stays down.

Right now he didn't know who the coach of the other team was, but he knew who was on the field. Doug Windsor, Jackie Smith, and Rich Macher. Windsor was on ice for now and he might just be more useful than if the planned extermination had happened. But the other two; they both had to go down hard.

He picked up his phone. He would make them wish they were never born—and anything either of them had ever done wrong or thought about doing wrong since they'd been born was getting ready to be public knowledge.

He had a good idea that Jackie Smith's past in particular would yield a great deal of tabloid fodder. Macher? If he couldn't find anything he would get creative. Maybe there would be some drugs hidden in his place.

DeVito smiled. By the end of the day, no one would believe a word either of those two said. The phone connected.

"Yeah, this is DeVito. I need a favor."

CHAPTER FIFTY-NINE

Macher and Jackie found the security shack empty and silent save for the buzzing of the industrial-strength fluorescent lighting. It was a letdown after they'd built themselves up for a confrontation with Jackie's fellow security guards.

Jackie said, "Must be short staffed today. The chief goes on rounds himself if we don't have enough guys to cover it."

Rich thought a moment and said, "You told me there were cameras in all the common areas and the parking lots. How about running through some of that footage to see if Tabitha walked out of here on her own?"

Jackie quickly agreed. Soon they were scanning the video feed in a closet-like control room just off the main security office. In the dark, cramped space, they searched for footage of the main entrance, looking for the day and time Jackie had seen the girl at the front desk in the other feeds he had searched previously.

"Here it is!" Jackie said, pointing to the date-time stamp on the screen. "This would be about the time she was there."

The video showed the hospital's front entrance and pull-up lane wet with rain and empty of cars. Running the tape at four times speed, Macher saw a flash of movement like a white blip on a radar scope.

"Stop! What's that? Slow it down and back it up, Jackie."

The younger man did so. In real time they saw the girl, shoeless and wrapped in a sheet, step through the sliding doors onto the concrete sidewalk. She paused and appeared to be considering what to do next.

Both men caught their breath.

"Like seeing a ghost, isn't it?" Jackie said.

"If what we believe happened really is true, we're looking at something more amazing than a ghost," Rich said. "It's… it's… it's the most amazing thing anyone ever saw. And we're looking at it. We're the first ones to see it."

"See what?" came an authoritative, husky voice from behind them.

They spun around like teenage boys caught watching porn.

"Chief!" Jackie sputtered.

"What's the deal, Smith? And who is this?"

The chief pointed a meaty middle finger at Macher, giving the gesture a subtly obscene twist. Jackie was a star employee, the best of the small force under him. He earned deference in many areas where others received none. Allowing a civilian to view security footage which might or might not be a violation of privacy depending on the day of the week, the particular people filmed, and the whims of the politicians in the hospital head shed, was close to the line on an average day. Today, given the shenanigans with the morgue hard drive and the public personalities who were in and out of the hospital for the past week, it was over the line.

"This is a friend. Rich Macher." Jackie said, trying not to sound like a school child called out of line for misbehaving. "He's a reporter for…"

"A… what the hell are you thinking, Jackie? Reporter?!" The chief cut him off. "Get out of there, the both of you. Jesus Christ, that's what I needed today. Reporter nosing through our videos."

Macher and Jackie stepped out of the cramped video monitoring room into the not-much-larger office. They found themselves backed up to the watch officer's desk, face to face with the chief, close enough to smell the onions on the hot dog he'd just eaten.

"Chief, it's not like that. He isn't... we aren't here to get a story."

Rich appreciated the shift in pronouns. If he went under the bus at least it was going to be a double thump. He jumped in.

"No, Chief. We aren't looking for a story." He hesitated and went on. "But we may have found *the* story. The biggest story imaginable—maybe it's better to say unimaginable."

Chief Harden's expression said he couldn't care less about stories. He wanted the reporter gone and he wanted to tear Jackie Smith a new one. He pointed toward the door and started to speak when Jackie said, "I've got the missing hard drive."

Harden stopped short. He turned on Jackie.

"What?! Where'd you find it? Who had it? Was it that little shit Hamilton? I thought he might've done something like that. He had a look when I questioned everybody…"

"Not Hamilton. No, Chief. It was me," Jackie interrupted the emerging tirade. "It was me. I snatched it that night to cover our asses. It was a snap thing. I didn't plan it. Once everything went down the way it did, uh, I didn't know how to get out of it."

This information stopped Harden cold. Jackie Smith. Not the guy you'd suspect of a stunt like this. His face went from blossoming red rage to slack and pallid. He walked around the desk and flopped into the watch commander's worn-out swivel chair.

Taking off his hat and running his fingers through his thick salt and pepper hair, he said "Jeez, Jackie. Jee-zuus. Do you know what's going down because of that missing hard drive? Let me tell you. Conspiracy! That's what. It's a conspiracy. They're saying the missing hard drive proves it. The Treeright girl was stolen as part of a plan to bring down the governor. Make him look bad or drive him nuts or maybe ransom her. Ransom a *dead girl's body*! That's what they're saying Jackie! And the hard drive is the heart of their theories."

He let out a stream of obscenities like a tea kettle boiling over until he stopped abruptly, eyes fixed on nothing.

"Chief, you need to see what I found on the video. It isn't going to make up for what I did but it's the real problem we need to work on right now." Jackie said.

Harden said, "There's no problem more real than you stealing that drive. There's no way around it or through it. When this comes out, it's my job, not just yours. And it's probably lawsuits against us personally."

"We're going to show you something that will make that look unimportant." Macher said.

Harden grunted.

Jackie leaned over the desk and turned his cell phone for the chief to see just as three day-shift security guards piled noisily into the room.

"Good," he said. "All of you need to see this."

The two men and one woman immediately took the temperature of the room by the chief's countenance. They stopped chattering, and as Jackie motioned them around, fell in behind the chief to see what Jackie Smith was showing on his phone.

Their faces went slack the moment they saw that it was video from the morgue. They glanced back and forth between themselves and Jackie and tried to glimpse Harden's expression over his shoulder.

Jackie narrated, looking alternately at the screen and their eyes. When he got to the segment of the video showing the girl at the info desk, the lone female security guard, an attractive young African-American, gasped.

"That's the girl we took into custody the morning after the incident in the morgue!" Her deep brown eyes were wide. "Harris. Thompson. You remember?! Ms. Franklin at the info desk called us to come get her. Said she was babbling about it being wet and dark outside and she was from another planet."

Harris and Thompson looked at each other with the "I'm not gonna say anything till you say it first" look.

The woman gave them a disgusted look and said sharply, "How many girls wearing nothing but a sheet have we ever found in the lobby? It was that girl." She stabbed a finger at Jackie's screen. "Chief, it was right after shift change that morning. We relieved Jackie and didn't even have time for a cup of coffee when the call came. Ms. Franklin was very upset."

She paused and looked at the chief expectantly. Harris and Thompson shifted uneasily on their feet, still unwilling to wade into this until they knew which way the stream flowed.

Finally, Harden spoke with an icy long exhale. Jackie detected something of resolution in the man.

"Smith. I know you're desperate to make it out of here—make it as a real cop. And I know you're disappointed at not getting my recommendation. But I'd of never believed you'd go to this length to make a name for yourself. Make up a case to solve. Burn down a house like an arsonist fireman."

His eyes flashed at Jackie, red with anger. Everyone in the room edged away from Harden like he was suddenly radioactive.

Jackie started "But Chief.."

"Stow it. I got a call this morning. A tip from a friend I trust. He said you'd be showing up sooner or later with a story about Tabitha Treeright. Yeah. He told me you'd try to pass off a fake video as the real thing. I guess you think I'm a hayseed? That I've never heard of deepfake? Even so I didn't want to believe it. Hell, I didn't believe it, but here you are and here's everything he told me would happen."

At the mention of the word *deepfake*, Macher growled in Jackie's ear, "This is DeVito. He's poisoned the well against us."

Fear flashed across Jackie's face but quickly morphed to anger. Macher tried to restrain him and get them out of the room. His mind was whirling with the implications of having a man like Syd DeVito mobilized against them. It was too late. Jackie jerked away from his grasp.

"Who are you in bed with, Harden?" The man's eyebrows shot up at the younger man dropping his title. "Who is filling your head with this shit? You know me." He gestured at the other three guards who were trying to melt into the floor. "They know me. There's never been a word said against me since I got here. Deepfake? I don't even know what that is so maybe I'm the hayseed!"

Harden rose to meet his subordinate's assault. "Hayseed? No. You're street. You're a stray dog somebody picked up off the curb. And you're playing to form now. Stealing and lying and snarling to get what you want."

The two men were nose to nose, leaning across the desk. Macher succeeded in pulling Jackie away and said in his ear, "Let's get out of here."

Overhearing this, Harden said, "Neither of you is going anywhere. You"—he motioned at Jackie—"You're gonna hand over the hard drive you stole from the morgue, and you"—he glared at Macher—"are under arrest for trespassing. Thompson, Harris, secure these two men. While I call this in." The portly chief reached for the desk phone.

Several things happened at once.

Jackie snatched the receiver out of Harden's hand and with blinding speed wrapped the cord around the man's head and uplifted right hand, pinning it to his face, leaving him involuntarily mimicking a pose of the Scream.

Shelton, the female security officer, stepped between Thompson and Harris, deftly tripping one man while simultaneously slapping a handcuff on the other's left wrist and jerking him backward before he could regain his balance.

Macher, edgy already with the intensity of the moment, cried out in shock as the cell phone in his shirt pocket went off, buzzing him like a miniature defibrillator paddle. He grasped at his pocket and answered the incoming call as the commotion in the room settled.

Jackie snatched a set of cuffs off the fallen guard sprawled face down beside the desk and secured his hands behind his back. The shock of what had just happened wore off Harden first and he tried to get to his feet, tearing at the phone cord around his face and neck.

Jackie shoved him back into the wobbly desk chair, nearly toppling him over. Shelton steadied it with a foot. They came face to face as Jackie jumped over the desk to ensure Harden didn't try to get up again.

"What are you doing Shelton?" he said with a surprised smile. "You're crazy, woman. You didn't need to get into this. You're sure as hell in it now."

Shelton was breathing hard with the exertion and still held the loose end of the cuffs restraining Thompson, who had fallen to one knee and stayed there more out of shock at what was happening than her forcing him.

"Help me," she said, pulling the man's free arm behind him to finish cuffing him. "I did what you did, Smith. Instinct."

Jackie shook his head. "You picked a side pretty quick. You better hope you're right."

Harden regained his senses enough to glare at them both and say, "You're gonna burn for this."

"Probably," Jackie said. "But I jumped off that cliff already."

Macher, who had been listening to his phone with one hand clamped over his free ear, looked shell-shocked. "That was my boss at the paper. He got a heads-up from a producer over at WRAL TV. A video of me soliciting sex with underage girls got delivered to them a few hours ago. It shows me asking a pimp for an underage girl. And"—his voice faltered—"and it shows me in a hotel room, ah, it shows me with what looks to be a girl who can't be more than twelve or fourteen years old… how?"

Harden chimed in, "The same way this asshole showed you a video of Tabitha Treeright walking around this hospital when she's dead, that's how. Getting a taste of it for yourself. Deep fake. You should educate yourself before you fall for a con. And," he added ominously to Jackie, "I've seen a video of you with a girl too who looks awful similar to the one your friend just described."

"Shut up, Harden," Jackie said. "The one thing doesn't prove the other." Looking at Macher, he said, "I'm the only person who touched that video from the morgue and it's on hundred percent real. I don't know anything about depth fakers…"

"Deep fake." Macher corrected.

"Deep fake, then," said Jackie. "I don't know what it is or how it's done. But even if I did, you just saw the girl on the feed that I never touched. And Shelton here says she saw the girl in the flesh. Nothing fake about that."

"It's pretty simple," Harden said, addressing the newsman. "Seems either all these videos are fake or all of them are real. You're going to need to decide. Maybe Jackie here is just a dupe and somebody else doctored the tapes. Maybe we can set this all right."

He fixed Macher in his gaze. "C'mon, Macher. You're smarter than this. You know what to do when the facts don't add up. You're gonna let your life—your work in this city and your name— you're gonna let that go on a fairy tale about a dead girl getting up and walking out of the morgue of this hospital? Because a pedophile found Jesus and called her from the dead?? Stupid. Stoooopid. Help me now and we can help each other."

Jackie narrowed his eyes. "What are you talking about, Harden? How do you know about deep fake videos and what do you have to do with setting anything right? Is your tipster Syd DeVito? Did he get to you? What's he promised you? You're the dupe if you think he won't throw you away when he gets what he wants out of you."

Harden sat still and smiled, tight-lipped. No need to stir this soup any more. Let it come to a boil.

"Jackie, this is my life," Macher said. "They told my boss the story runs at the top of the news tonight. I'm ruined if it does."

Jackie checked his watch. "It's three-thirty now. The story won't run till five. Give it an hour. That will leave us half an hour. Tell your boss we will deliver a bigger story than one about a couple of pedophiles." His tone was sure but his eyes were pleading.

Macher looked from Harden's smug countenance to Jackie's inquiring but firm expression. Was it possible that it was all a fraud? His years of experience chasing stories down weighed heavy on him. So many liars and lies and shades of truth and spin. And all of his work and reputation on the line over the most ridiculously impossible story of all.

Were his emotions in the way? Probably. He loved Jackie. He wanted to believe him.

Wanted. Love. Belief. Words. He'd made a life of putting words together into stories, and, he thought, telling the truth. Although he was no scientist, he had always thought of truth scientifically as an object; it stood on its own. Here he was in a proverbial moment of truth; and it felt anything but objective; it was all latticed through with feeling and possibility.

Looking one last time at Harden, he made his choice.

CHAPTER SIXTY

Tabitha yawned as she entered the room of adults. Getting into her own bed had been delicious and she'd instantly fallen into a drooling deep sleep.

She awoke after what felt like hours feeling disoriented. The shades were drawn and blinds closed. She heard a hard rain pattering the windows and the low murmuring of several people talking.

As she walked down the hallway toward the sound, she remembered both where she was and where she had been. It was comforting to be in her home, she thought, but it was also somehow less than being in that other place; the place she called Light land. A silly name, she admitted to herself, but then again it was the most simple and true way to give words to that place.

Since returning to this place—where the light was really so shabby as to not deserve to be called light—she had, it seemed, increasingly become more herself than when she woke up in the cold room in utter darkness. Bits and pieces of her felt like they found their way back.

It was like the old *Terminator* movie her dad loved to watch where the bad robot was shattered into a million pieces and they all spontaneously reassembled themselves. She smiled at this thought. She would have to tell her dad. She hated that movie but now she could share it with him and say she was a bad robot. He would laugh. She came through the door with this thought on her mind.

Three men sat facing her mom and dad. Two of them looked at her and then away with the typically dismissive "this is an adult conversation" body language. The third, an older man in a black suit with that weird white choker thing across his throat, did not look away. He met her eyes and they recognized each other. It was Hannah Taylor's priest from her church.

She watched his expression go from inquiry to recollection to shock. His mouth fell open, and without averting his gaze, he crossed himself slowly and deliberately with long pauses at each station. She read his wordless lips: *In the name of the Father. And the Son. And the Holy Spirit. Amen.*

She repeated the amen silently as one of the two other men, the fat one in the middle, gave a somewhat exasperated sigh, perturbed at being interrupted by the girl entering at the moment he was ready to fire a retort at Mullenix. "The church used claims of miracles and the miraculous to gain control and keep control over the people…"

He stopped mid-sentence as Tabitha passed between him and her mother and father, a look of disdain blooming on his face.

Daniel, who had just risen to his feet, done with the meeting and these unhelpful counselors, put his arms around the girl and embraced her tenderly.

"Tab, what are you doing up? You looked ready for a good long sleep when we got here."

"How long did I sleep, Dad? It felt like I was asleep for hours." Sensing Daly's glaring eyes at her back she said, "I'm sorry to bug you while you're in a meeting."

Wanda stood up and joined her husband's embrace of Tabitha. Taking the girl's face in both her hands, she pulled up her chin and kissed her. "You're not bugging us at all," she said.

Wanda looked to Daniel to see what he would do now.

Before her husband could react, Mullenix got up from his chair and thudded down on his knees, raising both hands over his bowed head. He began praying loudly in a clear baritone, "O Father, Lord of the heavens and the earth, Jesus the blessed one, resurrection and the life, Holy Spirit, gift of Father and Son, there is none like You. There is nothing too hard for you or too high for you…"

The other two men looked at the priest incredulously. Tabitha gently disengaged from her parents and joined the priest on his knees. She took one of his hands in her own and laughed a deep, rich laugh that echoed and lit the room aglow as if it were sunshine flooding in through an open curtain. Mullenix spontaneously joined her, and Daniel and Wanda fell in with them in a contagion of raucous, unrestrained belly laughter.

Hammond and Daly sat outside the ring of mirth looking in, Hammond with a stupid grin and Daly sucking in his lips as if he'd just eaten a lemon. Unaware and careless, the infected foursome went right on laughing in swells and fits and starts until they collapsed in various postures of repose on the floor, gasping for breath and holding their stomachs.

"Ohhhh," said Wanda. "That feels soooo nice. To laugh like that! I can't remember the last time."

Her husband said, "Never! I never laughed like that in my life!" He wiped tears from his eyes.

Mullenix, who had laughed louder and longer, and even, if the truth be told, howled a little, giggled. Seeing the older man in his dignified priestly suit giggling set such a contrast that the other three tittered in the edge of another laughing spasm. Their sore bellies were all that belayed them.

Hammond, still sporting a clueless grin said, "Wish I was in on the joke…" He trailed off wistfully, waiting for someone to let him in on whatever was so funny. When no one made a move to enlighten him, his expression darkened. He wasn't used to being on the outside and didn't know how to take the goings on.

Daly, offended by the inexplicable and undignified outburst, finally ejaculated, "What's wrong with you people? If I hadn't drunk the coffee myself I'd think you'd all been drugged!"

This set the four tittering again and groaning over their hurting bellies.

"She didn't drink the coffee," Hammond pointed at Tabitha.

"No, I didn't," Tabitha said.

"No, she didn't," agreed Daly, sourly. "And I'm not sure who she is."

Wanda, disliking Daly's tone toward her daughter, unfolded herself from the floor and stood up. "You don't? She's been to your church service with us quite a few times. More than to Father Mullenix's, I'd say. You don't recognize her? This is my daughter, Tabitha."

While she spoke Tabitha stood up and approached Daly, reaching out a hand to shake with him. Their hands touched at the moment her mother said her name. Daly jerked his hand away as if he had touched an electric fence. Tabitha, nonplussed, remained standing in front of the man with her hand extended, a pleasant smile on her face.

"Nice to see you again, Reverend Daly," she said. When the man remained frozen in place, looking half horrified and half angry, she turned to Hammond and extended a hand which he accepted in slow motion. She grasped his hand in a confident grip and looked him in the eyes as her father had taught her.

"I don't think I ever met you," she said. "I'm Tabitha Treeright. "Your name is?"

"Ah, aha, I'm Pastor Marty. Marty Hammond," he stammered. "No. Never met you, me." He shook himself comically. "Sorry. I mean we've never met."

Still holding his hand firmly, Tabitha said, "It's very nice to meet you."

The door slammed as if to punctuate her sentence. All eyes turned toward the sound. Jarry Daly had fled the room without a word.

CHAPTER SIXTY-ONE

Breathing heavy and moving fast through the rainy parking lot, Daly was reaching for the door of his black Buick LaCrosse when a strong hand grabbed him from behind.

"Shit!" he said.

"Take it easy, Reverend," a familiar voice said soothingly. "No need for all that."

He turned to see Syd DeVito, smiling smugly in a black raincoat and hat.

"What's got you so jumpy?"

Daly sketched out the strange meeting with the Treerights and its unsettling ending.

"So you've seen the doppelgänger too?" DeVito said.

"Dopple… what? Who?"

"The girl passing herself off as Tabitha Treeright. I already met her at the jail."

"But the governor… his wife... they introduced her as their daughter! You're saying that's not Tabitha Treeright?!"

Syd gave Daly's face an assessing glance. "I'm saying what everyone knows. Tabitha Treeright died in Duke Hospital. I saw her and I saw the death certificate. Now you tell me. Do dead people come back to life?"

He let the question hang in the air between them like a canary in a coal mine. Watching Daly's eyes, he knew.

"Right. I thought I had you pegged. So what explanation is there? Man on the verge of the presidency. Many political enemies. Few opportunities to hurt him or slow him down—and then this. What's more likely? A dead girl walking out of a morgue or a political trick to take down an invincible opponent?"

"But her own mother and father!? They know their daughter, don't they? How could she fool them? Who could pull off something like that?"

"Let me ask you a question. Do you believe in a literal resurrection? That Jesus literally and physically rose from the dead?"

"Of course not," Daly said without thinking. He looked surprised and afraid. He was used to speaking frankly among his trusted peers but was always more reticent with the unwashed masses.

"Of course not," repeated DeVito. "Because it is impossible. Don't fret. You're talking to a friend. So how do you explain the people who said they saw Jesus alive after he was dead? The ones who told everyone he was walking around and having meetings with them even after the crucifixion?"

Daly shook himself. He realized his heart had been hammering from the moment the girl walked into the meeting. It felt like he'd had a close call of some kind; a brush with insanity. This man he barely knew was throwing him a lifeline of cold logic and rationality. He took it, feeling his heart rate begin to normalize.

He felt foolish, the one thing he tolerated least in himself or anyone else, and found himself eager to distance himself from that feeling and that image. He shifted into a familiar academic identity and tone.

"Well," he said, "there are several theories about that. Some suggest he didn't die on the cross. He passed out or fainted or some such thing. Personally I don't care for this idea. What would they do with him when he woke up? I mean he would still have been a wanted criminal. And," the reverend paused and licked his lips, "don't men like you and I know we always have to ask who benefits from any given situation?"

Philips had never heard this before or given much thought to it. Heretofore he'd had little use for churches or clerics unless they presented opportunities for votes. Right now, every single vote might hang on something this pretentious egg head might know. And Syd knew how to get what he needed out of men like Daly.

"Yes. Men like you and I. So who would fake it? And why?"

DeVito could tell by the way Daly stood up taller that he'd read his man. It gave him a sense of control in the midst of the Tabitha shit-show that he could still push men's buttons. Familiar ground. Now just let him talk, see where it leads.

Daly said, "There's a lot to this. Some would say it's the greatest fraud in the history of the world. I guess you wonder why me and others like me would give our lives for it."

Syd shrugged. "No judgment here. I imagine you do it for the same reason people like us do most of what we do; the bigger picture."

Jesus, Syd thought, *the man's head actually looked like a balloon that might pop.*

Daly said, "Exactly! So what if the resurrection is a scam…that doesn't negate the man's teaching! The principles! These people who need the supernatural… they miss the purity of the message. The superiority of an exemplary life! They dilute it with miracles. It isn't Jesus's fault people took advantage of the moment and used him to promote their political causes."

Political causes. Syd's language. Yes. How could he turn this sham to his advantage? A new train of thought started up in his mind while the egg head droned on.

R. Kenward Jones

"The other theory is more modern and comes from a greater understanding of the human psyche. The people who followed Jesus around all those years invested their whole identities into him being the chosen one; the Messiah. The psychology of going from Jesus hailed as King of the Jews one week and the next seeing him arrested, condemned, and executed... it was too much. It caused a mental break."

Philips nodded. "So what did this break do to them?"

"It made them vulnerable. The shock and the sadness overwhelmed them. They couldn't accept his death as a reality. They took some of his sayings and decided he was telling them he was stronger than death. That he would conquer it. This set the stage for what came next. They became useful idiots for the movers and shakers."

Syd said, "So you're saying all the stories about Jesus rising from the dead are all made up from nothing?"

"I didn't say it was all made up. There are always elements of truth in all stories. It's what makes a good story good. What educated people have concluded is that the followers of Jesus wanted him to be the Messiah; they wanted him to come back to life and to validate all his teachings and their faith in him. They wanted it to be true so badly that they did see him. They projected him onto everything and everyone.

"There are hints of it in the Bible. The first woman to meet Jesus when he rises from the dead doesn't recognize him. He shows up with some people on the road and they don't recognize him until some magic happens and then 'poof,' there's Jesus. Jesus wasn't there but they saw him anyway. Their minds snapped. They needed him to be alive and so they made him alive."

Daly paused. DeVito stared through him. The silence grew. Finally DeVito said, emphasizing each word, "They needed him to be alive."

Daly said, "Yes. And so he was. To them."

"What about the body in the grave? Whoever disposed of it knew the truth," DeVito said.

"That's a rather difficult question."

"How so?"

"It's one thing for the followers of Jesus to need him to be alive and therefore see him, but it's another for them to perpetrate a hoax they were in on and then pretend to see him. That would blow up the psychological explanation. It would also mean his closest followers would have suffered horrible torture and execution knowing full well they were suffering for a lie. No. I don't think that's reasonable. But other explanations aren't easier. You're a man of politics. You see the issues I'm sure."

"Enlighten me," DeVito said, already fitting this into his own story; his own spin,

"Who would benefit by Jesus's body disappearing? Who benefits by the possibility that he was actually the Messiah? Not Rome. A fake messiah was trouble enough for them to stomach. The Jewish leaders? They had just done everything in their power to prove he was a fraud. His body going missing would only make them answer questions they didn't want asked. So who benefits from stealing his dead body? It can't be his followers. It can't be Rome. It can't be the Jews…"

DeVito nodded. "But according to you somebody did it. Either that or…"

"Oh, somebody did it. Dead people don't walk out of graves," Daly scoffed.

"So who risked it and what did they have to gain?"

"You only need to look at the Middle East today to get a clue. When you see these young Arabs who are barely into their teens blowing themselves up, what do you think?"

DeVito was puzzled at the non sequitur. He shrugged.

"They're trapped in powerlessness. They see no future. They don't see any possible change for their people. They're stuck. When I see a suicide bomber I see a person who decided that the risk of certain death—and what it may hold—is worth taking. It may bring change. I see a metaphor: it's better to blow it all up and start over in the rubble with whatever and whoever is left!"

"But aren't they motivated by a belief in their God?"

Daly sighed. "What God? They're as deluded as the Christians and the Jews. They manufactured their God and their leaders manipulated them just like every religion does. Nietzche was right when he said all truth claims are plays for power."

Fuck, Syd thought, *people actually talk like this? Nietzche? Power plays?* He watched Daly's eyes and kept the contempt out of his own. Useful idiots came in all flavors.

Daly went on, "These pawns are played by thinking men, not religious fools. There were people who saw in Jesus a way to burn down the system or blow it up; a system that wasn't working for them. They played him like a hand of cards. Who were they? I think it was a disenchanted group of the not-so-powerful nameless class of people just below the powerful. Ambitious but frustrated. Jews? Most likely. But I see no reason why it couldn't have been Romans too. These kinds of people find each other and are remarkably inoculated against the prejudices of other men by their love of power and money. You know the saying 'politics makes strange bedfellows'?"

DeVito nodded.

"These people found each other. They infiltrated Jesus's followers. And they had their inside man." Daly paused to see if DeVito would fill in the blank.

"Judas?"

"Judas. Yes. But he wasn't the only one, I'm sure. People like this never let a whole plan ride on the back of one mule. They probably had several close followers. There was, for instance, another disciple who gets very little ink but was the perfect person for the job. He was a Zealot. Simon. The Zealots were a group dedicated to the violent overthrow of Rome. To me he is a key. Zealots were outlaws to both the Romans and the Jews. Simon Zealotes. Right there under their noses," Daly mused.

"And so... what?"

"He kept them—the Zealots—in touch with the useful pawn, Jesus. He was there. He had the heartbeat of the little movement. He probably helped them stage the big public moments when the crowds created such a stir over Jesus. They had hopes he would bring on a spontaneous uprising which would throw off Roman rule and the religious hierarchy at the same time.

"If Jesus did surge to power on the tide of popular opinion, they would have their man on the inside still and they could manipulate him from there. But their hopes failed when the Jewish leaders forced a showdown with Rome. Put them on the spot. Planted their own agitators in the crowds and turned the tide against him. Jesus went too far too fast. The Zealots lost their chance and the pawn fell."

DeVito interrupted, "So what did this accomplish then?"

"Nothing. The opportunity passed..." Daly paused for effect. "But here's where the story turns. I believe it is the best explanation for all that happened next. Their attempt to start a coup failed but their determination didn't. They saw an opportunity in the failure. They remembered the claims Jesus made about rising from the dead and they hit upon a bold scheme: what would happen if they stole the body and made it look like he really did rise?!

"It would confound the Jewish leaders and it would stir the people up to stand up to the Romans. If they believed they had a leader who defeated death, what could make them afraid? They'd be emboldened to overthrow the systems the Zealots wanted torn down—they would do all the hard work for them!"

Bang! There it was. Syd heard it and saw it at the same time; a leader who defeated death… would be unstoppable.

Daly was still talking, "It was as if they'd been given this perfect gift if they could just take advantage of it. They had to move fast. I think at some point they added the idea of a body double. Find one of their number who looked enough like Jesus that he could pass the smell test.

"They had Simon to coach him up with some inside dope on how the man talked and the kinds of things he said. I believe it could have gone as far as buying his garments from the soldiers who stripped him and gambled for them at the foot of the cross. And the body double could always claim that dying and rising altered his appearance and voice. Makes sense right? Who could go through all that and not change?"

DeVito's brain buzzed with possibility. He said, "Could they pull it off? Wouldn't those closest to him see through all this?"

Daly said, "They did pull it off, didn't they? Not that it worked out the way they thought it would. It brought change all right, just not the change they were looking for.

"Like most revolutionaries they had courage to blow up the system but they lacked a coherent plan for what to do when the dust settled. And sometimes the explosion isn't big enough or isn't placed properly to bring the building down. Sometimes it's the equivalent of whacking a nest of yellow jackets with no idea what's going to happen next.

"They did get their war started. They got Rome's full attention. The Romans came and burned it to the ground, Jerusalem. The Jewish state for all intents and purposes ceased to exist from then until…"

"1948," DeVito broke in.

"Yes. Funny thing about what Rome did in Jerusalem," Daly mused.

"What?" said DeVito.

"By order of the emperor, they razed the city. Tore down the walls and burned it. But the thing that destroyed the Jews was the order to tear down the temple."

"Because it destroyed their most sacred place?"

"Yes, but it also had a major unintended consequence that doomed the Jewish religious leaders. It put a punctuation mark on the apocalyptic events Jesus seemed to have foretold." Daly smiled.

"Seemed to have foretold?"

"Remember what I said about the Bible having all the elements of mythology. This is part of how legends and myths grow up around a person. The people who studied this most—you ever hear of the Jesus Seminar? Probably not. It was a group of scholars who set out to study every word and deed of Jesus and discover if he really said or did it and to try to explain why these words and deeds ended up in the Bible.

"They also discovered the Bible was written much later than we originally thought. It had to be. Nobody could have predicted what was going to happen with Rome. What we learned is that some of Jesus's followers took some very obscure things he said about apocalyptic events and embellished them. Before you know it, the story gets started that the whole Roman-Jewish conflict was all prophesied by Jesus and especially the throwing down of every stone of the temple."

"How did that ruin the Jewish leadership?"

"The followers of Jesus already thought they had seen him come back to life. They gained a following and it grew, but when the temple came down and the Jews were at their lowest, the Christians not only had an explanation; they had a fulfilled prophecy. They had a story to tell to make sense out of all that happened. Stories are powerful things. People attach to stories. The best politicians know how to tell stories."

"So you're calling the Christian leaders politicians?"

"I'm saying they knew how to tell their story and help the people find their place in it. And they needed it. The Jews were done. They lost their national identity. Christianity gave them an identity. Look at what happened!

"Within three hundred years, the Roman Empire became a Christian empire and took over the western world. These people who had no power—who lived in an insignificant speck on the map; a backwater of a place like Jerusalem, who had no money or influence—these people had a story and nothing else and they turned the world upside down.

"Imagine what they might have done if they started out with some real advantages; influence, power, money, not to mention the ability to tell their story with the methods at our disposal."

"Hmmm, yes," DeVito said. "Imagine."

CHAPTER SIXTY-TWO

The cell was chilly. Doug pulled the scratchy wool blanket over his mouth and nose and let it warm his breath. He was alone.

He thought of the drive from Norfolk to Duke. The rain accumulating on the windshield precisely at a rate that no interval setting would work without that damnable skidding squeak. The loquacious woman. The money in the sun visor. The rip-off at the diner. And the voice.

All of the events of the past several days ran together. He tried to filter them. He tried to get them to play back with the audio tuned to only one channel. The voice. What did it sound like? Would he know it if he heard it again?

But he had heard it again. He heard it when the big man was going to hammer him to pulp. And again when the man in the interrogation room wanted to call the little girl a liar.

He told them it was God who spoke to him, but was it? *Why would God speak to a ChoMo like me?* he thought. *What does that say about God?*

Immediately another thought came. *Maybe it wasn't God. Maybe it was your perverted heart. You like to look at naked little girls. You wanted to touch them too, didn't you. And more...you like... Stop it!*

Images flooded his mind. He fought to keep them away. *No! I don't want to see this anymore!*

Sure you do. You want to remember the times you seduced them online. When you tried tricking them into meeting you. If you ever get the chance, you will meet them. You will touch them.

He broke out into a sweat. He threw off the covers, got out of bed, and stood in the middle of the cell. Try as he would, the faces of too-young girls bobbed to the top of his consciousness like apples in a tub of water. He felt the beginnings of arousal in his groin.

Coincidental with this attack he felt an overwhelming sense of vileness—of being filthy. The feeling pervaded his mouth as if he had suddenly fallen into that tub of apples and discovered they floated not in fresh water but in slimy, green, brackish swamp water.

He had fallen in with his mouth wide open and in his mind the taste and smell was so strong he gagged and spit on the cool concrete floor. He bent over, gasping, wondering at the realness of these sensations. He had never experienced anything like it.

The cell went from chilled to unbearably hot. All those girls. Their faces. Their bodies. He knew he was what they called in the meetings a "white knuckler," a dry drunk. He knew it because he spent a lot of time avoiding his substance of choice, which was underage girls.

Staying away from something was just as tiring as giving in to it; either way it defined your life. He learned in prison how to trade the one for the other. He learned it well.

The good side, the side that worked hard to stay away from child porn and seducing little girls was exhausting and left little room for any other identity, but the bad side got you locked away eating surplus government mac and cheese off tin trays three times a week and sleeping with one eye open to guard against the brutal justice of the criminal hierarchy.

He learned to keep all the memories in locked mental strong boxes in the corridors of his mind marked "no trespassing." He did it so well that it got him paroled. He did it so well, sometimes he even forgot those corridors were there.

But there were triggers, yes there were. And when those triggers got tripped he could find himself trespassing and checking the locks on those boxes.

That was different than this. This was a steamroller plowing through all the safeguards and bursting open the memories that no one knew, even the ones he hid from himself.

I'm no better than I was. I'm just as bad as I ever was, he thought. *I'm the same ChoMo they locked away. I'm worse. How can I be the person God would send anywhere to do anything? It doesn't make sense. It can't be true. It isn't true. I never heard anything but my own perverted heart.*

He thought of the pictures he had seen of the governor and his family before all this happened. He remembered the girl. She was just his type. Picturing Tabitha Treeright had been one of those triggers; one of those times he'd rattled the locks on his sobriety before running away, heart palpitating, to the safety of the good side.

She was my type. That's right. I never heard God. I heard me. And I wanted to see that girl. I wanted to touch her.

He gagged involuntarily and crumpled to his knees. "Oh," he said out loud in a cracked cry of a voice. "Ohhhhhhhhh." He sobbed uncontrollably and pressed himself into the smooth concrete, asking it to absorb him as if he had never been born.

Keys clanged in the cell door. Windsor had no concept of time; how long he had lain there. Long enough to feel the cold and stiffness in his joints. His eyes and nose were crusted with sleep and dried mucus from crying. A single guard came through the door and let out a shocked exclamation at seeing the prisoner prone on the floor. He rushed to him.

"Windsor! What happened?"

It was one of the guards from the previous day shift who had escorted Doug's would-be assassin.

"Nothing. Nothing." Doug said. "Old prison habit when my back was feeling about to go out. Sleep on the floor."

The guard looked doubtful at this, and scrutinizing Doug's face, helped him to his feet without further questioning. Doug rubbed his arms and legs, trying to get blood circulating through his extremities.

"Well, you might want to wash up a bit. You've got a visitor wants to see you and you ought to be presentable; it's a priest."

"A priest? Who sent for a priest? I'm not Catholic and I don't think I'm dying. At least not yet." Doug managed a half smile.

"He wasn't sent for, he was sent from."

"Huh?"

"No one here asked for him to come. He says the governor sent him over to talk with you. He's in Interrogation Room One"

Windsor questioned this with his eyes.

"Yeah, the boss said not to put y'all in the tank."

"Okay, let's go see what he wants."

CHAPTER SIXTY-THREE

Doug had never met a priest before. The person waiting in Interrogation One was the picture of a Catholic priest you'd have if you closed your eyes pieced together the images you'd seen on television and in movies.

"Mr. Windsor," he said, rising and extending his hand to Doug, who tentatively took it. "I'm Father Mullenix."

They scrutinized each other as they took chairs on opposite sides of the table in the middle of the brightly-lit room and sat down. Mullenix indicated that he wanted to be left alone with the prisoner and the guard stepped outside the door.

"Your first name is Doug?" the priest said. When Doug nodded, he added, "May I call you Doug?"

"Sure, ah, Father? I'm not sure what to call you, not being Catholic and all." Doug said.

"You can call me Father if you like. My friends call me Nexie... short for Mulli-nex. Goes all the way back to my grade school days on the playground."

Doug considered this. He never thought of priests as having a past. His image of them was as a fully-formed chunk of religious imagery that fell out of the sky or was delivered one day by some holy version of a stork. He smiled at this. The priest saw and guessed at where his mind was.

"Hard imagining priests as people with a past life?"

Doug looked embarrassed at having his mind read.

"You're not the first person to feel that way, by a long shot. And I guess a lot of people in my profession like to present themselves just that way... like they put away everything that came before when they put on the collar. But me, if you don't mind"—he reached up and snapped off the white collar at his throat and unbuttoned his top shirt button—"I've had this on too long in the past couple of days. I don't like to feel I'm hiding behind this thing."

He placed it on the table before them. Without the collar, the priest transformed in an instant into an average old man. Grey chest hairs sprouted over the top of a worn out t-shirt and untidy facial hair stood out around his otherwise well-groomed beard.

"Ahh. So much better," he said, rubbing his neck. "Where were we?"

"Having a past," Doug said.

"Right. I've got one. How about you?"

Doug thought he detected a slight upturn on the corners of the priest's mouth and decided to play along.

He deadpanned, "Me? You could say I'm not unfamiliar with our current surroundings…"

Mullenix chuckled warmly, spreading his hands before him on the stainless steel table.

"Furniture is classy at least. And you sure can't lose any of it." He faked straining to lift up the table from its bolts in the floor.

"Yeah, ah, Father—I think I'll stick with Father if it's okay— they like things to stay in their place when you're inside. Stuff that's out of place tends to get people nervous."

"I see," mused the priest. "Hence the reason I'm here." He let this fall between them, waiting for Doug to grasp it but the non sequitur left him flat footed.

"Dead people generally stay where they're put, Doug. Hmm? They don't move a muscle. It's the first thing I noticed when I first saw a dead body. The old lady that lived next door to me and my mom ran to our door one morning and said she thought her husband died in his sleep. When we ran over and went to the bedroom, I knew the man was gone. It was the utter stillness that spoke to me. Dead. There was no animation. That's a strange word for it—conjures up images of wild animals more than people—but it's a good word. I've seen a lot of dead bodies since then." The priest seemed to hitch and catch, like a broken DVD.

"I guess so in your line of work," Doug interjected.

"What? Yes. But more in Vietnam than in the collar."

"You? Fought? In Vietnam?"

"We all have a past, Doug. Lots of people came back from there and it turned them away from God, but there were also lots that came back with a renewed belief in God and a determination to find out about faith. In a funny way I guess seeing all that death led me to pursue the meaning of life. And when I did…" He shrugged.

"You found God?"

"Yes."

The two men considered each other momentarily like wrestlers about to go into the opening clinch. Mullenix moved first.

"What happened in the morgue, Doug? No, let's back up. Why were you in the morgue? How did you get here? What brought you here?"

Doug thought of backing away from this clinch, of closing down and keeping away from this man and every other human being. The filthy feeling of last night hung over him like body odor. He smelled his reeking self, its embarrassing stench.

Mullenix must smell it, too. There was no shower, no soap that would make it go away. Doug thought himself unfit for any contact with humanity.

Again he saw the priest reading him like a large-print book. He hung his head and put both hands over his face, hoping to disappear.

Mullenix slowly reached across the table and grasped his wrist with a warm hand. He gently pulled Doug's hands from his face. Doug kept his eyes turned down. Mullenix cleared his throat, continued to hold Doug's wrist, and waited.

Doug began to feel the weight of the silence like a heavy winter coat. He remained still under it; enduring it. There was nothing but the sound of the ventilator and their breathing.

He felt the warmth of the hand on his arm. He focused on it. Human touch. A choice. Remaining. Insistently gentle. Unrestrained keeping. And the silence bled away into stillness and the emptiness became full. He caught his breath as if breaking the surface from deep water. He let his gaze rise to meet the priest's. Tears pooled in the old man's deep-socketed grey eyes.

"Peace," the priest said, just above a whisper.

"Yes," said Doug. "Yes. Is there any? For someone like me?"

"Tell me your story, son. It's safe here now."

Without hesitation and without knowing why, Doug told him everything that had transpired. He brought him up to date to the breakdown he'd experienced the night before.

"I don't know what happened in the morgue, Father. I really don't. I thought I heard the voice of God in all of this but after last night… I don't think it's possible. I'm a child molester. I've done a lot of bad things. Things that no one knows about. Like I said, I thought I was following the voice of God but it was probably the voice I always listened to back then. The one that told me to look at little girls. And to touch them. Except it disguised itself better. That's all.

It got in under the radar. Made me think I was doing something good when really I was doing the worst thing ever... touching a dead little girl."

The peace that had compelled him to speak all that he had spoken evaporated with this last bit of confession. He pulled away from Mullenix's grasp and sobbed into his hands. The priest did not withdraw his arm but let it fall prone on the table.

"Doug? Doug? Did you touch Tabitha?" There was no accusation or malice in his voice. Not a hint of justice to be meted out, only a question to be considered. "Did you? Think Doug."

"I already told you what I am," Doug snarled at him suddenly, like a cornered animal. "What do you think? Stupid man. You came here to get a confession? Right? They sent you here to get me to say it. Okay. I touched her. I touched her." He put his hands in front of his downturned eyes, searching them for the filth he expected to see there. "I touched her. She was naked and cold and blue..." He choked on the memory of the girl's appearance and the clammy feeling of her skin.

"Yes. She was. And yes, you did. But why did you touch her, Doug? And what did you say to her?"

At the mention of this last question, Doug caught his breath. It arrested the spiral of condemnation. He reached out and took hold of it like a man grasping a vine as he tumbled over the edge of a cliff. It held. Pressing his arms around his chest to slow its heaving, he fought to control his voice.

"What... did they... tell you... I said to her?"

Mullenix, who had never retreated a hair's breadth, said, "The morgue attendant and the responding officers thought they heard you say something vile. They said you repeated her name and..." He hesitated only an instant and went on. "They said you were saying, 'Tabitha, cum,' Doug. And you repeatedly said it while you put your hands on her. It's why they nearly beat you to death. But I think you were saying something else." He paused and let Doug's breathing slow.

Doug slowly looked up. "What?"

Mullenix reached into his jacket pocket and pulled out a paperback New Testament. Doug recognized it as the one he had taken from the hospital chapel on the night he visited the morgue.

The priest held it out in both hands. "Wanda Treeright gave me this, just now. Look at what happens when I let this open naturally," he said as he fanned the pages. "It's new and appears to only have been opened to one page; one page that is folded over. You know what that spot is Doug, because this is your Bible."

Doug shook his head. "Not mine. I took it from the chapel. I would've given it back…"

Mullenix ignored this and went on, "It opens to a passage about Jesus raising a little girl from the dead." He ran his finger over the page and read it. "After he put them all out, he took the child's father and mother and the disciples who were with him, and went in where the child was. He took her by the hand and said to her, *Talitha koum*!' (which means 'Little girl, I say to you, get up!)." He locked eyes with Doug.

"It's what you were saying over the girl, isn't it?"

"It is."

"This is why you came here, isn't it?"

"I don't know why I came here. I told you what happened. I was driving and I thought I heard something. And that led to another something, and another. And there I was, standing in the chapel and the Bible was open to the place where it tells that story. So I went to the morgue and said those words. And…"

"And?"

"I got the shit kicked out of me not once but twice and I got thrown in here!"

"Didn't you tell Daniel Treeright that his daughter was alive? That you were sure of it?"

Doug looked miserably back at Mullenix. "I did. I did. I'm a con. I'll say anything to get out of a jam. It's what we do."

"But that's not all that you did. Didn't you stop a guy from tearing your head off with nothing more than some words? They tell me you dropped a killer like a tree. They say the man himself is telling the whole jail about you. You're a healer... a prophet. You can see secrets no one else could know. What about that? Did that happen? Is that a con?"

Doug looked confused and doubtful. "I… I… ah, don't know. It was clear and now it's not. It's like the voice. I thought I heard and now I don't know. Why would God talk with me? I'm a bad person. Very bad. It doesn't make sense for God to tell me anything… does it? Like I said before, a god who would talk with someone like me— a god who would use someone like me to do anything for him, would be a strange god.

"Think about it, Father. Would you send a liar to tell someone a message you wanted them to believe? Or send a thief to go and get a pile of money from the bank for you? Wouldn't the people on the other end have some real doubts about the message or the money? Rightly so. Rightly so. And"—he reached up and pulled back the hair on the right side of his head and tilted forward to show the priest the ugly black railroad tracks stitched into his scalp—"they'd be justified to show how unwelcome a messenger like that would be."

Mullenix was nonplussed. He continued holding out the Bible. "Doug, this book is full of stories about people like you, and me. There aren't any good guys in here."

The priest's self-inclusion wasn't lost on Doug. "You?" he said. "What do you and I have to do with each other?"

"You haven't been listening very closely, Doug. We all have a past. We all miss the mark; even people who look good to everyone else don't live up to their own standards. Why do you think so many 'successful' people kill themselves or wreck their lives with the pursuit of more and more when the rest of us would be happy to achieve half of what they've done? To answer your question directly, if God only used perfect vessels to do His work, nothing would get done."

"So are you here to get me to confess what I did in the morgue or not?" Doug asked. "Cause I'm confused. You come in here and ask me to confess—set me up real nice with all this talk about peace and now it seems like you're trying to talk me out of confessing?"

Mullenix's eyes widened as he finally caught on to the disconnect. "Doug, please forgive me. Even after all these years wearing this suit I still forget. I still see Nexie in the mirror and not a priest. I'm not here to get a confession out of you! I'm not here to hear a confession!"

Doug looked more confused. "Then why are you here?"

"Because of what happened in the morgue! The miracle! The resurrection! Tabitha!"

"What are you talking about? Nothing happened in the morgue other than an ass whoopin'."

"You didn't think so when you talked to the governor the night they brought you here. And you didn't think so when you met with the governor and his wife and Tabitha!"

"I've had some time to think since then. The other man, DeVito, didn't think it was her. None of it makes sense; least of all that I should have anything to do with a miracle."

"You're right about that, Doug. It doesn't make sense. What's happened is not rational. It's supernatural. Tabitha is alive. I've seen her and talked with her myself. I've touched her hand. She's alive! It did happen. You did hear from God! You were the one He called! She's alive! Daniel Treeright sent me here to ask you how it happened and what to do for you. You understand his hesitancy to come here again," Mullenix broke off with a small chuckle. "Strange isn't it?"

"What?" said Doug.

"God isn't ashamed to be seen with you. He isn't worried about associating himself with you... but the governor of the great state of North Carolina... he's a little more particular. Hmmm?! That's irony, isn't it?"

Doug wasn't interested in irony at the moment. "She's… alive. Alive? I uh… I thought so. I knew it and then I didn't. I think I'm going nuts. It's so hard to fit this in my head." He demonstrated the thought by taking his head in both hands as if it were about to explode. "You hear things and see things and they are so real and then in the next minute your brain seems to throw them out like you throw up a bad meal that's making you sick. It's brain puke. It's the brain saying 'Don't leave that in here or it'll make you sick.'"

"I understand, Doug. People always say seeing is believing, but that's not true. Believing is believing. Seeing only carries you to the edge of belief."

Mullenix's phone buzzed in his jacket pocket. "Excuse me," he said and answered it.

"Yes? When? Now? Okay. I'm with Doug Windsor now, Governor. I will ask him and get back to you. Yes, I think I can get the local channel streaming on my phone. Yes. I will get there as soon as I can."

Mullenix hung up and immediately opened the web browser on his phone and began searching for something. Doug looked at him inquiringly.

"Trying to get the local news to stream. Ah. Here it is." He got up and came around the table, positioning his screen so they both could view it.

"You'll want to see this as well."

CHAPTER SIXTY-FOUR

Syd DeVito was sweating. He wiped his brow repeatedly with a handkerchief that he stuffed in his pocket and retrieved again and again. He thought to himself how unusual this was for him.

He had spent hours in front of the camera in some of the most intense times imaginable without breaking a sweat, but he was sweating now.

He took huge gulps of air, trying to regulate his racing heart. Why this reaction? He considered. It struck him that he was on the cusp of a world-changing moment. He was the agent of a new world about to be born.

Yes. When he was done with this press conference, nothing would be the same again and he would be in the eye of a storm that reshaped political power. There had not been a moment like this one in two thousand years and when *that* moment came and went, the people involved had no knowledge of what was about to happen.

He knew. He was the great man at the great moment. The rare man taking history by the horns and being fully aware of it, turning it whithersoever he wanted it to go. But he had to play his part. It had to be done properly.

Sweating like a convict on a chain gang wouldn't do at all. He thought of the Nixon-Kennedy debate. The crisp coolness of the one and the pasty perspiration of the other. Winner-loser.

He had less than five minutes till he went live from the iconic spot he'd picked on the steps of the state capital. He was riding solo on this, not trusting even his closest staff or political allies.

The former were so worn down by the firestorm of the hospitalization and death of the first daughter that they'd all been sent away, and the latter, well, you couldn't expect sharks not to bite when there was this much blood in the water.

Politicians of any stripe were more likely to start a feeding frenzy than to help him build a shark cage. He would go it alone and alone he would take the glory coming to him.

He got water from the break room cooler. It was very cold in its tiny, dentist's-chair-sized cup. He filled it four times, throwing back the water like a gun fighter swallowing shots of whiskey in an old western saloon. Pulling out his handkerchief one more time, he dabbed his forehead and let out a long breath.

You are ready, he said to himself. *You've been ready. This is your time.* A calm came over him like a switch had been flipped and he knew he could do it. He saw it as a thing done already and all his anxiety left him.

He walked out onto the capitol steps precisely on time. The swarm of reporters from the aborted press conference at the jail had buzzed out of there and about the city in clusters of twos and threes without finding a place to light.

A few phone calls and texts to a few busy bees brought them together again. Cameras rolled and microphones sprouted in front of the podium kept there for these impromptu press conferences. Syd was besieged with shouted questions before he descended the steps.

"Where's the governor?!"

"Is it true the governor's daughter is missing?"

"When is the governor going to make a statement?!"

"What is the connection between the administration and Douglas Windsor?"

"Why did Governor Treeright meet with a known child molester?!"

All of this melded into a general roar in Syd's ears as he approached the mics, only picking out bits and pieces above the din.

He raised both arms in the universal sign for quiet. "Please! Please! I will have a statement and then I will take some questions. But you'll need to give me quiet so you hear exactly what I'm about to say. Please!"

He surveyed the field and identified the two national broadcast outfits he specifically wanted there; one from either side of the political divide. The swarm policed itself into a dull, manageable murmur.

"Thank you. I'm happy to tell you that you are going to be the first to hear a story that will go global within the next few hours."

A rowdy female reporter often hostile to the Treeright administration and candidacy shouted, "Pretty sure that's our call to make, Syd!"

A wave of subdued laughter filtered through the assembly. Syd smiled broadly.

"Right, Vivian. Right," he said. "And you'll be the first one racing to make my words come true in just a moment."

Something in the way he said this settled on the group like smoke on bees. They knew DeVito to be a vicious political fighter and a master of spin for his man, but they also knew he never pulled out his guns if he didn't mean to shoot, and the one thing he did not mince words about was publicity.

He lived and breathed it; he saved it and spent it. Whatever came next from Syd DeVito would no doubt be a bombshell.

He cleared his throat in the growing quiet.

"I'm going to address the happenings of the past week, its impact on our schedule and the governor's campaign. You all are aware that Governor Treeright arrived back here too late to be with his daughter as she passed away and that it was his expressed wish that no funerary action be taken before he returned. Accordingly, Tabitha, upon the certification of her death by three attending physicians, was moved to the Duke University hospital morgue, where she lay awaiting her father.

"I want to emphasize the point that no autopsy was performed at the time of death for more than one reason; first, her father's request not to perform one was honored by the hospital staff, but second— and this is in answer to some questions I've heard from some of you which are reasonable—she *is* the daughter of the man most likely to be our next president and therefore a suspicious death would be something we should consider as possibly politically motivated murder—the second reason we did not pursue an immediate autopsy is that the attending physicians were all in agreement that Tabitha's illness and demise were definitively caused by the so called 'brain eating amoeba.'

"Tests proved this conclusively from the time she was admitted and nothing occurred during her care that suggested any other cause for her condition. Tabitha Treeright died from a brain infection caused by *Naegleria fowleri*."

There was a restless shuffling in the crowd over the rehashing of details that had been endlessly cycled and panel discussed as the first daughter fought and lost the fight for her life. DeVito knew what he was doing; when to wind the engine, when to shift gears. Time for second gear.

"I personally met Governor Treeright at the airport the night he arrived from Africa. He wanted to go directly to see Tabitha, so I drove him to Duke. He was devastated, as you can imagine. I've known the Treerights a long time. They are family to me. We shed a lot of tears together as we drove. There are no words suitable for a time like that."

Here he paused and wiped away an imaginary tear from his eyes. He had them now. Smooth shift into third and close it out.

"Mrs. Treeright was at the Governor's Mansion. They spoke on the phone as we drove and they cried together. The Treerights are a special couple. Very strong. Very loving. It was touching and a privilege to listen in on such an intimate moment. A strong woman and a strong man consoling each other in the face of this tragedy. It was special.

"They hung up to each other just as we arrived at the hospital. I asked the governor if he was sure he wanted to see Tabitha right then. If he didn't want to go home first and perhaps let the funeral parlor make her more presentable. I know that sounds callous on my part but it's not. I was there at the end and I saw what Tabitha looked like and what she went through. She did not look like the girl we all know and love.

"The governor didn't answer me. He sat looking straight ahead. He had a look of utter calm. I've known Daniel Treeright since college and I can say as well as anyone what the man is like in private. He is what you see. I promise you. You've seen him get passionate and he is. You've seen him laugh and he does. People love what they see in him because it is real.

"All of that aside, I want you to know that I saw something in him I've never seen before that night. No matter what else is true of the man, he is a man of motion. He is moving and thinking and doing all the time. He wakes up that way and goes all day like that.

"Right then, in the car outside the hospital, it was like seeing the ocean go flat calm. It was strange to see. I thought he might be having a medical event and I started to get out of the car and go get help. He touched my arm and said, 'I'm fine.'

"Again, it was strange. It didn't sound like him but it was him. He got out of the car and we went into the hospital but we didn't go to the morgue. He led me straight to the hospital chapel. It was late and the room was empty. Governor Treeright is a good Christian man—he and his family attend Saint Mark's Lutheran here in town on a regular basis—but I didn't know what to make of this. Was he going to pray for the dead? For forgiveness for being away when his daughter got sick?

"I tried to stop him and tell him there was nothing to ask forgiveness for and that it was too late to pray for Tabitha, but it was as if he didn't hear me. There was a set to his jaw and a distant look in his eyes that was so intense I half expected him to be hot when I touched him. But he was cool and composed. He walked straight to the podium where there was a large pulpit Bible."

A woman reporter in the second row said loudly, "What's this got to do…" and was shushed down by the rank and file around her.

DeVito continued, "The governor went to it and began flipping pages, running his finger down each in search of something. He found it directly and stabbed it with an index finger. 'Here it is,' he said, and he picked up the big book, got down on his knees and placed it open before him. I had not followed him into the chapel, not knowing what he was doing and honestly wanting to guard against some unforeseen interruption if the man was going to pray. I blocked the door and waited to see what he would do."

DeVito paused and noisily took a long sip from a water bottle before continuing.

"Once he settled on his knees with the open Bible in front of him, he raised his hands and face to the ceiling. The governor did not move from that position for a long time. He didn't make a sound. I couldn't tell if he was in a trance or what was happening.

"About an hour passed. I knew Mrs. Treeright would be getting concerned and I was just getting ready to go to him when he let out a deep sigh and got to his feet. He took out a handkerchief and wiped his forehead with it. I saw as he folded it over on itself that it was stained with something red.

"I pointed at this and asked him if he was okay—what was wrong. He seemed to notice the stain for the first time and looked mildly surprised. I examined his forehead to see if he had cut himself somehow but there was no cut. Then I remembered something from my Catholic school days. The story from the Bible about Jesus praying in the garden on the night before his crucifixion. How he prayed so hard that he sweated drops of blood."

At this several of the reporters shuffled their feet and cleared their throats impatiently. None of them had shown up here to get a Sunday School lesson.

DeVito knew he had a trump card to play and knew he had time yet till he needed to show it. He wanted them to build up some frustration and irritation. He counted on it. When he slapped down the card it would make the contrast so much the sweeter.

Continuing on, he said, "I took the handkerchief from the governor and examined it closely. It was in fact smeared with blood. I asked him to examine it. I thought it might mean he was having a stroke or some medical event needing attention.

"He remained calm and had no appearance of distress. His eyes were clear and he said he was ready to go and 'get Tabitha.' Those were his exact words. Go and 'get' her. I was at a loss for what to say to this. The whole thing was disturbing. I decided to keep my own counsel and to escort him to the morgue, which I did.

"On the way out of the chapel, he saw a stack of paperback Bibles, the kind that are kept there to give away. He picked one up. We went to the morgue and the attendant let us in. His name is Romeo Carnel. He took us to Tabitha and showed us the body. I was prepared for this to be a shock to the governor but he remained calm and composed still. He asked if we could be left alone with the body and Mr. Cranel agreed.

"Once we were alone, the governor got down on his knees again as he had been in the chapel. He took out the small paperback Bible, thumbed through it to the place he wanted and folded it open on the ground. Again he held his hands up and looked up to the ceiling. This time he prayed out loud.

"Ladies and gentlemen, what he prayed was the most blood chilling thing I ever heard. You have to remember that I saw this child die a horrible death just over seventy-two hours before this. The governor... the governor was praying for his daughter to rise from the dead."

There were audible gasps in the crowd and a murmuring began and grew. Why would DeVito say these things? Had he decided Treeright was cracked and couldn't go on running for president? Was he genuinely concerned about the man's health?

DeVito let the murmuring build. He was content to let his story settle on the crowd. He was enjoying himself, playing this role. He reflected on how he'd felt so unsettled only a quarter of an hour ago and now... now as he surveyed these sheep and the vista from the state capitol steps, he looked beyond them all and saw himself in another capitol on another more impressive set of steps with a much larger herd eating up what he was feeding them. He smiled inside. *I was born for this,* he told himself.

"Yes. It was not what I expected either. I reacted much like you just did, although I have to admit that at the time—and I think if any one of you had been there you would agree—I actually looked at the corpse with some kind of expectation. Standing out here in the light of day it seems ridiculous or insane, but in that room with the man so sincerely praying at the edge of his little girl's bed as it were... it felt different.

"It wasn't crazy. The earnestness of his prayer. The stillness of the morgue and of Tabitha. The cold white lights. It was deadly serious. And for a moment I thought I had stepped into another world. A world where miracles were possible. I tell you I looked at the girl, half expecting her to sit straight up and start talking. But…"

He broke off and rubbed away non-existent tears from his eyes again.

"But nothing happened and the moment passed. I was back in the real world and I knew the morgue attendant would think it strange if we spent too much time with the body. I was genuinely concerned for my friend too. I thought it couldn't be a good thing for him to linger there.

"As carefully as I could, I got down on my knees next to Governor Treeright and put my arm around him. I told him that I love him and that we all loved Tabitha but it was time to go. I reminded him that his wife would be worried and needed him at home. He lowered his arms and head, softly repeated some phrase I couldn't make out, and got up. He bent over his daughter, holding the Bible, and he said '*talitha koum*.' I thought he was saying 'Tabitha, come,' as if she were going to get up and walk out with us.

"I said, 'Daniel, she isn't going anywhere,' and tried to pull him away. He said the phrase again. *Talitha koum*. Then I recognized it from my Catholic school days. This was what Jesus said over a dead girl. I've since looked it up. It's in the Aramaic language. Its literal meaning is 'little girl arise' or 'wake up little girl.'

"At the time I didn't know what to do. I felt like I needed to get the governor away from there. Get some space and let him come back to himself. Honestly, I was scared. This felt like a psychotic break without the raving or foaming at the mouth or folding up into a fetal position.

"Finally, the governor unbent himself and looked at me. He showed me the place he was looking at in the little Bible. It was the gospel of Mark. The story of Jairus's daughter. His finger was on the phrase I just told you. He said, 'She's on her way back'—or something along those lines. It didn't make sense to me until later. At this point I physically removed the governor from the morgue. I mean this. I dragged him out of the place and all the way back to our car.

"On our way out of the hospital, we ran into the man who was later arrested in the morgue. His name is Douglas Windsor. He is a convicted child molester from Virginia who was obsessed with Tabitha Treeright. It hasn't been confirmed yet but some law enforcement contacts in Hampton Roads tell me they have searched Mr. Windsor's apartment and discovered pictures of Tabitha taken from public photos plastered on his walls and a load of child pornography on his computers. Sick individual. Truly sick. He violated his parole coming here.

"We are working with Virginia to keep him here while we sort out charges. As I said, the man was obsessed with the governor's daughter. We believe when the news of her sickness and subsequent death hit the news, he snapped. He drove up here desperate to see her, even if she was dead."

There was a groan of disgust from the crowd.

"Yes. A sick man," DeVito said. "He broke into the morgue, found Tabitha's body and…" He cleared his throat. "And he proceeded to sexually assault her, ahhh, corpse.

"I hesitate here because it's going to get a little complicated. A lot complicated. For the moment, let's say Douglas Windsor, who knew Tabitha Treeright was dead, found her in the morgue, and touched her sexually. The morgue attendant, Mr. Cranel, caught Windsor in the act. He heard Windsor screaming vile things over the girl and that's what alerted him to the assault. Mr. Cranel forcibly stopped the assault. He then called both internal security forces and the local police who responded immediately and apprehended the perpetrator."

DeVito gathered himself for the key lie, or one of the key lies in the web of lies he was spinning.

"Today at the jail, many of you were made aware of the existence of a security video of the morgue on the night all these events took place. This is obviously a key piece of evidence and I want to get the record straight. We have reason to believe Windsor had help getting into the morgue."

He let that go for effect.

"Personally, I was unaware of how sophisticated the community of perverts can be and what I'm about to tell you shocked me. But it appears that our suspect Windsor was connected to at least two local people who knew he was coming to the hospital that night and were willing to help him. They were motivated, we think, by the possibility of getting video of Tabitha and Windsor which would bring a high price in the child porn circles.

"It is possible that the plan was set in motion by contact between Windsor and one of these people, who is a security guard at the hospital. The second individual is going to be harder for you to take, I'm afraid, but we have, just this afternoon, uncovered evidence which links him also to child porn. He is a long time member of our local media. We believe these two, working in concert, removed the security video from the morgue either in an attempt to cover for Windsor or to obtain some video of Tabitha Treeright's assault they could sell. Possibly both."

The murmuring in the crowd grew. DeVito thought they would break out into questions if he didn't keep up the pace of his account and he did not want questions. Not yet.

"I'm going to withhold the names of these two individuals at this time because they are not yet formally charged or in custody. We expect arrests within the next couple of hours. I want to move on and address a more significant development.

"Although we have not issued an official statement up to this time, for obvious reasons." This was an old trick DeVito used on the megalomaniac members of the media—telling them something was obvious when it was really as opaque as a smoked-out window on a moonless night, knowing they would each hold themselves as too intelligent to admit to anyone that they didn't see what he called obvious. He smiled to himself as he said it again.

"For obvious reasons, we have not spoken of the 'disappearance'"—here he actually gestured air quotes—"of Tabitha Treeright's body after the child molester Windsor was arrested and removed from the morgue. We are not certain of the exact time her absence was noted.

"Mr. Romeo Carnell was the first person who discovered she was missing and reported it. We were not immediately informed but when we did receive the information about both the assault and the disappearance, the governor, who was on his way home to the Governor's Mansion, decided to go to the jail to confront the suspect.

"I advised him against this, but I'm sure you can all appreciate how the governor felt at the time. He would not be dissuaded. We went to the jail and were allowed to visit the prisoner. All I'm going to say about that meeting at this time is that it was understandably intense.

"Windsor offered no explanation for his actions. He was remorseless and cold. He even smiled when the governor asked him where she was. I will put to bed the rumor that Governor Treeright got into a physical altercation with the prisoner. That is categorically false.

"We left the jail with no hint of where Tabitha might be. At this point, and I realize how this must sound, we began to form the working theory that she might have been taken away by co-suspects to some location where other perverts like Douglas Windsor could continue in private what he had been doing in the morgue. We believed it to be highly unlikely Windsor acted alone and when we got further information regarding the missing security video, it confirmed our hunches.

"We knew Windsor could not have taken the security video alone. He did not have it on him when he was taken into custody. This is what led us to begin checking for possible connections locally and the things I've spelled out to you just now.

"With no other leads to go on, the governor and I proceeded to the mansion. We felt it was the best course of action and the governor wanted to be the one to inform his wife of the goings on at the morgue personally. Mrs. Treeright was distraught. Inconsolable, but also determined to get answers about what happened to her daughter's body.

"The following twenty-four hours were very dark and very long. None of us slept. The police exhausted every avenue they could to trace Tabitha and whoever had taken her away. It was futile. We were looking in the wrong place."

DeVito took a sip of water, scanned the expectant faces before him and set the hook.

"There's a saying recorded about Jesus. Perhaps the key moment in all that went on around him. Some women went to the tomb to see him after the crucifixion and they ran into an angel. He said, 'Why do you seek the living among the dead?' It turns out this was the same problem we faced."

Nothing. No reaction to this seeming non sequitur. He let it wait anyway. Let them puzzle over it.

"I'm saying that Tabitha Treeright's body couldn't be recovered because she was not—is not dead! Actually I should say that Tabitha Treeright is no longer dead."

The reporters erupted in a cacophony of guffaws and gasps and some curses. This was the most outrageous presser anyone had ever attended. The curious and the angry elbowed and shuffled forward reflexively, surrounding Syd faster than he could retreat. He tried to speak but he had no control over the situation. His voice was drowned out as his body was swallowed up.

It was a full fifteen minutes before he could make himself heard again. He was losing his voice from yelling over the reporters.

In a hoarse voice he said, "Tabitha is alive and well and you can see her for yourself as soon as we get her completely checked over by her medical team. We are also going to have a counselor work with her to determine if she is ready for any public appearance. But we will share some video of her and proof that she is in fact alive. It's a miracle. There's no other explanation. If you will give me some room and quiet down I will answer as many of your questions as I can."

CHAPTER SIXTY-FIVE

Tabitha Treeright sat drinking tea across from her mother and father. They looked at her with unblinking eyes as if she would disappear if they lost focus for even an instant.

It was such a miraculously normal snapshot. Sitting. Sipping. Breathing. Normal. Miraculous.

The swelling of the sea of emotions inside Daniel and Wanda broke out of their eyes unbidden. Tabitha, noticing their tears, put down her cup, rose, and came to them, kneeling between their chairs and placing a hand on each of them.

No one spoke. It seemed a holy moment; too perfect for words. The antique clock on the mantle ticked cheerfully. Creaking footsteps on the wooden floor in the hallway announced an impending interruption but the three remained in their intimate triangle of life together even as the door swung open and Wanda's assistant entered.

"Sorry to disturb you, Ms. Wanda." It was obvious from the assistant's face she really was sorry; that she too knew she was seeing a holy moment. She waited to be acknowledged. After a long pause, the governor's wife lifted her eyes from her daughter to the woman.

"What is it?" she said in a voice that sounded distant to her own ears, as if she'd come down from a mountain too fast and the pressure hadn't cleared.

"It's... it's Mr. DeVito, ma'am. He's at the state house doing a press conference. And, ah, he's saying things that don't sound good. I, ahhh, I don't think he... it doesn't seem like..."

The woman was clearly frazzled and she wasn't the type to get frazzled. Wanda squeezed Tabitha's arm and she in turn squeezed her father's. He came down the mountain too and looked up, first at Wanda then at her assistant.

She continued, struggling. "Is he speaking for you?" With her eyes she included all three of the Treerights. "I thought we were keeping quiet for the time being and deciding what to do about..." She smiled at Tabitha. "About this!"

Daniel's eyes narrowed. "Syd?! Talking to the media? When? Where?"

"Sir, he's at the state house on the steps. It came on with breaking news about ten minutes ago. I was in the war room working on rescheduling meetings for Ms. Wanda when it came on. At first I thought he was doing a rehash of the last few days, just normal care and feeding of the press, but the things he's saying..."

Daniel was up and switching on a television on the far wall. The blackened screen flashed open to the scene Alicia Stoneman had been describing. It was muted. Daniel squeezed the volume button on the remote so hard it shot up to max level, instantly filling the room with the rumble of the sound of wind over open mics as the image of Syd DeVito filled the screen. He was drinking from a water bottle, eyeing the crowd in what Daniel knew to be a patented DeVito pause for effect. He placed the bottle down and began speaking.

Daniel stood, transfixed. He stared at the screen then back at his wife and daughter. They got up and joined him. Treeright made little gasping sounds as his longtime friend and chief political teammate made statement after jarring statement, his mouth opening and closing like a goldfish plucked from its bowl. Wanda too was frozen in place. She absently bit her finger like a patient biting down on a wooden peg awaiting a broken bone to be set, hoping it would end quickly.

Tabitha alone was easy in her posture.

She stood between her parents hearing all they heard. It washed over her with no effect. When DeVito reached the conclusion of his story and was swamped by the reporters, she reached out and grasped her mother's arm, pulled her hand down to her own and then did the same to her father.

They looked down from either side on her. They both realized they'd been holding their breath. Tabitha's expression was serene. It banished tension and ushered in a peace as real as the smell of freshly fallen rain. There was nothing to do. Nothing pressing. Nothing necessary. All they needed was to enjoy. The lies would untell themselves in due time. They always did. The struggle for a place and a name could go on without them for now.

They sat back down in the chairs across from each other. Alicia Stoneman watched this unfold and didn't know what she should do. She began as her mistress's aide-de-camp and confidant, protector of the political life of the First Lady and therefore the interests of the governor, but as she watched them watching Syd DeVito she had instead begun to feel she was an intruder in a family moment.

Many years ago this family had ceased to be a family in her eyes. They were pieces on a board game, she liked to think of it as Stratego. If you were in the right position you could see where the bombs and the flags were and you could see how it was all progressing.

The pieces were all just plastic, though, not flesh, not feeling, just useful markers interacting usefully to accomplish useful things. Those pieces included everyone and all the moves were table moves.

Tabitha was no exception. Syd DeVito, Wanda Treeright, the governor; all the same. She thought, no, she knew, when she came into the room with the news about DeVito giving a presser that was way off the reservation, the pieces were about to fly. They would go into motion. They would make moves.

Instead the pieces turned into people. Not only did they turn into people, the people they turned into were peaceful and calm and exuded love for each other. There was no sense of urgency in them. They could be sitting in the living room of a house in the middle of nowhere instead of in the Governor's Mansion on the way to the White House.

She hesitated as they took their seats, unsure of what this humanization of her boss's family meant for her. Then she backed out of the room and gently closed the door.

CHAPTER SIXTY-SIX

Jackie and Macher searched the security tapes while Shelton maintained a lookout for anyone trying to get into the security shack while keeping an eye on the prisoners. The chief sat sullenly at his desk and kept his mouth shut after Jackie threatened to gag him with some duct tape and his own sock.

They expanded their search from the obvious areas they expected to see the girl to the more obscure areas where the hospital had security camera coverage; the loading docks, the dialysis center, eventually they searched the common area feeds from the parking garage.

It was tedious work. Each level had several cameras and they had to spool through days of footage, not even sure what they were looking for. The system they settled on was searching the time stamps from two hours before the incident in the morgue to twelve hours after, the thought being that by that time Tabitha could no longer have been in the hospital.

Running through the tapes on eight times speed, they accustomed their eyes to the motion and looked for any anomalies. On the last angle of the third level of the parking garage, a popular spot for many of the hospital staff because of the easy access it offered to the main building, Macher caught a glimpse of something blurring past and said, "Whoa!"

Jackie backed up the tape and ran it at normal speed.

"Whaddya see?" he asked.

"Probably nothing, but it looked like there was a white coat walking away from the hospital to his car, or hers. Too fast to see it. Look. There." He stabbed a finger at the screen. "It's a male. He's a white coat all right. What's odd about it is it's after the morning rush and before the shift closed out. That's why it popped out to me, I think."

"Guy is just going to burn one in his car. They're freaks about smoking anywhere on campus so all the nicotine fiends dash out to their cars all day."

"Probably it," said Macher. Absently they watched the man walk across the screen as if they themselves had hit the pause button and the video was running them.

Jackie snapped out of the zone first and was reaching for the control to see a new video when Macher stopped him. Something in the manner of the man caught his attention; the way he walked and looked about him. He skulked like the cat who's eaten the pet parakeet.

"What're you doing the walk-o-shame for, Doc?" he said to the back of Jackie's head. "Hold up a sec. Let's see what he's up to. Can you zoom in? Tell who he is?"

The man got to the far end of the camera angle and it became difficult to see him clearly. Jackie scrolled to the next angle and forwarded to the same time stamp. This angle showed the man coming directly into the frame. His features were clear to see and with the high definition it was simple to blow up the shot and read the name on the right breast of his white coat.

Dr. Fred Robinson.

Macher wrote this down as they rolled tape. The man looked around several times and appeared to pause and listen for approaching vehicles before he popped the trunk of his car. As the lid swung up, he placed his satchel on the ground beside his car, bent over it, and rummaged through it briefly. They couldn't see what he was doing. When he stood up he was holding what appeared to be a white cloth.

Macher said, "What's he got there? Looks like a folded white cloth. A tablecloth? That's weird. A folded-up tablecloth? What's he got in it? Wrapped something up?"

"I dunno," said Jackie. "But he sure does seem anxious not to be spotted, doesn't he?"

"Yeah, he does."

What happened next puzzled them both even more. The man looked around again, clearing the area once more, opened the white cloth up to its full size, which appeared to be the size of a single bed sheet, shook it out, and carefully refolded it into a tightly compacted square.

Placing the square on the trunk of a car parked next to his own, he removed several items from his trunk, pulled up the cover of the spare tire compartment, and carefully placed the folded sheet in on top of the spare. He did this rapidly, continually glancing over his shoulder left and right as he worked.

Macher and Jackie reran the footage several times, trying to discern if the sheet was indeed the only item the man was hiding. They couldn't see anything that indicated otherwise. Once the man had placed the sheet into the compartment, he quickly replaced the cover and restowed the other items over it. Taking one final scan of the vicinity, he retrieved his satchel and walked back to the hospital.

"So he puts a common bed sheet in his satchel and walks it to his car? Then hides it in his trunk?" Jackie said.

"And shakes it out…" said Macher.

Jackie switched the video back to the first angle which showed the doctor coming back to the hospital. He paused it.

"Look at this bit right here," he said. Macher did.

"What?" he said.

"Watch the guy's eyes when he sees the camera."

The doctor glimpsed up at the security camera, obviously surprised to see it. His eyes widened noticeably and he craned his neck around, looking to the far end of the garage.

"I think the bastard's lookin' for other cameras. He knows he's busted," said Jackie. "But from what? What's a sheet got to do with anything?"

"Dunno," said Macher, studying the man's face.

"Any other cameras left to search?" he said. "I don't see how she left the hospital."

Shelton, listening from the other room said, "What if she didn't leave? What if she's still in the psych ward?"

Macher and Jackie locked eyes at the same instant.

"The doctor—he was from the psych ward!" they said to each other at the same time.

They took to their heels and started for the door. Shelton stopped them. "What are we going to do with these guys? You can't leave me here alone with them! We can't keep them here forever!"

"She's right, " said Macher.

"I'll go," said Jackie. "I know my way around here and I can get there and back faster than you. I'll scope it out and get back here. Then we can sort out what to do with them."

Shelton and Macher let Jackie out the door and secured it behind him.

CHAPTER SIXTY-SEVEN

Macher took the opportunity to check his phone. The little red notification on his messages said he had twenty-five new texts. He was a recipient on several group texts with fellow journalists and they were all blowing up. There was an impromptu presser starting at the Capitol with Governor Treeright's chief of staff.

He checked the time. It was ten minutes into the scheduled start time for the presser. He punched an icon on his phone, opening the web feed of a local television station. Live video popped up, showing the scene on the capitol steps.

DeVito was detailing the connections Windsor had with local pedophiles. Macher's mouth dropped open. He looked from the small screen to Shelton and back, speechless. Her eyes were saucers.

Harden, also listening in, stirred. "You freakin' pervert. You were in on it too." Speaking over his shoulder he said, "Shelton, I'll give you one more chance to get on the right side of this, now you know the score. Two pervs."

Shelton was shaking her head as she listened. She looked terrified, as if Macher might move up in his age preferences right now and start with her.

Several things happened at once. Shelton hesitated between freeing the chief and pulling her weapon on Macher. Macher threw himself at her in the moment of indecision. She was caught with the keys to the handcuffs in one hand and the service revolver half out of its holster in the other.

They crashed to the floor in a sprawl of arms and legs. Harden tried twice to get his bulk out of his chair, falling back onto it with a loud, grunted, "Humph."

One of the two guards secured to the pipes yelled and threw his legs out, attempting to kick Macher, but missed. The second guard got his legs around Macher's middle in a cage match move, squeezing a gasp out of him and holding him fast. Shelton, flailing to regain her balance, threw an elbow that caught the reporter under his chin with an audible crack. She retrieved the keys to the handcuffs and drew her revolver in one fluid motion.

"Don't move," she said to the stunned man.

"Keep him there!" she said to the guard, who squeezed another, louder grunt out of Macher.

"He ain't going nowhere," he said.

"Chief, put your arms up so I can get at those cuffs." Harden complied as best he could and Shelton snapped the bracelets off.

"Sorry, Chief. Guess I'm out of a job. I didn't know. But I'm not gonna be any part of helping people who hurt kids. My little sister is all kinds of broken up because of people like him."

Harden stood, shaking out his tingling hands and trying to restore some semblance of the command presence he never really possessed in the first place.

Trying to sound magnanimous, he said, "I don't see why this needs to be the end of your job, Shelton. There's a lot happening right now. Lots no one could know about. Let's clean up this mess ourselves, hmm? First we need to get his partner." Harden jerked a fat thumb toward Macher.

Harden assisted Shelton with securing Macher and freeing the other two guards. The journalist offered no resistance; the scuffle and blow to the jaw had deflated him physically and the things he'd heard at the press conference had taken the heart out of him. He didn't respond to Harden's gloating face shoved inches from his own. He barely heard the chief's guttural whisper between clenched teeth. "Stupid prick. You think you can put your hands into a fire and not get burned. We'll burn your life to the ground."

Macher looked blankly at the red face and crimson-rimmed eyes. One word registered: *We'll? We? What did that mean?*

Shelton looked to Harden for orders. It didn't occur to her until much later that the chief never called the police.

CHAPTER SIXTY-EIGHT

Jackie reached the psych ward via a service elevator rarely used by anyone other than security or housekeeping. His internal clock was running like a quarterback dropped back to pass. He had the sense that what he had to uncover had to be done quickly or he was going to be buried under crushing powers even now rushing in on him. He was sweating and out of breath when he pushed open the door to the psych ward reception room.

Dressed in civilian clothes without his identity badge, he had to hope he would meet with someone who knew who he was or it could get dicey. Of all the wards in the hospital, the identity of patients and goings-on in the psych ward was most jealously guarded. He had found that out when he happened upon a loud-mouthed state senator being restrained here one night. He'd been given the "no matter what you think you saw you didn't see anything" briefing by a charge nurse and sent packing.

The nurse on duty looked up as he entered; a pale, petite woman, twentyish with painfully tight curls in her shock-red hair. He didn't know her.

"Jackie!" she said. "Jackie Smith."

He inspected himself as if expecting to find some other Jackie Smith the girl recognized.

"Hey?" he stammered.

The girl pursed her lips in an affected pout.

"Don't recognize me?"

He didn't. Straining to see the name on her badge, he searched his mind for a name to match the face.

"Ahhh, I don't. Sorry."

The girl's face brightened with a friendly smile. "It's fine. I'm Carol. From oncology… I used to work nights over there…"

Jackie was still not making the connection.

"I used to be a bleach blonde and my hair was straight."

"Carol!" He saw the face pop into a new-old frame and he instantly knew her. "Wow, you threw me way off! You look great!"

She blushed. He regretted his enthusiasm immediately, feeling his compliment inadvertently pop out of the adrenalin and relief of finding a friendly face where he expected an adversary.

He stepped fully into the reception area and up to her desk.

"It's been a while. I wondered where you'd got to."

"Well, you know how those nights wear on you. Always on the flip side of life. Coming when everyone else is going, etc., etc. I saw this job come up on the internal jobs board and made the transfer in a week. Real quick. And you? Still on nights? You're not on duty I assume?" She eyed his civilian attire.

"Me? Ha! I'm as married to the night shift as I am to my wife."

Stupid analogy, he thought. *Get your head together*.

She continued to talk; a thing she could do prolifically as he recalled from many chats he had while passing her doing rounds.

"So what's got you all hot and bothered and up in the daylight? It took me two months before I got used to going home without sleeping in the sunlit hours like a vampire. I had to change my meal times too; even had to find a new hair person. You know how jealous hairdressers are? It was like leaving a boyfriend."

Jackie wondered at the way the woman could speak in a stream of words so solid that trying to find a way to insert a word felt like stepping into Niagara Falls. He had no time for this. It took a great force of will to shove into the torrent of words.

"So," she went on, "Melany Jurgenson said she had a girl..."

"Carol, I'm so glad to run into you again. I'm in a bit of a hurry and I need some help."

Knowing he wouldn't get far unless he matched her words per second, he plunged ahead like a man determined to give his drink and dinner order to a waitress all at once

"I'm looking for a doctor. Fred Robinson? Is his name. And I'd also like to know who the duty nurse was on Tuesday. Whoever was on nights and going off shift around seven. It's very important. I'm in a hurry. Bit of a jam. Could you help me out?"

Carol shared the characteristic of many of the loquacious bent that takes less offense at being interrupted than they take notice of their uninterrupted output of words. She smiled sweetly at Jackie and said, "Doc Robinson is out today, honey... let me look."

She thumbed through a white three-ring binder with 'Staff Schedule' printed on the front. "It looks like Marge Waddle was on that night. She's a sweetheart. Love her. She made me feel so at home when I came over from oncology. I..."

Jackie cut her off just as the word train started to leave the station again.

"Thanks, Carol. That's what I needed to know. Would you be able... I know it's not protocol, but you know me and you know I could look it up anyway, would you give me their contact info?"

The nurse looked doubtful.

Jackie went on, "Just between us. I'll tell them I looked it up. I won't mention you. Just saves me some time, that's all. And I'm in an awful hurry."

Carol brightened. "Sure, Jackie. It must be important?" Raised eyebrows invited him to let her in on whatever was going on. It was Jackie's turn to look doubtful.

"It's kind of an investigation, Carol," he said, instantly regretting it by the look that flashed across Carol's face. "No one's in trouble," he capered. "It's, ah, it's complicated. It's about a missing person and I can't, I don't..."

Carol bailed him out. "I trust you, Jackie. I know good people when I see them." She hesitated, a decision teetering on her expressive face, and said, "And I know the opposite when I see it too. Be careful of Robinson."

When Jackie raised an eyebrow, she went on. "You know what they say about seeing what a person is really like by the way they treat people they don't have to be nice to... you know, like waitresses or cashiers, or..."

"Or junior nurses," Jackie finished for her.

"Well, yeah," Carol said, a bit wistfully. "I know I can talk a lot sometimes, but I can take a hint. He's just not nice. Not nice to me or any of us nurses, junior or otherwise. I don't complain much and I'm not a whiner, really! But all of us get it from him and we talk about it. It isn't just the way most of them look down their noses at us either—I mean doctors to nurses—it's other stuff."

"Like what? Jackie asked.

"Like rewriting orders for patients after things went wrong. And blaming things that went wrong on people who aren't here anymore and can't defend themselves or contradict him."

"Rewriting orders?"

"Yeah, orders. The directions that doctors write for patients. It's hard to prove it, but several nurses told me he did it in two cases. And the strange thing about it is that neither case was really bad. No one got hurt. Both patients were fine. They just had bad reactions to the meds he ordered up for them."

"Why would he do that then? Sounds like he's altering official documents."

"I'm not certain. Patients here don't generally remember a lot of what goes on in their care. Most of them don't want to. They don't want anyone to know they're here; even their own self I guess. And most of the meds they use aren't deadly unless there's a huge overdose."

"Were the patients particularly important or something?" Jackie asked, not expecting an answer.

But Carol either forgot protocol or was so embittered by the way Robinson treated her and others that she responded immediately. "Yes! Both were politicians. Both were in here for pretty significant crack ups. They were in here about six months apart. You'd know them by name, Jackie. You'd recognize them. And Doc Robinson took special pains to be their primary caregiver. Even changed his vacation to be in charge of one of them. He was especially nasty to the girls assigned to that man."

Jackie considered this. Robinson was turning out to be a more enigmatic character than the enigma he'd seen on the video. While he was doing this, Carol handed him a sticky note with two cell numbers jotted in it.

"Marge is sweet. She'll help you if she can," Carol said, pointing to the woman's name with the tip of a black ballpoint pen. "Tell her we talked. This one"—she indicated Robinson's information—"I'd watch out for him."

Just as she handed him the slip of paper, the hospital intercom crackled to life.

"Code Silver. Code Sliver. This is not a drill. Code Silver"

Carol looked puzzled and grasped at the plastic card on her lanyard that showed all the codes and their meanings.

"Silver is a lockdown," Jackie said tersely. "Thanks for the help, Carol. Come and secure this door behind me."

He didn't wait for her to respond. He was out the door, heading for the stairway closest to the psych ward. His mind whirled. No one in the hospital could have called away a Code Silver without it going through the security shack first.

The only explanation was that their hold on the shack was gone and Harden was back in charge. The Code Silver was aimed at him or perhaps Macher if he'd made an escape, or both of them. He had to find a way out quickly.

Years of prowling the hospital and an understanding of how the lockdown procedures unfolded gave him an edge. He knew where the weakest point in the closing net was and how to get there.

In less than five minutes, he walked out of the laundry delivery bay and started down a concrete ramp that would lead him to a neglected walkway and into a back parking lot. He would be in the streets and on his home turf in moments. Halfway down the ramp he slowed and stopped. Something caught his mind like a protruding nail snags a sweater.

He went back into the laundry. He noted again something he'd thought many times walking through here on rounds; it wasn't really a laundry. No washing machines. No dryers. Just bins of soiled linen on one hand and stacks of folded linen on the other. He stepped into the middle of the room and paused, waiting for the subconscious snag to reveal itself.

Laundry. Sheets. Robinson! He noticed a label on one of the shelves. In black block letters it said MATERNITY. Next to it in the same lettering was a label reading MORGUE. He smirked at the irony and then a thought struck him. How would whoever worked here know which linens went on which shelf?

He strode to the shelf designated for the morgue and pulled out the first sheet in the stack. He shook it out to its full size and threaded it through his hands, examining it inch by inch. And there it was, stenciled in blue black ink:

Property of DUMC

Dec. Care Dept

He stared hard at the marking. Were all the sheets in the hospital marked this way? He pulled down a sheet from the pile on the shelf marked "Maternity" and searched it. He quickly found what he was looking for:

Property of DUMC

Maternity Ward

Jackie said out loud to himself, "What were you up to, Robinson?"

"Who are you talkin' to and what are you doin' in here?" A voice from behind him broke in on his thoughts. He jerked around, dropping the sheet.

The man connected to the voice wore the whites of the laundry workers and a firm but not unkind expression. His rich black skin set against the white clothing made it look as if he glowed.

Jackie had no mental capacity to make up a lie at this moment and didn't want to.

"Just curious. I've worked here for years and never noticed how all the sheets are marked with the department they come from. Has it always been that way?"

The man grimaced conspiratorially. "Maaan, you know how it is if you work here any 'mount of time. If we can make a simple job harder, we do it. I been here goin' on thirty years. True. Been here long enough to remember when the laundry was a laundry and not just this warehouse.

"'Bout five years ago they started with the stencils. Don't know why. Don't ask. Just know it used to be easy to put away the sheets 'at come back from the contractor and now we got to sort through 'em all and get 'em in the right stack."

"I see. Yeah. I know how it is. Any way to make it harder… So the sheets are all labeled with the department but that's all, right? Not numbered?"

The man gave him a sideways look that said, "Do not say such a thing out loud young man! Someone will think it's a good idea! And really what difference does one sheet or another make in this whole world?"

"Yeah," said Jackie. "What difference does it make?" He turned and walked out of the hospital.

CHAPTER SIXTY-NINE

Tabitha Treeright looked closely at herself in the mirror. It was only a few days since she awoke in pitch blackness and clawed her way out of what turned out to be a body bag in the Duke University Hospital morgue.

Her face looked alien in some ways and perfectly familiar in others. She tried to smile a camera smile; a thing she hated to do but had learned to be good at as the daughter of the most popular politician in the state of North Carolina.

She had perfected it as he became the most popular politician in the nation.

The difference between her real, natural smile, the one few people could illicit, and the camera smile, were the tiniest dimples that appeared when she genuinely felt joy. She was surprised and confused to see them emerge in the face in the mirror, but upon reflection she realized her heart felt light. She blushed at herself and then laughed. It felt good.

The past several years had been like living under water. *No, she thought,* it had been more like the medieval torture method she read about in history class, the one where the victim was placed between two flat boards and heavy rocks were placed one at a time on the topmost board until the weight eventually crushed the breath out of the victim.

Easy smiles became a thing of the past. Her parents' broken relationship was too heavy to hold up and too secret to let out, so she sat under it. The demands to appear like a picture book family; to be normal in an obscenely abnormal set of circumstances—to make the grades in school, dress the right way, and say the correct things—all choked her even though she was in fact a good student and a good girl and basically believed the things she said in public.

It was all the second guessing: am I me? Or am I playing a part they've written for me? And then to be a girl on the verge of puberty and all the fun things biology brought along. No. Easy smiles were not often to be had.

She looked again in the mirror, and smiled at her smile.

She had not understood the meaning of the meeting she interrupted with the ministers. Her father tried to explain why he invited the three men to the mansion. Even after he gave his reasoning, she still didn't get it. This need to gather information and "experts" was a puzzling part of watching her dad become something different than her dad, to see him become a public figure. She was cut off from discussing him with her mother, and the only other adult she trusted to explain political machinery was cut off by the equal but opposite end of the teeter totter they had landed upon.

Syd DeVito had been fun at one point. She never knew a time in her life that didn't include him. He was the person all kids need; close enough to be family and far enough away from titles like Mom and Dad to be trusted with the little secrets and questions that grew along with increasing shoe sizes.

He had been that person. The one she cried to when she got punished for sneaking cookies from the cookie jar, all the way up to the big cry when they'd had to move away from the only house she ever lived in to come here to this big, dark, old mansion. He had been that person. Then he wasn't. And now? Now he might be something worse.

She felt an icy bolt go through her heart as she recalled the way he had looked her over in the interrogation room at the jail. The flash of recognition replaced instantly by eyes so filmy and flat they fit a dead man's face; or a shark. It was a sight she never wanted to see again. It was unseeing; unbelieving, and she decided, deadly.

She didn't know what he meant to do next but she didn't want to see him alone. Not now and maybe not ever again. So she had lost him again, perhaps even more profoundly than she had when she discovered him kissing her mother.

Balancing this loss, it seemed her mom and dad had found each other in the midst of all that had gone on in the past week. Maybe it was the start of a new life or a restart of their old life. She didn't remember a time when they'd even looked at each other unless it was posed and public. When they were both just public figures.

Figures. What a funny but true thing to call the people her mother and father had become. Figures were what you wrote down on a math problem and lined up so you could add or subtract, multiply or divide. Everything had been like that for her family since the Treerights moved into this place and onto the stage of national politics—that's what they called it: a stage. Figures adding up or not; players reading lines. It was a confusing life for anyone.

And now this life, her life, had passed through death and come back again. At least that was what she guessed. No one had said this to her. No one asked. Like everything else that happened to her in these last few years, she was left to sort out death and life for herself.

She paused and thought about that. Was that true? She was sure that her life before dying had been that way, alone and on her own, but life after death was looking different. At least life in this old, dim world looked different. Her parents looked at each other and at her without the stage masks and without calculations in their eyes or on their lips.

The old priest from Hannah's church had hugged her like a friend hugging a friend on a happy day. His warm tears had fallen on her hand and reminded her of summer rain. It was the most authentic moment she'd ever spent with anyone in this house; the moment with her parents and the priest.

Maybe it was too real, for the other two had gone away without much fanfare. The round red-faced man actually seemed to flee and the younger bearded guy who tried to look like a hipster excused himself awkwardly. Then they all hugged and then they laughed a great belly laugh, the kind that leaves an uncomfortable ache that hurts so good.

Sending Father Mullenix to the jail was an example of unscripted living emerging for them. No one suggested it. They all thought it aloud at the same moment. It was the right thing because it was the right thing. They didn't know exactly why, but it was right. So the priest went and they stayed until Ms. Stoneman interrupted them with the news of Syd DeVito' news conference.

It was the first time Tabitha had heard someone say she had been raised from the dead. All the lies DeVito surrounded it with caused her to blush. She felt a twinge of anger but it was so out of place it flitted away like a bird finding no seed in a feeder.

Watching the reporters surge around Uncle Syd at the conclusion of his words gave her an odd feeling in her stomach. She was used to her father being the object of intense scrutiny, but she felt sure those people would soon surge around her.

For an instant, she flashed back to a time she and her mother and father visited New York City during the holidays. It had been before the governorship and the Secret Service; before anyone knew them from anyone else in that bustling mass of humans.

They had walked Times Square as if they were on a moving walkway in an airport except it was the pressure of the people that swept them along. Her mother suggested going to see a movie; anything to get out of the crowd and into a quieter place for a while. They got into the theater and barely squeezed in the doors. The lobby was packed with movie goers so close to each other, it felt like she was a potato chip in a Pringles can.

They tried to get to a ticket counter but it was very slow going. When the three of them were dead center of the lobby, several movies of the multiplex let out at once. Instantly the room overflowed from above. People poured down stairs and escalators like a torrent from a broken dam.

Tabitha had the panicky sensation they were about to drown. Her father sensed it at the same time and snatched her up into one arm. He took her mother by the hand and waded through people without apology until they broke the surface on a street that smelled like burned soft pretzels and car exhaust. It was the sweetest air in the world.

She had taken her father by the hand and remembered how good it was to be near him. The warmth of his grasp had pushed away the sickness in her gut.

Maybe his hands would be like that again now.

CHAPTER SEVENTY

Jackie knew his way around the city in ways that only a street rat or vice cop would. He knew how to be invisible because, unlike the movie about the man who turns invisible in a freak accident, he was born invisible.

It was only after his father-in-law and Macher saw him that he started to be visible even to himself.

He walked away from the hospital and into this invisibility as seamlessly as if he'd put on the cloak from *Harry Potter*. Making his way to one of the addresses Carol gave him, he thought about Macher and Poppie.

He wondered if he was about to make them wish they'd never known him. The situation was spinning fast and hard now; too fast and too hard for him to understand it or to stop it.

Doctor Fred Robinson's home turned out to be a disappointment. He imagined a mansion—it was a doctor's house after all—but the single family ranch at the address scrawled on a scrap sheet of note paper was nondescript. The house sat on a generous, immaculately kept lot in a decent neighborhood, but was unremarkable by any standard.

Jackie stood on the street outside the gate of the black wrought-iron fence and tried to remember what Carol had told him about the doctor. He was single, never married, and spent an inordinate amount of time at work. He was fussy about small details down to the placement of periods and commas in documentation. From where he stood, Jackie could see this carried over to at least as far as the exterior of the man's home.

The yard was mowed in a cross-hatched pattern only possible if the grass was mowed one way and then another, no doubt doubling the time it took to cut. Mulched flower beds lined the walk and fronted the house with various plants in regimental order in which no unauthorized weeds raised their heads. The windows facing the street gleamed, and black vinyl shutters stood out against a facade of cream-colored brick.

Jackie noted, as he swung open the gate and approached the front door, that Robinson had installed a video doorbell with motion-sensing capability. He hesitated, realizing he hadn't sorted out exactly how to approach the man.

Carol had mentioned that Robinson went off-shift the day of all the "craziness" in the morgue, as she put it. Jackie wondered just how much of the craziness the doctor was aware of.

Robinson sounded like a man who wouldn't respond well to the "bad cop" routine. Jackie had no real jurisdiction to throw around. Wearing civilian clothes and lacking even his hospital badge, he didn't have the means to fake it. He formed a line of questioning for Robinson assuming he knew all the "craziness," and decided to appeal to him with reason.

He pushed the doorbell button and heard the tinkling of its chime somewhere in the house. He waited. It was silent except for a light breeze rippling a wind chime on a neighbor's porch. He rang again. No movement. Sucking in his cheeks, he pondered his next move. He knew he wasn't leaving without seeing Robinson or assuring himself the doc was out. He checked to see if his presence had attracted anyone's attention. The street was dead.

He stepped off the stoop and walked to the garage door. It had little rounded windows just above eye level and he had to jump to see in. In the edge of the sunlight streaming into the garage he could see the back end of the car from the security video. Full-sized Beamer, spotless and glossy black. He wanted to see in that trunk. He tried the garage door handle, knowing it wouldn't budge, and it didn't. The car was sealed up tight like a big black cricket in a pantry.

Returning to the front door, he tried the doorknob. It turned but the door didn't budge. Deadbolt.

Jackie checked the street and surrounding houses for observers. When he had been a street rat, he regularly used brazenness to accomplish petty thievery. Don't go to the back door of a place in the middle of the night when you could go through the front in broad daylight. Look like you belong and go with it. Keep your head high and do it. Besides, daylight meant less gear and less need to worry about noise. People expect sounds of life in the daylight that set them on edge in the darkness; sounds that could get a person shot.

He pulled out his pocket Leatherman and used it to open the door as quickly and surely as if he had a key.

The door swung open into a spacious entryway. He stepped in and pushed it back enough to make it appear closed from the street but open enough for a quick exit. *Old habits die hard*, he thought. He stood silently for a moment, straining to hear any sounds of life. He heard only the low *wump wump* of a ceiling fan.

Advancing into the house, he abandoned thoughts of a friendly encounter with Robinson. It would be awkward now, but he hoped it wouldn't be ugly.

There was no sign of the occupant. Robinson never worked nights, according to Carol, so it wouldn't be likely he was sleeping at this time of day. But where was he?

Jackie advanced into the house and found himself in an antiseptic living room that reminded him of a neighbor's house he and

Maria visited where all the furniture was wrapped in plastic slip covers. This place was similar. It looked more like a furniture store showroom than a living room. Even the books on the coffee table, perfectly angled with crisp unnecessary dust jackets, had the appearance of props rather than reading material. Dust was as unwelcome here as weeds in the manicured flower beds out front.

The house opened wide to the left with the kitchen, dining area, and living room distinguished only by their outfitting. A hallway on his right led away into the personal quarters. Robinson was single, so the rooms he encountered on either side of the hallway would probably be repurposed.

Jackie was surprised to find the first room fully turned out in another furniture-store-display guest bedroom suite complete with throw pillows on the bed and a full-sized vanity taking up a sizable wall space. This room, like the inaptly named living room, looked untouched and untouchable. Robinson was certainly a clean guy. Weird for a middle aged bachelor, Jackie thought.

But what would he know of a life like this? The thought led him to think of where he was and what he was doing. He didn't like skulking around like the old street bandit he had been. He came here with honest intent and a good cause. As this thought clicked, he stepped back into the hallway and called out before he could change his mind.

"Doctor Robinson!" His voice sounded like a gunshot in the dimly lit hallway. He strained to hear any response. None came.

"Doc! It's Jackie Smith. I'm from the hospital security office!"

Nothing.

He advanced to the last door and paused outside, listening again. He knocked and opened the door simultaneously. A spacious master bedroom bathed in afternoon sunlight greeted him mutely. He could see through the open door of an equally generous bath that no one was here.

The bed was neatly made. The room smelled faintly of some hidden air freshener. The only place in the room or in the house that he'd seen so far that appeared to indicate anyone lived here was a desk on the far wall topped with a bookshelf reaching to the ceiling. The top desk drawer was slightly open.

A yellow legal pad sat on top of the desk with an ink pen beside it. Jackie approached the desk and looked at the yellow pad. It was blank but he could see indentations where someone, presumably Robinson, had written on sheets now missing, pressing hard enough at a few points to cause black ink to bleed through. He ran his fingers absently over the paper, feeling the ghost writing as if it were Braille.

Everything so neat. It was creepy. He scanned the book shelf. Most of the books had the pristine look of props in keeping with everything else he'd seen in this house, but on the lowest nook, just at eye level for someone seated at the desk, there were a few volumes creased with use.

A big paperback brick of a book with block lettering: *DSM-5* stood out from the crowd. Next to the brick were several volumes bearing the evidence of having been used. *God's Debris* by Scott Adams—that got Jackie's attention because the author had the same name as the guy who did the funny cartoons about Dilbert, *The God Delusion* by Dawkins, and the three volumes of *The Lord of the Rings*. Next to these there was a thin leather bound book he identified as a Bible without seeing any marking on the binding.

He pulled out the Adams book, curious to see if it was a comic book in disguise and was disappointed to see it had no Dilbert frames in it. The back cover showed that it was the same guy though. Jackie put it back in its place.

There was something about the blank legal pad that bothered him. He held it up at an angle to the light fading in the window. Most of the sheet bore the crisscrossed marks of several written-over sheets, but at the bottom of the remaining sheet, where little specks of ink showed up from the pressure of a pen, he could make out the indentation of a neat, cursive signature. It was Robinson. He took the pad with him as he retraced his footsteps to the entryway.

The kitchen was as equally untouched as everything else. He even thought he caught a whiff of the rubbery smell of new appliances as he passed through to what must be the door to the garage.

But he also sniffed something else that was as far from new and very out of place in this too well-ordered home. When he opened the door it got stronger. It was the sick-sweet smell of decay.

He flipped the light switch just inside the door and saw the source. Fred Robinson sat behind the wheel of his shiny BMW, a green garden hose snaked along the passenger side into the window, held there by several strips of silver-grey duct tape, the head of the deadly green snake forever perched inches inside the car where it had spewed its noxious poison.

The garage, suicide scene included, was a reflection of the house. All things in their places down to the doctor slowly rotting with his seat belt on and precise lengths of duct tape sealing the slight space between open car window and frame. The car must have run for a long time. There was a taste of exhaust fumes in the air, adding to the unholy palette for eyes, nose, and mouth.

Jackie approached the car solemnly. He had seen death on the street more times than he liked remembering, but only in the company of others. Walking alone into a lonely death unnerved him.

Suddenly the urge to leave surged into his chest like a rogue wave. He turned to go but noticed two things as he did; a sheaf of yellow paper paper-clipped neatly together on the passenger seat next to the dead doctor, and the car keys in the center cup holder.

Then he remembered the sheet. He wanted that sheet and whatever it might be wrapped around. And he wanted to read what

Robinson had written on that legal pad before he came in here and strapped himself in for a one-way ride out of this world.

Jackie tried the passenger-side door. Locked. He moved to the driver's side and wondered what he would do if it was locked too. His law enforcement brain began to kick in. While this had the air-tight look of a suicide, he'd broken into the house. Breaking into the car would disturb evidence and leave it at the same time. The last thing he needed was to be implicated in a bizarre murder/suicide investigation.

Thankfully, the door was not locked. He slowly opened it. The smell of decay grew. How long had the doctor been here alone, dead and unlooked for? He judged by the smell and the state of the body it couldn't have been more than a few days. Long enough for the decomposition to get going but not long enough for it to reach the stage when the weight of all the body fluids found their way out and made a real mess.

He'd seen that before when he and his gang found a homeless junkie who became a misshapen skin sack puddled on an abandoned couch. He hesitated, taking in the scene and looking for signs that could suggest anything other than the obvious cause of death.

Robinson, as Jackie had already noted, was wearing the seatbelt. His eyes were closed and his head rested back on the headrest. Jackie realized that the doctor had inclined his seat slightly. Taken with the presence of the belt he decided that Robinson wanted everything in place even after he left. He wanted to be found upright and slotted into his spot like one of the books on his shelf.

Robinson's hands and upper arms protruded from the sleeves of the white doctor's coat which bore his name. The same coat Jackie and Macher saw on the security camera video. There was a bulge in the right breast pocket where a brown-orange plastic prescription bottle poked out.

Jackie reached out gingerly and removed the bottle and popped the lid. Xanax. Three quarters of the pills were there. Jackie knew little about Xanax but he doubted taking a quarter bottle of it would kill a person.

The label said it should be taken twice a day as needed for anxiety. Strange that a man who helped people with mental illnesses was himself on meds for a mental condition. Or maybe it wasn't. Seeing crazy people all day must be stressful.

He replaced the bottle. The picture was getting more clear. Robinson had arranged everything to take his own life, got in the car, strapped himself in, and taken a few pills to ease himself into eternity. The car must have run till it emptied itself of fuel. And here he was, as peaceful as sitting on a park bench.

The odor jogged Jackie back into the moment. He retrieved the key fob from the center console along with the paper-clipped sheaf of yellow papers. Realizing he had left prints inside the car, he looked around the garage for a rag to wipe things down. Finding nothing evident to accomplish the task, he remembered the sheet he wanted to examine. That would do just fine if it was still in the trunk.

He closed the door on the doctor and used the fob to unlock the trunk, which obediently clicked open and silently raised a few inches like the mouth of a crypt. It was tight quarters between the car and the garage door. Jackie stood with his knees pressed against the rear bumper while he emptied the contents.

There was little there; a first aid kit—ironic in a dead man's car—a combination emergency radio/jumper cable/air pump that showed a green fully charged light, and a full sized umbrella. The dead doctor had been a thoroughly prepared guy.

Laying all this aside while mentally mapping where each item had been, he found the pull tab for the spare tire cover and pulled it up, half expecting the sheet would be gone. But there it was, peeking out from beside the spare, bone white against Treadstone black.

Jackie stooped over to retrieve the sheet, expecting to feel the weight of whatever was wrapped inside it. He lifted the square of folded cloth. It was like an empty envelope. He frowned. What was this then?

He carried the empty cloth pouch to the center of the garage directly under a bright fluorescent light. Maybe it contained something small. Maybe a bit of paper. He slowly unfolded it, assuring himself he wasn't missing something in each successive fold, but when he had opened the sheet fully there was nothing to see, not even a stray thread or piece of lint. He returned to the trunk and got out his phone to use its flashlight.

The screen popped on, showing five missed calls from Maria and an equal number of texts. He didn't understand how he missed all this activity. Must have been so focused on finding the doc he didn't feel the buzz.

The texts made his heart skip a beat and accelerate. Maria was watching some press conference and wanted to know if Jackie was watching. From there the texts became more and more frantic interspersed with missed calls.

Was he the person Syd DeVito was talking about? Why wasn't he answering? Did he know Rich Macher had been arrested?

The police are here looking for you! Please call me. I'm taking the kids to Dad's house. He is making calls asking what people in the force know. Please call me I'm scared.

Jackie felt sick to his stomach. He began to hit Maria's speed dial and stopped. He didn't know all the ins and outs of cell technology and how to trace where phones were when they connected but he didn't want to chance originating a call or for that matter a text from inside this house. He also thought it likely Maria was being watched, even in Poppie's house.

He didn't want her to worry and he didn't have any answers to stop his own worries right now. Better finish finding whatever he could find here and get out. What was that about Syd DeVito? This day had gone from a life-changing—no, world-changing—discovery to a wrecking ball swinging randomly through his world.

He searched the spare tire compartment and the rest of the trunk. Empty. Like the sheet itself, there wasn't a thread or speck of lint. It was as if Robinson had banished all unauthorized objects from his world, and only left room for the things he wanted in the order he wanted. No wonder the guy chewed on the nurses at the hospital. A man used to keeping a car trunk so completely in line would not take well to having a coworker miss a comma in a report.

Jackie let that sink in for a moment and asked himself the obvious question: what got so out of order that Robinson couldn't put it back again? What could be so disorderly that he would decide to die rather than force it back into place?

He returned to the sheet. The sheet? Robinson went to a lot of trouble to bring that sheet away from the hospital. Jackie and Macher had assumed it concealed something. But there it was, naked and empty like a white shadow on the slate gray floor. He picked it up and smelled it reflexively; a habit he had gotten into when he and Maria put fresh sheets on their bed.

A whiff of something strange triggered his memory. Where was it? Fresh and starchy but something else too. Then it connected like an electrical circuit. It smelled like the hospital morgue.

Of all the hospital smells—Pine Sol and hand sanitizer, blood and urine—the morgue was most distinct. It was like all those other smells were not allowed there. Everything there had a very particular place and it didn't move. And it had a smell that got in you and stayed on you when you left. The guys joked about it, called it dead stank, but it was creepy and it wasn't what death smelled like at all.

The garage was just beginning to smell like death. No, the morgue smelled like bright lights and formaldehyde. A chemical smell that pronounced lifelessness more than it did death. Dead things trying not to be dead. And the sheet smelled like the morgue. Jackie reexamined the sheet, pulling it through his hands like a skein of yarn, knowing what he would find before he saw the purple stamped words. They were there plain to see:

Property of DUMC
Dec. Care Dept.

CHAPTER SEVENTY-ONE

Doug stirred on his bunk. It was late afternoon but he didn't know how he knew. Time came to him like faint whispers.

Since leaving the meeting with the priest he had been moved to a tiny single cell in the innermost section of the jail; the city jail's equivalent of solitary. The warden told him it was for his protection but it was difficult sensing the difference between being safe and being punished. He took his meals alone in the cell and had not been allowed out since his visit with Father Mullenix. As a ChoMo he'd been through this routine plenty of times before. It wasn't something he ever got used to; now was no exception.

He reflected on his situation since DeVito had gone public with his version of the Tabitha story. Clearly he was in trouble if this came from the top. If DeVito convinced the governor to use the miracle to propel his political career forward, Doug couldn't expect help from him. The priest had turned white as a sheet listening to DeVito, mumbled something Doug didn't understand, and bolted out of the interrogation room.

And here he was, falling deeper into the Chateau D'if. He thought about his favorite story. The Count of Monte Cristo had his priest, his Abbé Faria who helped him unlock his mind and his prison cell. Mullenix didn't seem like the man to fill the spot at the moment.

Doug felt heavy, as if gravity itself had increased as he went further into the jail and the story got darker. He knew they couldn't keep him in a city jail indefinitely, but they had also sent someone here to kill him.

Justice became more and more elastic with increasing power; it was clear to anyone who followed politics. Doug was a nobody from nowhere and his life intersected the life of the country's most powerful politician. He expected what he learned in prison and in politics to show itself here and now: power is reality from the prison courtyard to the steps of the courthouse; justice, well, it was more of a concept riding along on the back of the big black horse named Power. He could expect as much justice as he could demonstrate power, and that left him little hope at present.

He opened the paperback Bible Mullenix had left with him and thumbed to the passage that got him into so much trouble. *Talitha koum.*

But that wasn't true, was it? It wasn't the Bible that got him into this cell. It was the voice. That insistent voice.

Drive. Drive west. Drive to Durham. The hospital. The chapel.

Yeah. It was the voice that got him to that place. There was something both reassuring and infuriating about this knowledge. Hearing a voice meant he was either a crazy person, or he was hearing a person. People speak. Voices aren't detached from a person; even one who is coo-coo.

It was reassuring because the person who led him to Tabitha and the morgue could not have been Doug. And the person who told him what was ailing the assassin and what to say to him couldn't have been Doug. So he wasn't crazy. But man, c'mon. The same voice; the same person got him into this place. *Maybe I didn't have much but at least I wasn't caged up like this back in Norfolk,* he thought.

This person, the one behind the voice, was dangerous. He could get you killed. Doug read the passage about the little girl again. Jesus. The voice must be Jesus. But that was weird.

Where is he? How can I be hearing his voice? Is Jesus in my head?

The guys he met in prison who told him about Jesus and salvation said he needed to invite Jesus into his heart, and he'd done it. He'd said the prayer they asked him to pray. He guessed he had a picture in his mind of a red valentine-shaped heart with a little door in it. He imagined himself opening it and inviting in this tiny little guy in a white robe.

In truth it was comical to him. He wanted to laugh, but the guys around him were so somber; heads bowed, eyes pressed shut so hard it looked like it hurt. They took turns praying after he prayed. When they were all done they each looked hard into his eyes as if they were trying to see Jesus there.

But Jesus was supposed to go in through the heart, not the eyes, right? He tried to reflect back and see whatever they were looking for but he wasn't sure he did. He had felt lighter. He remembered that. Prison was weighty. It was heavy on the lightest day.

He felt a streak of that familiar sorrow dance through his chest at the recollection of prison gravity. Reliving it now in this place after following that little, white-robed guy out of his nice light apartment with no bars on the windows into solitary confinement... infuriating.

He didn't deserve this. Or did he? Mullenix didn't say so, and he was a professional Jesus follower. The guys in prison said Jesus forgave all our sins when he died on the cross and all he had to do was accept Jesus and it all went away.

He believed it. He didn't know why he did, but he believed it. So he prayed. And then they gave him a Bible like this one and told him to read it and pray every day. And he had to quit smoking and cussing and jerking off to pictures of naked girls or even thinking about naked girls. He had to go to church meetings and Bible studies. They called it the walk. Or was it the Walk? They said it was what you did if you were Christian.

He saw this much like the other gangs in prison; there were the blacks, Hispanics, and Muslims who all had their code and community. He tried to keep up with the rules, tried to be a good Christian, but he always felt something was wrong with him.

He was never good at reading and this walk seemed to revolve around that one activity more than any other. They were always talking about "being in the word" or quoting bits of the Bible he didn't understand.

It reminded him of trigonometry class. He sat there like a bird on an airstrip with planes zipping over his head so fast he couldn't see them, only hoping he wouldn't get hit by one, but also knowing he was supposed to fly. His wings looked puny compared to what was around him, and it was all so meaninglessly loud. He decided the safe thing to do was stay on the ground and pray there wasn't going to be a test like the ones he failed in high school; the ones that blasted him right out of higher math into vocational math class.

The tests in his new gang turned out to be more subtle than math class and no one talked about making him leave, but he could see in their eyes he wasn't making the grade. When they asked if he memorized the Bible bits or if he was too heavy in his heart or head to make it to a required meeting.

Yes. He saw it in their eyes. Maybe that little Jesus never went in the valentine heart. That's what their looks made him feel like. Maybe that's why he was here now and not free. The Chateau D'if.

He looked back and saw that even though he tried to do the things the other Christians said he needed to do, he could make a long list of failures. Lots of impure thoughts about sex. Lots of angry thoughts, even hateful thoughts toward people. Yeah, he was not passing the course.

"I'm sorry if I missed the point," he said out loud. "I'm sorry if I did something wrong." Then he corrected himself. "I know I've done so much wrong. They told me you would forgive all my sins, but that was before. Now what do I do? Was it you that brought me here? Did you know I'd end up in jail again? I belong here so you set me up?"

He waited in the silence of the cell. He was cold. He took the scratchy green wool blanket off the cot and draped it over his head and shoulders like a shawl. It was so still and quiet in the inner cell he could hear his heart beating.

"Well? Where are you now?"

Nothing but his beating heart and the mechanical hum of the building.

"I know you can hear me!" he shouted. "I know you can speak. I know you can talk to me. I believe it. I have heard you. Please. Let's talk. I don't like this place. I want to go home. All I did was listen and follow…"

As these words came out of his mouth, the floor of the cell rumbled. He felt a disorienting lull in the atmosphere as if for an instant the whole sentence of the world came to a comma, and then began again. Simultaneously the door of the cell rattled and swung outward. From under his makeshift prayer shawl, Doug peered into the brightly lit passageway, expecting to see a guard. No one was there.

"Hello?"

He strained to hear any movement. Nothing. He got up and went to the door and stuck his head out, looking either way. No one was in sight. His heart rate increased. He knew it was foolish to leave the cell. Where would he go? What would he do? Certainly there was nothing ahead but dead ends and more locked doors.

"Well? What now? Is this you? What should I do?"

He heard a whisper so small it was barely discernible.

What do you want to do?

It scared him. He stepped back into the cell and pressed himself against the wall. He took in a few big gulps of air.

"Me? Is that just me? Is it you? Would you ever say that to me? What do I want to do? That's got to be me. This is going to drive me nuts. How do I know you from me? Me from you?"

What do you want to do?

He put one hand on his chest and pressed it there, just feeling its reality and willing his heart to slow down.

"I... ah, I don't wanna be here. I don't like this place. I want to go."

He listened but heard only the steady hum of the building restored from its lull as if nothing ever happened and ever would again.

"Okay. Okay then. I'm going to go now."

He stepped into the passageway and stood squarely in the middle before the open cell door. He had no idea which way led out or further in and he still couldn't believe he was going anywhere farther than the next cell block and a locked door.

He turned to the left and shuffled gingerly along on the white tiles. A dotted line consisting of roughly-torn segments of red tape ran down the center of the passageway. He tried to concentrate on staying in on it. One block at a time to the end. Only a right turn available, so he went right and ran right into the door separating the isolation block from the gen pop common area.

He could see through the thick glass in the door that there was a short passageway between this door and another door that looked like it could double as part of a tank. He glanced up and saw the security camera pointed on the spot he occupied. The red indicator light blinked steadily. Couldn't be long now till the guards noticed one of the sheep was out of its pen.

He placed his hand on the first door and lightly pushed. It didn't move. He pushed harder. Solid. Might as well be pushing on a wall.

"Oh, well. I didn't really believe I was leaving anyway," he half whispered to the door.

Pull.

"Wha?"

You quit too easy.

"Huh?"

Pull.

Doug looked at the door and laughed a barely audible snigger. The ridiculous journey from Norfolk to Durham and the ridiculous miracles of the morgue and the jail telescoped backward in an instant.

He remembered suddenly a day long ago standing at a pullover on the Blue Ridge Parkway with his family. The whole world opened up before them. He was so small and everything was so big. You could see forever up there. You could see it all.

He came back to himself. He saw it all in an instant. Pushing when he should have pulled. Quitting when the answer was near and simple. Believing he was locked down by others when in fact he could walk away with ease if he was willing to try something new.

He laughed aloud and full. It felt good and real and rich and genuine.

He saw it all; even the ugly shadows of the worst of himself, but from up here they blended in with the whole and looked like they belonged. They were part of him too. The laughing turned to a choked cry and racked him.

It dawned on him that he liked his life. He liked himself. And it was right. No shame or guilt or lack. Whole. It was something he never forgot the rest of his life. The first time he felt he was himself and himself was enough.

He stepped back and pulled the door handle, knowing before he did it would yield. It did. And the next door also opened easily. He proceeded across the common area with its lingering scent of Pine Sol-coated prisoner funk.

The guards. What about the guards and the staff and the front end of the jail that would be full of people? His khaki jumpsuit and white rubber shower shoes over white tube socks was not an outfit lending itself to blending in.

He kept walking, his shuffling footsteps incongruent with the confidence he felt rising in his chest. He was going where he wanted to go and he was leaving this place. He didn't have to know how, he only had to keep going.

When he reached the last door opening into the non-secure area, he didn't hesitate. His heart rate was slow and steady. He looked straight ahead as people passed him in the narrow hallway leading past the interrogation rooms.

He met a well-dressed middle-aged lady he recognized from one of his trips back and forth in the jail. She was reading a paper on top of a stack of manila folders. She glanced up and met his eyes. He expected to see recognition morphing into alarm; instead she gave a nod of acknowledgement and went on reading her paperwork.

Doug proceeded, wondering what he looked like to the woman; obviously he must not look like an escaping con. He met two men as he turned the corner to the left leading to the huge front desk where the watch captain sat. One wore khaki pants and a blue sports coat that all men of uniform wear as a non-uniform uniform. Detective. The other was a uniformed cop. They continued a conversation without giving him a glance. People saw him but didn't see him. He kept walking and decided he would take the last hurdle differently than all the others he passed.

The watch captain was a wisp of a man who looked like he could have been a cut-out paper doll from an old fashioned child's play set. Doug pushed through the swinging half door at the side of the elevated desk and let it flap its way back to its place noisily. The paper cut-out cop turned to him, gave him a once-over, and returned to pursuing a sheaf of documents on the desk before him. His flat expression remained unchanged. Doug might as well have been the cleaning lady carrying out the trash.

Only the double glass doors opening on the street remained ahead. He could see the red-pink edge of a gorgeous sunset fading into a bruised purple dome of sky as it peaked between the buildings of downtown.

Where would he go from here? Push or pull? A man turned in from the sidewalk and opened the doors—they were doors you could either push or pull—ah, another concept to remember. He held the door for Doug and grunted "no problem" when he thanked him. As Doug was about to step through, a thought struck him and he paused.

"Mister, I'm not from here. Could you tell me the way to the bus station?"

The man gave him the same up and down as the paper cut-out cop.

"Sure, friend," he said, and his expression matched his words. "Take a left out the door, go down three blocks and then go left again. Station's on that street. Just keep goin' till you see it." He gave a funny twitch of his nose. "Probably smell diesel before you get there if you got a sniffer like mine."

The man had kind eyes in a forgettable face. He looked at Doug hard for a second, held up a hand and pointed at him as his expression changed. Doug thought for an instant he was about to realize who and what he was looking at.

"Listen, friend," he said, shaking the finger in the air. "It may sound weird but I felt like I heard, well,…" He looked embarrassed. "…a voice this morning. I'm not crazy or anything," he quickly added as Doug's eyes widened slightly. "It's just something that happens now and then to me. I try to listen. I pray I guess. I'm a Christian, you see…"

Doug could see the man struggling. He said, "I am too. A Christian. I hear voices too. I mean I hear a voice."

The man looked relieved. He continued. "Anyways, I felt like I heard I was going to meet someone today and they would be in need and I should help them. I forgot about it till just now. Busy day. Hard day."

He reached in his back pocket and pulled out a worn billfold, all the while holding eye contact with Doug. "I kind of have a rule of thumb that when I feel I'm supposed to give a gift to someone, I give them everything I have on me." He opened the wallet and pulled out a neat little stack of cash that Doug purposely didn't look at. The man pushed the bills into Doug's hands.

"Take it. It's not much really. And it won't buy me what I need anyway."

Doug looked closely and saw creases around the man's mouth and eyes and the grey pallor of sleeplessness; a young man with worry aging him. He heard himself speaking as if it were someone else.

"She's not in Raleigh. Chrissy. Your girl. Look for her in Atlanta. Alpharetta. She is with a girl named Kim on Dunlow Avenue. By the time you get home, there will be a call asking you to come get her. Don't be afraid. The fight isn't over and don't expect her to be happy about coming back here. Rest. She won't run forever. She will hear for herself when she is ready."

The two men were face to face. Doug wrapped his arms around the stranger. The man began to cry.

He said, "I hear things too. Don't ask me how. I don't know. Go home. I'm sure it's all true."

The man turned and hurriedly walked away, pulling out his cell phone as he did. Doug looked at the cash wadded in his hand and stuffed it into a pocket. No need to count it. It would be more than enough. He was sure.

CHAPTER SEVENTY-TWO

Syd DeVito drove himself to his office. He was sure the frenzy over what he said at the press conference was just the beginning.

He decided to give Daniel space to digest what he had done. He knew by now the governor must be aware of it. He also knew his initial reaction would be anger. They had gone through enough political fights together that Syd could read him. He rarely went off on his own like this, making Treeright follow, but his instincts were sharp and he had never led his man down a dead end path; only up and further up.

Treeright always came around to seeing Syd's moves as being for the best. It would be so this time too.

And Syd was positive he had pulled off the master stroke of all master strokes. They might rewrite the constitution for Treeright. Not only would he get elected, he would be, beyond question, the most powerful president ever to sit in the Oval Office, or for that matter the most powerful leader of a nation since the Ceasars.

Treeright was going to be a god, and Syd had created him. What would that look like? His mouth twitched with anticipation.

But there remained some messy little details to clean up. He felt confident his stories about Windsor and Macher would grow legs and run those two into the ground. They would be ruined. At the very least he had created so much smoke around them that everything either of them said would be painted with a bright red stripe of suspicion.

He smiled to himself at the masterful way he had wrapped those two into a single lie, connecting them with an anchor that would sink them. *When you're good you're good*, he thought to himself, and there was no denying he was good at this kind of work; maybe born for it.

The second mess was much more sensitive. It temporarily wiped the smile off his face. How would he find and dispose of Tabitha Treeright's body? He knew he was in a forced position. He needed to use his network of resources to locate her body, but every person he used became a liability; another potential leaker who could bring down the whole scheme on his head.

Sooner or later, Daniel would see what Syd knew from the start; Tabitha was dead and the girl living in his house was an imposter. It was inevitable; a matter of time and exposure. She would slip up sooner rather than later.

He mulled that over. Well, if she wanted to play a high stakes game, she had to be willing to pay the price. She was in now, no turning back. She was Heinlein's *Double Star*, a book Wanda insisted he read, useless at the time, but growing more useful by the moment. That girl, whoever she had been, was never going to be anyone but Tabitha Treeright. And if she ever thought about backing out; well, rising from the dead didn't make her immune from another tragic accident that would be more permanent.

He thought of the old mummy movie he watched late one night as a kid. He couldn't remember the name; some variation of mummy plus return or curse or revenge. It was black and white which made it scarier somehow.

The most vivid scene had come to him several times in the weeks after he watched it. An army of workers dug the tomb of a pharaoh in a secret place to keep it hidden. They were all dressed in loincloths. When the tomb was complete, all of them marched out of the hidden tomb into a valley in the desert. While they rested, another army of Egyptian soldiers rode up in chariots and slaughtered every single one of them, even the foremen and the designer of the tomb. No one remained alive to tell the secret.

All it takes is the will to act, he thought, and he had it.

He set his jaw, chewing the inside of his cheek. If only he could rub out any trace of the deception. He thought back to the conversation with the red-faced Reverend Daly. Had he mentioned how the church managed to tie up their loose ends? They had the same problem he had: a dead body that needed to stay off the radar forever.

He knew from watching enough crime shows, and from a few personal experiences he never dwelt upon, that dead bodies had a nasty habit of floating to the top no matter how thoroughly they were disposed of. He preferred bodies that were found and explained. It was easier to control that outcome and made for a neat end no one felt the need to keep tracking.

This was new ground. This body had to really and truly disappear without a trace. But he had to find it first.

Phillip's phone buzzed in his pocket. He scrambled to retrieve it. It was an unknown number. Unlike most people, he never let calls like this go to voicemail if he could help it. He had many associates who only used burner phones to conduct business.

"Go," he said.

"Thought you'd want to know Windsor skipped," said a familiar gravelly voice.

"Skipped? When? How?"

"No details yet. He's gone, is all I know. This is fresh though. Couldn't be more than a few hours. He was holed up with a Catholic priest 'at come from your man Treeright with orders to set 'em up and let them alone."

DeVito mulled this over. "Got a name for this priest?"

"No, but I can get it."

"Do that. What's the department doing about Windsor?"

There was a pause. "That's the strange thing. They aren't followin' protocol. Hasn't gone out on the wire. All that's happened so far is a search of the jail and questioning some guards. My guy tells me it's like the whole place is asleep." Gravel Voice coughed and cursed. "So what do you want to do?"

"What about Macher? He get processed yet? And Smith?"

"That's the other big news. The chief of security there, Harden's the name, is one of our guys. You ain't gonna believe what happened. The two of them, Macher and Smith, got caught creepin' around the security shack in the video room."

"Good. Good. They arrest them?" DeVito interrupted.

"That's the thing. When they got caught they knocked down a couple guards and tied them and the chief up."

"This is too good." DeVito said.

"Yeah, well, from the sounds of it they were looking through the tapes for something. They had control of the thing until a report came in about how the two of them were involved in child porn." Gravel Throat gave a raspy snort of a laugh. "But you already know about that. Anyways, that's when a third guard, who was helpin' them for some reason, lost her nerve and turned on 'em."

"So we have them in custody?"

"Macher, yes, but Smith left the shack before it flipped on them. Harden says Smith was on his way to the psych ward to ask questions about some doctor. He didn't get the name. They called for a lockdown but Smith didn't turn up. It's a big place and there's plenty of room to hide, so it's possible he's holed up in there."

"No," DeVito said. "He's sharper than that. And he knows the gaps in the system. Have to assume he got out." He didn't like the way this was shaping up; two liabilities in the wind and no idea which way it was blowing them.

"Okay. That's all good info. Here's what I need from you. Smith is the priority. I want him found. Send someone up to that psych ward and find out what he did there. And the guard that flipped, I want to know why he..."

"She."

"What?"

"The guard that helped them was a girl."

"Alright. I want to know who she is. Full detail. You know the drill. Take whatever assets you need."

"What about Windsor?"

DeVito hesitated.

"Well?"

"I don't want him recaptured."

"Roger that."

DeVito ended the call. His phone immediately buzzed. He was surprised to see it was Treeright. He considered sending it to voicemail. He had anticipated a cooling-off period before his boss confronted him. At the fourth ring he accepted the call.

"Daniel," he said in what he hoped sounded like a flat monotone.

"Syd I've got to hand it to you." The warm, rich voice of national fame flowed into his ears, catching him completely off guard. But, wary old pro that he was, Syd managed to catch himself before leaning into this opening. He remained silent, pursing his lips.

"Yes. No one plays the game like you do, Mr. DeVito. No one. Sometimes I'd like to have a little window at the back of your head so I could see those little gears turning, meshing, clicking until they come up with the precise movement for the moment." Treeright waited with the bait in the water. DeVito didn't bite. He gave it a twitch.

"You like press conferences? A lot can happen in a short time. It doesn't even take a big stage or a big group of hungry reporters to change everything. Remember the offhand comment at the end of the presser in that little town in backwater Virginia? What was the word? Macaca? And it was enough. And nowadays?! We don't even need a microphone or a camera. We... only... need... a cell phone." This last was muffled as Treeright evidently moved his phone away from his face and shifted it to put the call on speaker.

DeVito tensed at this, a feeling of dread building. Treeright gave the bait one last tantalizing twitch.

"Yes. We only need a cell phone, and a Twitter account. Change the world in one-hundred-forty characters or less."

"What are you doing, Daniel?"

The sound of digital keyboard clicks was all he could hear.

"Daniel?!"

"Hold your horses, Syd. I'm finishing up a tweet. Composing on a little screen isn't my forte."

There was another spate of clicks, then a long exhale.

"Let's talk before you send anything. I can be there in ten minutes." Although he tried to suppress it, Syd could hear the desperation in his voice.

"So you want to talk now? You didn't want to talk before your presser. Guess you've got a different set of rules for what you put in the public ear and what I do."

"God damn it, Daniel! This isn't about rules!"

"Strange choice of words, Syd. I've been thinking a lot about God... what he damns and what he doesn't. What he might be doing and what I should do about it. You said I'm a praying man, didn't you? Not just a praying man, but evidently I'm a praying man who knows how to raise the dead!"

"C'mon Daniel! You've got to see how powerful this story can be!"

"Story? It depends on what you mean by "story," Syd. Stories are powerful as much as they point to a truth or as much as they reveal something true. I'm afraid you mean something entirely different when you say "story." You mean lies are powerful. And I think you're in line with some really awful people when you use the term. You're much more like the Nazis. The bigger the lie, the more effective it can be, right?"

"Give me a break, Daniel. We both know how many lies it took to get where we are. Don't act like you're lily white. Don't pretend you all of a sudden got religion."

Daniel laughed. "No, Syd. I'm not white, lily or eggshell or any other shade. So tell me. How is it that my prayers are so powerful? How is it that in your story a guy like me gets an answer like a dead daughter coming back to life? That's your story, isn't it? That I'm some kind of messiah? Tell me how this plays out? Saint Daniel the great hope of the world? We know better. I know better!"

Syd interrupted. "Just slow down, Daniel. I didn't say you were a saint. This isn't just about us. It's about our movement! And we're on the edge of history. We can... *you* can redefine the course of the world. Don't do anything rash…"

"Rash?! Like calling a press conference to lie about raising someone from the dead?"

"So you see it now? You see it's a set up? What did she do to tip you off? I told you…"

"No, you fool! Tabitha is alive. She's alive. For a moment I thought you believed it too. You're good in front of the cameras, Syd. Damn good. I thought you'd gotten a clue. Maybe you just couldn't stand the idea that a vagabond like Windsor would get the credit for her miracle.

"Maybe you even convinced yourself I prayed when we went to the morgue that night. But when you started in on the child porn angle it all came clear. You're a good actor on their stage, but we've played too much political poker. I know your tells. And I know the truth."

DeVito sneered. "Who cares about Windsor? He's not even going to be a footnote when this story is written. Truth? Keep your truth. Truth belongs to whoever is powerful and brave enough to shape the facts into something useful. What does it matter if I believe Tabitha is alive or not? You believe it and I'm glad for you. Now leave the truth to me and let me make it useful to us."

There was a long silence. DeVito strained to hear. "Daniel?"

"I've got a lot to atone for, Syd. I played the game rough and ready all these years. I played it. I played it with my conscience, with my friends and my enemies. I even played it with my wife. I let her be just another piece on the board. And my daughter too, I let myself believe she wasn't on the board, that I drew the line at Tabby. But that was a lie. There was nothing and no one I didn't put on the board. When she died... when she died I saw it all in a flash..."

"What? What did you see? That you've given your life for the cause? For things bigger than yourself? Made sacrifices so that millions could have better lives, be more free, have equal justice?! Did you see that?!"

Daniel sighed deeply. "Syd, I love you. I do. Despite all that's happened. And I forgive you. It's actually easier to do that than to forgive me. Listen closely. This may be the last time we speak for a long time; maybe forever."

"Daniel, what..."

"Listen, friend. Starting out well doesn't mean going along or ending well. Great ideals don't guarantee great outcomes. I've thought about it a lot over the past several days. It's like weddings, isn't it? Why do people spend so much money, time, and effort on a wedding? Is it really out of love and excitement? Or is there a little bit of superstition in it? Maybe if we tee this up just right, we will have a good marriage. If we get a perfect beginning, we might not lose the coin flip chances of a marriage succeeding. But look at what happens! Even with all that, marriages still fail half the time."

Treeright gave a rueful laugh. "We had great intentions, Syd. We started well. But the revelation is this: sacrifice isn't the problem; it's motivation. When I saw that I'd placed everything in my life on the table, I saw that it included me! Tabby was the last little part of me I'd pretended to hold back. Seeing her there, laid out in that morgue was like seeing myself. It was all I had. I put all I had into the game. And I asked a simple question: why? Why? Was it for one of our policies? A plank in the platform? Why did I lay down my life?"

DeVito couldn't contain himself and broke in. "Because you're a good man! Because you want to do good!"

"Good?" Treeright laughed. "Good? Is that what I am? Is that what we're doing? How do we know? Are you going to tell me it's good to sleep with another man's wife? To outright lie in order to get what we want? To destroy people's names? And," he hesitated, "and to 'remove' men who are in our way? Syd? That's a good man? That's doing good?"

Treeright's voice got distant again as he navigated on his phone. "I'm going to do you a favor, Syd. But you won't see it that way. Check your Twitter feed."

DeVito did so, switching to speaker phone as he did it.

The official Treeright for Our President account popped to the top of the feed. DeVito' heart raced at the first words:

"Today I am ending my campaign for the office of President of the United States. I have also informed Lt Gov Henry and the NC State legislature I am stepping down as governor effective immediately. Our family is grateful for your support and love. God bless us all."

He heard Treeright speaking as if through a long, dark culvert. "You're fired, Syd. I made that official just after your presser. I directed security to remove your access from all official computers and from entering buildings.

"I also directed IA to investigate the claims you made about Rich Macher, Jackie Smith, and Doug Windsor. I'm certain they will find out that the evidence you presented against them was manufactured, especially since I gave up all the information I have about your contacts with your fixers. In case you don't know it, your phones have been tapped ever since you took up with Wanda. I'm not proud of it. I wouldn't use it now except you've put three completely innocent bystanders under the bus and I can't leave them there."

He added, "If I were you, I'd get away somewhere and think hard about all that's happened. There's still time to change for all of us. There's still room to believe."

Syd pulled his car onto the shoulder of the road and turned off the ignition. A ghostly quiet fell. His hand trembled as he reached to push the red end call button. He saw the line was still open and heard a scratching sound.

"Uncle Syd?" A familiar voice.

"Uncle Syd?" It was an electric current to his head and heart. He almost dropped the phone.

"It's me, Tabby. I know it's hard. I love you, Uncle Syd. You can come home. I asked Mom and Dad. I told them you are family. You don't have to be alone."

Syd DeVito listened to the voice from the grave. He wanted it to be her. The closest thing he'd ever had to his own flesh and blood. His heart ached like the open ocean, vast and empty. He longed for it all to be true; for some sign of life in the endless deep blue depths.

"Tabby? Tabby girl?" He choked on a sob. "I miss you. I'm so sorry I couldn't keep you safe."

"I am safe! I'm safe at home! I'm with Mom and Dad! Uncle Syd? Don't cry!"

Vehicles sped past, vibrating the car with their insistent voices, hurrying to somewhere, mocking him. Syd had no more somewheres to be. His head ached with the sound. A text came up in his notifications. It was from the same number his fixer had just used. He swiped it open and read it at a glance.

It read: Eyes on Windsor. Confirm orders.

"Uncle Syd?"

He read the text over. Did he want Windsor to disappear? What good would it do now? He thought it over. Windsor was the link to whoever set this up and now they would get their wish. With Treeright gone, the race would break wide open again. The dogs in the pack would eat each other. And one of those dogs wrecked his life.

The emptiness in his heart began to fill with fire. He did have somewhere to be. It was driving a crane with a wrecking ball on it through the middle of that pack and watching them howl. If he couldn't have the bone, he'd make sure none of them would, and Windsor was the starting point. He had some specialists who would get the information he wanted out of the pervert.

"Uncle Sy-"

He broke the connection.

"Stupid man. The little bitch almost had me," he said out loud as he hit the callback button for a burner phone that held Douglas Windsor's fate.

CHAPTER SEVENTY-THREE

Jackie Smith wiped down every surface he had touched twice before leaving the doctor's house. He thought of making an anonymous call to alert the police of the suicide, but decided against it.

Halfway out the door he remembered the neatly stacked suicide note, forgotten in the discovery of the sheet from the morgue and the urgency of reconnecting with Maria. He was torn between sitting and reading the note, which was several pages long, and getting away from the scene of the suicide. He was also undecided as to what to do with the sheet.

He made a snap decision to leave the sheet and used his phone to take photos of the pages of Robinson's note before giving the house a last sweep for evidence of his presence and slipping out the side door of the garage.

It was a quiet neighborhood and he got off of Robinson's street quickly, unseen by anyone. He made good time toward home, using back streets and cut throughs. No one seemed to be following him, although he got a scare when a passing squad car turned around and flipped on its lights. His heart rate raced, but the patrolman was only after a red light runner.

Jackie changed directions discreetly, leaving the cop to his work ruining some poor slob's evening. His change of course brought him to a strip mall with a Walgreens and a TJ Maxx—two of his mainstays.

Stopping to orient himself, he saw a man in a set of tan coveralls walk out of the clothing store carrying several bags. He looked uncertain which way to go. Jackie's eyes were drawn to the man's feet. He did a double take. The man shuffled along in shower shoes.

As Jackie registered this information, several things happened at once. The man made up his mind to go to his right and started on a path leading him to an alleyway behind all the stores, and two men broke away from a conversation they were having at the store next to TJ Maxx and split up, one following Tan Coveralls and the other sprinting toward the other end of the strip mall where the alley looked into the parking lot.

It clicked in Jackie's head that he was seeing an escaped prisoner about to get taken down by the two men. One wore khakis, a white t-shirt with a black knit ski hat; the other wore jeans and a lightweight windbreaker. They didn't look it, but they had to be cops.

The brazenness of an escapee walking into a store still wearing prison clothes amused him and made him think of the videos he watched about the world's dumbest criminals. But the cops were blowing it. There was another end of the alley they would leave open if the escapee saw them coming.

He couldn't help himself. *Maybe I'm a candidate for the same show*, he thought. *I'm running from the law myself and I'm going to get involved in a police foot chase?* But it was like a moth to a flame for him. He ran to the opposite end of the strip mall to close off the last route of escape for the prisoner.

As he ran, a strange feeling came over him. It was as if this scene were playing out on video and he was watching it rather than in it.

From his video vantage point he saw the four players moving at once; the two people he assumed were lawmen, the man in the tan jumpsuit, and himself. The hunters had guessed right; he could see it as he focused on the lawmen moving to tighten the noose around the prisoner, who was now between them.

They didn't draw their guns. *That was odd,* he thought. *Why wouldn't they?* When they got to the alley, the two men took out long black batons of the kind Jackie recognized from European crime shows.

Advancing deliberately, the two made eye contact. One gave a sign to the other that their man was between them hiding beside a couple of green dumpsters behind the Chinese No. 5 restaurant.

Jackie made the far end of the alley and slowed to a walk as he turned toward them, mesmerized by the double vision of reality overlaid with the odd video surveillance in his head.

The prisoner shed the jumpsuit and laid it in the ground like a floor mat. Stepping onto it, he removed one white shower shoe and tube sock. The man, unaware of approaching danger, stood naked with the exception of a pair of tighty-whities and the remaining shower shoe and sock.

It was like watching a game-hunting show, except the deer in this show wouldn't be felled by a bullet from afar, but set upon by dogs he never sensed were there. Jackie was crossing the point where the alley divided when the dogs jumped their prey.

The double vision faded at the same time Jackie sighted the ambush; in years that followed he would never be quite sure which "eye" saw what happened, the surreal or the real, In either case he saw an image that he remembered the rest of his life.

Both the attackers—for that is how he immediately recast the situation—hit the nearly-naked man with their nasty looking black rod batons at the same time. He stood defenseless, empty-handed except for the new sweat shirt he had removed from the shopping bag.

The blows were to both legs. The man to the right wound up like a spring and unleashed himself with such force that the baton shattered the naked man's shin with a sickening thud. Jackie saw the white of bone punching through thin flesh as the man cried out and crumpled to the ground. The smell of urine added itself to the sweetly sickening scent of rotting food in and around the dumpsters.

"Hey! Hey Glenny!," said the bone-breaking thug. "He pissed himself!"

The second attacker stood over their writhing victim. He said nonsensically, "Better to be pissed off than pissed on, they say. He's gonna get the rest of the piss beat outta 'im once we get 'im to the boss."

Jackie stood frozen half a dozen paces from the spot. He knew plenty of violence from his life on the street. He had used it to get what he wanted and he had never been squeamish about shedding a little blood or breaking a few bones, but he prided himself on using force as an adjunct rather than a primary means of accomplishing his goals.

These two weren't violent; they were cruel, and it disturbed him. But he had other things to consider. He didn't want to test the two-on-one odds when his wife needed him home in one piece. He quietly began to retreat back the way he'd come when the bone breaker spoke again as he dropped a knee into the middle of the prone man's back, eliciting a gasp.

"Hear that, Windsor? You got another party to attend tonight." He laughed.

Jackie's head was spinning as he turned back. The prisoner managed to get one elbow under him and push his head up. He spotted

Jackie between the legs of his attackers and pleaded with his eyes for help.

It was him. Jackie saw the man from the morgue, bruised and cut, several days' growth of unshaved stubble, but no doubt about it: Doug Windsor.

Jackie hit the thug closest to him squarely in the temple. There was no thinking, no plan of action, only action. The man went down like a building toppled by explosives.

Knit Cap, kneeling on top of Windsor, tried to rise to the surprise counter attack, but like the majority of his ilk, he was only an effective fighter against unarmed or unsuspecting opponents. He was halfway between standing and kneeling when Jackie shattered his jaw with a crushing right-handed blow that shut his eyes and would have him eating through a straw for the better part of the next year.

Jackie's heart raced as he stood over the two men, face-down on the greasy asphalt. The sound of groaning snapped his head around and brought him down from the high of battle.

"Windsor?" he said, kneeling down beside Doug.

"My leg…" was all the man could say, gasping, his eyes rolling up into his head in agony.

Going into shock, Jackie realized, thankful now for the insight of a hundred painfully boring but mandatory first-aid training sessions at the hospital.

He needs warmth and he needs me to stop the bleeding. And I've got to get him to a…

Jackie realized the hard spot they were in instantly. An escaped prisoner and a fugitive from the law couldn't present themselves at the nearest patient-first and expect to leave free men.

Obviously these weren't cops he just knocked out, and that meant they must be working for some bad people in the city who wanted Windsor for themselves and their own reasons, probably the same people that wanted Jackie out of circulation.

Jackie checked the pockets of the two unconscious men. He found two cheap cell phones, obviously burners, and a wad of cash rolled in the fashion familiar to the street. Nothing else. No identification of any kind; another mark of professional and expendable muscle. No way to connect them to their overlords if they were caught up with an unforeseen difficulty.

It made Jackie smile a bit to add "like me." Knit Cap groaned and began to stir.

"Gotta move," Jackie said to Windsor, who looked anything other than able to move.

"Arrgh," was all he got in response.

Jackie made a snap decision. Using one of the burner phones, he dialed. He was surprised to get an answer on the first ring.

"Poppie? I need your help… no time for explaining."

CHAPTER SEVENTY-FOUR

Rich Macher felt like he had fallen into a pinball machine. He remembered his favorite table in his high school days, called Firepower; a machine that let you capture five balls in sequence, then a robotic, gravelly voice pronounced *Fy-re Pow-er* before launching them all at once in a ricocheting silver flurry.

These past few days… Firepower.

Bounced between the cold, hard edge of take-no-prisoners politics and the law, the firm grip of friendship and the surreal possibility of an earth-shaking, world-reorienting miracle. It was getting to be too much to handle, especially on four hours sleep and a shot-sized Styrofoam cup of burned-down coffee he had grabbed ages ago in the police station lobby. The same police station he was leaving after spending a half hour getting booked only to be unceremoniously released without explanation.

He stood at the top of the worn concrete steps holding a manila envelope containing his wristwatch, wallet, and cell phone and wondered if the silver balls were done or if he should just wait right here for the next bounce.

Glancing at his cell, he saw thirteen missed calls, twelve from his editor and one, less than five minutes ago, from a number not in his contacts. *Probably a robocall*, he thought.

He massaged his forehead, trying to forestall the beginnings of a headache that was related to lack of food or sleep or both. Putting on his watch, he noted the time and pocketed his wallet before crumpling up the envelope and tossing it in the combo butt/trash can at the base of the steps. He dialed his editor.

"James. I'm out. Whatcha got for me? Did you bail me out? I'm dipped if I know what just went down. Never saw a judge or bondsman or…"

"Macher!" The man screamed into the phone so loudly Rich recoiled and almost dropped the device.

When he held it back up to his ear, he was met with a stream of profanity-laced chronic updates on the events of the hours he'd been incommunicado. From the sound of it, Rich Macher went from respectable local citizen and well-loved reporter, to child porn kingpin and wanted criminal, to the victim of a high-level political hit job in just over the amount of time it took to catch a movie.

Too bad this wasn't a movie, he thought. No way to put this genie back in a bottle. He knew enough about the ebb and flow of these kinds of stories in the Information Age to foresee his future would be full of conspiracy and counter-conspiracy claims forever. Rich Macher was no longer himself; he was a story or part of a story.

Treeright out, DeVito under investigation, Windsor on the lamb; incredible developments all.

It took him a moment to process what he heard and realize the absence of information he most wanted to know.

"What about Tabitha Treeright?"

"What about her?" James asked.

Macher rubbed his forehead again, subconsciously trying to massage all the events his editor had just sprayed on him into his head.

He repeated the question. "What about Tabitha Treeright?! She is the story!"

James didn't miss a beat. "Oh, you mean the girl coming back to life thing? Yeah, the thinking on that is DeVito knew he was gonna get canned over the handling of the girl's body going missing, or maybe he knew Treeright was getting ready to pull the plug on the campaign, so he called a Hail Mary—try to force the governor to stay in the race. Sounds crazy, but the whole thing is crazy, it'n it? And DeVito had to know he was going under the bus if Treeright was gone.

"Man, you can't believe the dope we got on him. People are scramblin', Macher. Big names. Untouchables. It's unbelievable. Who knew? Raleigh is like a mob town. It's like I went to bed and woke up in Jersey. Anyway, we got plenty of ripe fruit. How you feelin'? Ready to go to work? Lots to do. Need you…"

"What about the video of the morgue?! The girl walking out of there? The people who saw her…"

"No one is claiming to have seen her. At least no one will go on record as seeing Tabitha Treeright. Videos? With what they pulled on you and that friend of yours, uh, what's his name? Smith? Yeah, with what they pulled on you guys, everyone believes all the footage from the morgue is more deepfake video. Makes sense. Obviously can't be real. When you coming in? We're gonna be going 24-7…"

Rich Macher punched the end call button and sat down on the steps. He re-tied his shoes, loose from the rapid job he'd done hastily leaving the jail. When he glanced up, a well-dressed man was standing in front of him surveying the street as if looking for someone. When they made eye contact, he said, "I know it's not likely…" He sputtered haltingly, obviously embarrassed.

Macher got up and looked him over.

"Well?"

The man dropped his eyes and held up one hand. "Never mind," he said.

Macher started to walk away, muttering as he did, "'Not likely.' Brother, you could put this whole day in that category."

It sparked the businessman, who looked like a little boy with a secret he just had to tell or he'd burst. "Bet mine's a crazier story than yours," he said.

Macher, tired as he was, couldn't resist. Curiosity was his line of work. "Let's hear it," he said.

"You won't believe it. I can't believe it myself. I think it's why I came back here looking for him."

Macher saw something in the man's face he'd missed in his fagged-out haze. It was joy that snuck up around his cheeks and filled his eyes with life. It was so intense it made the already handsome man look beautiful, like a natural wonder; a sunrise or the blue in a bluebird's back. Macher knew before he continued speaking this would be more of the Ripley's Believe it or Not world he'd fallen into.

"My name is Brian Lands. I came here a few hours ago, desperate. I needed help. I have a daughter named Chrissy…"

Lands poured out the account of his meeting a man on these very steps who told him where to find his daughter, and how everything he said about her had been true. He had come back here knowing it was foolishness but hoping to run into the stranger again to thank him.

Macher listened patiently as Lands tracked and backtracked through the tale, remembering new details that rerouted him back and forth circuitously. When Lands landed on his return to the scene of the crime, looking intensely into Macher's eyes, he couldn't think of anything to say, but his reporter-conditioned mind ejaculated a question.

"And to what do you attribute this?"

"Attribute?"

"Yes. It's an incredible story. How did the man know what he knew?"

The man's face brightened even more, like he'd discovered the last bit of intensity on a dimmer switch. "God!"

"God?"

"God. How do you explain it? I can't think of another way."

Macher considered this. He looked in the man's face again and thought of all the religious numb nuts he'd run into over the years; how he avoided them and their oversimplified explanations of every damn thing that happened.

God. He didn't believe in God and had no use for the trappings of the religious life. He realized even in the midst of following the story of Tabitha Treeright that he didn't consider God as an explanation. He also realized he wasn't looking for an explanation at all; he was looking for that elusive thing called "the story."

He was convinced, one way or another, she was the story, not an election or corruption, but the girl. He was convinced whatever happened in the morgue was the thing he needed to pursue. Jackie had him believing the girl was alive, but that was as far as Macher could go. With the videos released showing him doing and saying things he never did or said, his hold on the authenticity of Jackie's tape was tenuous.

"Hey?" Brian Lands broke in on his reverie. "You have another way to explain it?"

Macher gave the man a weary grin. "Nope," he said. "I don't. But I wouldn't say I'm firing on all cylinders right this minute. I'm glad you found your daughter at any rate. Hope things work out."

Lands reached out a hand to Macher and grasped his shoulder. "I'm sure it will work out. The same guy that told me where to find Chrissy told me it would take time but it would work out. He was right about the first thing, seems like a good idea to believe it all."

Macher thought of something. "This guy. Did he shake you down for money?"

"No. But I gave him all the cash I had on me."

Macher smirked and Lands caught on. "You've got it wrong, brother. He only asked where the bus station was and he was ready to shove off. I stopped him and gave him all my money before he told me anything about Chrissy."

Macher didn't change his mind or his expression. "Are you in the habit of giving away all your money to strangers for no reason?" he asked in a tone more sour than he felt toward the man and immediately regretted.

Lands was unfazed. "No. I don't do it often. I hardly ever give money to street people. In fact, I never do. But sometimes I feel like I'm supposed to do it."

Macher held up a finger to stop him, "Let me guess... God tells you?"

"Yes. I guess I'd call it that. Although it's something I hear in my head. Nothing crazy. Just an impression or something like it."

"You said the guy was a street person? Why would he need a bus? Most of the homeless folks I know in town live on a few blocks and never move too far from their own nest."

This was the first thing that seemed to dim Lands' countenance. "Good point."

Macher went on, in his investigative persona. "And why come back here to find a guy you bankrolled for a trip out of town?"

"Right again." Lands pursed his lips in thought. "On the second point, I think I came back here because I wanted to remember the meeting since it turned out to be the most important thing that's happened to me, maybe ever. I don't think I really expected to find him. On the first... now that I think of it, he wasn't dressed like a street person at all."

Lands rolled his eyes side to side as if getting mental power point images to flip backward. A surprised look dawned on his face. "Don't know how it didn't occur to me!" he said. "It's almost like I had blinders on."

"What?" said Macher.

"I think the guy was a convict! He had on a tan jumpsuit and shower shoes!"

Macher's eyes grew wide. "Are you sure?"

"Sure. Tan jumpsuit and shower shoes. Remember those because of the way he kinda shuffled when he walked to keep 'em from falling off." He paused again, contemplating his slideshow memories, then started to continue, "And the other thing I see now, too…"

Macher heard himself finishing the thought, "The guy was beat up… face bruised. Had a cut over his left eye."

CHAPTER SEVENTY-FIVE

The burner phone he had taken from the thugs rang. Jackie paused to check the number before answering. It was strange not having contact information come up with incoming calls, but this number he knew by heart. It was a number he had memorized when he was still a street thug himself using burner phones.

The number was a steel thread stitching him into a relationship with the one person who saw him differently than he saw himself. The first person who ever loved him for no good reason and believed in him in spite of many reasons not to.

"Macher?! Where are you?"

"Just skipped. Don't know how or why but I'm out. Where'd you go—no, let's not do this over the phone. For all I know they put a tap on me to get to you. What number is this? I knew it'd be you. I got thirteen missed calls and twelve of 'em were my editor. You're the only other person 'at cares enough to look for me."

"Long story, Macher-man. I'll explain in person. Where are you? We'll come get you. It'll be better if you keep out of sight. Only go with the guy if he knows our handshake." Jackie put the slightest lilt in his voice on this last word. Macher gave him the name of a bar close to the police station and hung up.

Thirty minutes later. a young black man approached Macher. He was a detective he knew, a man from a story he'd done about a sting on a city councilman using public money to fund a gambling habit. Macher reached out, shook his hand, and performed a series of flicks and flutters that looked like a fish in its death throes. The man's eyebrows arched crossly.

"What the hell, Macher? You old white dudes just get weirder every day."

Macher smiled. "Just had to check."

The detective grimaced. "Don't even wanna know what that means. Let's go."

They climbed into a black Chevy sedan and drove in silence. Macher knew enough of surveillance technique to realize they were driving a pattern to discover a tail and to lose it.

At a Wawa just off Interstate 40, the detective pulled in to a fuel pump, got out, and told him to wait. Just as he saw him disappear into the store, Macher was startled by a rap on the window so loud and close it felt like the blows were to his head and not the glass. Angry, he reached for the window switch and looked up, ready to go off on whoever was responsible for scaring him half to death. Framed in the window was the grave face of Poppie Rodrigues.

"C'mon, Rich," he said in his gravel-filled Spanish accent.

Before he gave it a second thought, Macher stepped across the fuel island into Poppie's car parked on the opposite side. The switch from one car to the other happened in less than a minute.

"Mike gave me the all-clear when you pulled in," Poppie said. Macher remained silent. Poppie leaned forward as he drove, taking in his passenger.

"You must feel like the last kernel in a popcorn popper," he said. "Sorry to bounce you around more. Believe me, when you see what we got at our house, and hear the story, this cloak-and-dagger stuff will make sense."

"Poppie, I trust you. But I'm about done. If there's not a couch or a bed at the end of this drive, shoot me and push me out the door now. Don't know what's more worn out, my body or my head, but both are cooked."

Poppie gave a nod and a tight-lipped smile. "Don't worry, Rich. Only a few minutes to the house. Suzette will set you up."

True to his word, in less than five minutes they pulled into the Rodriguez home, a seventies-style split-level ranch, and pulled into the only garage on the residential street that hadn't been converted to living space. Poppie's wife met them at the steps up to the house, and as if on some unseen cue, showed Rich directly to a guest bedroom just off the kitchen. Without a word, Macher collapsed into dreamless sleep.

He awoke, disoriented, to the sounds of silverware clinking on dishes and muffled conversation. The room was dark, but as his eyes adjusted he saw gray light framing the blinds of a single window.

Poppie's house. I'm in Poppie's house, he told himself as the fog began to lift. He got up and shuffled to the bedroom door. One arm was filled with needle pricks. It refused to answer the call to wake up and join the land of the living. He rubbed it as he followed the sound of voices and the smell of bacon cooking to the kitchen.

"Hey. Here's the man," said a familiar voice as he entered the room.

"Jackie!" he said, glad to see his friend. At a glance he took in the roster at the Rodriguez table. Jackie Smith and his wife, Maria, Poppie himself, and a man he knew but had never met: Douglas Windsor.

Windsor looked like he was recovering from an MMA match gone very badly. Face swollen. Fresh stitches over an eye. Leg wrapped in a makeshift splint, propped on a chair.

To Suzzette Rodriguez, who busied herself serving breakfast, Macher saic, "Ms. Suzzette, I don't know if you're running a triage or setting up to film an episode of *Raleigh's Most Wanted*!"

Suzzette, a stately-looking middle-aged woman who smiled as much as she moved, which was perpetually, said, "A little of both, Richard. Would you like some eggs? Pancakes? Help yourself to the coffee."

"All the above, please," Macher said as he poured a cup of wonderful-smelling brew and took a seat.

"Go ahead, Jackie," Poppie said.

Jackie said, "I was filling everyone in on what happened at the hospital when we went there, Macher-man. Once we got Doug here and you called, we all hit a wall. I was too loopy to tell the story. Poppie and Momma kept an eye on Doug here and I crashed."

"Thank you," Doug croaked in a pain-racked raspy voice.

Everyone looked his direction. He shifted in his seat and winced.

"What are we going to do with him?" Maria said with a look that reflected Windsor's discomfort.

"We can't take him to any hospital. Not now."

"What happened?" Macher asked.

"The short of it is that somebody wants him and sent some guys to get him. They broke his leg as an introduction," Jackie said, grimly.

"Who?" Macher said.

Jackie looked at the slumping man. "Doug?"

Windsor stirred himself. "I don't understand why any of this has happened, to tell the truth." His words were punctuated by little grunts of pain. "Never saw those people before."

Poppie, lathering butter on a biscuit, spoke. "My guys tell me it's DeVito 'at wants 'em." He paused to take a bite and continued as he chewed. "DeVito don't tie his shoes without thinking about poll numbers."

"What do I have to do with poll numbers? And why is somebody trying to kill me twice in one week?" Doug said.

"Twice?" Jackie said.

"They put a man in my cell with me right after they arrested me. He was there to kill me." Doug looked from face to face to see if they believed him. Their expressions were passive. He went on. "Huge man. Tall as that door frame." He pointed. "As soon as they closed the cell door, he came at me. Had to be a set up."

"Is that how your face got so messed up? I thought that was from the beat down in the morgue." Macher asked.

Doug touched the cut over his eye gingerly, and surprised everyone with a laugh. "No. He didn't lay a hand on me. It's getting a little hard keeping track of where all my beauty marks came from." He ran a hand around his face like a sales woman showing her wares. The tension in the room lifted.

"How'd you get out of that one, Windsor?" Jackie asked.

"I healed him of liver cancer," Doug said, deadpan.

Nervous laughter tittered around the table as they each in turn glanced at one another and then Windsor, expecting him to give the joke away with a grin. He didn't return the looks. He stared at his hands, now folded on the table before him.

"You... healed him... of liver cancer?" Suzzette said, taking a chair and sitting down next to her husband.

"Yes. No. Yes," Doug stammered. He wrinkled his nose, thinking. "It's not me that did it, but I did what I heard. Hard to explain."

"We're all ears," Macher said for the group.

"It's the same thing that happened in the morgue. I didn't do anything but what I heard."

"Heard? From?" Macher asked.

"God. Jesus. The Holy Spirit." Windsor said, growing agitated. "I hear a voice. I heard a voice. It's why I came here. At first I didn't think about it as God, I thought... well, I didn't think, I just felt like I should go for a drive. After that I started to hear instead of feel."

"Great!" Maria interrupted. Her pretty features were contorted with anger. She broke like a thunderstorm. "Great! Jackie! Our lives are ruined and you're going to jail because of a man who hears voices! Voices, Jackie! There's a word for that! It's called schizophrenic!"

She slapped the table with a flat-handed *thwop*. "My children are gonna be without a father because of this lunatic who thinks he can cure cancer!"

No one moved. Doug said calmly, "Not voices. A voice. And I never said I can cure cancer."

Jackie put an arm around his wife, who had spent her anger. She dropped her head into her arms in a heap and sobbed.

Doug looked at the crying woman and awkwardly continued, needing them, her, to hear his story.

"The voice got me to Durham and then to the hospital and the morgue. I did what it said. That's all I did. I've been beaten black and blue and now gotten my leg broken in the mix. But I'm sure who it is now. It is not an it or a voice. It is Him. It is God. Tabitha Treeright is alive. Rolly is healed of liver cancer. I walked out of jail without anyone stopping me or a key to open any door..."

"And Brian Lands found his daughter," Macher interjected. All eyes turned to him.

"Who?" asked Windsor.

"The man you met on the police station steps," Macher said. "Everything you told him was true. I know because I met him there myself."

Doug squinted at Macher for a second, then smiled as he connected the dots. "Ah! I'd forgotten him. That's how I ended up in an alley behind TJ Maxx! I didn't know his name. I was going to go to the bus station and find a way out of Raleigh. He emptied his wallet. Gave me four hundred bucks, so I got in a cab instead and went to get some clothes." Windsor paused, then mused, "He found his daughter. Good."

The room fell silent. Jackie caressed Maria's back tenderly. Poppie sipped coffee. Macher squirmed in his seat. Suzzette folded a stray strand of hair behind an ear.

Doug took in the thoroughly domestic scene and felt a stab of melancholy. It was family. It was home. He could not remember the last time he'd been in a place like this; a place that smelled and tasted like belonging, if belonging had a smell and taste. He liked it.

It made him sad to know nothing in his life tasted and smelled like this. It made him sad to think his presence here changed it all for the worse. He started to voice his regret, but Suzzette, with a mother's sensory perception, cut him off.

"You are welcome here, Doug." Looking at Jackie and her daughter, then smiling into her husband's eyes, she said, "We believe in miracles in this home. We know that chance meetings on the police department steps lead to daughters and sons finding their way home or finding a home for the first time." A teardrop glistened in her eye. She let it roll down her cheek onto the table.

Macher was surprised to discover his own eyes were wet. He said in a hoarse whisper, "It's true."

Jackie said, "Doug? I just had a thought. Maybe it's mine or maybe I'm starting to hear voices—a voice I mean—too." All of them looked at him. His eyes were bright with a childish, almost mischievous look. "Doug, you've been handing out miracles." He held a hand up when Windsor started to protest. "My words, not yours. You've been handing out miracles for others. Why not ask for one yourself?"

"What do you mean?" Doug said. "I think walking out of a locked jail cell is a miracle for me."

"Okay. True," Jackie said. "But you haven't walked far enough to be safe! And you ain't walkin' out of here without a lot of help." He scanned the group to see if anyone was tracking with him yet. Nothing. He plunged on, "Why not heal yourself? Why don't you just heal your leg?"

Doug's blank look made Jackie laugh. "What?! Haven't you even thought about it?!"

"No. I guess I haven't. I'm not sure it works like that," he said.

"Why not?" Macher asked, joining in. "If you raised a girl from the dead and healed a man of liver cancer, and if you walked out of a locked cell, I would think you'd at least think about it." Although he tried to keep it out of his voice, Macher's inflection on the word "if" made them all shift in their seats.

Poppie cut his eyes at Macher and said to Doug, "How does it work, Doug?"

Windsor took a deep breath, held it, and slowly exhaled. "It doesn't feel like I do it. I mean it doesn't feel like I decide to do it. It's like it comes through me." He ran his fingers through his hair as he gathered his thoughts. "And I know when I'm supposed to do the thing—ah, it's so hard to describe."

"Try," Macher said, again displaying an edge.

"He doesn't owe an explanation to you or anyone in this room, Rich." Jackie said.

"Oh?" Macher said. "I think he does. My life is in pieces no matter what comes of this. A lifetime working in this city is in the toilet because he's here. If he's telling the truth, at least it's for something. It will give me plenty to think over. But if it's smoke and mirrors…"

Poppie said, "A second ago you told us he brought a man's daughter home to him. Now you doubt him? You're the one who sounds loco."

Macher doubled down. "It doesn't matter what I said before. I want to see it. Show us, Windsor! Heal that leg of yours and solve our problem of hiding an escaped prisoner who's a cripple! No?! Can't do that? Too much?! Just heal that cut over your eye! Show me. I need to see my life isn't shredded for no damn reason."

Windsor didn't respond. He took the blood-splotched white towel wrapped around his shattered leg in both hands and gingerly removed it. The ugly split in the skin of his calf where the broken bone pierced him showed angry red beside the jury-rigged splint. The swelling and discoloration spread from his toes and disappeared into the shorts he wore. A slathering of an entire tube of Neosporin added a yellowish lube-oil patina to the gruesome sight.

Doug looked at his ruined leg with surprising detachment. The air went out of the room. Nobody moved or breathed. Jackie gave a sideways glance at Macher. His eyes were bulged wide. Doug leaned forward in his chair with an effort. He closed his eyes. The clock over the kitchen sink clicked away one minute and then two more. Finally, Doug sat back in his chair.

"No," he said softly.

The room relaxed like a group of runners called off the starting line after a false start.

"No," Macher said to himself. He got up and left the kitchen. They heard the back door open and shut.

Jackie realized he'd been holding his breath. He gulped in a big breath, got up, and refilled his coffee cup.

Windsor slumped in his seat. Sweat beaded on his forehead. The clock ticked along glumly.

Maria broke the silence. "What's this mean?" she said to no one in particular.

"Nothing," Poppie said. "It means nothing. It means we have a man who needs help in our home and it's up to *us* to help him."

The subtle emphasis on the word "us" in his father-in-law's answer pricked Jackie's heart. He put down the coffee cup. Without a word, he rounded the table and crouched over Windsor. He took the kitchen towel that had covered the man's ruined leg and gently replaced it.

"Us," he said. "I believe he's here because God told him to come to Durham. I believe it. I believe Tabitha Treeright is alive. I saw it. I saw her." Jackie spoke in a monotone without looking around. He stared at the towel.

"I spent my whole life on the street with no one caring whether I lived or died, yet here I am. Here I am. If I can't believe in miracles, who can? But we forget quickly. I forget." Tears flowed down his cheeks as he leaned over Windsor's prone figure.

"Maybe God speaks to us, too. Maybe just now when I thought of Doug healing his leg it was really me He was talking to. Doug says he's no one special. I believe that, too. He says it's Jesus. God is Jesus and Jesus is God. Okay. Then it's Him who did these things, not this guy." He nodded toward Windsor, who was looking at him through weary, half-closed eyes, head back.

"Okay. Okay," Jackie said. "Jesus. I believe you did these things…"

He paused a long minute. Poppie, Maria, and Suzzette looked on wordlessly.

"Jesus, I believe it was you that got me off the street and put me in a family. I don't know that I ever knew till now but I do. Jesus, we need help now. Please help us. Heal this leg."

No one moved. The clock ticked. Jackie couldn't bring himself to lift the towel and see the leg. What if it were the same? What if nothing happened?

His mind darted from image to image like a sparrow unable to find a suitable place to light. Windsor's leg, the melee in the morgue, the security camera video, the confrontation in the security shack, the jail, the hospital, Maria's face, Robinson's house, the dead doctor. *Bounce, bounce, bounce.* He flashed to the sheets folded in the hospital laundry, the single folded-up sheet in the trunk of the dead doctor's car, the suicide note.

The note. The neatly-written lines on yellow legal pad paper. In his hurry to get to Maria, he'd walked into Windsor's brutal ambush. The letter was forgotten.

He took out his phone and pulled up the photos he'd taken before departing the garage-turned-gas-chamber.

It seemed far away now, but he shuddered with the realization that here in his phone was the evidence he had been in that place with that dead man and no one knew those lifeless eyes still stared blindly into eternity. He began to read Robinson's final words.

CHAPTER SEVENTY-SIX

"I am going. I am leaving NOW. GOOD-BYE! Bilbo Baggins said it. He had his magic ring. He was tired. I am tired. I think the word he used was "stretched." I am stretched. He made all the arrangements for a long holiday and didn't expect to come back. I don't have a magic ring but I've made the arrangements. All is in order and I KNOW I'm not coming back. There is no coming back from where I'm going because there is no place to go. There is no there and here will not last either. No one dies and comes back. No thing dies and comes back. All we see will die. I'm tired of denying it. I'm tired of helping people deny death. The people who are the most afraid of death come to me and I convince them to live. It's my job. I've done it well for many years. I've lied. The ones who are most afraid are the only ones who see clearly. The more I "helped" people get over their fears, the more I took them away from reality.

Thirty years ago I saw all of this in a lightning flash of insight, and I attempted to take my own life as painlessly as possible. This time, I think I shall have better luck. The people who "helped" me back then said my mind was broken. They convinced me to live when I wanted to die and tried to die. They stabilized me and normalized me, but they never gave me any good reason to live. I thought they wouldn't have worked so hard on me if they didn't have a reason for living. Maybe they just didn't share it with me. I thought if I learned everything they knew, I would find it. And so I went to school and became a psychologist myself.

They call what I do a "helping profession." Help. That's a strange word. Help. When I say it out loud it sounds like an animal sound. Help. I looked it up. It means "to make more pleasant or bearable." It has roots in the word "heal" and "health." So I worked these many years in helping and healing human animals, at least that's what it's called. But what for? All my patients die. When they die they rot in the ground. The enviros get all poetic about it. They love to spew nonsense about death giving birth to life in a beautiful cycle that goes on and on. It doesn't. The sun will melt and extinguish all life. It will erase every page of every story. No record will remain of humanity and no marble slab will mark our grave. When I take a seat in my car in just a few minutes, I'm going to drive over a cliff into nothing and nowhere.

I got here accidentally like the rest of the creatures who climbed up from the ooze, but I see now the only proof of evolutionary advantage, the only evidence the human animal did rise to a new consciousness, is to choose to die. All other animals show their inferiority by struggling to live meaningless lives. Choosing death is the only meaningful thing a creature can do; it reveals a fully evolved being. The lesser beings stand in fields with bovine contentment unaware of their fate.

Fear is the proper response to our true state; cutting it off is the rational response. Why choose to live in meaningless fear and suffering?

I know what will happen over the next days and weeks as people mourn the loss of a public figure; especially a young person like Tabitha Treeright. I've seen it play out many times. Lady Di is a good example. The public grief, the pouring out of meaningless trinkets like the flowers that rot alongside roads where the less famous died in their cars. Talking heads pontificating endlessly on the value and brevity of life. And none of it faces the truth. None of it opens the eyes of the "healthy" and the "helped." No, I won't help any more of the rightly delusional to become less delusional. Not even one who claims to be returned from the grave like the last young lady I met who wrapped herself in grave clothes and took on the identity of a dead girl. Let her go on with her delusion and let the world mourn without me. Let her be Tabitha Treeright for as long as she likes and let the whole world believe that she is returned from the dead. Others have lived out their meaningless existence embracing greater deceptions than this. As for me, I am fully awake and my eyes are fully open. I choose to die. I only wish that no one mourn me and so dishonor the sole meaningful act I will ever perform."

CHAPTER SEVENTY-SEVEN

Jackie scrolled to the bottom of the picture he'd taken of the final page. Robinson had not signed it; it simply ended. He felt drained. He thought the letter was the most awful thing he had ever read. The room felt flat and devoid of life, as though light had been sucked out of the place through those words.

He put the phone down on the table and rubbed his eyes hard with both hands as if to squeeze out the image of the yellow pad pictures. As his eyes cleared, he realized Maria, Suzzette, and Poppie were looking at him. Then he saw they were not looking at him, but at something over his shoulder.

He craned his head around to see what they were looking at. It was Windsor. He stood a little unsteadily behind Jackie, like a thin tree on a breezy day. The towel that had covered his broken and bloodied leg lay on the floor in a discolored puddle. He smiled a little boy's grin; a mischievous glint in his eyes.

Jackie felt an electric shock in his head that went ear to ear. It was accompanied by a freight-train roar. He staggered to his feet and tried to face the man, but he fell back into his chair, clumsily, off balance. He found himself on eye level with Windsor's thigh. It was creamy white, the color of a white man not accustomed to ever wearing the shorts he now wore.

He let his eyes trace the white limb down and back. No scar. No bruising. No blood. As he watched, Windsor unbuckled the two belts of the now-expendable splint. Doug took them and handed one to Jackie and the other to Poppie.

"Wrong," Poppie said with mock sternness.

Windsor looked confused.

"Have you seen this belly? You think that fits me? Takes a whole cow to make me a belt."

Windsor saw the mistake and laughed.

"Here, Jackie," he said, switching the belts to their rightful owners.

Maria crossed herself solemnly. "My God! My God, what does this mean, Jackie?!"

Her husband had no words for her. She looked to her mother, who sat back in her chair looking like a strong wind was blowing in her face.

Poppie spoke for them all. "It means…" he started and then cleared his throat, coughing up a lifetime of healthy police skepticism with the next sentence, "it means we've all got a lot to reconsider."

Jackie found his voice. "Where's Macher?! Rich!"

They searched the yard and house for him. He was gone. He'd missed the miracle by fifteen minutes and in the years to come would not entertain any discussion of it in his presence.

CHAPTER SEVENTY-EIGHT

Daniel Treeright's departure left the nomination process in tatters. It was unprecedented. He had accumulated an insurmountable lead in delegates to the convention. By law those delegates were committed to voting for a man who would not be there; or for that matter, a man who had somehow disappeared.

Attempts to locate the Treerights proved futile. Speculation ran rampant. The family was in Brazil. They were in Norway. They had been murdered and dumped at sea. The dead girl come back to life was a stunt by the campaign that went wrong or a plant by another campaign to wreck his campaign.

A well-known Hollywood producer claimed to have examined the so called "resurrection video" and determined the girl was an actress he had discovered, but he would not reveal her identity. The world's foremost expert in digital video manipulation and "deep fake" videos studied the morgue video and could come to no definite conclusions. He would only say it was "likely" the video had been altered.

The unclaimed body of a Jane Doe found dead of an overdose in Chicago was purported to be that of Tabitha Treeright. When DNA testing failed to match the Treerights, a conspiracy theory immediately spread, claiming the lab involved in the testing was either incompetent or had surreptitiously switched the samples in a cover up.

The news cycle spun out tales so quickly that cable news shows empaneling sets of "experts" to discuss the current story were regularly overtaken by a new one mid-episode, leading to some comical results.

CNN was live in their Atlanta headquarters with a set of party officials discussing a theory that Daniel Treeright would appear on the opening night of the convention and claim the nomination when the network ran a chirographic banner announcing the governor had been sighted in a downtown Atlanta MARTA station. As the officials bantered back and forth, first one and then another saw the scrawling graphic, looked agape at each other, and ran out of the studio, leaving no one on camera but a sputtering, speechless anchor. It was a false alarm, just one of the many Treeright "sightings" from a public anxious to see what they wanted to see.

Incredibly, a man who was an eyelash from taking the presidency, with a face familiar to the entire nation and growing familiarity around the globe, had simply walked away from the Governor's Mansion and disappeared with his "resurrected" daughter and beauty queen wife. It strained belief on any and every level.

Americans generally don't associate their New World with monasteries. They have imagery of European Catholic practices that are musty and out of line with their way of life. There are, however, many monasteries in the United States, some of which are very much Old World and more lost in time and inaccessible than the Amish of Pennsylvania and Ohio.

Just off the Appalachian Trail in central North Carolina, barely a four-hour drive from Raleigh, a self-sustained community of twenty monks and seventeen nuns occupied a piece of land donated to the church by a rich northeastern railroad man in the late 1800s.

They lived there solely to pursue prayer and intimacy with God and had never, in their 125 year existence, allowed any person not under vows to enter the cloister. Candidates for the community had to have lived under vows in less restrictive communities for a minimum of ten years before they were considered for inclusion in Holy Spirit Abbey on the Mount.

The Prior of Abbey on the Mount walked with a pronounced limp. He was a perpetually smiling man who had a face wrinkled like a topographic map. He kept his ash gray hair cut in a Marine Corp-style that was offset by an unruly white cloudburst of beard.

He went by Jacob, a name he took to himself after surviving a land mine explosion as a grunt infantryman on his first tour in Vietnam. A navy chaplain visiting the field hospital where he was recovering told him the story of the Jewish patriarch who wrestled with God all night long, and as a result, walked with a limp the rest of his life and got the name "Israel," meaning "struggles with God." Prior Jacob liked to say, "No one ever meets the real God without a struggle."

Jacob hobbled into the Abbey dining hall where the community was gathered. The Prioress, Sister Madalyn, met him with a nod, indicating all their people were there. She was a wiry sixty-year-old with a roughhewn, simple face of placid beauty, like an undisturbed and undisturbable pond.

All eyes turned to Jacob as he eased himself onto a stool at the front of the room. The aged structure smelled of cedar . It was so quiet the sound of his knees cracking could be heard as he settled himself.

"Brothers and sisters," he began in a gently rumbling tone, "we are a community dedicated to prayer and seeking the face of God. We represent generations of seekers who came here to live and to die pursuing Him. Simplicity is our way. Taking away distractions so we can hear clearly. We are not hiding from the world, we are pursuing the other, invisible world."

Jacob paused for a murmur of agreement running through the group. "The Church is our home both now and in the life to come. We are never alone. While we ourselves live in this place, we do not live here for ourselves. Our prayers are for the love of God to impact us and for the words of God to penetrate us in ways that will help the church and the world.

"The songs and the sermons we write pass out of the Abbey into the church and the world as relics dug from Holy soil. They are not ours to keep. They are priceless things the Holy Spirit gives us in the quiet life we are privileged to live. The things Jesus teaches us as we live here together are passed down not only to those who come here, they are passed out to those who oversee us."

The Prior sat up and cleared his throat before continuing. "And the church has been glad these many years to leave us to this work. She has never asked us to bring anything into the Abbey except those who are called to live here under vows." He paused and drew a deep breath. "But now we are being asked to do something unprecedented."

He scanned the room, face by familiar face, making eye contact with each of them in turn. He made a sign to Sister Madalyn, who passed through the gathered monks and nuns to the back of the room. She opened a door to a room that normally served as a sick bay for the community. The men and women shifted collectively in their seats, craning to see what Madalyn was doing. She gestured and held the door open as three people stepped into the meeting hall and followed her to Jacob's side.

The room resonated with low murmurs of surprise. Where had these people come from? Who were they? Jacob silenced the room with a look that was neither stern nor mild as he stood and placed himself in the midst of the strangers.

"This is Daniel and his wife, Wanda," he said as he reached his right arm behind the couple. "And this," he said placing his left hand lightly on the young girl's shoulder, "is their daughter, Tabitha."

The family stood before the group with awkward, closed-lip grins, unsure of what was about to happen.

A severely bent-over old nun stood up unsteadily in the front row. Two nuns quickly rose to support her at either elbow. She shuffled to the family, who glanced back and forth at one another with eyes wide. When the two nuns brought her to a point uncomfortably close to Daniel, with great effort, as if cranking an invisible wire of a crane, she raised her face to his.

Daniel realized the old nun was blind. Her filmy white eyes, sunken into their sockets, were like milk spilled in the aged landscape of her face. Without a word, she suddenly reached a surprisingly supple hand to his face. He caught himself in time not to recoil and let her explore his features with her gentle fingers. When she was done, the two supporting nuns repositioned her before Wanda and lastly Tabitha.

The cabin and all the woods around seemed to be holding their breath; even the birdsong ceased. Finally, they escorted her back to her seat.

"These are the people I saw," the nun said in a voice that cracked and sang with age. "The girl is the one I saw pass through darkness into light and back."

A thrumming sound filled the room like the passing of a train. The ground trembled. Every person experienced it personally. Each would tell it differently in the years to come. Each would agree it was the most peaceful moment they'd ever known, even while it felt like they were in motion while it happened. When it passed they all felt a sense of connection and belonging to one another—both the community of the Abbey with each other and the strangers with them and each other.

Jacob said, "This family is now our family. They will stay with us until it is time for them to go. The infirmary will be their quarters and they are free to go anywhere in the Abbey."

Turning to the Treerights, he said, "You are family. Tell us what you need and let us serve you."

Daniel glanced at his wife and daughter. Wanda's face showed the strain of the past ten days. Her eyes were bright, but tired. Tabitha stepped forward and wrapped her arms around herself in a typical Tabby pose, girlish and un-prepossessed. She surprised Daniel by speaking for the family.

"I'm Tabitha," she said in a confident tone that also surprised her parents. "I've been baptized in light. Hmmm. No, I've been baptized in the Light. These aren't my words. I hardly know what they mean or how I know to say them. They're just"—she unfurled her arms and pointed both hands at her chest, fingers first like, blades of knives that could open her up and let them see—"they're just in here. I found them here after I woke up and came back to myself."

No one stirred. The monks and nuns looked on with upturned, expectant faces.

"They tell me I died and came back to life. I don't know what that means either. I left here"—she pointed to the floor—"and I went to a place of light. When I came back I didn't know who I was for a while.

"Actually, that's not true. When I was in the light I knew who I am more than I do right now. This is a shady place and I feel like a shadow. There I felt like I was real. Here I feel less real. The words are the only way I know to tell what happened.

"I may have died. People are curious about that and some are very angry about it—they seem to believe whatever happened was make believe. People keep talking about death and dying, but dying isn't the biggest thing. I was baptized in light. That's the big thing."

Tabitha stopped. She had such a simple little-girl expression in contrast to the profound words she spoke that it made her look even younger than her twelve years. Daniel and Wanda instinctively moved to her and framed her on either side. She spoke again, this time with some weariness in her voice.

"We are here to ask for help. We need a place to rest and we need people who will help us understand."

Daniel, used to commanding and persuading rooms full of people, felt the need to speak. Wanda, who was holding his hand behind their daughter, sensed his anxiousness and squeezed gently in a wife-to-husband manner they were rediscovering.

He held back and saw why Wanda restrained him. The entire community of nuns and monks were rising in ones and twos and making their way to the front of the room where the family stood with Jacob and Madalyn. They surrounded them, coming close and reaching out hands to touch each of them. The outer rings of men and women reached out to touch the inner rings.

Soon everyone in the room was connected in this spontaneous act. The Treerights looked at each other, eyes wide. Daniel nodded for Wanda to look at Tabitha, who had turned up her face as if letting rain fall on it. Joy was written there in unmistakable brilliance. It was like watching a clear chalice filling with liquid sunshine. She glowed.

Low, indistinct voices began to rise from the men and women clustered around them. Daniel was surprised to hear distinctly foreign languages. German. Spanish. Dutch. It hadn't occurred to him that anyone from another country would be here in the remote mountains of North Carolina.

Although it was jumbled together in clumps, he began to pick out repeated phrases and words. *Jesus, Holy Spirit, God our Father*, and *kingdom* bubbled up to the surface like effervescing water.

Daniel and Wanda and Tabitha simultaneously lowered themselves to the floor. It felt to Wanda like they were stepping into a bathtub, bathing in the rhythmic prayers of these people. It washed away the fatigue, anxiety, and disorientation of leaving their familiar world behind. The gentle touches of the stranger's hands changed them from outsiders to insiders.

When the praying trickled to a stop, they wiped their eyes and knew they were part of a family, and they were safe.

CHAPTER SEVENTY-NINE

Syd DeVito examined the cold piece of steel in his lap as he drove west on Interstate 40. He wore a shabby pair of farmer's overalls, and a stained and torn chambray shirt. The start of a scraggly beard itched his face.

The used F-150 pickup truck he had procured for $1500 cash at a used car lot sported tags lifted off a car impounded in a Raleigh tow yard. It was as nondescript as any of the thousand such rusty buckets found on the backroads of North Carolina.

The weapon was a reliable old revolver, as untraceable as Syd himself. *Treeright isn't the only one with an insurance policy*, he thought. *And he doesn't have the kinds of friends I have.* No, not the black Mr. Clean, Daniel Treeright. It was Syd's job to get dirty when it was called for, and he knew people who were the dirtiest.

It had taken a few persuasive conversations and twisted arms, but he had gotten himself a new identity and a new look in just enough time to stay ahead of the net Treeright had tried to throw over him on his way out the door. A bug-out bag was a good idea for an average guy; for a guy like Syd, who played with people who only played for keeps, it was a necessity.

He had fifty thousand in cash, a flash drive full of interesting documents and pictures that could make some very important people look very bad, and this gun. He didn't think he'd need all the cash. He planned to use up the bullets before he used up the money. *And really*, he thought, glancing down at the gun, *five rounds might be one too many.*

The old priest had been a harder nut to crack than he'd anticipated.

It was a stroke of inspiration—DeVito mused on that word a moment—to visit the person he knew was last with Treeright before the press conference; the fat Lutheran priest, Daly. He had given him the names of the other two men in the Treeright religious confab.

DeVito left Daly to himself. The man obviously believed everything they discussed at their chance meeting in the Governor's Mansion parking lot. He knew what Syd had tried to accomplish with the "resurrection" presser and he knew the Treeright move had destroyed that plan. They had an understanding; he saw it in the man's red rimmed beady eyes. No need to cut that cord.

Hammond had been another matter.

The hipster wannabe megachurch pastor had sounded like he might pee himself when Syd called and asked to meet him. He knew the type of man. Plenty like him in the political world. Always looking at people like living stepladders; evaluating the potential to elevate themselves by finding a handhold.

The more hungry for position, the easier to manipulate men like Marty Hammond. And Hammond was hungry. Well, he had been. He wanted to tell Syd how much he admired the courage to talk publicly about Tabitha and the governor's role in raising her from the dead. It would sure be great if Syd could arrange for them to visit his church. But on the primary issue, the whereabouts of the governor and his family, Hammond proved to be a dead end,

Syd had him deposited in a Motel 6 in north Raleigh, filled to the gills with heroin and in the company of a couple of working girls. If he recovered, which was doubtful, the pictures of the Right Reverend Hammond cavorting with the prostitutes would keep him busy with credibility problems for a long time.

But Mullenix… Yes, a tough nut to crack.

Who would've thought the stringy old gray man was an ex-recon Marine? It took serious persuasion to get him to talk. Hours. Unpleasant hours it had taken with the most unpleasant men Syd had at his disposal. Waterboarding didn't get it done. All the usual interrogation double talk, backtracking, and confusion couldn't dull the priest's sharp mind. The man was singularly unafraid of death; more than any man he'd ever known. And his toleration of pain, well it was superhuman.

The chance discovery on Mullenix's desk of a half-written letter to his mother gave them the only leverage point that worked. It was amazing, at his age, that the man's mother should still be living, but there it was; a neat, handwritten scribble to "Dearest Mother" and an addressed envelope, stamped and ready to receive it.

Syd shuddered in spite of himself remembering the pitiful look on Mullenix's bruised and battered face when his chief interrogator held the missive before his eyes. The game was up; resistance drained out of him like a gashed tire as the thugs explained what they would do to the woman in graphic detail. Syd might have had doubts about their veracity, but the priest didn't.

In a last ditch effort to keep his secrets, Mullenix lunged for a knife already stained with his blood and tried to slit his own throat. It was amazing to see and caught his torturers off guard. They barely succeeded in preventing the suicidal move, kicking him in the groin. The spontaneous body spasm caused his hands to grasp at his crotch and drop the knife.

"Idd'n dat what ya call a marrtal sin 'der, padre?" one of the thugs said. "Killin' ya self?"

Writhing in new depths of pain, Mullenix had only groaned a long, wheezy groan like an old freight train's wheels grinding excruciatingly to a stop. The other man, the one Syd only knew as "Cheese," leaned down on one knee next to his head. He hissed through his wired-shut jaws, "Try that again and we will visit Mother no matter what you tell us or don't. Send yourself to hell. Good. I will *take* her to hell. And it will be a long, slow ride."

Mullenix talked then. He knew another priest who had been a recon Marine like him. Served in Vietnam. Wounded. Spent time together in hospitals from the field to the States. He ran an abbey in the mountains out in the western part of the state. His name was Mike Ryland, but since entering the priesthood he went by Jacob. No one was allowed to enter the abbey unless they were under vows, but Jacob made an exception for Mullenix; the first in the history of the Abbey.

The Treerights were there.

DeVito made a snap decision then. He never got his hands dirty. Ever. Being present at the priest's interrogation was the closest Syd DeVito had come to the dark side of the political game in fifteen years. He found it disconcerting how non-disconcerted it made him. Watching a man being broken had no noticeable effect. He wondered at it. He couldn't watch a plastic surgery reality show on cable because it made him squeamish, yet here he saw the wounds and smelled the blood and looked on placidly, unblinkingly.

He decided then; this was the last chapter. No one else would write it but him. He instructed Cheese and his companion to remain with Mullenix while he, DeVito, drove out to the abbey and confirmed the man's story. Once that was done, they could finish him up and plant him wherever they wanted.

If the story were true, if Daniel Treeright and his wife and the girl were actually in the abbey, they would be like an ellipsis; three little dots before he became the last word in the book. It was a revelation to him that he could seriously consider putting bullets in three people and then a final one in his own head, but he knew, pulling away from the priest's secluded home, that he had it in him. He felt it as surely as he felt the gravel driveway crunching up through the old truck's tires and into the steering wheel he grasped.

A state patrolman whizzed past him, breaking his reverie. It was getting late. Checking the time of arrival on his maps app, he realized he would reach the little town closest to Holy Spirit Abbey on the Mount too late to ditch the truck and make his way through the woods in the dark. He silently cursed the priest for taking so long to finally give up the inevitable information.

Now that he was set on this climatic course, he was anxious to see it through, but when he arrived there was nothing to do but hole up for the night near the entrance to the old logging road that served as access to the isolated abbey.

He pulled over and made a quick call to Cheese, who assured him Mullenix was still alive and kicking. DeVito warned the goon about punching the priest's time card before Syd gave the word, and hung up.

He set a wake-up alarm on his phone and tried to find a way to lie down for some shut-eye. He was soon as frustrated as a lovesick redneck trying to find a way to make it with his girl inside on a rainy night. The bench seat defeated him both in length and width. Finally, he slouched over the steering wheel using both arms as a bony thin pillow. He dozed.

CHAPTER EIGHTY

Rich Macher left Poppie's house with no clear idea of where he was going. His footsteps on cold cement sidewalks felt as pointless as his whole life had become in the last twenty-four hours. A reporter with no place to go and no story to tell; forever tainted by association with the Treeright affair and the manufactured video of him soliciting underage prostitutes. Raleigh seemed to his eyes to be a foreign city; every familiar corner obscured with doubt and sadness.

He didn't deserve this, he repeated to himself over and over. He was a good man. He used his place in society to do good things; to help good people and to question bad ones. Why had all of this happened to him? How had he been fooled so badly? It was as if a lifetime of useful skepticism and objectivism had been swept away like so much sawdust spit from a saw.

The price was enormous. Even if he recovered from DeVito' smear job, how would he ever regain his stature as a reporter? Taken in by claims of resurrection and healings—no one in the profession would take him seriously ever again.

He trudged along, wandering in these thoughts. His body, on autopilot, led him to his apartment. Standing in the shower, he let hot water cascade over his body until his fingers looked like prunes.

He started to throw on his bed clothes and disappear into oblivious sleep.

Are you going to quit?

He heard the question in his head and shook it groggily. *Man, he thought, I'm beyond fatigue. Voices in my head. Or is it just me?*

He heard the next sentence distinctly and it felt like an icy hand gripping his throat.

If you lie down right now, you'll never get up again.

Macher choked a little on his own spittle. *True*, he thought. *Doesn't matter where that voice emanates from; me, or mental illness, or an angel or the devil.*

Tired as he was, he felt it in his bones. Lying down right now was a metaphor for giving up and giving in. The bed may as well be a coffin. As he looked at the folded edges of the sheets pulled back he imagined them forming the lid to a sepulcher; the headboard a headstone.

He quickly threw on street clothes, grabbed some cash he'd randomly thrown in the nightstand drawer, and headed out the door.

There was a way out of this, he thought. The way out was to be the one who broke the real story. And he had a leg up on anyone; he was already *in* the story.

It took a day and a half pounding the streets to lead him to pick up the trail. It had not been a straight line; no true story ever was. Through one of the surreptitious occurrences so often attending a reporter's trade, Macher remembered the name of the woman who worked the front desk of the hospital the night the Treeright girl's body disappeared and tracked her down.

Ms. Sherry Franklin, a sixty-something angular woman with steel grey hair and thin, perpetually-pursed lips, mistook Macher for a man who attended her church. Before he could dissuade her, she went on to commiserate with him about her good friend Alicia Stoneman, who was out of a job because of all the craziness at the

Governor's Mansion. And didn't he know that Pastor Hammond had been called to consult with the Treerights over some very important issues?

Once the woman began, the string of words flowed so seamlessly, Rich found no place to interrupt. He mused silently as Franklin bloviated that people really liked to talk about themselves; a most useful fact of human nature making his job as a reporter both easier and more enjoyable for a personality like his.

In thirty minutes he obtained a fair sketch of the religious confab that had taken place the day the Treerights disappeared, as well as a thorough rundown on the social lives of a number of the good people of Accelerate Church. When he asked whether or not Pastor Hammond kept office hours anywhere, Sherry Franklin didn't think it odd that a man she supposed to be a member of the church wouldn't know this without being told.

"He does. He does," she said in her youthful voice that felt out of place coming from her well-aged face. She paused for the first time and a look of concern cast a shadow. "But, it's odd. You know how last Sunday Pastor Hammond wasn't there?"

Rich nodded, although he had no idea even of the location of the church.

"We were ready to start a new series of talks. All the serve teams had new t-shirts with a special logo. We at the information desk were supposed to hand out miniature toy cars to every guest to promote the talks. It was all planned out and then..."

"Then what?" Rich asked.

"Well, you saw it didn't you?! No Pastor Hammond! And the associate pastor... well, he's a nice man, but the poor man should never try to fill those shoes."

She looked sheepish, then added apologetically, "He tried his best I'm sure, but he looked lost up there and he didn't talk about anything to do with our promotion. If you ask me it looked like he was thrown into speaking at the last minute. Usually when Pastor Hammond is gone we get someone really good in his place. You remember the last one? The man who is on the religious TV station?"

Rich nodded again and squinted his eyes in fake remembrance.

"Sherry?" he said. "I didn't make it to church last week. Ah, wasn't feeling well."

"Oh. Sorry, dear."

"Yes. Better now. But did anyone mention where Pastor Hammond was? Doesn't he usually let the church know when he leaves town?"

Sherry Franklin pursed her lips even more than usual.

"Mmm. That's the strangest part. In all the times he's been away, his wife has always gone with him. He's even talked about it in a sermon. He says the Bible teaches it's not good for a man to be alone and he believes it. So when he travels he takes his wife. Helps to keep him from being tempted like what happens to so many men who spend too much time alone in hotel rooms."

She paused to give Rich time to agree with these obviously wise words. He bobbed his head again, not feeling good about the continuing deception with this talkative but nice woman.

"But last Sunday, Mrs. Hammond was there. And—I'm not trying to be unkind—she looked horrible. She's such a beautiful woman," Franklin said with a tone of veiled cattiness, "but without makeup…"

"Did anyone ask her about Hammond?"

"I'm not part of the leadership. I guess someone must have asked her. But you know they're a very private couple for people who lead such a large church. Not many people seem to be friends with them."

It took another ten minutes of Accelerate Church gossip for Rich to extricate himself from Sherry Franklin. When he got to his car, he sat and thought through his next move. A quick check of the names of the other two religious men the woman knew attended the meeting with Hammond showed that the Catholic priest's church was on the northeast side of the city; about a thirty minute drive.

The Lutheran minister's church was barely five minutes. He decided to start there and see what more he could uncover. He called the church offices, and using a fake identity as producer for a national news program, arranged a meeting with Jarry Daly.

Passing through the dim, empty sanctuary on the way to the office had been disquieting to him. He entered the sanctuary from the rear and walked up the center aisle like a tourist in a foreign land.

Nothing here was familiar to him. The smell of religion was in the air; snuffed candles, musty books, wilted flowers. The diffused light from the multifaceted stained glass windows was strangely sorrowful in the dim room. He had never been in a sanctuary without people—and rarely with them.

Halfway up the aisle, a square of light opened at the right side of the ornate dark wood stage. Reverend Daly hailed him, his voice booming in the acoustically-tuned room.

Macher sat in the office of the Reverend Jarry Daly, pastor of Saint Mark's Lutheran Church; the photo-op church picked out for the Treeright family by Syd DeVito. Macher scanned the walls and bookshelves. Daly didn't have many pictures on display; a blown-up snapshot of him in running clothes with a group of similarly clad people, a posed photo of a wedding, and a studio portrait of what appeared to be him and his wife and children. These were placed in fairly inconspicuous spots on either side of the big mahogany desk where the Reverend sat.

Prominently displayed on the wall behind him were three oversized diplomas; Bachelor of Arts and Master of Arts in religion from a couple of schools Macher never heard of, and centered directly above his head, a PhD in Philosophy from the University of North Carolina.

The Reverend was a fortyish man with a round red face and blond, thinning hair. He wore sweatpants and a long sleeve dri-fit shirt which did a poor job holding in a bulging midriff.

"Mister Upland," he said in an overly officious tone mismatched to his casual attire. "What can I do for you?"

Pleased that his assumed name had been so easily accepted, Macher cleared his throat. He picked his form of address off an ostentatious desktop gold nameplate, and his approach to the man from a fine-tuned instinct for human nature.

"Doctor Jarry."

The man waved his hands as if to wave off the title, but allowed Macher to continue.

"There's been so much in the press about truly profound issues lately... issues that impact the highest levels of our politics and at the same time touch our most deeply-held beliefs. Ah, I thought it would be a good idea to interview a person who, as it were, stood astride both and could speak to both with authority."

He paused to let the thinly-veiled flattery sink into Jarry. He could see instantly this fish would be easy to catch. He went on.

"Doctor, Governor Treeright and his family attend your church? Members of your congregation?"

"Yes and yes, Mr. Upland. Although I'm sure you'd understand that a governor is a busy man, and our governor, well with running for president, it makes it hard for him to attend services regularly."

"Of course. Sure." Rich smiled. "Very busy. But he obviously values you... I mean the church. A man like that! Making time to be here at all tells me this must be an important place for him."

The fat face glowed under this pronouncement like a steak under a restaurant heat lamp. This was almost too easy. Rich continued.

"I took the liberty of listening to your latest message as prep for meeting you, I've forgotten the title…"

Macher had done no such thing. He'd simply taken a half minute on his way from Sherry Franklin's home to look up the Lutheran church's website online and found a prominent link to Doctor Jarry's sermons. The latest one had a title about the strength of the human spirit in times of political turmoil. He knew his man would gobble down this bit of ego bait and fill in the blanks.

"Oh, yes! My message on our response to political upheaval."

The man looked as if his head might actually pop like a cartoon bubble from his pride. He pronounced the word "upheaval" with a particular relish that turned Macher's stomach. He fought to keep the feeling from making its way to his face.

"Uh-huh. That was so insightful and appropriate to the times. Ah, I was wondering,"—*time to set the hook*, he thought—"it sounded to me like you've had some extensive experience with these issues. Seems like Governor Treeright would be wise to consult with you. Have you been in touch with him during all that's gone on?"

A sly look flashed Jarry's eyes, and for an instant Macher thought he had moved too fast. But Jarry leaned back in his chair and laced his fingers behind his head.

"As a matter of fact, Mr. Upland," he said in a conspiratorial tone, "the governor and his chief of staff sought me out."

Fish on! thought Macher. Now to play it out and find out how big it was. He decided to give this one plenty of drag and let it run.

Jarry did not disappoint. In the next twenty minutes, the loquacious reverend filled in the details of the meeting at the Governor's Mansion, as well as a meeting between Jarry and DeVito, which was a new twist.

The chief of staff's impromptu presser took on a different light. Jarry took full credit for DeVito' move to credit Treeright with the faux resurrection. Jarry thought it was brilliant. A move that would sweep Treeright into the realm of unassailable in the national election and give all his policies the texture of divine mandates. When Macher pressed him on the morality of such a move, Jarry finally paused.

"Morality? Mr. Upland, what do you think morality is?"

"Well, Reverend, that isn't my area of expertise. Maybe you should tell me."

"Morality is whatever does the most good for the most of us. Elevating a man like Governor Treeright to the most powerful office in the world and ensuring he has the mandate to enact the things he believes in... isn't it obvious that's what's best for us?"

Macher bit off the desire to say this was the same definition of morality that led Germany to elevate another man in another era. Instead he turned to the big question.

"You're obviously very close to the situation. But I guess you're in the dark like everyone else when it comes to knowing why Treeright stepped down and where he is right now."

He delivered this with a pitch-perfect challenge to Daly's pride and watched it blossom in the man's countenance. If he knew anything, it would come out now.

"I'm not at liberty to share everything I know," he said. Macher noted the eye movement up and to the left. Daly was making up something, but maybe there would be a bit of truth to whatever he said next.

"The governor is reassessing his whole life—at least that's what this latest move was all about for the purposes of public consumption. But it is actually meant to have the effect of building the mystery. It's all part of the plan. Can't you see? When he re-emerges it will be all the more dramatic. He's a good actor, or better yet a good singer. Leave the crowd wanting more. Make them hungry for the encore."

"So you expect him to return to the public and run for president even though he said he's done? Surely you haven't been in contact with him?"

Again the sly look, but this time with another upper-left-eye movement.

"I won't say. But since he's been gone, I have met with the chief of staff." He locked onto Macher's eyes. This was true, Rich sensed. He arched his eyebrows in response.

"Yes. We met here and discussed the press conference and how we might continue working together. I'm not sure," he added with a conspiratorial whisper, "but I don't believe he trusted the other two men who were there when the girl came into our meeting. He wanted to sound me out about them and what I thought they might do as the plan unfolds."

This bit of information, a meeting with Syd DeVito, here in this office, set Macher's mind spinning. He failed to realize Daly was done talking for a pregnant ten-second silence.

The reverend cleared his throat, bringing Macher back to the present. He got up and said, "You've been very generous with your time, Reverend Daly. And very informative. No one else has been here? To talk? No other press people?"

Something in the phrasing or tone Rich used with this last question finally waded through Daly's incredible ego and struck close to his equally-sizable instinct for self-preservation.

"No. No. No other members of the press. Guess I should have said before." He waved his hands in a childlike, embarrassed gesture. "This is all off the record, eh?" More of a request than a statement. Rich decided to ignore it. He had no intention of letting any of this hit the cutting room floor when it was time to write this story.

"Curious," he said, more to make Daly squirm than to get anything more from this fat fish flopping on the pier. "Why would DeVito risk coming to see you when he's got half the Raleigh PD looking for him?"

He let that fall on Daly. The man had a stupid, vacant look. He had suddenly lost his appetite for self-disclosure.

"And how does it make sense for Treeright to give up every bit of dirt he had on DeVito—share it with the press and every level of law enforcement—if he's coming back to run for office?"

He left the room, gently closed the door to Dr. Jarry Daly's office, and made his way back through the dark echoing sanctuary.

CHAPTER EIGHTY-ONE

Syd DeVito woke from a confused, uncomfortable sleep. He was surprised to see the start of a sunrise after day upon day of rain and cloudy skies.

He was more surprised when he checked his watch. Quarter till nine. He would have sworn he never went to sleep in this pickup truck cab which was only suited for contortionists.

He shook himself and rubbed each arm to get the blood flowing. *I could use a cup of coffee,* he thought. Immediately, he realized the time for coffee was passed. Forever passed. His errand up this mountain and through the forest would preclude any more creature comforts. No time now and there would be no time after. No time forever after.

He pondered the fact and found another surprise; he mourned the loss of coffee and the rich brown smell that grasped the nose insistently. He mourned the loss of a slice of bacon; the sight of sizzling grease and the scent of invitation to sit down at a breakfast table and enjoy.

Weird. Only hours to live and I'm contemplating these things. I always assumed at the end I'd be remembering someone, not some things.

He got out of the truck, coughed, and spit on the ground, clearing out the morning phlegm. The cell phone buzzed. He hit the green accept call button and said tersely, "Go."

"Checkin' in. Give the old guy his last rights? Glenny's gettin antsy to blow this place."

DeVito let out a long breath, rubbing his eyes as he thought.

"Yeah. Didn't plan on getting such a late start last night. I haven't put eyes on the target yet, but I will."

DeVito paused. He saw a hole in his plan. There wouldn't be anyone to call the final shot when he was done today.

"Here's the deal; it's what, just nine? If you haven't heard from me at eleven, punch his ticket, right?"

"Right," Cheese grunted.

DeVito ended the call.

That easy to end a life. Strange.

He flipped open the revolver, checked the rounds, and closed it. He tossed the phone in the glove compartment along with his wallet. He hid the keys under a bush a few paces from the truck after locking it. He didn't think he'd be needing any of these things again, but he remained the same man, even when he went for his last walk; the man who always had a backup plan; a way out when things went sideways.

He started up the mountain, looking for a trail that wasn't there.

CHAPTER EIGHTY-TWO

Daly's disclosure of Syd DeVito' visit bounced around in Macher's head like a cue ball after the break. It hit several other bits of data before it came to rest. When it did, it left him with an obvious shot.

The dead psychiatrist may or may not have been the victim of suicide and a coincidence, but the missing mega church pastor couldn't be. And if Marty Hammond was missing, the next obvious question was: where was the priest?

He looked up the name. Mullenix. Couldn't be that many Catholic priests with that name in Raleigh. His search proved harder than he thought. The Catholic churches in the area appeared to be a bit behind the technology curve their Protestant counterparts embraced.

It took wading through several pages of search results to locate a parish nearby with a priest named Mullenix. The church web presence consisted of a static info-only page with an address for the building and a main number to call.

Several tries to the number got him a recording sounding so much like the old SNL skit's Church Lady he swore they must be trying to imitate her. Giving up on Mullenix for the moment, he turned his attention to the missing megachurch pastor. From the conversation with Sherry Franklin he felt sure no one at the church would be helpful. The guy's wife didn't know where he was, from the sounds of it.

Macher thought it over and decided the best way to proceed was to treat it like a missing person case. True, the pastor had not been missing for long enough to call it in as such, but he didn't need the police. He had his own contacts he used over the years to track down "missing" people.

In Macher's experience, grown adults, especially those in high-profile jobs, seldom went missing. If they could not be located, it was a matter of choices, usually poor ones involving questionable activities, people, or substances. Sometimes all three.

As he scrolled through his contacts looking for a particular number, he had a sense of foreboding. The Treerights were missing. DeVito was missing. Where would Hammond turn up?

He found his contact and two others. He quickly located a photo of Marty Hammond on the Accelerate Church website—it was almost the first thing that loaded on the site, prominent and unavoidable—and shot off three text messages including the photo while he drove in the general direction of the address listed for Mullenix's church.

I'm going to kill someone if I don't stop reporting while driving, he thought. Texting? Bah. He composed entire features single handedly and utterly distractedly, often arriving at a destination with no recall of how he got there.

One of these days it's going to catch up to you.

His phone rang so quickly after hitting send on the last text message, it startled him.

"Yes?" he said.

"Rich!" a nasally, distinct voice popped from the speaker. "Who's the stiff in the picture you just sent?"

"Hey, Bart. Why? Stiff? You know anything?" Macher said.

"If it's the same guy I think it is, you need to turn on a tv cause it looks a helluva lot like the nut job freakin' preacher 'at turned up dead in a hotel."

Macher cut the connection. He pulled his car into a Citgo. The late local news was just finishing up. He scrolled through several sites till he found the segment. One look at the picture associated with the newscast showed him it was Hammond.

Heroin overdose. Questionable hotel known as a location prostitutes frequented with customers. But one crucial detail his contact had asserted was wrong.

Hammond was not a stiff.

Not yet anyway. He was in critical condition in Sisters of Mercy Hospital ICU. Macher checked the location of the hospital and plugged it into his phone. He knew Hammond would be useless for questioning but there were always crumbs that fell around the table of all his stories.

And he was sure now this was his story. The coincidences had thrown him off the scent before, but everything in him screamed that he was on the trail of something big. And, he told himself, he was on the road to setting his own place in the story right. He would change the narrative when he sorted this out. He would no longer be the alleged underaged porn king who alleges innocence. He would write his own headlines. All this whirled through Rich Macher's head as he sped to Sisters of Mercy.

He used an old maxim he'd learned over years of chasing stories to gain access to the ICU; walk fast and act like you belong. He was helped by the late hour.

There were relatively few occupants in the ICU. He guessed most anyone in Raleigh needing acute care ended up in Duke. He knew that would be his choice.

The macabre anonymity of ICU patients, be they eight or eight-eight years old, slowed him down for a bit. Each person was veiled in tubes and wires connected to whizzing, whirling boxes with colored lights silently contradicting the impression the occupant of the room was expired.

Almost by chance he walked into the last room on an aisle full of empty beds and came close to bowling over a frazzled-looking blonde. He reached out instinctively to keep her upright. They ended up face to face in the curtained doorway of the room.

She would be a pretty woman, Rich thought, *but for the raccoon eyes from crying away too much mascara, and disheveled hair that was too blonde to suit her.*

He settled her and said, smoothly, "Watch it, Mrs. Hammond!"

He saw immediately he'd hit his mark. He took in the room, empty save this woman and her unconscious husband. Running on pure instinct, he forged ahead. "I know no one is supposed to visit your husband." He emphasized this, widening his eyes. "Alicia Stoneman spoke with the governor and he sent me to help you any way I can."

At the mention of Wanda's aide, the Hammond woman visibly relaxed.

She said, "The governor?"

"Yes, Mrs. Hammond. Governor Treeright is grateful for the time your husband spent with him talking over the, ah, unusual occurrences, as of late."

Macher let that lay, seeing if she would pick it up.

"Oh. Yes. Oh. Ah, please, let's go and sit? I would like a drink of water."

The ICU waiting area provided them with some privacy and her with a cup of water from a water cooler. As the water glugged into her paper cup, Rich contemplated the conversations this old-fashioned-looking water dispenser must have heard over the years. Probably a lot of sad things had been said in this room.

"Mrs. Hammond—"

"Donna," she interrupted. "Please. Call me Donna."

"Donna. As I was telling you, Governor Treeright was grateful for your husband's help. I'm here to do whatever I can for you."

The less said the better when you're making up stories, Macher thought. *Let the woman fill in the blanks and spill whatever she knows.*

The miserable look on Donna Hammond's face as she began to speak made Macher feel bad for taking advantage of her misfortune. But maybe there would be redemption for all of them if he could get to the bottom of this story.

"We appreciate it. Marty, he was so…" She wiped her eyes and caught a cry in her throat. "He was so excited to meet the governor. And to see, you know, to see…"

"What? Mrs. Hammond?"

"Donna."

"To see what, Donna?"

"To see the girl." Donna Hammond leaned toward Rich and whispered this last phrase.

"Of course. Yes," Rich said, pursing his lips.

"Marty told me the governor told them to keep their meeting confidential. Marty said the girl needed time to"—here she made a quizzical face as if considering something she'd not thought before—"she needed time to recover from rising from the dead." Donna gave a pleasant little laugh at this. "Strange sounding, isn't it?"

Rich nodded in agreement but said nothing.

Donna continued. "Marty was sure we would be the first to get her."

"Get her?"

"Yes. Of course. God wouldn't do such a thing unless He had a plan to use her!" Donna Hammond managed, even in her frazzled, disheveled condition, to look the part of a southern-belle-cum-televangelist gently scolding a clueless non-believer.

"Of course." Rich said. "But Mrs... Donna, this can be discussed later. How can I help now? What's Pastor Hammond's condition? Can you tell me what happened?"

She snapped back to sober reality. The tears came in a flood. She tried to choke off the sobs but they came in great gulps between stifled cries. Macher thought it was more awful to see the exertion to hold back the tears and cries than the tears and cries themselves. What could it be that possessed a person in such a way they couldn't even grieve freely?

The pastor's wife wrapped her arms around herself to calm the shuddering in a self-swaddle. Macher leaned in, but let the woman settle on her own. He wasn't the nurturing type, and the awareness that he was not here as a friend kept him from reaching out to her. They'd both have less to think about when and if the true nature of why he was here tonight came out.

"He's... he's in a coma." Donna finally said. "They told me he was full of heroin. Heroin! I don't believe it. No." She set her jaw in a defiant line and bit off her words. "No. Way. They also said two 'women' dropped Marty off at the ER. Prostitutes! That's what they meant! They didn't say it but that's what their eyes meant. I could tell! Marty?! Heroin and prostitutes?? Who do they think he is?"

The last caught Macher off guard, as Donna Hammond starred defiantly in his eyes with a look demanding an answer. He had none. He clucked his tongue and wagged his head slightly.

The woman went on, "They don't know. They don't know who he is! Marty Hammond is a good man. A great man. He would never even look at a woman like that! And drugs?!! He led the mission the church did to Afghanistan. We went there to talk to the poppy farmers and tell them they needed to stop selling drugs and they needed to know God!"

Rich failed to see the connection but decided to let it go and see where she would take this.

"Would the governor call on a whoring druggie to advise him?! No! These people are incompetent. Obviously. Marty is having some kind of episode. It's an episode. I'm getting him moved to the university. Now! Tonight! We've got friends in the church there. They will help us. They won't believe in this heroin prostitution nonsense."

She paused, and the deadliest, most sincere expression yet to cross her face appeared. "The church. The church has to be protected from lies like this. They always want to destroy the church. Any way they can. I'm not going to let them."

Again Rich failed to see how this made sense but he also didn't care to be enlightened. He wanted to look for a few little scraps and get out of here.

The meeting with the three religious men was now clearly established. Hammond's wife might have an overblown opinion of her husband, but his sense of lies and liars told him she wasn't hiding any major character flaws for him either.

If Marty Hammond was a whoring druggie, he had his wife fooled. Whoring he could believe a man could hide; a serious habit for smack, no.

"Donna, did your husband have contact with anyone from the governor's office in the past few days?"

She screwed up her face in thought. "Marty did tell me about someone calling to follow up about that meeting they had." She reached into her purse, sitting on a chair next to her, and retrieved a phone.

"Here's Marty's phone." She shook it in Machers direction. "Prostitutes? If a guy gets rolled by hookers they steal everything he's got. Everybody knows that. Every crime show shows that. But Marty had his phone, his wallet... with the five hundred dollars cash he usually has. How's that for a guy that was rolled by hookers?"

Rich barely registered any of this, his eyes fixed on the cell phone. He did catch the mention of five hundred in cash. Who carried that regularly? But he wanted to see that phone. Badly. His hands itched. Keeping a steady tone, he asked, "Anything there give you a clue to what's going on with Pastor Hammond?"

"Well, there is a call from an unknown number the afternoon Marty went missing." She scrolled through the list of calls, stopping at a number with no name. She held it out for Macher to see. It was a local area code, he noted.

He said, "Let me take that number down. I, uh, the governor has contacts that may be able to find out who that call came from..." He saw a look flash across her face and shifted gears smoothly. "But we aren't doing a criminal investigation are we? We need medical advice, don't we?"

Donna Hammond relaxed. "Yes. That's right. It has to be right. Marty isn't involved in anything criminal."

"One more question, Mrs. Hammond. Did Marty say who it was that contacted him? To follow up on the meeting with the governor? And do you know if Marty met them?"

Again the scrunched-up brow. "Mmm. Yes. It was the man that was on television that day. The one who said the girl really rose from the dead. I remember because Marty was surprised at what the man said. Marty said it didn't sound right. No. What he said was it didn't feel right. He said the governor wouldn't have liked it."

"Wouldn't have liked what?"

"The whole thing. He said the governor was adamant about letting his daughter have space to recover and it didn't make sense for that man... ah! I remember now! DeVito! I think he's part of the governor's staff—you must know him?"

"Syd DeVito is the governor's chief of staff, if that's who you mean."

"Yes. That's him."

"So you're saying Syd DeVito contacted your husband as follow up to the earlier meeting in the mansion? And Marty met with him?"

"Yes. Except the last part. I know it was DeVito that contacted Marty. I don't know if they met."

Macher felt he had all he needed to put this together.

DeVito was cleaning up loose ends. Hammond was one he decided to cut. Daly was a different case. His mind wandered to the third man that had attended the religious confab. The Catholic priest, Mullenix.

He had the feeling the man was in grave danger if he was still alive. It was probably too late, but his whereabouts was the next link in the trail of his story.

"Thank you, Mrs. Hammond. I will leave you to tend to your husband. If we can help you, please let us know."

"Okay. Mr...." She paused and looked sheepishly at him with the realization she had poured out her life before this person and never bothered to get his name. She let the phrase trail off for Rich to fill in the blank.

He instead smiled and touched her on the shoulder. Looking into her eyes, he said sincerely, "I hope your husband will make a full recovery."

CHAPTER EIGHTY-THREE

Macher drove north and let the phone tell him the way. The crumbs he'd collected were enough to let him know he was going into danger now.

He had no way of knowing how DeVito was working his problem. Had he dispatched thugs to each loose end at once, or was he dealing with them one at a time?

The Lutheran priest had been personal. DeVito visited him. Windsor had been taken down by professionals with no sign of the chief of staff. Hammond? His case had the earmarks of a professional working over, but was DeVito there when it went down?

Macher thought of the phone number scrawled on the scrap of paper in his pocket. He was sure it would be DeVito or one of his "associates."

The timeline was not clear yet, but it was getting there. If the Catholic priest had been first on DeVito' list, or if all the loose ends had been targeted at once, he could be dead by now. If he was last on the list or if he'd slipped through their hands somehow, he could be fat, dumb, and happy anywhere.

Churches of any flavor were not Rich's purview, but his impressions of the Catholic church were more dark and hazy than Jarry's dim Protestant sanctuary.

It was the imagery that did it to him.

The dead man staked out in the unnatural posture they hung at the front of their halls. It reminded him of a scene from a western he watched as a child that haunted him.

A cowboy captured by savage Indians, stripped and beaten, stretched out on stakes with leather thongs binding his hands and feet; baking in the sun as the leather shrunk but by bit. Dying of thirst. Leather biting into his wrists and ankles. It was horrible. It was only a moment in the movie but a splinter in Macher's mind.

The Catholic Jesus was a vertical version of the tortured cowboy. It haunted his childhood dreams. He felt the shame of fascination at not being able to turn away from the pain inflicted by men on other men. These dark thoughts accompanied him as he drove north in search of Mullenix's church and hopefully the priest.

St. Mark's Holy Catholic Church of the Ascension was not an impressive structure. Macher wondered at its diminutive size compared to its expansive name. A small white pill box perched on a hill overlooking nothing but a grove of walnut trees.

The sign and grounds were well kept, both with crisp lines he could see in his headlights. He wasn't expecting to find anyone in the middle of the night but he had no other leads, so this was as good a place as any to park and wait for some sign of the priest.

Pulling into the lane leading around to the back of the church, he saw a gravel road leading further up the hill and deeper into the walnut grove. Wakefulness waning, but curiosity piqued, he pulled into the lane to see where it would lead.

Without knowing why, he turned off his headlights and eased along, letting sporadic moonlight show the way. It was a spooky scene. The dark windows on the rear of the white church stared blankly back at him in the rearview mirror; the sound of gravel crackled under his tires and bounced off the trees making it seem as if he were driving across a giant frying pan.

Entering the woods, it became momentarily so dark he let up on the gas entirely and drifted a few feet, afraid of running off the road. Before the car came to a complete halt, he realized he could see again.

A dim light shone at the end of the tunnel of trees. At first he took it to be moonlight returning, but the unnatural pink-orange tint of an exterior security light soon showed him he was approaching another structure.

Parsonage? This was an old church and probably did have a house for the priest when it was built.

That would be too fortuitous, he thought. *Maybe I won't have to wait to find the priest.*

The house was as nondescript as the church. It was in fact just a smaller white pill box with symmetrical, darkened windows on either side of the front door.

The moon leaked through a cloud just as Macher eased to a stop outside the arc of the security light. In the light, he saw there were two cars parked at the steps leading to the concrete slab front porch. A small black subcompact was parked with its driver's side to the steps. That must be Mullenix.

But the second car was a tricked-out metallic lime-green machine with a black vinyl top. Not a priest's car. Not a priest's first car or second car.

Macher noticed his heart rate going up even as he reached for his door handle and got out of his car. He sensed it before he knew it; he'd managed to catch up with the story.

No lights showed in the house. He walked around the side closest to the woods and discovered the home had been built into the side of a hill. At the rear, the basement opened onto the back yard. He could see the corrugated steel semi-circles framing several windows. These old basement windows always made him think of World War II bunkers. A faint glow illuminated the window wells.

He walked to the side of the house and approached the light. He reminded himself to breathe as he crouched down and looked in.

A man was strapped to a wooden chair, facing the window. His head drooped to one side, leaving half a grossly-swollen face exposed. His arms were tied to a stanchion over his head. There was a grey bucket with something foul-looking in it at his feet. The man was laboring to breathe, each intake of air causing his head to convulse upward grotesquely.

The weak light came from a bare incandescent bulb in an overhead socket. Deep shadows fell over the rest of the open, unfinished basement. There was no sign of the person or persons who had done this to Mullenix, for that was who he was assured the man was.

Macher's heart hammered away so loudly his ears thrummed with its sound. Where were they? Had they heard his car? Were they stalking him even now?

As these thoughts rushed his mind, he heard the front door open and shut with a thud. Muffled voices drifted around the corner of the house. They would see his car and the game would be up.

Without thinking, he turned and shuffled clumsily down the sloping yard to the exposed backside of the basement. A small deck overhung the entrance, throwing it into darkness. He stumbled over a stray garden hose, tripping and cursing as he did. On all fours on the ground, he tried to still his breathing long enough to listen for any indication the goon squad had seen his car or heard him fall.

Nothing.

He found the door to the basement and pushed it open noiselessly. All senses hyper alert, he smelled the dank cellar smell of wet concrete that never saw sunlight long enough to properly dry, but also a whiff of something much worse; urine and vomit.

To his left, the light he'd seen from the window shed its pitiful light on its pitiful view. He ran to the bound man and knelt in front of him, trying to untie his feet. Mullenix stirred and opened one eye wide in surprise.

"Who are you?" he choked in a whisper.

"Macher. No time. Gotta get us out of here before…"

The sound of the front door opening and closing again stabbed Macher in the chest like an icicle. The old priest's one good eye went wide. He flicked his head up to his hands. "Get those loose. Knife." He indicated with a nod.

Rich looked down where Mullenix gestured. His stomach churned. A wickedly curved buck knife lay on the concrete beside the bucket he'd seen from the window. The blade was stained black with dried blood.

At the same moment he heard another door open and someone begin to descend the basement steps, he realized the bucket contained one of the priest's ears. It floated atop a scuzzy-looking dark fluid. His stomach revolted as he grabbed the soiled knife.

The footsteps grew louder, closer. Macher stepped behind the stanchion to get at the zip ties holding Mullenix's arms. A man coughed somewhere behind him. He tried to cut the ties. They were so tight they bit into the priests thin wrists, disappearing in angry red tracks.

Several things happened at once. The man descending the stairs—it was Glenny—saw Macher and yelled. It was something between calling for Cheese to help and a curse. It came out as "Mwwoootherrrr - Cheeeeese!!!!!"

The sound of the enraged man exploded in the echo chamber of cement block and hit Macher like a physical blow. He dropped the knife and turned to see Glenny, a shadow demon, eyes white and wide, rushing at him.

Cheese, who had been at the top of the stairs, heard Glenny's cry, took one step, and whiffed on every other step as he came down like a sailor's sea bag tossed down a gangway.

Macher tried to meet the headlong charge of his assailant but he was twenty years older, a head shorter, and fifty pounds lighter.

It was no match. Glenny hit him full speed, throwing a shoulder into his gut and landing on top of him. Macher's world got very small very quickly. There was only one thing and it was the thing that was absent.

Air. Air. No air. All the air in the universe was gone. Why wouldn't his chest rise, his lungs work? Blackness edged into his field of view from both sides. The snarling, grinning face of his assailant would be the last thing on earth he ever saw, he thought.

He started to go out like a burned-down candle. Dimly he heard a dull *thwunk* just over his face. Glenny's eyes rolled back in his head, grotesquely showing the whites before shutting completely in a tight wince of pain. He rolled to one side and off of Macher's chest.

Light and air returned to the world in a painfully sweet rush. Macher took great gasping gulps of air, trying to drink it in like water. Strong hands jerked him to his feet. He bent over, head down, hands on knees.

A commanding male voice: "Take this. Be ready to defend yourself." A knife shoved into his unsteady hand.

"Wha?" he managed to gasp. But a shadow form moved away from him in the direction of the stairs. A man there was screaming; cursing, crying. He heard the same commanding voice but couldn't discern the words. He examined the knife in his hand. It was the same knife he'd picked up moments ago and dropped in the feeble attempt to free the priest.

The priest! He lolled his head to look over his shoulder. It took much more energy than it should have, he thought.

He started to return to the priest to finish freeing him so they could flee this place with their rescuer, whoever he was.

The chair was empty. The priest was gone.

He heard what sounded like a warning issue from the foot of the stairs and then another *thwunk* like the one that turned Glenny's lights out.

A figure emerged out of the gloom. It grew into Mullenix. The priest had a grim expression. He carried a baseball bat loosely in his left hand. Black streaks of blood from the hole where his right ear should have been disappeared into the stained collar of his shirt. Matter-of-factly he answered the question in Macher's eyes.

"Pulled a gun on me. Lying there with a broken leg. Believe it? Still thought he was in charge. Had to give 'em a tap." He slapped the bat gently against his palm. "Shouldn't be too damaged. Be out for a while though. And who are you?"

Macher slowly raised himself from his crouching, doubled-over position to face this incredible man. A man who sounded as if he'd just gotten up from a good night's sleep instead of escaping a sleepless night of torture. The question lost its meaning. *Who am I?* Compared to this man, Macher had no idea who he was. He stared dumbly back, speechless.

"Well?" the priest said. "Are you hurt?"

At this Macher stirred himself. "Me?! Your ear! They… they… they."

The priest put a hand to the bloody stump of an ear hole. He made a strange face, a remembering face. "Yes. They did. Father forgive them."

Macher blinked. These words pinged off his ears like hail on a tin roof. Unreal. Rote. Impossible.

Mullenix seemed to be reading this in his expression. He said, "You're not always seeing what you're looking at. Bad grammar, but truth doesn't always conform to grammatical law... or law, period." He looked hard into Macher's eyes and repeated, "Are you hurt?"

"No permanent damage that I can tell. Ah, Father? Reverend? Mullenix? Right?"

"Yes. People I know call me Nexie or Father Nexie." He gave him another up and down glance. "But I'm pretty sure we've never met."

"I'm Rich Macher. I'm a reporter for a paper in Raleigh." He offered a hand awkwardly. Mullenix took it and returned a surprisingly firm handshake. The man's hand felt like it was made of stone.

Who is this guy? Macher thought, all his puerile images of clergymen in general and Catholic priests specifically dissolving in the crush of the old man's handshake.

There was no hint of recognition of who Rich was in the priest's eyes. He shook his head slightly. "Sorry. Can't place you. We haven't met? How is it you've managed to find me and save my life?"

Rich gave a much-abbreviated account of his involvement with the Treeright affair and its aftermath. He told of his relationship with Jackie Smith and their search for answers. He told of the attacks on Hammond and on the man, Windsor, who supposedly raised a girl from the dead but couldn't heal his own broken leg. He concluded with the trail of destruction that led directly from Syd DeVito to this basement.

Mullenix listened intently. When he was done, to Rich's surprise, the old man went to the grey bucket, retrieved his severed ear, and held it up with a grim, noiseless chuckle. "Guess I could use a meeting with Windsor myself. Not sure even the best surgeon could reattach this."

Rich couldn't grasp how to respond.

"Didn't you hear what I just said? The man's a fraud! It was probably these two thugs that broke his leg!"

Mullenix didn't look Macher in the eye. He only looked down at the grotesque object in his palm as if he hadn't heard him. He maintained the curious look Macher had just noticed. The look of someone remembering something unpleasant.

The silence had begun to grow uncomfortable before he broke it with a low monotone voice Rich had to strain to hear. There was a dangerous note in this; a hard, flat edge like the knife he still held in his shaking hand.

"No. Windsor isn't *the* healer. But he isn't a fraud either. He's just a man who got in the way. Tabitha Treeright is alive. It's hard to accept... to believe. Even when I saw her myself.

"I admit it. I saw her and I knew her and it's still hard for me to keep it in here." He touched his head and then tapped his chest. "And here. It's too big, I think. If I think about it, it leaves no room for thinking about much of anything else. But I have to think about other, little things and even just one little thing, driving to the store or talking to a friend, just pops it like a soap bubble. Isn't it odd that a thing so huge could be so fragile? So hard to hold?"

Rich felt many things at once. Anger that this man, who was living in the same story as he was—who had been literally and permanently mauled by it—was so calm and peaceful and contemplative; curiosity at what Mullenix had seen that would convince him the girl was alive; and a hint of growing fear that he, Macher, was missing out and couldn't get in on the story in the story. He swallowed it and pushed it down.

"Lies are fragile," he said. "Big lies are more fragile than most, but there aren't many brave enough to risk poking the bubble; of calling out the naked emperor."

Mullenix looked up and met Macher's gaze passively. "You think I'm convinced because I saw her. And you think the girl I saw is someone other than Tabitha Treeright. But you're wrong and you're wrong. I did see her and I do know it is her, but it isn't seeing her that convinced me." He paused and gave a wry smile. "It was meeting him."

Macher could barely contain himself. "Him! Windsor?! The pedophile?! A child porn king?! A man who diddles little girls like Tabitha Treeright? What's wrong with you?! Why would you believe someone like him?"

"Who said Windsor is a 'child porn king'? Isn't it the same people who said you were too? Or did I miss something? I'm pretty sure the stories about you, and your friend Jackie, and Windsor all hit at the same time. How's that? What did they get right? Was it one for three? Two out of three? Windsor and Jackie are perverts and you're the innocent who got splashed in their mud? Hmmm. Isn't it all so queer? Lies are fragile? I agree. The whole counterfeit kingdom sits upon a foundation of lies; the throne is occupied by the Father of lies. Your problem is you think you know the truth but you've never asked the right questions."

"You don't know me or anything about me," Macher said harshly.

Mullenix raised one eyebrow. "I know why you're here and it's not to rescue me from these two." He nodded at the prone man and pointed toward the stairs. "You want your name back. You want it back in more ways than one. You are the man of facts who got fooled by a scam."

He threw this sentence like a master dartsman, gently, firmly, precisely, into the double bullseye. Then he stuck another dart right beside it. "And you are the good man, the man who rescued the street urchin out of the goodness of your heart, but the city you gave your good works to forgot that in an instant with one fantastic lie about you. I know you. I know what you're looking for. A name. Good man. True man."

Mullenix let the darts stick. He gestured toward Glenny, who was stirring. "Cheese isn't going anywhere even when he comes to. But this one... he won't know enough to behave himself. We need to secure him to something. Give me a hand."

He strode over to Glenny and with surprising dexterity flipped him onto his stomach. Glenny let out a half conscious "umph."

"There's a roll of duct tape on the bench over there. Grab it for me?"

Rich mechanically retrieved the tape. In moments they had Glenny taped to the same stanchion and chair Mullenix had just vacated.

"I'm going to get Cheese tied up on the opposite side of the basement. Do you have a phone on you?"

Macher nodded.

"Ok. Call it in. Address is 905 Deerpine Road."

Mullenix began toward the steps, then turned back. "Second thought. Go upstairs and use the landline. It's in the kitchen. Just call it an attempted robbery… and when you've gotten through, leave the line open. Don't hang it up. We've got to get out of here. No time to wait on them to send a unit."

Rich's face conveyed the question.

"You want the end of your story, don't you? I'm going to take you to it.

CHAPTER EIGHTY-FOUR

The path to Holy Spirit Abbey on the Mount proved harder to follow than DeVito expected.

His intention had been to parallel the abandoned single-lane logging road which served as the only access for vehicular traffic. It was used so infrequently that grass grew high enough in the middle and sides of the road to mask its existence from all but close range.

Having to detour around a large cluster of thorny, intertwined blackberry bushes, Syd lost sight of the road. He had never been an outdoorsman, nor was he in particularly good condition for the uphill trek. Before long he was completely disoriented. The only semi-coherent plan he could derive was to keep going up, believing this must necessarily lead him to the summit where he would either find the abbey or a vantage point high enough to spy it out.

Mopping his brow with a handkerchief, he swore under his breath. He fingered the cold gun in his pocket. The coveralls he wore fit too loosely, causing the slab of metal to slap his thigh with each step. Added to the rising sweat of the excursion, the uneven ground and the inability to walk a straight line for more than a few yards without having to avoid trees, bushes or both, DeVito was growing more and more irritated.

Like many people who find themselves in uncomfortable situations, he focused and blamed his discomfort on an illogical but proximate object. Daniel Treeright.

He had started up the mountain with homicidal thoughts to be sure, but there was a cool arithmetic to his murderous intentions. His plan was clear: the first bullet went into the girl's head; he didn't care that she was a plant, a fake, a political dirty trick and probably mentally unstable—really, who could be convinced to play this role besides a sick person? What mattered was that Treeright and Wanda believed she was Tabitha, and that served his purposes. Let them watch the girl die. It would be a suitable payment to them both for abandoning him.

After the girl, it was a toss-up between who he hated more, who he needed to see suffer more. Was it the friend or the lover from whom he needed to exact a higher price to make the math add up?

He had settled on Wanda. She had been more used than loved by Syd until lately. It was a fresh wound and strange. He convinced himself he took her and kept her as an act of pure politics. She was a chess piece; lifeless and useful only as he stretched out his hand to move her, and immobile unless he did.

But the events that had upturned the chessboard of a lifetime, scattering all the pieces, had jolted his well-controlled emotions. He discovered that losing Wanda was losing something very much alive; maybe the only real living part of his life. It hurt and it hurt in a way he couldn't see a cure for other than a bullet in her faithless heart. She would be second.

But now, with sweat dripping off him, these damned hick-clown clothes chafing, and the gun slapping out the unsteady rhythm of his upward march, it was Daniel Treeright he wanted most.

He had been the last, the period in the sentence, but this hike was bringing a sense of clarity to Syd.

Daniel Treeright was nothing when Syd met him in college. A womanizer and a pothead who was too smart and too smooth and too... *too.* Sure, he had natural gifts that were remarkable, but he lacked the killer instinct.

Syd laughed to himself at the irony of the thought. Yep. Treeright lacked killer instinct and along came Syd. Before Syd, Daniel was like a talented basketball team that always played down to the competition, lost games they should have won easily, and gave up double-digit leads late in the game because they didn't want to run up the score.

Syd thought back to the time he'd taken Daniel out on a trail behind the dorms one afternoon. He'd brought along a BB gun to shoot at frogs in a scummy little pond along the way. It was the closest thing to outdoorsmanship Syd had ever participated in.

Sitting near the pond, talking about women in their classes, Syd had handed the BB gun to Treeright and showed him how it worked. After a few practice shots, they'd tried without luck to locate a frog to shoot. Then a sparrow landed a few feet away on a low-hanging branch and began to chirp.

At Syd's prompting, Daniel had raised the gun and took a shot at the bird. It fell to the ground flopping around spastically, seriously but not mortally wounded. The two of them approached the creature who tried to escape but could only make circles in the dirt like a ship with a jammed rudder.

"Finish it," he'd told Daniel.

"What?"

"You can't leave it like that, finish it."

Treeright had cocked the BB gun and stood over the bird but couldn't get a bead on it with all the commotion.

"Naw. Don't waste a BB. Just step on its head."

The look on Daniel's face that day was still vivid in his memory. Syd could see the man didn't have the stomach to do what needed to be done, then as now. He'd crushed the sparrow's skull with his foot. It gave a diminutive crunch. Done.

Daniel's face had contorted with disgusted horror. No killer instinct. No stomach for the necessary dirty work. But talented. Yes, very talented. With the right help he could go places, maybe even the highest places.

Syd had talent for the other things; the necessary things. He discovered he had a talent for identifying those who also could do the necessary things and how to motivate them. Like Cheese and Glenny waiting to finish off the worthless old priest.

It was true, Syd built a network of people to do the dirty work, a network good enough to keep his own hands clean. That was another necessary thing. Couldn't let his connection to Daniel become a liability or the whole house of cards would fall. Because they needed each other.

But now? Now it was over. And he would get his hands dirty.

Treeright was going to get the first bullet. Syd smiled through the sweat. The thought both soothed and invigorated him. It clarified the path that wasn't there in the woods but was plain in his mind.

He would step on Daniel Treeright's head and crush it. A poetic ending. Maybe even a complete ending. With him dead, the other two became so much flotsam on the pointless river of existence. Maybe even let them go. Who cared where they drifted?

CHAPTER EIGHTY-FIVE

Daniel stirred early. Before he could make out the shapes of his wife and daughter, he rose, dressed silently, and slipped out of their makeshift bedroom.

The mountain morning air was chilly, but refreshing, the kind of pure air that felt like you could drink it as well as breathe it. He zipped his Carolina-blue hoodie up to his chin and buried his hands in his pockets. He chose one of the trails—paths for contemplation was what Jacob called them—and followed it absently.

The urge to light a cigarette came from nowhere. He hadn't smoked in years. *Strange,* he thought, *why now?*

Considering this while he walked in the dense darkness of the trees, he tumbled over an object in the path. For a panicked second, he thought he'd stepped on a sleeping animal. A "whummmpf" and a surprised exclamation told him he'd somehow run over a person.

"Whoa! Who's that?" A scuffling sound was followed by a pale yellow beam from an old flashlight pointed at the ground then sweeping upward into his eyes.

"Da-Daniel Treeright," he sputtered, regaining his footing and shielding his eyes.

"Oh! Governor!" A rich, full baritone came from the dim shape behind the flashlight. "Sorry!"

The beam lowered from his face and then shone upward on the face of the speaker. "Brother David. I was resting against this tree with my feet in the trail. Are you hurt? I didn't hear you coming!"

"No, no. I'm fine, Brother David. I'm sorry to break up your rest. Ah, what were you resting from? A little early for chores, isn't it?"

"You'd be surprised. Our days start early around here. Lots to do. But…" He hesitated as if considering what to tell Daniel.

"But what?"

"Well, Jacob decided it would be a good idea to set a watch for a few days since you and your family came."

"Oh." Daniel considered this. More to the old prior than he'd thought. "How long have you been watching, David?"

"I came on at midnight. We have three watches and three sections. Covers all the approaches to the abbey. The place isn't very accessible. You'd be surprised. In fact, if you don't know the area, Governor, I'd be careful walking the trails in the dark."

"Animals?" Daniel asked. "Bears?"

"Yes, there are bears. And believe it or not, mountain lions. But they generally keep their distance. It's the cliffs I'm talking about. Might not know it but right here we are set against some of the prettiest overlooks along the Appalachian Trail. But there are some spots… well, it doesn't look like it, but the edge of a cliff is a step away. Every couple of years we have a hiker wander off and tumble over a cliff. Matter of fact, this trail we're on now goes very close to the edge of a cliff called Sliver Stone."

"Silver Stone? I didn't know we had silver in Carolina."

David laughed. It was a happy, hearty laugh that made Daniel want to laugh with him.

"Not silver; sliver. It's a finger of rock that sticks out twenty feet or so over the edge of a cliff. It's like the mountain's pointing a finger to the west. Beautiful place to take in a sunset."

"Sounds like something worth seeing."

David clicked his tongue against the roof of his mouth, making a bird like sound. "Just wait a few hours till you've got good light. The way onto the rock is hidden and not easy to find if you don't know it's there. On either side of it there are places you could fall a long way if you make a wrong step." He made that clicking sound again and said, "But do go. It's a special place. We call it a 'thin' place."

"Thin?"

"A place where the veil between this world and the other world isn't so thick and dark. A place where it's easier to meet with God and to hear His voice."

Daniel couldn't see the monk's face. He had turned off the flashlight and they stood in total darkness. He took a deep breath and let it out. "Do you need to keep a watch on me? Or am I free to go?"

"Oh! You're free to go of course! Jacob never said to watch you. He wanted to keep watch for anyone who might try to hurt you or your family."

Daniel left the monk before the man could think through the logic of what he'd just said. He found the man's back and patted him as he stepped around and felt his way along the path.

Despite the monk's warning, he made his way to Sliver Stone. He wanted to see if the 'thin place' would be thin for him. It was hard to find in the dark. He became aware of a vast open space more by sound and feel than sight, and he got down on all fours and felt his way through the hidden entrance. It was exhilarating to climb out on the slender slab of elephant-grey-brown rock.

As the light grew, the vista before him came into focus like a slowly developing Polaroid. It was wonderful. He couldn't remember the last time he had been so still and so alone. He moved to the very edge of the rock and sat with his feet dangling over into nothing. The rock was cold to his touch and slightly damp from morning dew. The sun rose full and bright behind him in the east.

Time flickered and went out of his mind like a snuffed candle. He thought nothing more of it, sitting in a mindless, sun-warmed trance until a shadow fell across him and he heard a distinct click, not unlike Brother David's clicking tongue from the dark morning.

He craned his neck and looked into the glare, shading his eyes as he did. The infusion of light forced his eyes to slits, darkening the figure standing behind him into a barely discernible shadow.

"Good morning, Governor Treeright," said the shadow.

Syd DeVito lowered his cocked revolver in Daniel's face.

CHAPTER EIGHTY-SIX

Daniel's senses came all awake at once. He twisted to rise but Syd put a firm hand on one shoulder, forcing him back down.

"Stay put, Daniel. Not a lot of room to maneuver out here. Don't want any accidents."

"How'd you find me, DeVito? What are you planning to do with that gun?"

Daniel talked over his shoulder, trying to distinguish where DeVito was, relative to him and to either side of the rock. His mind flashed to the story of some young American mountain climbers taken prisoner in Afghanistan by armed rebels. How they escaped by throwing one of their captors off a mountain.

DeVito seemed to read his mind. He stepped a pace away from Treeright and centered himself on the narrow stony finger.

"Whatcha thinking, Syd? Going to persuade me to get back in the race with a gun to my head? That's out there, even for you."

"The race?! The race? Brother, the race is over and this is the finish line for you."

DeVito looked out over the blue mountains and hills and green pastures far below. "All in all, not a bad place to die. Better than the final view of the old bastard priest 'at got you here will be."

Daniel clenched his jaw. "Killing priests, Syd? Low, lower, and lowest. Turning innocent people into child porn kings? Diddling your best friend's wife? Plenty of other unmentionables. And now you killed a priest? You're digging a hole in the basement of filth, Syd. How much lower?"

"Yes, Daniel. Unmentionable, but never unnecessary. All to get you to the finish line. But now? Well, I'm gonna get you there one way or another."

Daniel felt Syd's emotional kettle coming to a boil, working up to the fatal moment. He threw the only cold water on it he could think of. "Tabitha loves you, Syd. She isn't stained by any of this. She…"

"Save it. She's dead. And in fifteen minutes, that bitch that has you and Wanda fooled is going to be dead too. I hadn't decided till now what that final roster looked like, but I'm thinking Wanda last so she can see the miracle girl isn't so miraculous."

Syd saw Daniel's reaction coming, had provoked it to get himself over the edge, completely ready to do what he'd come here to do.

He had decided to let the girl and Wanda live, but Daniel Treeright didn't need to know it. Daniel Treeright needed to die with an emotional kick to the groin and a bullet in his head.

Several things happened at the same time. Treeright rolled to his right, flattening himself against the rock in an attempt to move out of DeVito' line of fire. DeVito pulled the trigger an instant late. The bullet creased the left side of Treeright's head in a neat line that drew blood but was only as deep as a cat scratch.

The sound of the revolver discharging penetrated the thin mountain air, echoing into the valley. The acrid smell of gunpowder mixed with the sweetness of honeysuckle.

Daniel never felt the wound of the initial shot. He continued his roll, clinging to the edge of the outcropping and simultaneously stretching out his left arm to grasp at DeVito' legs, trying to pull him to ground.

The explosion startled a turkey buzzard that was roosting unnoticed on a crag below Sliver Stone. It took flight with a raucous cry, unwinding its huge black wings in a flapping whirl of motion to DeVito' left.

With Daniel clutching at his legs and the great black bird squawking and flapping, DeVito staggered and came close to dropping the gun, but he regained his balance, kicking Treeright's arm aside. He turned and fired off a second round in the direction of the buzzard purely out of reflex.

As the bird flapped away and the second gunshot echoed, Daniel Treeright gained his feet. He charged DeVito like a linebacker, head down, fully intending to take the man over the cliff regardless of whether or not he could keep from going over the edge with him. DeVito saw what was happening and fired his third round. It hit its mark with terrible effect, shearing off a chunk of bone and flesh just over Daniel Treeright's right eye.

A pink mist lingered momentarily in the flat mountain air, marking the spot where he fell. He went down like a dropped rag, inanimate, flat.

DeVito never saw his handiwork. Startled by the huge bird and lunging man, he staggered backward as the gun discharged. The first two rounds he'd fired two-fisted and poised; the last he'd fired one-handed and off balance.

The kick from the gun was nominal—anyone who handled guns would have mocked a man who couldn't control it easily under normal circumstances—but Syd DeVito never handled guns, and this was a deadly confrontation on a narrow finger of stone.

His heel caught on a small shelf of rock. He threw his hands up in an acrobatic twirl like a high wire walker, trying to pluck something stable to hold out of thin air. He hit the ground, his back on the edge of the cliff. There was a resounding thud and an involuntary gasp as all the air in his lungs escaped in a rush.

For a fraction of a second, he hung on the edge of Sliver Stone before his momentum carried him over and down. The first drop was not dramatic, only twenty or twenty-five feet, but it had a dramatic effect on Syd's body.

He fell at an almost perfect perpendicular to a ragged spine sticking out from the rock face. He landed on his left side, crushing three ribs and puncturing a lung. From there he bounced like a penny dropped from a moving car, careening off bits of rock and scrub trees for another hundred feet before he hit his head against a flat rock with such force it made a sickening sound like a baseball bat hitting a ripe watermelon.

Lying on an outcropping some hundred-and-fifty feet from where he'd fallen, he looked up to the ledge with dimming eyes, his ragged last breaths sounding like a screech owl in his ears. He saw a shadow pass, then another. Someone was there above. So he'd missed his mark after all. Daniel must be standing there.

Could he see him? Should he call out? As Syd fell into darkness, he realized he didn't care. He remembered he'd come up this mountain ready to die; ready for the end. He tasted the coppery blood in his mouth. Dark and getting darker...

CHAPTER EIGHTY-SEVEN

Brother Jacob, an early riser even by the rooster-challenging standard of the abbey, spent several hours praying in his private quarters before muted voices outside his door told him a problem existed that likely required his attention.

It was a hard and fast rule never to disturb any member of the community engaged in contemplative prayer; a rule the men and women of Holy Spirit Abbey took even more seriously when it came to their leader. Jacob had tried unsuccessfully over the years to make his charges see that he did not mind being called from prayer—that the sacred and the holy were not separate but the same inside or out of the prayer closet. The closest he had been able to get them were these not-so-silent gatherings outside his door.

He opened the door to find one of his youngest monks, Brother David, looking chagrined, in an animated discussion with the Prioress and Wanda Treeright. The governor's wife was agitated, afraid, and incredulous. She wanted to see her husband; this man knew where he was, but would not tell her how to find him. Who did he think he was?!

David, looking down at his feet while he talked, told Jacob of his encounter with Daniel in the night watch and that the governor had taken the trail to Sliver Stone. When he had been gone a couple of hours, David trekked to the Stone to check on him. He found him sitting silently out on the stone, obviously engaged in prayer and contemplation. When approached later in the morning by the Prioress with Wanda Treeright in tow, David applied community rules to the man. He was safe and he shouldn't be disturbed. Finishing his story, David looked in Jacob's eyes for approval. Jacob put an arm around him and told him it was fine.

The Prior then explained to Wanda what the Prioress and Brother David already told her, but agreed to go and check on her husband himself. Just another little fire to put out in the day-to-day life of this gathering of God's people. The tension he'd felt upon opening the door to his prayer closet and seeing their worried faces drained away as he and David began the walk to Sliver Stone.

Halfway there, the unmistakable sound of a gunshot shattered the calm air.

The men glanced at one another and broke into a run. The trail was on uneven ground gnarled with tree roots ready to catch a toe. It slowed their progress. The second and third shots came close, one upon another, when they were still a good distance from the hidden entrance to Sliver Stone.

David, the younger man by twenty years, marveled at Jacob's speed and agility. The old Prior outdistanced him over the last hundred yards. The overgrown path out to the rock slowed him down enough so both men scrambled out onto the sunlit outcropping at the same moment.

Taking in the scene, they thought the gunshots must have come from someplace other than the rocks. There didn't appear to be anyone here.

They walked cautiously out to the end of Sliver Stone where they discovered the body of a man sprawled facedown behind a small stone knuckle in the stone finger.

Jacob held out an arm across David's chest and halted him. He had been haunted by things he'd been unable to unsee for the better part of his life. The remains of men taken apart by metal and gunpowder. If he could spare the younger man from seeing something like that, he would.

"Stay back," he said in a hoarse whisper, wondering why he felt a need to keep quiet, sensing it was the presence of death that demanded it.

David obeyed. Jacob advanced to the body. *Please don't be Daniel*, he repeated to himself, knowing at the second pace it was a forlorn request. He recognized the Carolina-blue hoodie the governor had been wearing when he arrived.

A dark stain on the rock around the man's head was ominous. Blood. He could smell it and the lingering scent of gunpowder; together the two formed a pungent cocktail so strong in his memory it pulled him to the ground like gravity.

On hands and knees, he crawled the few remaining feet to the body. It was Treeright. He lay flat on the brown-grey rock, his head turned away from Jacob, the right side of his face to the ground. Even from this angle, Jacob could see the devastating wound the man had suffered. But as he got near enough to see this, he also could see Daniel Treeright was still breathing.

Weak rises and falls in the tightly-stretched fabric of the hoodie clearly showed life. Jacob turned to cry out for David and found him hovering over his shoulder.

"I... I saw you fall. I,. Ah... I. His eyes grew wide as he looked over Jacob's shoulder. "What happened!? Did he kill himself?" He went to his knees and grasped his stomach, turning his eyes away.

Prior Jacob shed fifty years in an instant. USMC Staff Sergeant Mike Ryland emerged from the distant past. He barked at David.

"Get back to the abbey! Tell the Prioress to get Sister Francine and Sister Grace and set up the infirmary for a head wound. Send a runner down the mountain to call for Doc Bremer in town. Tell him we will need a Medevac. Go!"

The man had a blank look in his eyes, as if Jacob were speaking a foreign language. Jacob took him by both arms and shook him.

"David." He looked directly into his eyes. It relit the light of recognition. "David. You have to move quickly. This man is not dead. We can help him."

Jacob stood.

"I've got this. Go! And bring back three of our youngest men and a blanket we can use for a litter."

David stumbled away, glancing a final time over his shoulder at the stranger who was Prior Jacob.

Jacob removed Daniel Treeright's hoodie, trying not to move his head. He could see, through the bloody pulp above the still-opened right eye, grayish bits of matter.. He fought to keep down his bile and his past from claiming him all over again as it almost had back then.

He could do this. He could help Daniel Treeright without becoming Mike Ryland again. He just needed to borrow from that man and that time long enough to get Daniel stable and off this rock.

His hands were too weak to rip the seams of the hoodie. Taking a piece of rock laying nearby, he slammed it to the ground. It broke, forming a jagged edge he used it to cut the garment into strips. He field dressed Daniel's wounded head quickly, moving him as little as possible. As he did this, he ran through the best possible scenarios to get the patient off the mountain and to the intensive care he needed.

He looked around. Could a helo put down here? A combat pilot might have risked it back in the day but he didn't think a civilian would try it. Maybe they could hover. In fact this was probably the only place on the mountain they could attempt that kind of rescue.

While he thought this he became aware that he had not given any thought to how Treeright got shot. The adrenalin rush had all gone one direction and it was all toward the downed man.

How had he ended up face down on Sliver Stone? Where was the shooter? Jacob was sure he'd heard small arms fire, so this had happened at close range and not from a rifle. He reprimanded himself for not thinking clearly. What if the shooter was hiding out waiting for someone to come?

Slowly, Jacob stood and turned to the base of the rock, expecting to see someone pointing a gun at his chest. No one was there.

Was David right? Had Treeright shot himself? He searched around and under the inert form but could find no gun. He had not expected to find one. The wound was too oddly placed to be self-inflicted.

He retraced his steps back toward the entrance to the rock, looking for clues. Halfway along the length, it struck him that there had not been time enough for anyone to make an escape from here and avoid him and David. They had arrived mere moments after the third shot.

Occam's razor. The simplest explanation was the shooter was still on this rock and since there was no place to conceal a person on the bare outcropping, the next simplest explanation was they went over the edge.

He moved cautiously to the edge closest to where Treeright lay and looked down at the sheer drop. There didn't appear to be a way to climb down from here, and no evidence of a person hiding. He switched to the other side. As he approached, he noticed scuff marks three feet from the edge where something had been dragged across the thin scrabble of rock dust.

His heart rate increased. Not knowing if he would find an armed killer hiding in a cleft, he stooped down and picked up a loose stone. Before leaning out to see beyond the edge, he yelled and tossed the stone over, hoping to distract anyone hiding there.

As his yell echoed off the adjoining rock face, he heard the stone slapping and cracking as it hit the ledge below; the same ledge that broke Syd DeVito' fall while all but breaking him in half. He saw DeVito himself, unmoving, lying in a black pool of blood.

David and three men burst onto Sliver Stone gasping for breath, pulling his attention away from the sight.

Their eyes inquired of him. No one wanted to approach Treeright but all were willing to be commanded. Taking the blanket he'd requested, he gave new orders. David was to go himself into town and retrieve the sheriff. While he was there, he was to inform him they needed a helicopter for a Medevac on Sliver Stone immediately for Governor Treeright.

Don't ask them. Tell them. Jacob said. *Do not take no for an answer.*

The other two men were to fetch the doctor and Wanda Treeright and bring them here. Once David was sure the sheriff was arranging for a helo, he was to bring him and whatever men he might need to recover a body at the bottom of the rock.

The men nervously followed Jacob's gaze to the body at the bottom of the cliff, then responded as if they were soldiers. No questions. All action.

When they'd gone, Jacob tore himself away from the sight of the mangled man and returned to Treeright. He wondered at how quickly a human being, vital, moving, thinking, speaking, could become little more than a fleshy trash bag of broken parts tossed to the ground. It was a thought from a past he'd wanted and expected to leave undisturbed until his own body assumed room temperature. Of course death visited the abbey, but not like this. Not in violent bursts but in slow retreats.

He knelt down and placed a hand on Treeright's back, feeling the still-steady rising and falling of breath. He had seen strange things on the battlefield. Men with no visible wounds who died from a shell burst just near enough to permanently stop their heart, and then men like this; grotesquely torn, who nevertheless breathed on.

He prayed a wandering, formless prayer; heartsick and confused. He was still praying when Wanda and the Prioress ran breathlessly onto the rock with Tabitha in tow.

He had not wanted her to see her father like this, but Tabitha seemed to take the situation in hand more readily than her mother or the Prioress or Jacob himself. She took Daniel's hand in hers and began to pray earnestly and simply. Wanda, who had begun wailing upon seeing her husband lying face down and the black blood staining the rocks around him, instantly became calm.

"This place is a close place," Tabitha said. "It's close. I feel it."

The three adults looked at each other quizzically. Prioress Madalyn caught her meaning. "You mean heaven is close? Tabitha? We call this place a 'thin' place."

Tabitha nodded her head yes. "But not heaven. It's not heaven. It's the other world. It's the real world. The land of Light. You can feel it here. I can feel it. It's close. My father is going to be okay. He will be fine."

She said this without a hint of doubt or fear. She said it as if the man lying face down before them had fallen there because of a twisted ankle.

Again the adults looked from one to another, not knowing how to react. They were interrupted by two men led onto Sliver Stone by another monk. Jacob turned, surprised that either the doctor or the sheriff should have gotten there so quickly. He was even more surprised when he saw instead Nexie Mullenix accompanied by a man he didn't recognize. The monk looked apologetically to his superiors.

"They wouldn't stop! They came to the entry of the abbey and walked right in!"

"It's okay, Timothy," Jacob said. "Any word from town yet?"

"David sent one of the brothers back to say the helo is being dispatched. We are having a time finding the doctor though, and the sheriff is getting some climbers together before he comes."

Jacob nodded and turned to his old friend. He took in the haggard look and blood-stained wrap covering the wounded ear. "Looks like we ended up back where we started, Nexie."

Mullenix's mouth was a tight red ribbon.

"I'm sorry…" he started to say.

Jacob held up a hand, gently silencing him.

"Not your doing. I knew what we were getting into when I opened the abbey.

"Still. I'm sorry," Mullenix said.

"Who is this?" the prior asked, indicating Macher, who stood several paces back.

"This is Rich Macher. Reporter. Saved me from a couple of thugs working for Syd DeVito. We drove all night to get here. I knew he was headed this way but…"

"He did this?" Macher said numbly. "Where'd he go? He got away?"

"No. That explains the body at the bottom of the cliff." Jacob gave a nod toward the spot where DeVito went over the edge. "He didn't get away. Not a pretty sight."

Macher and Mullenix took turns looking over the edge.

"It's him," Mullinex said.

As they took this in, the sheriff, along with four men toting backpacks and ropes, burst out of the covered entrance to the rocks.

Simultaneously, the distinct *whump whump whump* of a helicopter approaching reached them.

The next forty-five minutes were a blur of activity. A life flight crew from Duke rappelled down as their helo hovered some fifty feet above. Wanda fought off the idea that she and Tabitha would ride back to Durham any other way than with the governor.

In the end, she had to concede to the crew that only one of them could go on the helo. Tabitha stayed with assurances that Macher and Mullenix would deliver her to the hospital as quickly as they could go. The sheriff volunteered patrol cars to clear the way on the road. In an instant, Wanda was hoisted aloft, and a litter securely lifted her husband just after her.

Then the helo was gone. An eerie silence descended, broken by the clinks and clanks of the men climbing down to recover DeVito' body.

Soon Jacob and Madalyn stood alone on Sliver Stone, numb, silent, feeling as if they'd been in a dream atop the mountain. The day was clear and crisp. The air was sweet. The only indicator of the events they'd just seen was the stain of sticky blood drying on the stony ground.

"Will this ever be a thin place again?" Madalyn said.

"Close. It's close, the girl said. If it ever was, it always will be," Jacob said.

CHAPTER EIGHTY-EIGHT

Macher found himself flying down the interstate he'd just traversed in the opposite direction, his body exhausted, his mind buzzing. In the back seat, the old priest and the young girl conversed excitedly.

The incongruous pair struck the newspaper man as bizarrely similar and he couldn't understand how. The two should not be in the same car together, let alone able to speak the same language. But there they were, even in this headlong rush across the state to what would most likely end in a funeral, chattering away, seemingly oblivious to that fact and seemingly happy.

Rich had seen enough of the wounded governor to know the man would either be dead or braindead before the helicopter landed.

And then there was the girl herself. There was no question in Mullenix; no skepticism whatsoever as to this girl's identity. The priest addressed her as Tabitha; had even introduced her to one of the police escorts now zipping along, blue lights flashing, a hundred yards out in front of them. Macher's ear, adeptly tuned to any ironic tone, caught none.

The drive through the night to Holy Spirit Abbey on the Mount with Father Mullenix had been uneventful and quiet. Mullenix dozed off and on and Macher grew sleepy as the adrenalin buzz from escaping DeVito' thugs wore off.

He hadn't known what to expect at the abbey. Mullenix only told him they needed to get there and it was the next place DeVito would strike. The priest then called a nursing home and got assurances his mother was safe before he passed out.

Now he was refreshed; animated, gesturing wildly with his hands. The girl likewise responded to him. They talked as if they'd known each other a long time; old friends. This didn't make any sense to Macher, who still saw the girl as an inanimate cog in the machinery of a huge political scandal; almost a mannequin placed in the frame to dress up a story someone wanted to tell. He felt their banter building up on his ears and mind like a bucket left under running water.

It overflowed.

"You're Tabitha Treeright?!"

It came out as an accusation. He immediately regretted the lack of control in his voice. The priest and the girl ceased talking mid-sentence, meeting his eyes reflected in the rearview mirror.

The mirror didn't let him see their full expressions, eyes only. But there was nothing coming back at him in those eyes except... except, what? What was it?

He barely remembered he was driving at a high rate of speed down the interstate, the eyes held him so completely in their spell. He broke away with a glance forward, realizing the word as he did. It was *serene*. The eyes were serene. Her eyes. The priest's eyes. Absolutely peaceful. The absence of either defense or animosity.

No one spoke for what seemed like a long time. Shadows of trees lining the road flashed through the car, giving the scene the feeling of a flickering old movie.

Macher's brain spun around the immovable eyes in the back seat and revolted against a rising sense of fear. He'd fallen down into the pit of naive guilelessness with Jackie and it cost him everything. He'd crawled back out to get his life back. That was why he was here now. Those eyes were not going to pull him back into the incredible without a fight.

The incredible was what he made a living destroying. The credible, the facts, that's what he needed to live and to restore his life. And it was a fact that Tabitha Treeright was dead. Witnessed and signed. Dead. Fact.

The priest broke the silence. "Rich, you told me about a young friend of yours. I believe you said his name was Jamie, ah, no, it was Jackie. Right?" This had been part of Macher's hasty narration of how he'd ended up in the priest's basement. He nodded in agreement.

"Yes. You said he'd convinced you that Tabitha Treeright was alive, but now you know he was mistaken."

Rich again nodded, adding in anticipation of the priest's direction, "It wasn't his fault. The deepfake technology in videos these days—"

Mullenix interrupted. "I'm sorry, Rich. I'm not up on those kinds of things; your explanation would be wasted on me. But I am curious about something. You are an old-fashioned reporter. You seem like it to me. What they call 'hard boiled.'"

This made Rich smile.

Mullenix said, "Am I right? Is that an apt assessment?"

"Yes. I've been called something equivalent to that, only"— he shifted his glance to the girl—"a little more vulgar."

This made both the girl and Mullenix smile.

"My question is this: how is it that you, the hard boiled 'expletive omitted' reporter could be fooled into believing the most outrageous tale ever told? You did believe it, didn't you? How?"

The question caught Macher leaning the wrong way. He'd been looking for the questioning to run toward his reasoning for disbelief, not belief. His unguarded answer surprised him. "Because of Jackie. Because he told me. No one else could have told me that story and made me believe it."

"Did he make you believe it? Or did you just believe it because it was him?"

Macher paused to consider this. Mullinex went on. "I would think in your line of work people present evidence and make you believe things before you believe them, but what you just said sounded like the opposite. You believed in Jackie before you could have believed the things he said."

Macher considered this in silence. Mullenix continued. "I'm not trying to put words in your mouth. I'm just trying to get you so see something most people pass over because it's so obvious."

"What's that?" Macher asked.

"That there is no such thing as facts without faith." Mullenix let that lay in the air between them, then added, "All facts are discovered by people of faith."

Macher arched his eyebrows at this.

"Or maybe a better way to say it is: we have to believe something before we can know anything."

Tree shadows continued flickering through the car. They felt for the moment like they flickered through Macher's whole being.

"Tell me, Rich, why did you believe Jackie when he told you about Tabitha? Wasn't it because you believed in him? But you didn't just believe in him without knowing him. Right? Go back to the beginning. When you first met him. How did you meet Jackie? Was it at work or the hospital? How long have you known him?"

Again this was taking a different turn than anticipated. Macher fought to keep the focus on the obvious contradiction sitting in his back seat; the ability to blow up this farce of a story and recover his name and his mental stability in one stroke. Jackie was not untouched by all of this himself. He wasn't going to let his friend get buried under the muck flying from the ring where political giants struggled.

"That's got nothing to do with this girl and this story," he grumbled. "A lie is a lie no matter who's mouth it comes from or how well intentioned or honest they might be. Jackie is a good boy. He didn't deserve to be thrown in the middle of this."

Mullenix's ears were well trained to hear empathetic notes sung from even the hardest hearts. Macher wasn't as hard boiled as he liked to let on. It was easy to hear.

"A good boy? He's a grown man with children of his own, isn't he? You must have known him a long time. Back to when he was a boy. And you love him."

The plain statement hit Macher like a punch. Love Jackie? Unspoken. Never said. But true. Since his parents had died in consecutive years two decades ago, Rich had not uttered these words aloud or in his head about anyone, and no one said them to him.

He felt heat rise in his cheeks. He gripped the steering wheel tighter. He would not let this distract him from the point. And he would not, by God, let a tear fall in front of these people.

Mullinex saw he'd hit the mark. "How did you meet Jackie?" he pressed.

Macher gathered himself and fended off this side bar. "How I met Jackie, or if I love him, has nothing to do with the story that girl and her handlers are trying to tell. She's the one who should be answering questions. Where did she come from? Why do you believe her? When did you meet her?" He glared at the faux Tabitha, but she maintained her serene countenance and said nothing.

"Rich, Tabitha will answer any questions you have. She isn't hiding. I just think you need to consider some things before you talk with her."

"Like what? I didn't take you for one of those side-show con-artist faith healers, Father, but it's looking more and more like either you are or you're a fool. My choices are narrowing."

Mullinex did not rise to the insult. "Like the relationship between faith and fact that you've probably never considered." He paused, then added, "I completely understand why you believe this girl is not who she says she is, and I'm willing to hear your reasons. But would you first let me tell you my reasons for believing she is actually Tabitha Treeright? Isn't that fair?"

Rich nodded soberly.

"Do you know how it was that Einstein came to the theory of relativity? Not the scientific machinations, but the thought process itself? It was through deciding what to believe and where to look for answers. You are an educated man. You see the result of his exploration of physics; atom bombs and nuclear power. The world changed entirely. Yes?"

Again Rich nodded.

"Personally I didn't give much thought to this until I read a book by a man named Leslie Newbigin. I was always embarrassed about being a person of faith. I felt like I couldn't enter the arena of ideas and facts. But he helped me see things differently. Rich, in your line of work, you have to ask a lot of questions, don't you?"

Rich grunted agreement.

"How do you know what questions to ask? How do you know where to look when you start to look for the story?"

Rich decided to go along with the old man. They had a long drive ahead of them. Maybe if he did, he could get the girl involved.

"It's a good question, Mullenix. I guess I'd say I've developed a nose for it. It's an instinct."

"Ah. An instinct. Yes. Years of experience. Would you say you're good at it? At 'getting the story' and 'getting it right?'"

Rich allowed himself a wry smile. "I'm pretty good. I've found stories others missed."

"That's good!" Mullenix said. He sounded as if he genuinely believed it and was glad for it. "Asking the right questions... it's a great skill. It's what Copernicus did. It's what Einstein did. But it wasn't all they did. They had to know where to look and they had to believe there was something to find. Do you see? They couldn't ask and look unless they believed!"

Mullenix didn't wait for Macher to respond. "Yes. The search for truth begins with belief. It begins with a faith commitment; a prime belief."

He licked his lips.

The man's enjoying this, Macher thought.

"Do you want to know what it is? The thing you believe—the thing you can't prove, yet you base your life and work upon it? It's this: we ask questions because we believe there are answers that make sense!"

This supposedly great insight burst from the priest's mouth with the enthusiasm of a schoolboy scoring a winning basket. It fell flat on Macher's ears. He rolled his eyes at the man.

"What?! You don't see it?" the priest said. "The search for knowledge assumes that it exists and it exists in some orderly fashion. You are part of a culture of doubt, Rich. Skeptical of everything except your own skepticism! How can you doubt everything but your own doubts and call it honesty? And how can you explain your belief in order and logic? You just said you found stories that others missed. What really happened was that you believed something was there when others didn't. You believed. You didn't know. If you hadn't believed you never could have known anything."

Despite his impatience, Rich's mind began to stir. It was true. He had no counter argument. He said, "Okay. What if I agree with this? What difference does it make? When I see things that obviously don't add up, what are you suggesting? I push the 'I believe' button and move on? If someone tells me two plus two is five, I point out the mistake, I don't say, 'Let me see if I believe in some other math where it does.'"

"No! Right! But the point isn't the denial of facts. The point is, that as humans we have no way to access facts without faith. There was a time when you did not 'know' arithmetic. You didn't know two plus two. Someone told you it was true. If you had maintained the skepticism our culture is so proud of, you would not be able to say that you know anything! You believed a teacher and it led you to a fact. I'm saying there is a place between skepticism and knowing, a step; it is a leap of faith. Without it we can't know anything!"

"What if the leap lands us in something false? What if I believed and then found out I was lied to?" Rich was thinking about how foolish he felt to have fallen for the resurrection story and the sting of seeing the impotent Doug Windsor who couldn't heal his own broken leg.

"There's no avoiding faith commitments, Rich. All we can do is hold them honestly and let go of them humbly when proven wrong."

"That's what I'm trying to do. Let go." Macher cut his eyes in the girl's direction.

"Why now? What have you seen that is compelling enough to let go of your belief? And what made you believe in the first place? It was Jackie, right? Has Jackie lied to you?"

This sent a hot streak through Rich that surprised him. "No! Jackie never lied to me, not even when he was a punk street rat. Never lied. It was one of the reasons I decided I was going to help him get a real life. It was what made him different."

"So what is it then? You did believe him? And now you don't. I said we hold to our faith commitments. But we know why we do and we can give a good defense of them. That means we also need to have good reasons for letting them go."

"It was a lot of things. It was the videos that surfaced of me doing things I've never done that were so real looking. It was the arrest. It was the insanity of the whole story." Macher paused before going further, replaying the scene in the Rodriguez kitchen. "It was seeing Windsor face to face and realizing he's nothing special. It was so... so flat. So flat. No power." Macher ended, murmuring, "Couldn't even heal his own leg."

"Did it ever occur to you that your reasons for not believing that Tabitha Treeright returned to life are the same reasons Germany was able to butcher millions of Jews in World War Two?"

"What?! That's ridiculous! That's more insane than anything you could've said."

"Is it? The reason Jews went to their deaths almost uniformly without resistance was simply unbelief. They had plenty of evidence the Nazis were exterminating people. There were even films showing gruesome scenes in concentration camps and documents detailing the plan.

"Yet they couldn't believe it. No matter what they were told, no matter what stories were told, they would not accept them. Why? Something beyond human experience was happening. It didn't fit into their heads. Not only the Jews, but the whole world rejected the evidence of the slaughter. Even today there are people who will not believe it happened when there is a mountain of evidence that it did.

"Why do they reject it? Because it doesn't support their worldview. There you have it. Beyond human experience and outside our worldview. What could I offer you that would change your mind, Rich?"

"People don't come back from the dead!" Rich almost yelled it. In his own ears it came out sounding like he was trying to convince himself.

Tabitha spoke unexpectedly. "Do people recover from gunshot wounds like my father has?"

All the air went out of the car. Rich felt it physically. He cracked his window involuntarily. The wind whipping into the speeding car thrummed. No one spoke.

"When we get to the hospital, Mr. Macher, my father will vouch for me. He will tell you himself that I'm his daughter. Will that clear this up for you? Will that make you believe? I guess not. You already think I've fooled them into believing I'm their dead daughter. What about a DNA test? Would that prove it? Or would you insist that was faked too?

"The trouble with miracles is that they're miraculous, isn't it? They are hard to believe. I don't know why I'm here or how it happened. I can't explain it. My father is going to be waiting to talk to me when we get there. I know it but I don't know how I know it. It will be another miracle because he should be dead. It will be hard for me to believe too."

Rich looked from the girl's face to Mullenix. He tried to convey with a glance that Mullenix should let the air out of the girl's prediction, but Mullenix wasn't returning his glance; he was focused on her.

Macher sighed. "It's not likely. I'm afraid the word we get when we arrive will be 'the governor is dead.'" Again this came out more bluntly than he intended, and again the priest and the girl seemed to take no notice.

She said, "Mr. Macher. If that is what we hear, I will be so happy for him."

No one spoke another word the remaining thirty minutes of the drive to Durham.

CHAPTER EIGHTY-NINE

The information that the lost Governor Treeright had turned up would have been enough in itself to set off a tidal wave of media. Sheriff Findstein, of the little town at the foot of the mountain abbey, unused to dealing with situations much larger than a lost hiker or a runaway dog, used an open radio circuit to alert his two deputies about the need for rescue and recovery at Sliver Stone.

He identified the gunshot victim by name as the deputies asked him to repeat it several times.

A widow in the suburbs of Lancaster, Pennsylvania had recently discovered a free app for her phone allowing her to entertain herself listening in on police scanners all over the country.

She was a Treeright supporter replete with signs in her yard and stickers on her car. Randomly flipping through localities in her app, she heard the call go out from Findstein to his men. She went to her desktop computer and "did the google" as she told her son, to find the location of the transmission.

The Treeright family flight from the national stage was the hottest thing in all media. Still, it took her an hour to get anyone at the local television station to talk to her and another half hour to convince them she heard what she heard.

The result was that just about the time Daniel Treeright and his wife were hoisted into the Medevac chopper, the station manager of the Lancaster ABC affiliate called his counterpart in Raleigh with a tip, demanding he get credit for breaking the story if it turned out to be real.

Tight-lipped as they were with their exclusive information, the mere movement of two of the station's remote news coverage vans was enough to set media dominoes falling. Seeing the ABC vans rolling, a snitch paid fifty dollars a month to keep an eye out for just such occasions by the NBC affiliate called it in.

Soon there were two caravans of news vans rolling, one following the ABC team headed to Durham, the other to the west with a second ABC crew who were still plugging in the name of a town they'd never before heard of at the foot of the Smoky Mountains.

The ABC crews themselves were sketchy on what they were doing and where they were going. They weren't the frontline shock troops, but the wannabe weekend warriors of the business, more used to talking about puffy bits of stories that fell from the table of hard news than the main course. Still they weren't very excited about being rousted out on what was, from all they could tell, probably no more than a prank call.

The possibility that the lost governor might have turned up troubled the local newsmen enough that they decided, at almost the same moment, to kick the ball up to their national organizations. From there, all the dominoes fell. They fell on Durham at the hospital and on the sleepy little town of Sugarfoot. They came on these two locations from the air and by cars and on foot.

When Tabitha was a patient in the hospital, a certain level of decorum governed the men and women seeking out bits of information. The unwritten rule of politics was a candidate's family was off limits. They mostly kept that in mind.

But the immensely interesting twists in the story had built a worldwide curiosity; a wreck on the highway so irresistible that there were no more lines or limits. Stop in the middle of the road. Drive on the opposite side of the highway. Run your own car in a ditch. Whatever it takes, get a look at this story.

The Medevac chopper made it to Duke Hospital barely an hour before the fringe of this media flood got there. By the time the three-car motorcade carrying the girl, Mullenix, and Macher arrived, there was no getting through the frenzied ring around the hospital. They drove away before the crowd spotted them and sped all the way to Raleigh where they arranged to get the three on a police chopper which delivered them to the hospital rooftop on an improvised second landing pad.

CHAPTER NINETY

Doug Windsor sat on a bus at the Greyhound terminal in Raleigh, not far from the state police helicopter pad where Macher, Mullenix, and Tabitha took off. He heard it whine into the sky and pass overhead while he awaited departure.

He had been concerned about coming to this high-visibility place as a fugitive, but it turned out to be uneventful. No one gave him a second glance, even two squad cars that passed him. One of the cops in the second car had made eye contact with him and nodded with zero recognition.

Maria and her mother had sent him off in style. They insisted on buying him new clothes and shoes, and picked up both a sling-style backpack, which he now had in his lap, and a slightly scuffed-up Samsonite rolling suitcase, which was stowed with the other passenger luggage under the bus carriage.

The sling was stuffed with home-baked food, carefully packed in plastic containers and zip-locked bags. It was much too much for him, he'd insisted, but there was no denying them their contribution to his journey.

Two days after his leg was healed, about the time Macher was gearing up to go looking for the end of the Treeright saga, Doug had awoken from a vivid dream with an urgent need to move on from the Rodriguez home.

In the dream he had seen an indistinct darkness descend upon their house that he connected with his presence. In his dream he had tried to go back to Norfolk, but he encountered a huge wreck with cars and tractor trailers piled high.

Each detour he explored to get around the pile up was blocked; sometimes by fire, others by flood, and one way was blocked by an immense herd of cows that would not move.

The dream ended when he saw a beach he recognized. It was north of Jacksonville, Florida. He knew it from a trip there in early childhood. It was the place he had first found a fossilized shark's tooth, black on the white sand. In his dream he saw himself walking the surf line, leisurely looking for more. He awoke knowing he was leaving and the direction was south.

Jackie and Poppie monitored police activity and the news for anything indicating Doug was being sought. They were both surprised at the lack of activity but both agreed that it was true; the authorities and the media seemed to have forgotten he existed.

Doug was greatly relieved. He wanted his life back and he wanted to disappear. The dream at first created a conflict, for he felt the need to go home before he went south, but after a long walk around the neighborhood he discovered there was nothing in his apartment that he wanted or needed to get on with living his life.

It made him smile when he finally came to this conclusion. He came back to the house humming the "I Got No Strings" song from Pinocchio, wondering to himself where that came from and thinking he'd never tell it to anyone because it seemed so childish and stupid.

He realized Norfolk had never been home and had no hold over him. The more he reflected on the term—home—the more he thought Poppie and Suzette's house gave him a feeling he'd never known; a feeling of warmth and belonging. It was a feeling he guessed must be what home was supposed to be like.

The feeling of release from Norfolk and the revelation that he'd found something he'd always wanted but couldn't begin to define, much less find, mixed with the sorrow of having to leave it immediately.

The dream was clear enough; his presence in this home endangered it. He let that drive him and force the issue with the family, who were firmly against him leaving.

And so they'd provisioned him. Poppie and Jackie knew how to get things done in this city.

Included in his provisions were a new North Carolina driver's license and matching social security card identifying Doug as Mark Ferrin, an organ donor with their guesses as to his age (they had him two years older) and height (they had him a few inches taller).

All in all, a passable fake. They also set up a bank account with a debit card for Mark Ferrin with five hundred dollars in it. When he tried to protest, Suzzette shut him down cold.

"Let us be part of the miracle, Doug. Don't take away our little part."

Doug let it go and let them do for him. It was a strange feeling, being loved without really being known. He struggled with it.

Let the others struggle with resurrections and healings, he thought. *Those were easy to believe in. But people loving you for no good reason? Unbelievable.*

It was with this thought heavy upon him that Doug Windsor, aka Mark Ferrin, climbed the steps of the bus that would carry him to Jacksonville.

Half an hour later he was dozing, head against the gently vibrating window, the black knapsack hugged against his chest like a child's stuffed animal, the evidence of a loving family that he'd known for less than a week.

It was to be an enduring family for the rest of his life.

CHAPTER NINETY-ONE

It was a full week before Fred Robinson's body was discovered. The doctor didn't show up for his shift, which prompted the hospital to call. When none of his phones gave anything other than messages saying he was unavailable, an intern newly assigned to rotations on the psych ward was volunteered to go to his house.

The intern, a vertically-challenged young woman, got to the house, knocked on the door, and getting no response, tried to peer in the garage windows just as Jackie had several days earlier. When she saw she was too short to see, she decided to drag the city trash can around and proceeded to climb up on it. A neighbor saw her and came over to investigate. The man almost startled the girl to death when he came up behind her and asked what she was doing. He had to catch her to keep her from falling.

"Looking for Dr. Robinson," she gasped as the neighbor helped her to the ground. "I was trying to see if his car is here."

"Yep. It's here," the man said, drawling out the words in classic Carolina style.

"Ain't seen 'im come nor go these several days. An' I'd know. Retired. Got nothin ta do but sit an' snoop."

She ventured a glance at his face to see if this was humor. His eyes said it was.

"Well, he's not been to the hospital for his shift and they sent me to look for him."

The man assessed her. "Yep. Expect you drew the short straw. Not a friendly man, the doctor. Bit of a strange one. Here, let me take a look."

The neighbor was a tall man. He easily stood to the garage windows and cupped his hands around his eyes. When he turned back to the intern, the eyes were wide.

"You got your phone on you?"

She nodded.

"Call 9-1-1," he said. "Looks like the doctor's here, but it's not right."

He didn't wait for her to say anything. He elbowed the nearest pane of glass, shattering it. He reached a long, spindly arm in through the jagged hole. The garage opener release dangled down just close enough for him to stand on his tip-toes, reach through the jagged hole, and pull it. As she dialed he ran the door back. The smell of decay hit them both instantly.

"No need for an ambulance. Better send for the detectives and the morgue," he said matter-of-factly as the girl gagged while trying to talk with the 911 operator.

The detectives did come; so did two units and a van outfitted for recovering bodies. It took less than an hour for the death to be declared a suicide and the doctor to be on his way to the county morgue.

The suicide note was deemed by the lead detective to be too detailed to be a fake. It went into a plastic evidence bag. The only item that gave anyone pause was the folded up sheet they found carefully tucked away in the trunk of the car. They unfolded it and found the embossed-ink identifying mark for Duke Hospital's morgue.

A forensics expert, bored out of his skull on a call that obviously didn't require his talents, took the sheet to his van and discovered traces of blood on the sheet, barely visible to the naked eye. Questioning the intern as to why a doctor from the psych ward would have a sheet from the Morgue in his possession produced a moon-faced stare.

The girl was experiencing the weird sensation of being both hungry and sick to her stomach at the same time and only wanted this random side trip into the macabre to end. She had nothing to contribute. So the sheet went with the forensics man who decided to do some checking around and some testing on it.

Barely two hours from the intern's call, the only indication anything unusual had happened at Doc Robinson's house was a broken pane of garage window glass and some yellow-and-black plastic police tape in big Xs across both the front and garage doors. The house and the street were quiet as a graveyard.

CHAPTER NINETY-TWO

The entourage that met Tabitha, Mullinex, and Macher on the rooftop landing pad of the hospital consisted of the hospital administrator and two security guards Their rather grim, unwelcoming expressions at first led Rich to conclude either that the governor was already dead or that the identity of the girl he and Mullenix accompanied might be in doubt with these people.

He was dissuaded of the latter thought when he realized their sour expressions were focused on him. The two guards were remembering his face from the standoff in the security shack. It was him they had doubts about, not the faux Tabitha Treeright.

The administrator hurried up to the group. As she approached Tabitha, however, the woman's grave face morphed instantly to joy. Then she said the most remarkable sentence Rich Macher had ever heard or ever would hear for the rest of his life. She shouted to be heard above the roar of the helicopter.

"Oh, Miss Tabitha! Governor Treeright is asking for you!"

The girl didn't respond to this the way Rich expected, but then again nothing he'd seen in this story had gone the way he expected.

She didn't smile. A melancholy look spread across her face. Her eyes momentarily went blank as if seeing through the scene. For her there were no whirling helicopter rotors, no people, no gray sky.

He saw a glow reflected there as if a blazing yellow-red sun of another world was piercing this one—perhaps it was what the monks called a thin place here and now. Then it was gone and Rich knew what was beyond knowing. He knew he was staring into the eyes of the girl, Tabitha Treeright, who had been not just to the border of that world but over and back.

His knees buckled slightly.

Her melancholy look persisted an instant longer.

She said, "He would have loved it there."

CHAPTER NINETY-THREE

Afterword

The convention for the RNC that year was a raucous affair. The unprecedented events in the month leading up to the convention generated more questions than answers, for the simple reason that they were questions never before considered by a major political party in the nation.

Did Daniel Treeright still control the massive majority of delegates he'd accumulated in the primaries after he resigned and disappeared? Would those delegates support him since he'd reappeared and announced his intention of claiming the nomination? Would the governor's public statements of policy changes since his incredible recovery from the gunshot wound drain away party or public support?

Emerging from the hospital after a single week, Treeright had stepped onto the public stage beginning at the front doors. The surging crowds of people, supporters, media, officials of all stripes, were beyond restraint. They overran all barriers and security personnel by sheer numbers.

Without a thought, Treeright climbed on top of a police mobile operation center van, borrowed a bullhorn from one of the officers attempting to keep back the crowd, and addressed those gathered for twenty-five minutes. When he began to speak, the raucous noise faded to pin drop silence.

Tabitha and Wanda looked on from the ground. The policy issues addressed in that first public statement were no surprise to them. Daniel had not stopped speaking and outlining his ideas since waking up from the drug-induced sleep in the Medevac helicopter.

Bringing him up out of that coma to check the extent of brain damage done by Syd DeVito' bullet, the medical team was astonished at this completely unexpected volubility.

They had to restrain Treeright, who not only wouldn't or couldn't stop speaking, but also swung his legs over the side of the bed and began shedding various bits of life-sustaining medical paraphernalia he did not want or need.

In the end, a procedure to close the wound in his forehead using a metal plate and some plastic surgery to lessen the appearance of a scar was the extent of anything close to treatment.

These procedures were carried out under local anesthesia mainly for the reason that none of the medical staff felt comfortable with any act that might affect the man's brain activity which was beyond medical explanation.

It was like a mechanic found a car running that shouldn't run and was afraid to shut it down because he had no confidence it would ever start again by his hand.

The people hearing Treeright for the first time were astounded. It wasn't just the old power and persuasion and charm coming from the miracle man and it wasn't just the presence of the miracle girl somewhere close, just out of sight; it was the things he was saying.

There were no boilerplate RNC talking points. There were flip-flops about cherished party issues that sounded like the opposition party. There were clear articulations of other issues with more reason and passion than they'd ever heard; so much so that members of the opposition party publicly praised him if not outright agreeing with him.

More than anything else, there was a quality of vulnerability and humanity in Treeright that brought a hushed awe over the crowd. They weren't hearing a stump speech; smooth and calculating. They were hearing a man sharing his heart.

When asked during subsequent appearances about his daughter and the press conference by his deceased chief of staff, Daniel Treeright was more coy.

Those who watched him most closely and those who knew him best (and also knew the truth) discerned the slightest shift in his posture and tone of voice, and the bullet-scarred forehead, which gave an oddly Frankenstein-like aspect to his handsome face with its square of lighter colored skin grafted over a titanium plate, would turn a bit darker.

Treeright would not deny the DeVito version of Tabitha's resurrection; the version giving him credit for praying over his dead daughter. He "let it run"—his own term.

Wanda asked him about this only once and Tabitha never did. His reasoning was that it was no one's business but their own what had really happened in the morgue. It was family. It was their privacy and if he opened up that conversation it would be open season on all of their family life.

Besides, he concluded, would they be doing Douglas Windsor a favor by throwing him into the swirl of people hungry to feed on this story? They were public people, used to such things. Windsor? It would ruin his life.

Tabitha managed to steer clear of the feeding frenzy. This was made easier by the fact it was summer and she did not have to navigate attending school. While Daniel returned to full campaign mode within a month of leaving the hospital, Wanda and Tabitha holed up in the Governor's Mansion.

The family only made two appearances together outside their home between the shooting and the convention. One they were able to keep from being detected; the other turned into a fiasco.

There was an assumption on the part of the governor's staff that interest in Tabitha had waned in light of the shooting and subsequent recovery of the candidate—that the continuation of the campaign restored traditionally observed unspoken rules about pursuing a candidate's family.

This notion blew up when Wanda's aide, Alicia Stoneman, pleaded for help for her pastor, Marty Hammond.

Hammond was still fighting an uphill battle from the heroin overdose administered by DeVito' thugs. Tabitha overheard the conversation and insisted on visiting him in the hospital.

Daniel was campaigning nonstop, but was home for one night between fundraisers in New York and Las Vegas. He decided they should all visit the man who was paying such a high price simply for being willing to offer them some advice. The family slipped security, a feat Daniel was perfecting, and made the trip to Durham.

Undetected with the exception of the surprised hospital staff, they spent an hour with Hammond and his wife.

Tabitha took the lead, praying for Donna Hammond, who looked haggard and sleepless, and for the unconscious pastor with such simple assurance that the adults were left speechless and teary eyed.

She gave the pastor's wife her cell number and asked to be kept informed of Marty Hammond's progress.

She also gave her the number of a Catholic priest to call who would be glad to help them.

Leaving the ICU, it was immediately obvious that news of their visit had leaked. They were surrounded by a ring of doctors and nurses from all over the facility who wanted to see the two miracles, one of whom was looking more and more each day like the man who would be the next president.

Politely weaving their way out of ICU, they got in the elevator which opened on a ground-floor lobby stacked with members of the media. Cameras were rolling and questions were shouted. It was a melee.

Daniel snapped the door closed and hit the button for Sublevel Zero. Making their way to the morgue, Romeo Carnell met them, wide-eyed and smiling. He abandoned his post in the morgue to shuffle the three into a hearse parked at the back loading dock.

And so the Treerights, two of whom should have left Duke University in a hearse lying down dead just weeks before, were driven away huddled under a blanket in the proverbial long black limousine.

The other family excursion came just a week later with no drama. The three met Prior Jacob early in the morning at the foot of the trail leading to Holy Spirit Abbey on the Mount and enjoyed a leisurely hike to the abbey.

The community of monks and nuns gathered for their visit and greeted them warmly. Daniel and Wanda thanked them for sharing their place and apologized for bringing the world to their doorstep.

It was a relaxing day for the Treerights in the midst of the craziness of nonstop campaigning and scrutiny. Wanda and Daniel begged off when Tabitha suggested a visit to Sliver Stone. She went alone just before the late sunset.

Sitting with her legs dangling over the furthest ledge, she was yards away from the spot where Syd DeVito surprised and shot her father. The sense of peace she felt, fingers outspread on the warm rocks, slight evening breeze beginning to stir, was disturbed by a feeling of being watched.

Several times she glanced over her shoulder expecting to find someone there. But no one came and she eventually lay back full and dozed lightly. She had a vision of an old, bent woman with whitened, blind eyes. It was the nun who'd been there the day they first came to the abbey.

The old nun was speaking but Tabitha couldn't hear the words. Her deeply-lined face looked troubled. Tabitha tried to comfort her but it seemed there was a boundary through which they could not speak or hear each other.

Slowly the boundary solidified and became visible, at first only a flat shadow line, but like an object turned in the daylight, it began to grow and take shape.

It was the shadow of a man.

Then the shadow was gone and the man was there. It was her father. The woman's expression went grave and she ceased trying to speak as Daniel Treeright stood there, towering over them both.

The vision was gone.

Tabitha opened her eyes to see her flesh-and-blood father standing there on Sliver Stone, smiling at her. For a fraction of a second between vision and reality, that smile appeared as an iceberg; concealing something, a politician and not her father.

Tabitha shuddered involuntarily and Daniel Treeright stooped to pick her up in his arms. The thought came to her then and repeated itself often in later years: this is a thin place, a place where hidden things come near.

The National Convention was an intense affair.

It took three ballots to nominate Treeright despite the fact that no other candidate held a claim to his delegates. Hardliners managed a near coup on the first ballot by rallying a coalition of party-faithful superdelegates around a man Syd DeVito had warned Daniel about and who was top on his list of potential conspirators behind the plot to steal Tabitha's dead body.

They circulated a story that the girl was actually a plant that would be exposed during the presidential campaign. It was a bizarre twist to an already bizarre campaign.

Bowing to pressure, Daniel agreed to let a selected group of delegates meet Tabitha in what turned out to be a very uncomfortable meeting with the candidate and his wife and daughter.

Tabitha, for her part, remained unflappable, but Wanda exploded during the meeting, threatening to take the whole thing public and saying to Daniel in front of everyone that they could run independently.

The second ballot following the meeting moved Treeright within a whisker of the nomination, and a maneuver to quickly insist upon a third ballot within hours of the second left undecideds with no time for intrigue from party bosses still reeling from the shift to his camp.

He was nominated comfortably without time to even identify a running mate. The picture of Daniel, Wanda, and Tabitha hand in hand accepting the nomination carried the headline: DO YOU BELIEVE IN MIRACLES? RNC SAYS YES!

Mark Ferrin watched the convention that evening at a bar mostly frequented by sailors just outside the Mayport Naval Base.

He smiled wryly at being carded upon entry. He felt much older than his twenty-eight years, or the twenty-seven showing on Poppie's ID.

He was enjoying Florida. He'd even found a couple shark's teeth on his first weekend walk on the beach. The heat everyone complained about seemed mild to him.

Working outside for so long had its advantages. Contractors were singularly uncurious people when it came to hiring workmen who would simply show up for work each day and put in their eight to ten hours without making a fuss.

The stitches on his forehead and back of his head were gone. He'd plucked them out himself. The little nest egg of money from Poppie and Suzette had set him up nicely, and the first wad of cash from his boss felt good in his pocket. Maybe this would be a place to set up shop and stay, make a home.

No one at the bar noticed his eyes glistening and the ever-so-slight upturn of his mouth when the Treerights made the stage. He froze the picture in his mind's eye and examined it again and again for many years afterward.

Leaving the bar, he slid behind the wheel of a grey-green Ford Futura with way too many miles and years near the ocean. He wondered what had become of the car he'd abandoned at the truck stop in Emporia what seemed like a lifetime ago.

The Futura started easily. He rolled on to Kennedy Avenue reaching for the knob to the radio. Nice night for a drive along the oceanfront. He still liked the road as a place to do something while he did nothing. The wheels whispering soothing sounds in harmony with the wind gliding past the open windows.

It was just cooling off. A Florida thunderstorm was in the air. The old songs on the radio—no more talking heads, no more news for him—unwound. "Goin to Kansas City, Kansas City here I come."

Kansas City?

"Goin to Kansas City, Kansas City here I come."

The old artist's voice faded and an older voice said it.

Kansas City.

Doug heard it and sighed.

Once you hear it you know it, he said to himself.

He turned off the radio but the repetition grew louder in the silence.

Goin' to Kansas City.

Well, maybe he would.

The forensics inspector called Poppie Rodriguez. He was troubled over a matter.

Poppie had been a mentor to the man when he started out with the force. Could they get together? On a whim, Poppie took Jackie along, thinking the son-in-law might enjoy talking shop with someone from a different side of police work. Jackie jumped at the chance.

They met at the local diner where Jackie and Rich Macher had forged their friendship and only months before had discussed the existence of the Tabitha Treeright video.

Following a greasy spoon lunch consisting of overcooked burgers topped with fried eggs and a side of steak cut fries, the forensics man, who sported a disturbed look from the moment they sat down and barely picked at his food, unburdened himself.

He told them about the suicide scene at the Duke psychologist's home and the unusual package found in the dead doctor's trunk; the folded-up sheet from the Duke morgue.

Jackie strained his neck with the effort to not look at his father-in-law while they heard this revelation.

The man told them about the faint blood stain he discovered on the sheet. At this, Poppie and Jackie couldn't help but look at each other, but it didn't matter. The forensics guy wasn't looking at them; he was focused on a spot somewhere in the vicinity of the shiny silver napkin dispenser in the middle of their table.

He went on in a steady monotone, as if determined to get out what he had to say and not be interrupted.

"It bothered me," he said. "It didn't make sense. The doctor didn't have any cuts on his body—he'd checked out by suffocating himself—but I ran his DNA against the trace anyway to make sure. Not his blood. Then I wondered if we might have missed a murder victim. What if the doc killed himself out of guilt? But to be honest, that seemed far-fetched, too. I went over the sheet with a fine-tooth comb and came up with some hair. The hair and the blood didn't match. Now it's really got me going."

Poppie and Jackie locked eyes, waiting for the punchline.

"So I was dead asleep and I had a thought just come and shake me awake. What about the girl in the morgue that supposedly came back to life? And the guy who got arrested that night? His DNA was easy enough. We took a swab when he got booked. The girl was a little tricky. I had to do a little recon in the hospital. I've got a friend over there who works in the lab. They still had some specimens from her." He slowed down, emphasizing each word.

"The blood, a match for him. The hair, a match for her." He looked to Poppie and then to Jackie.

"There's only one way that could happen and it isn't the story that DeVito guy told. I went back and watched a video of his press conference. He said that perp never got close to the girl. That he got beat down wandering around the morgue looking for the body. But the blood on the sheet says different. It says Windsor was close enough for his blood to end up on the sheet. It says this story about Treeright being the one who somehow raised a girl from the dead isn't the whole truth at all."

Poppie cleared his throat to speak. Jackie cut him off. "So what is the whole truth?"

The man hesitated, then shook his head. "I don't know, man. There's missing evidence. Not enough to tell the whole story. If only someone hadn't stolen the security footage, we'd know wouldn't we?"

Jackie looked hard at the man for a long time; so long it got uncomfortable. He looked away. Poppie again began to speak, but Jackie broke his silence.

"I'll tell you the whole truth," he said. Poppie stirred as if to stop his son-in-law, but Jackie held out a reassuring hand.

"The whole truth is that no amount of evidence can tell the whole truth. There's always going to be a place where we decide to believe something. And when we do it may be in spite of the evidence, not because of it. Videos can be faked. DNA samples cooked. Even dead bodies stolen. Seeing isn't believing, only believing is believing. And there never will be a way to know some things until we believe them.

"I don't know what to tell you about Daniel Treeright or Syd DeVito or a girl coming back from the dead. But I will tell you this: the only reason I'm here with a father who loves me and not still living on the streets is that a few people believed I was something I was not and chose to treat me like I belonged in a family. Dead come to life? I believe it because I'm living it."

Two days before the presidential election, Poppie, Suzette, Jackie, and Maria attended church downtown. Rich Macher joined them at Jackie's request. It was the first time they'd all been together since the day Douglas Windsor sat in the Rodriquez kitchen, unable to heal his mangled leg.

The polls indicated Daniel Treeright was headed for the Oval Office in an unprecedented landslide. The running joke was that Wanda had spent the last six weeks of the general campaign picking out furniture for the White House and looking for schools for Tabitha in DC.

Marty Hammond, looking frail and sounding like a much different man than the one who stalked this same stage like a hungry tiger in years gone by, addressed the congregation with an odd message from the book of Revelations.

He prefaced his talk with a confession that he rarely even read the hard-to-understand last book in the Bible. He talked in low unemotional tones. He said he wasn't sure why this was the message of the day, but that he had promised God if he ever returned to this pulpit he would only give what he was given.

With this ominous word he opened a small black Bible and put on reading glasses before reading the passage:

"And the dragon stood on the shore of the sea. And I saw a beast coming out of the sea. He had ten horns and seven heads, with ten crowns on his horns, and on each head a blasphemous name. The beast I saw resembled a leopard, but had feet like those of a bear and a mouth like that of a lion. The dragon gave the beast his power and his throne and great authority."

Pastor Harmond paused and wiped a damp handkerchief across his forehead. He swallowed hard before continuing.

"One of the heads of the beast seemed to have had a fatal wound, but the fatal wound had been healed. The whole world was astonished and followed the beast. Men worshiped the dragon because he had given authority to the beast, and they also worshiped the beast and asked, "Who is like the beast? Who can make war against him?"

R. Kenward Jones is a disruptive teacher, writer, podcaster (who isn't these days?), counselor, husband, father and grandfather. He holds a bachelor's degree in mechanical engineering and master's degrees in biblical studies and counseling.

His debut novel, Buried at Sea, was published by Penmore Press in 2022. Daily, he writes proverbs, parables and prayers and shares them on his Facebook page and website to inspire and encourage.

R. Kenward Jones is a US Navy veteran and served as both an enlisted man and officer for 12 years before he left the military to become a pastor. After a 13-year long bout with treatment resistant depression he left the ministry to reset his life. He knows the Valley of the Shadow of Death and the power of personal Creativity as the way through it and out of it.

Currently he works as a counselor and teaches the 515A "zero excuses" bootcamp at the local YMCA. He and Tina, his high school sweetheart, have been married for 40 years, have two children and one grandchild, and live in Southeastern Virginia although they still consider the Shenandoah Valley to be their "home."

R. Kenward Jones enjoys life and joy tempered by suffering and more than anything wants to help other sufferers experience the same.